Edmund Spenser, Alexander Balloch Grosart

**Complete Works in Verse and Prose**

Vol. 9

Edmund Spenser, Alexander Balloch Grosart

**Complete Works in Verse and Prose**
*Vol. 9*

ISBN/EAN: 9783337366605

Printed in Europe, USA, Canada, Australia, Japan

Cover: Foto ©Andreas Hilbeck / pixelio.de

More available books at **www.hansebooks.com**

THE

# COMPLETE WORKS

IN

## VERSE AND PROSE

OF

# EDMUND SPENSER.

*EDITED, WITH A NEW LIFE, BASED ON ORIGINAL RESEARCHES, AND A GLOSSARY EMBRACING NOTES AND ILLUSTRATIONS.*

BY THE

REV. ALEXANDER B. GROSART, LL.D. (EDIN.), F.S.A.,

*St George's, Blackburn, Lancashire;*

IN ASSOCIATION WITH

PROFESSOR ANGUS, LL.D., LONDON.
THE REV. THOMAS ASHE, M.A., CREWE.
PROFESSOR CHILD, LL.D., HARVARD UNIVERSITY, CAMBRIDGE, U.S.A.
THE RIGHT HONBLE. THE LORD CHIEF JUSTICE OF ENGLAND.
PROFESSOR EDWARD DOWDEN, LL.D., TRINITY COLLEGE, DUBLIN.
EDMUND W. GOSSE, ESQ., LONDON.
THE REV. WILLIAM HUBBARD, MANCHESTER.
PROFESSOR HENRY MORLEY, LL.D., LONDON.

DR. BRINSLEY NICHOLSON, LONDON.
GEORGE SAINTSBURY, ESQ., LONDON.
FRANCIS TURNER PALGRAVE, ESQ., LL.D., LONDON.
AUBREY DE VERE, ESQ., CURRAGH CHASE, ADARE.
PROFESSOR WARD, M.A., OWENS COLLEGE, MANCHESTER.
THE REV. RICHARD WILTON, M.A., LONDESBOROUGH RECTORY.
WILLIAM ALDIS WRIGHT, ESQ., M.A., LL.D., TRINITY COLL., CAMB.,

ETC.            ETC.            ETC.

*IN TEN VOLUMES.*

VOL. IX.

PROSE :

A VEUE OF THE PRESENT STATE OF IRELAND.
LETTERS, ETC.

PRINTED FOR PRIVATE CIRCULATION ONLY
1882-4.

100 *copies only.*]

*Printed by Hazell, Watson, and Viney, London and Aylesbury.*

# CONTENTS OF VOL. IX.

## PROSE.

I.

# A VEUE OF THE PRESENT STATE OF IRELAND.

1596.

# NOTE.

Dr. Morris, in his 'Globe' Spenser, thus writes (in Preface) of his text of the 'View of the Prefent State of Ireland' :—

"The prose Treatise on Ireland, as printed by Sir James Ware, and followed by all recent editors, was found on examination, to be very inaccurate and incomplete. It seemed scarcely fair to Spenser's memory to let this single piece of prose remain in so unsatisfactory a state. I have therefore re-edited it from three manuscripts belonging to the library of the British Museum. The text itself is from the Additional Manuscript 22022, the oldest of the three manuscripts ; and, according to Sir James Ware's account of some of the best manuscripts seen by him, the Ad. MS. is evidently a very good one. Harleian MS. 1932, which very closely resembles, even in its omissions, Ware's text, and Harleian MS. 7388, are very fair manuscripts, and have been collated throughout with the Additional Manuscript and Ware's text " (pp. iii-iv).

There is abundant evidence that Dr. Morris must have spent considerable pains in the collation of the two MSS. named, as compared with his adopted MS. The 'various readings' recorded in his Appendix (pp. 703-5) are creditable to his industry. None the less is it surprising that he should have adopted for text an anonymous and unauthenticated and undated MS., and with such supererogatory minuteness given us the various readings of the other MSS.—manuscripts that only a slight examination shew to be perfunctory and unreliable. The surprise is increased because Dr. Morris incidentally reveals that he was aware of the Lambeth MS., though he gives no evidence of having so much as looked at it ; in this differing from Todd, who must have (at least) dipped into it. Without any hesitation I have elected the Lambeth MS. for my text, because (*a*) It was the copy submitted by the Author to the Archbishop of Canterbury for License ; (*b*) It is initialled E. S., and dated by him ; (*c*) It gives by far the most satisfactory readings throughout, albeit, having been transcribed by several writers, it has certain easily-corrected clerical mistakes. I have to return his Grace the Archbishop of Canterbury my right hearty thanks for allowing me the loan in my own study of this important MS. (J Θ. : 10 4to vol. 92, Bibliotheca Lambeth :, 111 folios = 222 pages and 1 blank at beginning and end), that I might leisurely *verbatim et literatim* transcribe and collate.

My procedure has been as follows : I reproduce the Lambeth MS. as my text fundamentally ; but in footnotes record anything that seemed to call for

notice in comparing it with (*a*) Dr. Morris's, (*b*) Mr. J. Payne Collier's text.
But neither yields much of any great moment—*id est*, so as to be preferred
to the Lambeth MS., my own text: *e.g.* the orthography differs repeatedly,
and small words, as ' of ' and ' the,' which our MS. drops, are inserted —
as illustrated on the first page of the ' Vcue ' ; but it were mere pedantry to
record these. In only two little things have I ventured to depart from literal
reproduction of our MS. : viz., 1 have extended contractions, as 'y*' for
'the,' ' y' ' for ' that,' ' w·h ' for ' which,' and ' & ' for ' and,' and the like ;
and I have punctuated more frequently, the comma being, (as was then the
mode, almost the entire punctuation of the MS. Otherwise, the Author's
own text, in its quaint and varying orthography, etc., is given in integrity.
In the Glossary (Vol. X.) will be found Notes and Illustrations, under all
noticeable words. See for more in the new Life and related Essays in
Vol. I., where I give examples of the superiority of our text to Dr. Morris's,
as to all.

A. B. G.

# A

# Veue

of

# The Present State

of

# Ireland.

1596.

# A Veue of the preſent State of Ireland.

### DISCOURSED BY WAY OF A DIALOGUE BETWENE EUDOXUS AND IRENIUS.

*Eudoxus.*

UT if that country of Ireland, whence you lately came, be ſo goodly and commodious a ſoyle as you report, I wounder that no courſe is taken for the tourning 10 therof to good uſes, and reducing that ſalvage nation to better goverment and civillity.

*Irenius.* Mary, ſo ther have bin divers good plotts deviſed, and wiſe counſells caſt alredy about reformation of that realme ; but they ſay it is the fatall deſtiny of that land, that no purpoſes, whatſoever are ment for her good, wil proſper and take good effect : which, whether it proceede from the very genius of the ſoyle, or influence of the ſtarrs, or 20 that Almighty god hath not yet appoynted the time of her reformacion, or that he reſerveth her

*⁎* The various readings placed underneath are drawn from Dr. Morris's text, when not otherwise stated—a few only accepted. See Introductory Note.

in this unquiet ftate ftill, for fome fecret fcourge,
which fhall by her come unto England, it is hard
to be knowne, but yet much to be feared.

*Eudox.* Surely I fuppofe this but a vaine conceipt
of fimple men, which judge things by ther effects,
and not by ther caufes; for I would rather thinck
the caufe of this evel, which hangeth upon that
country, to proceede rather upon the unfoundneffe 3c
of the counfell, and plotts, which you fay have bin
oftentimes layd for her reformacon, or of fayntneffe
in following and effecting the fame, then of any fuch
fatall courfe or appoyntment of god, as you mifdeme;
but it is the manner of men, that when they are
fallen into any abfurdity, or theyre actions fucceede
not as they would, they are ready alwayes to impute
the blame therof unto the heavens, fo to excufe their
own folly and imperfections: fo have I alfo heard
it often wifhed, (even of fome whos great wifedome 4c
in [my] opinion fhould feme to judg more foundly of
fo weighty a confideracon) that all that land weare
a fea-poole: which kind of fpeach, is the manner
rather of defperate men far driven, to wifh the utter
ruine of that which they cannot redreffe, then of
grave counfellors, which ought to thinck nothing fo
hard, but that through wifdome, it may be maiftered
and fubdued; fince the poet fayth, that the wifeman
fhall rule even over the ftarrs, much more over
the earth: for weare it not the part of a defperate 5c
phifition to wifh his difeafed patient dead, rather
then to imploy the beft indevours of his fkill for
his recovery: but fince we are fo far entred, let us

l. 52, '*applye.*'

I pray you, devife of thofe evills, by which that country is held in this wretched cafe, that it cannot, as you fay, be recured. And if it be not painfull to you, to tell us what things during your late continuance ther, you obferved, to be moft offenfive, and impeachfull, unto the good rule and government therof. 60

*Iren.* Surely Eudox., the evills which you defire to be recounted are very many, and almoft countable with thofe which were hidden in the bafket of Pandora : but fince you fo pleafe, I will out of that infinit number, reckone but fome that are moft capitall, and commonly occurrent both in the life and condicions of private men, and alfo in the manage of publique affaires and pollicie. The which you fhall underftand to be of divers natures, as I obferved them : for fome of them are of very 70 great antiquity and long continuance ; others more late and of leffe endurance ; others dayly / growing and increafing continually, as the evill occafions are every day offred.

*Eudox.* Tell them, I pray you, in the fame order that you have now rehearfed them : for ther can be no better methode then this which the very matter it felf offreth. And when you have reckoned all the evills, let us heare your opinion for redreffing of them. After which ther will perhaps of it felf 80 appere fome reafonable way to fettle a found and perfeʄt rule of government, by fhunning the former

l. 54, '*a litle devife,*' but is abfurd, as the Difcourfe was meant to be a lengthy one : l. 66, '*current*' : l. 67, '*as*' : l. 68, '*managing*' : l. 75, '*then.*'

evills, and following the offred good. The which methode we may learne of the wife Phifitions, which firft require that the malady be knowne throughly and difcovered : afterwards do teach how to cure and redreffe it : and laftly do prefcribe a diet with ftreight rules and orders to be dayly obferved, for feare of relaps into the former difeaie, or falling into fome other more dangerous then it.

*Iren.* I will then according to your advifement, begin to declare the evills which feme to be moft hurtfull to the comon-weale of that land : and firft, thofe which I fayd were moft ancient and long growne : and they are alfo of 3 kinds ; the firft in the lawes, the fecond in cuftomes, the laft in religion.

*Eudox.* Why, Irenius, can there be anie evill in the lawes ? can things which are ordayned for the fafetie and good of all, turne to the evill and hurt of them ? This well I wote both in that ftate and in all other, that were they not contayned in doutie with feare of lawe which reftrayneth offences, and inflicteth fharpe punifhment to mifdoers, no man fhould enjoy anie thing, everie mans hand would be againft another. Therfore in finding fault with the lawes I doubt me you fhall muche over-fhote your felfe, and make me the more diflike your other diflikes of that government.

*Iren.* / The lawes Eudox., I doe not blame for them felves, knowing that all lawes are ordayned for the good of the common weal and for repreffing of licenfioufneffe and vice : but it falleth out in lawes,

l. 89, ' *a* ' : l. 92, ' *me* ' : l. 96, ' *third* ' : l. 111, ' *right well.* '

no otherwife then it doth in Phifick, which was at
firft devized, and is yet dayly ment and miniftred
for the health of the patient : but neverthcleffe we
often fe that cither through ignorance of the difeafe,
or unfeafonableneffe of the time, or other accidents
comming betwene, in ftead of good it worketh hurt,
and out of one evill, throweth the patient into many 120
miferies : fo the lawes were at firft intended for the
reformacon of abufes, and peaceable continuance of
the fubjects : but are fince either difanulled or quite
prevaricated through chang and alteration of times,
yet are they good ftill in them felves: but to that
common wealth which is ruled by them they worke
not that good which they fhould, and fometimes alfo
perhaps that evill which they would not.

*Eudox.* Whether do you meane this by the comon
lawes of the realme or by the ftatute lawes and acts 130
of parliament ?

*Iren.* Surely by them both : for even the comon
lawes, being that which William of Normandy brought
in with his conqueft and layd upon the neck of England, though it perhaps fitted well with the ftate of
England then being, and was readily obeyed through
the power of the comander which had before fubdued the poeple to him, and made eafy way to the
fetting of his will ; yet with the ftate of Ireland
peradventure it doth not fo well / agre, being a 140
poeple altogether ftubborn and vntamed and, if it
were once tamed, yet now lately have quite fhaken
of ther yoke and broken the bands of ther obedience.
For England, before the entrance of the Conqueror,

l. 123, '*fithence*' : l. 141, '*or.*'

IX.                                                                    2

was an unpeaceable kingdome, and but lately entred
to the mild and godly goverment of King Edward
furnamed the confeffor ; befides now lately growne
unto a lothing and deteftation of the unjuft and
tirannous rule of Harold, an ufurper, which made
them the more willing to accept of any reafonable
condicons and order of the new Victor, thincking
furely it would be no worfe then the latter, and
hoping well it would be as good as the former : yet
what the proofe of the firft bringing in and eftablifhing
of the lawes was, was to many full bitterly made
knowne.   But with Ireland it is far otherwife : for it
is a nation ever acquainted with warrs, though but
amongeft themfelves, and in ther owne kind of military difciplin, trayned up even from their youths :
which they have never yet bin tought to lay afide,
nor made to learne obedience unto the law, fcarfely
to know the name of law, but in ftead therof have
alwayes preferved and kept ther owne law, which is
the Brehon law.

*Eudox.* What is that which you call the Brehon
law ? it is a word unto us altogether unknowne.

*Iren.* It is a certaine rule of right, unwritten,
but delivered by tradition from one to an other,
in which oftentimes ther appereth great fhew of
equity, in determining the right betwene party and
party, but in many things repugning quite from
gods law and mans, as for example, in the cafe
of murther.   The Brehon that is there judg, will

1. 146, '*goodly*' : l. 152, '*later*' : l. 155, '*hath beene*' : ib., '*after*' :
l. 164, '*Brehons*' : l. 165, '*it . . . unknowne*' not in our MS. :
l. 171, '*both to.*'

compound betwene the murtherer, and the frends
of the party murthered, which profecute the action,
that the malefactor fhall give unto them, or to the
child, or wife of him that is flaine, a recompence,
which they call an Iriach ; by which vile law of
thers, many / murders are amongeft them made
up and fmothered. And this judg being, as he 180
is called, the Lord Brehon, adjudgeth for the moft
part a better fhare unto his Lord, that is the Lord
of the foyle, or the head of that fepte, and alfo
unto him felf, for his judgment, a greater portion
then unto the plaintifes or parties grieved.

*Eudox.* That is a moft wicked law indede : but
I truft it is not now ufed in Ireland, fince the
kings of England have had the abfolute dominion
therof, and eftablifhed ther owne lawes there.

*Iren.* Yes truly, for ther are many wide countries 190
in Ireland, in which the lawes of England were
never eftablifhed, nor any acknowledgment of fubjection made : and alfo even in thofe which are
fubdued and feme to acknowledg fubjection, yet the
fame Brehon law is privily practifed amongeft them
felves, by reafon that dwelling as they do, whole
nations and fepts of the Irifh together, without any
Englifhman amongeft them, they may do what they
lift, and compound or altogether conceale amongeft
them felves ther owne crimes, of which no notice 200
can be had by them which would and might amend
the fame, by the rule of the lawes of England.

*Eudox.* What is this which you fay? and is ther
any part of that realme, or any nacõn therin, which

1. 178, '*Breaghe* : *ib.*, '*bi law.*'

have not yet bin fubdued to the crowne of England?
Did not the whole realme univerfally accept and
acknowledg our late Prince of famous memory,
Henry the eight, ther ownely King and liege Lord?

*Iren.* Yes verily: in a parliament holden in the
time of Sir Anthony Saint-Legar, then Lord Deputy, 2
all the Irifh Lords and principall men came in, and
being by faire means wrought therunto, acknowledged
King / Henry for their Soveraigne Lord, referving
yet, as fome fay, unto them felves, all their owne
former privileges and fignories inviolate.

*Eudox.* Then by that acceptance of his foveraignety
they alfo accepted of his lawes: why then fhould
any other lawes be now ufed amongeft them?

*Iren.* Trew it is that therby they bound them
felves to his lawes and obedience, and in cafe it had 2
bin followed againft them, as it fhould have bin,
and a goverment therupon prefently fetled amongeft
them agreeable therunto, they fhould have bin
reduced to perpetuall civillity and contayned in
continuall duty: but what boots it to breake a colt,
and to let him ftreight run lofe at randome? fo
were this poeple at firft well handled, and wifely
brought to acknowledg allegance to the King of
England: but being ftraight left unto them felves
and ther owne inordinate life and manners, they 2
eftfones forgot what before they were taught, and
fo fone as they were out of fight by them felves,
fhooke of ther bridles, and began to colt anew, more
licenfioufly then before.

*Eudox.* It is great pitty, that fo good an opportu-

l. 212, '*fure*': l. 221, '*upon.*'

nity was omitted, and fo happy an occafion fore-
flacked, that might have bred the eternall good of
that land : but do they not ftill acknowledg that
fubmiffion ?

*Iren.* No, they doe not, for now the heires and 240
pofterity of them which yeilded the fame are, as
they fay, either ignorant therof, or do wilfully deny,
or ftedfaftly difavow it.

*Eudox.* How can they fo do juftly ? doth not
the act of the parent, in any lawfull grant or
conveyance, bind his heires for ever therunto ? Sith
then the / anceftors of thes that now live yeilded
them felves their fubjects and liege men, fhall it not
ty ther children to the fame fubjection ?

*Iren.* They fay no : for ther anceftours had had 250
no eftate in any ther lands, Seigniories, or heredita-
ments, longer then during ther owne lives, as they
allege : for all the Irifh do hould ther lands by
Taniftrie : which is to fay, no more but a perfonall
eftate for his life time, that is Tanift. By reafon
that he is admitted therunto by election of the
country.

*Eudox.* What is this which you call Tanift and
Taniftrie ? they be names and tearmes never heard
of or knowne to us. 260

*Iren.* It is a cuftome amongeft all the Irifh, that
prefently after the death of any ther chiefe Lords
or Captaines, they do prefently affemble them felves
to a place, generally appoynted and knowne unto
them, to chofe an other in his ftead : where they do

l. 236, '*fore-ftald*' : l. 240, '*Now*' : l. 245, in our MS. miswritten
'*prlament*' : l. 248, '*then*' : l. 254, '*as fay they*' : l. 255, '*Tanifth.*'

nominate and elect, for the moſt part, not the eldeſt
ſonne, nor any of the children of ther Lord deceaſed,
but the next to him of blood, that is the eldeſt and
worthieſt, as commonly the next brother unto him,
if he have any, or the next couzine germane, or ſo
forth, as any is elder in that kindred or ſept : and
then next to him do thoſe choſe the next of the
blood to be Taniſt, who ſhall next ſuccede him in
the ſayd Captenry, if he live therunto.

*Eudox.* / Do they uſe any ceremony in this election ? ffor all barberous nacōns are commonly great
obſervers of cerimonies and ſuperſtitious rights.

*Iren.* They uſe to place him that ſhall be their
Captaine, upon a ſtone alwayes reſerved for that
purpoſe, and placed commonly upon an hill : in many
of the which I have ſene the fote of a man formed
and graven, which they ſay was the meaſure of ther
firſt Captaines foot, wheron he ſtanding receiveth an
oath to preſerve all the former auncient cuſtomes
of the country inviolable, and to deliver up the
ſucceſſion peaceably to his Taniſt, and then hath
a wand delivered unto him by ſome, whoſe proper
office that is : after which, diſcending from the ſtone,
he tourneth him ſelf round, thrice forwarde and thrice
backward.

*Eudox.* But how is the Taniſt choſen ?

*Iren.* They ſay he ſetteth but one foote upon the
ſtone, and receiveth the like oath the Captaine did.

*Eudox.* Have you ever heard what was the occaſion and firſt beginning of this cuſtome ? for it is
good to know the ſame, and may perhaps diſcover

l. 289, ' *aboute.*'

ſome ſecret meaning and intent therein, very materiall
to the ſtate of that goverment.

*Iren.* I have heard that the beginning and cauſe
of this ordinance amongeſt the Iriſh, was ſpecially for 300
the defence and maintenance of ther land in ther
poſterity, and for excluding all innovacõn or aliena-
cõn / thereof unto ſtrangers, and eſpecially to the
Engliſh: for when ther Captaine dieth, if the
Seigniory ſhould diſcend unto his child, and he
perhaps an infant, another might perhaps ſtep in
betwene and thruſt him out by ſtrong hand, being
then vnable to defend his right, or to withſtand the
force of a forrayner: and therfore they do appoynt
the eldeſt of the kin to have the feigniory, for that 310
he commonly is a man of ſtronger yeares, and better
experience to maintain the inheritance, and to defend
the country, either againſt the next bordering Lords,
which uſe commonly to incroch one upon an other
as each one is ſtronger, or againſt the Engliſh, which
they thinck ly ſtill in wayte to wipe them out of
ther lands and territories. And to this end the
Taniſt is alwayes ready knowne, if it ſhould happen
the Captaine ſuddenly to dy or to be ſlayne in
batayle, or to be out of the country, to defend and 320
kepe it from all ſuch doubts and dangers. Ffor
which cauſe the Taniſt hath alſo a ſhare of the
country alotted unto him, and certaine cuttings and
ſpendings upon all the inhabitants under the Lord.

*Eudox.* When I heare this word Taniſt, it bringeth
to my remembrance what I have read of Tania, that it
ſhould ſignify a province or Seignory [as] Aquitania,

l. 304, '*dyed*': l. 326, '*mynd and.*'

Lufitania and Britania, the which fome do thinck to
be derived of Dania, that is, from the Danes : but, I
thinck, amiffe, for fure it femeth, that it came anciently 33(
from thofe barberous nacons that overranne the world,
which poffeffed thofe dominions, wherof they are now
fo called.　And fo it may well be that from thence
the firft originall of this word Tanift and Taniftry
came, and the cuftome therof hath fithence, as
many others els, bin continued : but to that generall
fubjection of the land, wherof we formerly fpake, me
femes that this cuftome or tenure can be no bar nor
impeachment, feing that in open parlyament by ther
fayd acknowledgment, they waived the benefit therof, 34(
and fubmitted them felves to the ordinance of ther
new foveraigne.

*Iren.* Yea but they fay, as I earft tould you, that
they referved their titles, tenures and feigniories
whole and found to them felves, and for proofe
alleged that they have ever fince remayned to them
untouched, fo as now to alter them, they fay fhoul'd
be a great wrong.

*Eudox.* What remedy is ther then, or means to
avoyde this inconvenience, for, without firft cutting out 35(
this dangerous cuftome, it femeth hard to plant any
found ordinance, or reduce them to a civill goverment,
fince all ther evill cuftomes are permitted unto them.

*Iren.* Surely nothing hard : for by this act of
parlament wherof we fpeake, nothing was given to
King Henry, which he had not before from his
aunceftors, but onely the bare name of a King :
ffor all other abfolute power of principallity he had

l. 330, ‘*for*’ is miswritten ‘*but*’ in our MS. : l. 350, ‘*of.*’

in him felf before derived from many former Kings,
his famous progenitours, and worthy conquerors of 360
that land, the which fince they firft conquered and by
force fubdued vnto them, what nede he afterward to
enter into any fuch idle tearmes with them to be
called ther King, when as it is in the power of the
Conqueror to take upon him felf what title he will
over his dominions conquered : for all is the conquerors, / as Tully to Brutus fayth : and therfore me
femes in ftead of fo great and meritorious a fervice,
as they boaft they performed to the King, in bringing
all the Irifh to acknowledg him for ther liege, they 370
did great hurt to his title, and have left a perpetuall
gall in the mind of that people, who before being
abfolutely bound to his obedience, are now tyed but
with tearmes whereas both ther lives, ther lands, and
their liberties were in his fre power to appoynt what
tenures, what lawes, what condicions he would over
them, which were all his : againft which ther could
be no rightfull affiftance, or if there were, he might,
when he would, eftablifh them with ftronger hand.

*Eudox.* Yea, but perhaps it femed better vnto 380
that noble King to bring them by ther owne accord
to his obedience, and to plant a peaceable goverment
amongeft them, then by fuch violent means to pluck
them under.  Neither yet hath he therby loft any
thing that he formerly had : for having al before
abfolutely in his owne power, it remayneth fo ftill,
he having neither forgiven nor forgon any thing
therby vnto them, but having received fomething

l. 374, '*wheras els*': l. 378, '*refiftance*': l. 383, '*keepe*': l. 386,
'*ftill vnto him.*'

from them, that is a more voluntary and loyall
fubjection.    So as her Majeftie may yet, when it fhall  3(
pleafe her, alter any thing of thos former ordinances,
or appoynt other lawes, that may be more both for
her own behoofe, and for the good of that poeple.

*Iren.* Not fo: for it is not fo eafy, now that things
are growne into an habit and have ther certaine
courfe, to change the channell, and turne ther
ftreames an other way; for they may have now a
collourable pretence to withftand fuch innovafion,
having accepted of other lawes and rules alredy.

*Eudox.* But you fay that they do not accept of 4(
them but delight rather to leane to the ould cuftomes
and Brehon lawes, though they be much more vnjuft,
and alfo more inconvenient for the common poeple,
as by your late relacon of them I gathered.    As for
the lawes of England, they are furely moft juft and
moft agreable both with the goverment and with the
nature of the poeple : how falls it out then, that you
feme to diflike of them, as not fo meete for that
realme of Ireland, and not onely the common law,
but alfo the ftatutes and acts of parlament, which 41
were fpecially provided and intended for the onely
benefit therof ?

*Iren.* I was about to have tould you my reafon
therin, but that you your felf drew me away with
other queftions, for I was fhewing you by what
means, and in what fort, the pofitive lawes were firft
brought in and eftablifhed by the Norman Conqueror:
which were not by him devifed, nor applyed to the
ftate of the realme then being, nor as it might beft
be, (as fhould by lawgivers be principally regarded,) 42

but were indede the very lawes of his owne country
of Normandy : the condicon wherof, how far it
differeth from this of England, is apparent to every
leaft judgment.  But to transfer the fame lawes for
the governing of the realme of Ireland, was much
more inconvenient and unmete : for he found a better
advantage of the time, then was in the planting
of them in Ireland, and followed the execution of
them with more feverity, and was alfo · prefent in
perfon to overloke the magiftrates, and to over awe 430
the fubjects with the terror of his fword, and countenance of his Majeftie.  But not fo in Ireland : for they
were otherwife effected, and yet not fo remayned, fo
as the fame lawes, me femes, can ill fit with their
difpoficion, or work that reformacon that is wifhed :
for lawes ought to be fafhioned unto the manners
and condicons of the people, to whom they are
ment, and not to be impofed upon them according
to the fimple rule of right : for then, as I fayd,
in ftead of good they may worke ill, and pervert 440
juftice to extreame injuftice : ffor he that would
transfer the lawes of the Lacedemonians to the
poeple of Athens fhould find a great abfurdity and
inconvenience : for thofe lawes of Lacedemon were
devifed by Licurgus, as moft proper and beft agreeing
with that people, whom he knew to be inclined
altogether to warrs, and therfore wholy trayned them
up even from ther cradles in armes and military
exercifes, cleane contrary to the inftitution of Solon,
who, in his lawes to the Athenians labored by all 450

1. 428, '*Ireland*' miswritten '*England*' in our MS.: l. 433, '*affected*':
*ib.*, ' *doe.*'

means to temper ther warlike courages with fwete
delights of learning and fcienfes, fo that as much as
the one excelled in armes, the other exceded in
knowledg : the like regard and moderation ought to
be had in tempering and menaging of this ftubburn
nation of the Irifh, to bring them from their delight
of licenfious barbarifme unto the love of goodneffe
and civillity.

*Eudox.* I cannot fe how that may better be then
·by the difcipline of the lawes of England : for the
Englifh were, at firft, as ftoute and war like a poeple
as ever were the Irifh, and yet ye fe are now
brought to that civillity, that no nacon in the world
excelleth them in all godly converfacon, and all
the ftudies of knowledg and humanity.

*Iren.* What they now be, both you and I fe very
well, but by how many thorny and hard wayes they
are come therunto, by how many civill broyles, by
how many tumultuous rebellions, that even hazard[ed]
often times the whole fafety of the kingdome, may
eafily be confidered : all which they nevertheleffe
fairely overcame, by reafon of the continewall prefence
of the King, whos onely perfon is oftentimes in ftead
of an army, to contayne the unruly poeple from a
thoufand evill occafions, which that wretched kingdome, is for want therof daily carried into. The
which when they fo make head, no lawes, no penalties can reftraine, but that they do in the violence of
that fury, tread doune and trample under foote all
both divine and humane things, and the lawes themfelves they do fpecially rage at, and rend in peces, as

l. 479, '*theyr.*'

moſt repugnant to ther liberty and naturall fredome, which in ther madneſſe they effect.

*Eudox.* It is then a very unſeaſonable time to plead law, when ſwords are in the hands of the vulgare, or to thinck to retaine them with feare of puniſhments when they loke after liberty, and ſhake of all goverment.

*Iren.* Then ſo it is with Ireland continually, for the ſword was never yet out of ther hand, but when they 490 are weary with warrs, and brought dounc to extreame wretchedneſſe, then they creepe a litle perhaps, and fewe for grace, till they have gotten new breath and recòvered ſtrength againe : ſo as it is in vaine to ſpeake of planting of lawes, and plotting of pollicies, till they be altogether ſubdued.

*Eudox.* Were they not ſo at the firſt conquering of them by Strangbowe, in the time of King Henry the ſecond ? was ther not a thorowe way then made by the ſword, for the impoſing of the lawes upon 500 them ? and were they not then executed with ſuch mighty hand as you ſayd was uſed by the Norman Conqueror ?  What ods is there then in this caſe ? why ſhould not the ſame lawes take as good effect in that poeple, as they did here, being in like ſort prepared by the ſword, and brought under by ex- tremity ? and why ſhould it not continew in as good force and vigor for the contayning of the poeple ?

*Iren.* The caſe yet is not like, but ther apperes great odds betwene them ; for by the conqueſt of 510 Henry the ſecond, trew it is that the Iriſh were utterly vanquiſhed and ſubdued, ſo as no enemy was

1. 496, '*are.*'

able to hould up head againſt his powre : in which there weakeneſſe he brought in his lawes, and ſettled them as now they ther remaine, like as William the Conqueror did : ſo as in thus much they agre, but in the reſt, that is in the chiefeſt, they varie : ffor to whom did King Henry the ſecond impoſe thos lawes, not to the Iriſh, for the moſt part of them fled from his power into deſerts and moun- taines, leaving the wide country to the conqueror, who in their ſtead eftſones placed Engliſh men, who poſſeſſed all the land and did quite ſhut out the Iriſh, or the moſt part of them : And to thoſe new inhabitants and Colonies he gave his lawes, to wete, the ſame lawes under which they were born and bred, the which it was not difficulte to place amongeſt them, being formerly well entred ther- unto : unto whom afterward ther repayred divers of the pore diſtreſſed poeple of the Iriſh for ſuccor and relieſe : of whom ſuch as they thought fit for labor, and / induſtriouſlie diſpoſed, as the moſt part of theire baſer ſort are, they received unto them as theire vaſſalls, but ſcarcelie vouchſafed to imparte unto them the benefite of thoſe lawes, vnder which them ſelves lived, but everie one made his will a coṁandment and a lawe unto his owne vaſſall. Thus was not the lawe of England ever properlie applied unto the Iriſh nacon, as by a purpoſte plott of goverment, but as they could inſynuate and ſteale them ſelves under the ſame by theire humble carriage and ſubmiſſion.

*Eudox.* Howe comes it then to paſſe, that havinge

l. 528, '*inured*' : ll. 536-7, '*will and commandment a lawe.*'

ben once fo lowe brought, and, thoroughlie fubjected
they afterwards lifted them felves fo ftronglie agayne,
and fithence doe ftand ftifflie againft all rule and
goverment ?

*Iren.* They faie that they contynued in that
lowlyneffe untill the time that the divifion betwene
the houfes of Lancafter and Yorke arofe for the 550
Crowne of England : At which tyme all the greate
Englifh lords and gentlemen which had greate pos-
feffions in Ireland, repaired over hither into England,
to fuccor their ffrendes here and to ftrengthen theire
partie for to obtene the Crowne : others to defend
there landes and poffeffions againft fuche as hovered
after the fame uppon hope of the alteracon of the
kingdome, and fucceffe of that fide which they
favored and effected. Then the Irifhe whom they
before had banifhed into the mountaynes, where they 560
lived onlie uppon white meates, as it is recorded :
feeinge nowe there fo difpeopled land weakened,
came downe into all the playnes adjoyninge, and
thence expellinge thofe fewe Englifhe that remayned,
repoffeffte them agayne ; fynce whych tyme they
have remayned in them, and growinge greater,
have brought under them many of the Englifhe,
which were before theire lords. This is one of the
occafions by which all thofe countries which, lyinge
nere unto any mountaynes or Irifhe deferts, which 570
had bin planted with Englifhe, were fhortlie dis-
planted and loft. As namelie / in Mounfter, all the
landes adjoyninge unto Slowlougher, Arlo, and the

1. 550, ' *two* ' : l. 552, ' *fome* ' : l. 556, ' *here* '; l. 558, ' *fucceffion* '
l. 568, ' *was.* '

bogg of Allon.    In Connaght, all the Countries borderinge uppon the Culvers; Montroo, and Orourkes
countrie.    In Leinfter all the landes neighboring
unto the mountaynes of Glanmulls, unto Shellelagh,
unto the Brifkbagh, and Poulmont.    In Ulfter, all
the countries nere unto Tirconnell, Tyronne, and
Hertellagh, and the Scottes.

*Eudox.* Surelie this was a greate violence: but yett
by your fpeche it femeth that onlie the Countric and
vallies nere adioyninge unto thofe mountaynes and
defertes, were thus recovered by the Irifhe : but
howe comes it nowe that wee fee almoft all that
Realme repoffeffed of them ?    Was there any more
fuche evill occafons growinge by the troubles of
England ?  or did the Irifhe, out of thes places fo by
them gotten, breake further and ftretche them felves
out thorough the whole land ?    But nowe for ought
that I can underftand, there is no parte but the bare
Englifh pale, in which the Irifhe have not the greateft
footing.

*Iren.* Bothe out of theis fmale begynnynges by
them gotten nere to the mountaynes, did they
fpreade them felves into the Inland Countrie ; and
alfo, to theire further advantage, there did other
like unhappie accidentes happen out of England,
which gave harte and good opportunitye to them to
regayne theire oulde poffeffions.    Ffor in the reigne of
Kinge Edward the fourth, thinges remayned yet in
the fame ftate that they were after the late breakinge
out of the Irifhe, which I fpake of : And that noble

l. 575, ' *Mointerolis* ' : l. 577, ' *Glaunmaleerih* ' : l. 578, '*Brifkelah* ' :
l. 589, ' *for.* '

Prince began to caft an eye unto Ireland, and to mynde the refermacon of thinges there rune amiffe : for he fent over his brother the worthie Duke of Clarence, who having married the heire of Larie, and by her havinge all the Erledome of Ulfter, and moche in Meathe and in Mounfter, verie carefullie went about the redreffinge of thofe late evills : and 610 though he could not beate out the Irifhe agayne, by reafon of his fhorte contynuance, yet he did fhutt them upp within thofe narrowe corners and glennes under the mountayne foote, in which they lurked, and foe kept them from breaking any further, by buildinge ftrang holdes uppon everie border, and fortefyinge all paffages : Amongeft the which he built the caftle of Clare in Thomond : of which Countrie he had the inheritance, and of Mortymers landes adjoyninge, which is nowe by the Irifhe, 620 called Killalowe. But the tymes of that good Kinge growinge troublefome, did lett the thorowe reformacon of all things. And thereunto foone after was added another fatall mifcheife, which wrought a greater calamitie then all the former. For the faid Duke of Clarence, then Lord Lief-tenant of Ireland, was by practize of evill perfons about the Kinge his brother, called thence awaye : and foone after by fynifter meanes was cleane made awaye. Prefentlie after whofe deathe all the North 630 revoltinge, did fett up Oneale for theire Capten, beinge before that of fmale power and regard : and there arofe in that parte of Thomond, one of the

---

l. 607, '*Earle of Ulfter*' : l. 614, in our MS. '*they lurked . . . further*' has got misplaced.

O-Bryens, called Murrogh en ranagh, that is, Morrys
of the ffarme, or wafte wylde places : who, gatheringe
unto him all the relickes of the difcontented Irifhe,
eftfones furprifed the faid Caftle of Clare, burnt and
fpoyled all the Englifhe there dwellinge, and in fhort
fpace poffeffed all the countrie beyonde the river
of Shenan and nere adjoyninge : whence fhortlie 6
breakinge forth like a fudden tempeft, he overran
all Mounfter and Connaught, breakinge downe all
the holdes and fortreffes of the Englifhe, defacinge
and utterlie fubvertinge all corporate Townes that
were not ftronglie walled : for thofe he had no
meanes nor engynes to overthrowe, neither indede,
would he ftay at all about them, but fpeedilie ran
forwarde, counting his fuddennes his moft vantage,
that he might overtake the Englifhe / before they
could fortefie or gather them felves together.    So 6
in fhort tyme he cleane wyped out many greate
townes, as firft in Chegin, the Killalowe, before
called Clarryfort, afterward Tharles, Mourne, Butte-
vant, and many others, viz.    [blank of nearly a line]
whofe names I can not remember, and of fome of
which there is nowe no memorie nor figne remayning.    Upon report whereof there flocked unto him
all the fcume of the Irifhe out of all places,
that ere longe he had a mightie army, and thence
marched forth into Lynfter, where he wrought greate 6
outrages, waftinge and fpoylinge all the Countrie
where he went : ffor it was his pollicie to leave
no holde behinde him, but to make all playne and

---

l. 635, ' *Fearne*': !. 640, '*Shannon*' : l. 648, ' *accounting*': l. 651,
'*fpace*': l. 652, ' *Infhequinn* ' : l. 653, ' *Thurles.*'

wafte.   In the which he fone after created himfelfe
Kinge, and was called Kinge of all Ireland ; which
before him I doe not reade, that any did fo
generallie, but onelie Edwarde lee Bruce.

*Eudox.* What, was there ever any generall Kinge
of all Ireland ?   I never heard it before, but that
it was alwaies, whileft it was under the Yrifhe, 670
devided into fower, and fometymes into five kingdomes or dominions.   But this Edward lee Bruce,
what was he, that he could make him felfe Kinge
of all Ireland ?

*Iren.* I would tell you, that in cafe you would not
challendge me for forgetting the matter which I had
in hand, that is, the inconvenience and unfitnes which
I fuppofed to be in the lawes of the land.

*Eudox.* No furelie I have no caufe, for neither
is this impertynent thereunto ; for fithence you did 680
fett your corfe, as I remember, in your firft parte, to
treate of the evills which hindereth the peace and
good orderinge of that land, amongeft which that
of the inconvenience of the lawes was the firft which
you had in hand, this difcourfe of the overrunninge
and waftinge of the realme is verie materiall there
unto, for that it was the begynnyng of other evills,
which fithence / have afflicted that land, and opened
a way unto the Irifhe to recover theire poffeffion,
and to beate out the Englifhe which had formerlie 690
wonne the fame.   And befides, it will give greate
light both unto the feconde and third parte, which
is the redreffinge of thofe evills, and plantinge of
fome good forme or pollicie therin, by renewinge the

l. 666, ' *remember*' : l. 676, ' *anone*' : l. 679, ' *occafion* ' : l. 687, ' *all.*'

remembrance of thofe occafions and accidentes, by which thofe ruynes hapned, and layinge before us the enfamples of thofe tymes, to be compared with ours and to be rewarded by thofe which fhall have to doe in the like. Therefore I praye yow, tell them unto us, and as for the point where you lefte, 7ᵢ I will not forgett afterwardes to call you backe agayne thereunto.

*Iren.* This Edward le Bruce, was the brother of King Roberte lee Bruce, who was Kinge of Scotland att fuch tyme as King Edwarde the fecond reigned here in England, and bare a moft malicious and fpitefull mynde againft King Edwarde, doinge him all the fcathe he could, and annoyinge his territories of England, whileft he was troubled with civill warres of his Barons att home. He alfo, to worke him the more 7 mifcheife, fent over his faid brother Edwarde, with a power of Scottes and Red-fhankes into Ireland, where, by meanes of the Lacies and of the Irifhe with whom they combyned, they gott footinge, and gatheringe unto him all the fcatterlyn[g]s and out-lawes out of all the woodes and mountaynes, in which they longe had lurked, marched forth into the Englifh pale, which then was cheiflie in the North, from the point of Dunluce, and beyonde unto Dublyn : havinge in the middeft of her Knock- 7: fergus ; Belfaft ; Armagh ; Carlingforde, which are nowe the moft out-boundes and abandoned places in the Englifhe pale, and fome no parte thereof at all : ffor it ftretcheth nowe noe further then Dundalke towardes the North. There the faid Edward lee

1. 698, '*warned*': 1. 708, '*hurt*.'

Bruce fpoyled and burnt all the old Englifh pale,
puttinge to the fworde all the Englifhe inhabitantes,
and facked and raced all Cytties and corporate
Townes, no leffe / then Murro en Ranagh, of whom
I earft tolde you : ffor hee wafted Belfaft, Greene 730
caftell, Kiells, Beltalbott, Caftletowne, Newtowne,
and many other verie good townes and ftronge
holdes : he rooted out the noble ffamilies of the
Audleys, the Talbottes, the Tutchites, the Cham-
berlynes, the Mandevilles, and the Salvages, though
of the Lord Salvage there remayne yet an heire,
that is nowe a verie poore gentleman dwellinge at
the Ardes. And cominge laftlie to Dundalke, he
there made him felfe Kinge and rained by the fpace
of one whole yere, by the name of Edwarde kinge 740
of Ireland, untill that Kinge Edwarde of England,
havinge fett fome quiett in his affaires at home, fent
over the lord John Bermingham to be Generall of
the warres againft him, who, encountringe him nere
to Dundalke, overthrew his armye, and flewe him
felf, and prefentlie followed the victorie fo hotlie
upon his Scottes, that he fuffred them not to ftaye,
or gather them felves togeather agayne, untill they
came to the fea coaft. Notwythftandinge, all the
waie as they fledd, for verie rancor and difpight, they 750
utterlie wafted and confumed whatfoever they had
before left unfpoiled ; fo that of all townes and
caftells, fortes, and bridges and habitacons, he left
not any ftick ftanding, nor any people remayninge :
for thofe fewe, which yett furvived, fledd frŏ his

---

l. 737, '*of verie meane condition*' not in our MS. here : l. 743,
'*Bremmegham*' : l. 747, '*breathe*' : l. 753, '*they.*'

furye further into the Englifhe pale that nowe is.
Thus was all that godlie Countrie utterlie wafted and
left defolate. And as [it] yet remayneth to this
daie, which before had ben the cheife ornament and
beautie of Ireland. ffor that parte of the northe 7ʹ
fometyme was as populous and plentifull as any parte
in England, and yelded unto the kinges of England,
as yett appeareth by good recordes, thirtie thowfand
markes of olde money by the peece, befide many
thowfand of able men to ferve them in their warres.
Suer it is yett a moft bewtifull and fweete Country
as any is under heaven, feamed thoroughout with
many godlie rivers, replenifhed with all fortes of fifhe
moft aboundantlie : fprinkled with verie many fweete
Ilandes and goodlie lakes, like litle inland feas, that 7
will carrie even fhippes uppon theire waters, adorned
with goodlie woodes, fitt for buildinge of houfes and
fhipes, fo comodiouflie, as that if fome princes in the
world had them, they would foone hope to be lordes
of all the feas, and er longe of all the worlde : alfo
full of verie good portes and havens openinge uppŏ
England [and] Scotland, as invitinge us to come unto
them, to fee what excellent comoditics that Countrie
can afforde, befides the foyle it felfe moft fertile, fitt
to yelde all kynde of fruit that fhalbe comitted 7
there unto. And laftlie the heavens moft milde and
temperate, though fomewhat more moyfte then the
partes towardes the Weft.

　*Eudox.* Truly Irenius, what with the prayfes
of your countrie, and what with the lamentable
Dyfolucon thereof made by thofe ragtailes in

　　　l. 764, '*yeare*' : l. 786, '*defolation.*'

Scotland, you have fylled me with a greate
compaffion of theire calamities, that I doe moch
pittie that fweet land, to be fubject to fo many
evills, as everie daie I fee more and more throwen 790
upon her, and doe halfe begynne to thinke, that it
is, as you faid at the begynnynge, her fatall mis-
fortune, above all countries that I knowe, to be thus
miferablie toffed and turmoiled with theis variable
ftormes of afflictions : But fynce wee are thus far
entred into the confideracon of her mifhappes, tell me,
have there ben any more fuch tempeftes, as you
terme them, wherein fhe hath thus wretchedlie ben
wracked ?

*Iren.* Verie many more, god wot, have there 800
ben, in which her principall partes have ben torne
a funder, but none that I can remember, fo
univerfall as thefe. And yet the rebellion of Thomas
ffitzGarrett did well nighe ftretche it felf into all
partes of Ireland. But that, which was in the tyme
of the governement of the Lord Gray, was furelie no
leffe generall then all theis ; for there was no part
free from the contagion, but all confpired in one to
caft off theire fubjeccon to the Crowne of England.
Nevertheles, thorough the moft wife and valiant 810
handlinge of that right noble Lord, yt got not that
head which the former evills found ; for in them the
Realme was left, like a fhipp in a ftorme amiddeft all
the raginge furges, unruled and undirected of any :
ffor they to whom fhe was comitted either fainted in
theire labor, or forfooke theire charge. But he, like
a moft wife pilott, kept her corfe carefullie, and helde

l. 804, '*Fitz Gerrald.*'

her moſte ſtronglie againſt thoſe roaringe billowes, that he brought her ſafelie out of all ; ſo as longe after, even by the ſpace of xij or xiij yeres, ſhe rode 8. at peace, thorough his onlie paynes and excellent endurance, how ever envye liſt to blatter againſt him. But of this wee ſhall have more occacon to ſpeake at an other tyme : now (if it pleaſe you) lett us return agayne unto our firſt corſe.

*Eudox.* Trulie I am verie glad to heare your judgement of the governement of that honourable man ſo ſoundlie ; ffor I have heard it oftentymes maligned, and his doinges depraved of ſome, who, I perceyve, did rather of malicious mynde, or private greevance, 8. ſeeke to detract from the honor of his deedes and counſells, then of any juſt cauſe : but he was nevertheles, in the judgement of all good and wiſe men, defended and maynteyned. And nowe that he is dead, his imortall fame ſurviveth, and floriſheth in the mouthes of all the pœple, that even thoſe which did backbite him, are choked with theire owne venom, and breake theire galls to heare his ſo honorable report : But lett him reſt in peace, and turne wee to oure more troublous matters of 8. Diſcourſe, of which I am right ſorie that you make ſo ſhort an end, and covet to paſſe over to your former purpoſe ; for there be many other partes of Ireland, which I have hearde have ben no leſſe vexed with the like ſtormes, then theis of which you have treated. As the Countrie of the Byrnes and Tooles nere Dublyn, with the inſolent outrages and ſpoyles of ffeagh mã Hugh, the countries of Carlo,

<hr>

l. 822, ‘ *bluſter* ’ : l. 848, ‘ *Katerlagh.* ’

Wexforde, and Waterforde, of the Cavenaghes:
The countries of Leix, Kilkennye, and Kildare, of 850
the Moores. The countries of Offalie, Meath and
Langford, of the Conhours. The countries of Weſt-
meath, Cavan, and Louth, of the O Relyes, the
Kellies, and many others. So as the diſcourſing
of them, beſides the pleaſure which ſhould redound
out of your hiſtorie, be alſo verie proffitable for matter
of pollicye.

*Iren.* All theſe which you have named, and many
more beſides, often tymes have I right well knowne,
to kyndle greately ſyres of tumultuous troubles in 860
the countries bordering uppon them. All which to
rehearſe ſhould rather be to Chronicle tymes, then
to ſearche into the reformacon of abuſes in that
Realme: and yet verie nedefull it wilbe to conſider
them, and the evills which they have ſtirred upp, that
ſome redreſſe thereof, and prevencon of the evills to
come, may thereby rather be devyſed. But I
ſuppoſe wee ſhall have a fitter oportunity for the
ſame, when wee ſhall ſpeake of the particler abuſes
and enormities of the goverment, which wilbe next 870
after theſe generall defeﬅes and inconveniences, which
I ſaid were in the lawes, cuſtomes, and religion.

*Eudox.* Goe to them in gods name, and followe
the courſe which yee have purpoſed to your ſelfe, for
yt fitteth / beſt I muſt confeſſe with the purpoſe of
our diſcorſe. Declare your opynion, as you begon,
about the lawes of the Realme, what incomoditie you
have conceived to be in them, cheifly in the comõn

---

l. 849, '*Kevanaghs*': l. 850, '*Leis*': l. 860, '*broyles*': l. 873,
'*Goe to then a Godes name*': l. 874, '*promiſed.*'

lawe, which I would have thought moſt free from all
ſuch diſlike.

*Iren.* The comon lawe is, as I before ſaid, of it
ſelfe moſt rightfull and verie convenient, I ſuppoſe,
for the kingdom for which it was firſt devized ; for
this, I thinke, as yt ſeemes reaſonable, that out of
the manners of the people, and abuſes of the countrie,
for which they were invented, they tooke theire firſt
begynninge, for elſe they ſhould be moſt unjuſt : for
no lawes of man, accordinge to the ſtraight rule of
right, are juſt, but as in regard of the evills which
they prevent, and the ſafetie of the comon weale
which they provide for.   As for example, in the true
ballancinge of Juſtice, it is a flatt wrong to puniſhe
the thought or purpoſe of any, before it be enaᵉcted :
for true juſtice puniſheth  nothinge but the evill aᵉcte
or wycked worde ; yet by the lawes of all kingdomes
it is a capitall cryme, to deviſe or purpoſe the death
of the King : the reaſon is, for that when ſuch a
purpoſe is eᵉffeᵉcted, it ſhould be to late to deviſe
of the puniſhment thereof, and ſhould turne that
comon-weale to more hurt by ſuche loſſe of theire
Prince, then ſuche puniſhment of the malefaᵉctors.
And therefore the lawe in that caſe puniſheth his
thought: for better is a miſcheif, then an inconvenience.   So that *jus polliticum*, though it be not of it
ſelfe juſt, yet by applicacon, or rather neceſſitie, it is
made juſt ; and this only reſpeᵉct maketh  all lawe
juſt.   Nowe then, if theſe lawes of Ireland be not
likewiſe applied  and fitted for that Realme, they· are
ſure verie inconvenient.

*Eudox.* You reaſon ſtrongelie : but what unfitneſs

doe you fynde in them for that Realme ? fhewe us fome particulers.

*Iren.* The comon lawe appointeth that all trialls, afwel of crymes as titles and ryghtes, fhall be made by verdict of Jurye, chofen out of the honeftift and moft fubftancall free-holders : Nowe, all the ffree-holders of that Realme are Irifhe, which when the caufe fhall fall betwene an Irifhe man and an Englyfhe, or betweene the Quene and any ffree-holder of that countrye, they make no more fcruple 920 to paffe againft the Englifheman, or the Quene, though it bee to ftrayne theire oathes, then to drinke milke unftrayned. So that before the Jury goe togeather, it is all to nothing what theire verdict will be. The tryall thereof have I fo often fene, that I dare confidentlie avouche the abufe thereof : Yet is the lawe of it felfe, as I faid, good ; and the firft inftitucon thereof being given to all Englifhe-men verie rightfull, but nowe that the Yrifhe have ftepped into the rowmes of the Englifhe, who are 930 nowe become fo hedefull and provident to keepe them forth from thensforth, that they make no fcruple of confcience to paffe againft them, it is good reafon that either that corfe of the Lawe for trialls be altered, or other provifion for Juries be made.

*Eudox.* In foothe, Iren : you have difcovered a point worth the confideracon ; for hereby not onelie the Englifhe fubject fyndeth no indifferencie in decidinge of his caufe, be it never fo juft ; but alfo the Quene, afwell in all pleas of the crowne, 940 as alfo for all inquiries for efcheate ; landes attainted,

l. 920, '*they*' miswritten '*that*' in MS.

wardſhipps, concealementes, and all ſuche like, is
abuſed, and excedinglie endamaged.

*Iren.* You / ſaie veric true ; for I dare undertake,
that at this daie there are more attainted landes,
concealed from her Majeſtie, then ſhe hathe poſſeſſions
in all Ireland : and that is no ſmale Inconvenience :
for, beſides that ſhe looſeth ſo moche land as ſhould
turne ther to her greate proffitt, ſhe beſides looſeth
ſo many good ſubjectes, which might be aſſured 9
to her, as thoſe landes would yelde inhabitantes and
living unto.

*Eudox.* But does that people, ſaie you, make no
moer conſcience to perjuer them ſelfes in there
verdictes, and to dampne there ſowles ?

*Iren.* Not onelie ſo in there verdictes, but alſo
in all other there dealinges, ſpeciallie with the
Engliſhe, they are moſt wilfullie bent : for though
they will not ſeme manifeſtlye to doe it, yet will
ſome one or other ſubtile headed fellowe amongeſt 9
them, pick ſome quirke, or devyſe ſome ſubtill
evaſion, whereof the reſt will lightlie take holde of,
and ſuffer them ſelves eaſilie to be ledd by him to
that them ſelves deſired : ffor in the moſt apparant
matter that can be, the leaſt queſtion or dowbt that
can be moved, will make ſtop unto them, and put
them quite out of the way. Beſides that, of them
ſelves, they are for the moſt parte, ſo cautelous and
wylie headed, eſpeciallie beinge men of ſo ſmale
experience and practize in lawe matters, that you 9
would wonder whence they borrowe ſuche ſubtilties
and ſlye ſhiftes.

*Eudox.* But mee thinke, this inconvenience might

be moche helped in the judges and cheif majeftrates which have the choofinge and nominatinge of thofe Jurors, yf they would have care to appoint either moft Englifhemen, or fuche Yrifhemen as were of the fowndeft difpofition ; for wee dowbt not but fome there bee incorruptible.

*Iren.* Some there be in dede as you faie ; but 980 then woulde the Irifhe partie cry out of partialitie, and complayne he hathe not Juftice, he is not ufed as a fubject, he is not fuffered to have the free benefitt of the lawe : And theis outcryes the majestrates there doe moche fhunne, as they have caufe, fynce they are fo reddelie harkened unto here ; neither can it indede, although the Irifhe partie would be content to be fo compaffed, that fuch englifhe freeholders, which are but fewe, and fuche faithful yrifhemen, which are in dede as fewe, fhall 990 alwaies be chofen for trialls : ffor beinge fo fewe, they fhoulde fone be made wearie of theire freeholdes. And therefore a good care is to be had by all good occafions to encreafe theire nomber, and to plant more by them. But were it fo that the Juries could bee picked out of fuche choife men as you defire, there would neverthelles be as bad a corrupcon in the triall : ffor the evidence beinge brought in by the bafe Irifhe people, will be as deceiptfull as the verdictes : for they care muche 1000 leffe then the others what they fweare, and fure theire lordes may compell them to faie any thing : ffor my felf have heard, when one of that bafe fort, which they call charles, being challenged, and re-

l. 976, '*juryes*' : l. 978, '*judgemente and.*'

prooved for his falfe oathe, have anfwered confidentlie, that his lord comaunded him, and that it was the leaft thinge he could doe for his lord, to fweare for him : fo inconfcionable are theis comon people, and fo litle feeling have they of god, or theire owne fowles good.

*Eudox.* It is a moft miferable cafe : but what helpe can there be in this ? ffor though the manner of the triall fhoulde be altered, yet the proofe of every thinge, muft nedes be by teftimonies of fuch perfons as the parties fhall produce : which if they fhall corrupt, hower can there any light of truthe appeare ? what remedy is there for this evill, but to make heavie lawes and penalties againft jurors ?

*Iren.* I thinke fure that will doe fmale good ; ffor when a people are inclyned to any vice, or have no towche of confcience, nor fence of theire evill doinge, yt is booteles to thinke to reftrayne them by any penalties or feare of punifhment ; but either the occacon is to be taken awaie, or a more under-ftandinge of the right, or fhame of the fault is to be imprinted : For if Lycurgus fhould have made it deathe for the Lacedemonians to fteale, they beinge a people which naturallic delighted in ftealth, or if it fhoulde be made a capitall cryme for the Fflemminges to be taken in drunkennes, there fhould have been fewe Lacedemonians foone left, and fewer Fflem-minges : fo unpoffible it is to remove any fault fo generall in a people, with terror of lawes or more fharpe reftraintes.

*Eudox.* What meanes may there be then to

l. 1033, ' *moft.*'

avoide this inconvenience? for the caufe fure femes verie harde.

*Iren.* Wee are not yet come to that point to devyfe remedies for the evills, but onlie have nowe to recompt them; of the which, this that I have 1040 tolde you is one defect in the common Lawe.

*Eudox.* Tell us then, I praie you further, have you any more of this forte in the common Lawe?

*Iren.* By reherfall of this, I remember alfo of an other like, which I have often obferved in trialls to have wrought greate hurt and hinderance, and that is, the excepcons which the common Lawe alloweth a fellon in his triall: ffor he may have, as you knowe, xxxvj excepcons peremptorye againft the Jurors, of which he fhall fhewe no caufe, and as many 1050 as he will of fuche, as he can fhew caufe. By which fhifte there beinge, as I have fhewed you fuche fmale ftore of honeft Jurie men, he will either put of his triall, or drive it to fuche men as perhapps are not of the fowndeft forte, by whofe meanes, yf he can acquite him felf of the cryme, as he is likelie, then will he plage fuche as were brought firft to be of his jury, and all fuche as made any partie againft him, and when he comes forth, will make theire cowes and garrons to walke, yf he doe not other mifcheif 1060 to theire perfons.

*Eudox.* This is a flye device, but I thinke might fone bee remedied : but wee muft leave it a while with the reft: in the meane tyme doe you goe forward with others.

*Iren.* There is an other no leffe inconvenient then

l. 1054, '*leaue*'

this, which is for the triall of acceffaries to felony :
ffor, by the comon Lawe, the acceffarie can not be
proceeded againft till the principall have receyved
his triall.   Nowe the cafe often falleth in Ireland,
that a ftealth beinge made by a rebell, or an outlawe,
the ftolen goodes are conveyed to fome hufbandman or gente, which hath well to take to, and yet
liveth moft by the receipt of fuche ftealthes, where
they are found by the owner, and handled : where-
uppon the partie perhapps is apprehended and
comitted to gaole, or putt uppon fuerties, till the
Seffions, at which the owner, preferring a bill of
Indiftment, proveth fufficiently the ftealth to have
ben comitted vppon him by fuche an outlawe, and
to have ben found in the poffeffion of the prifoner,
againft whom, nevertheles, no caufe of Lawe can
proceede, nor triall can be had, for that the principall
theife is not to be gotten, notwithftandinge that he
likewife, ftandeth perhapps indifted at once with the
receyver, beinge in rebellion, or in the woodes, where
peradventure he is flayne before hee is taken, and fo
the receivor cleane acquited and difcharged of the
cryme.   By which meanes the theeves are greatlic
encoraged to fteale, and theire mainteyners imboldned
to receive theire ftealthes, knowing howe hardlie they
can be brought to any triall of lawe.

*Eudox.* Trulie this is a greate inconvenience, and
a greate caufe, as you faie, of the maintenance of
theeves, knowinge theire receivors alwaies readie ;
ffor, would there be no receivors, there woulde be no

l.  1070, '*falleth out*' : l.  1073, '*gentleman*' : l.  1074, '*goodes
ftolen*' : l.  1082, '*courfe*' : l.  1087, '*ftowne.*'

theeves. But this, me femes, might eafelie be provided for by fome act of Parliament, that the receivor,
beinge convicted by good proofes, might receive his
triall without the Principall. 1100

*Iren.* You faie verie true, Eudox : but that is
almoft impoffible to be compaffed. And herein alfo
you difcover an other imperfeccon in the courfe of
the comon Lawe, and firft ordynance of the Realme ;
for you knowe that the faid Parliament muft confift
of the peeres, gentlemen, freeholders, and burgeffes of
that Realme it felf. Nowe theis beinge perhappes
them felves, or the moft parte of them (as maye feeme
by theire ftif with-ftandinge of this act) culpable
of this cryme, or favorers of theire friendes, which 1110
are fuche by whom theire kitchins are fometymes
amended, will not fuffer any fuche ftatute to paffe.
Yet hathe it oftentymes ben attempted, and in the
tyme of Sir John Perrott verye earneftlie, I remember,
labored, but by no meanes could be effected : And
not onelie this, but many other like, which are as
nedefull for the reformacon of that Realme.

*Eudox.* This alfo is furelie a great defect, but wee
maye not talke, you faie, of the redreffing of this,
untyll our feconde parte come, which is purpofelye 1120
appointed thereunto. Therefore procede to the
recountinge of moe fuche evilles, yf at leafte you
have any more.

*Iren.* There is alfo a greate inconvenience which
hath wrought greate dammadge both to her Majeftie,
and to that Common wealth, through clofe and
collorable conveyances of the landes and goodes of
Traytors, fellons, and fugitives : as, when one of

IX. 4

them myndeth to goe into rebellyon, he will convey away all his landes and Lordſhips to ſcoffes in truſt, wherby he reſerveth to himſelfe but a ſtate for terme of lief, which beinge determined either by the ſword or by the haulter, theire Lande ſtreighte com̃eth to the heire, and the queene is defrauded of the intent of the Lawe, which layed that grivyous puniſhment upon Traytors to forfeite all theire landes to the Prince, to the ende that men might be the rather terrefied from com̃yttinge treaſons : ffor many which would little eſteeme theire owne lyves, yet for remorſe of theire wyves and children, ſhoulde bee withhelde from that hayneous cryme. This appeared playnelie in the late Earle of Deſmond ; ffor before his break-inge forth into open rebellyon, he hade conveyed ſecretelie all his landes to ſeoffes of truſt, in hope to have cutt of her Majeſtie from the eſcheate of his landes.

*Eudox.* Yea, but that was well ynoughe avoyded ; ffor the ac̃te of Parliament which gave all his landes to the queene did, (as I have hearde,) cutt of and fruſtrate all ſuche conveyaunces, as had any tyme, by the ſpace of xii yeres before his rebellyon, bene made: within the Compaſſe whereof, that fraudulent feoffement, and many other the like of his accom-pliſſes and fellow-Traytors, were contayned.

*Iren.* Very true, but howe hardlie that ac̃te of Parliament was wrounge out of them, I cann wytnes : and were yt to be compaſſed againe, I dare undertake it would never be compaſſed. But were yt foe

---

1. 1132, '*eſtate*' : l. 1154, '*attaynted*' [for '*contayned*'] · *hath bene made voyd*' : ll. 1157-8, '*I dare . . . compaſſed*' not in our MS.

that fuch actes might eafilie be brought to paffe
againft Traytors and fellons, yet were yt not an 1160
endles trouble, that no Traytor nor fellon fhould
be attaynted, but a Parliament muft be called
for bringinge his landes to the queene, which the
Comon Lawe geveth her.

*Eudox.* Then this is no faulte of the Comon Lawe,
but of the perfons which worke this fraude to her
Majeftie.

*Iren.* Yes mary, for the Comon Lawe hath left
them this benefitt, whereof they make advantage, and
wreft yt to theire bad purpofes. Soe as they are 1170
thereby the bolder to enter into evill accons, knowinge
that yf the worfte befall them, they fhall loofe
nothinge but themfelves, whereof they feeme furely
verye careles, like as all barbarous people, as Cæfar
in his Commentaryes fayth, are very fearles of death.

*Eudox.* But what meane you of fugitives herein ?
or how doth this concerne them?

*Iren.* Yes, very greatly : for yee fhall underftand
that there be many ill difpofed and undutyfull perfons
of that Realme, like as in this pointe there are allfo in 1180
the Realme of England, too many, which beinge men
of good inheritance, are for the diflike of religion, or
danger of the law into which they are run, or difcontent
of the prefent government, fled beyond the feas, where
they lyve under Princes, that are her Majefties profeffed Enemies, and converfe and are confederate with
other Traytors and fugitives which are there abidinge.
The which nevertheles have the benefitt and profittes

ll. 1174-5, ‘ *as Cæfar . . . fayth* ’ not in our MS. : ll. 1182-4. ‘ *diflike*
. . . *of the* ’ (2nd) not in MS.

of their landes here, by pretence of fuche cullorable conveyances thereof, formerlie made by them to theire pryvie frendes here in truft, whoe fecretly fende over unto them the faide revenewes, wherwith they are there mayntayned and enabled againft her Majeftic.

*Eudox.* I doe not thinke that there bee any fuch fugitives which are releived by the profitt of theire lands in England : ffor there is a ftraighter order taken. And yf there bee any fuch in Ireland, yt were good yt were likewife looked unto : for this evill may eafelie be remedied : but proceede.

*Iren.* Yt is allfo inconvenient in the Realme of Ireland, that the wardes and marriadges of gentle-mens Children fhould be in the difpoficon of any of thefe Irifh Lords, as nowe they are, by reafon that theire landes are helde by knightes fervice of thofe Lords, as now they are. By which meanes yt cometh to paffe, that thofe faid gentlemens chil-dren, beinge thus in the warde of thofe Lords, are not only thereby brought up lewdlie, and Irifhe like, but allfo for ever after foe bounden to theire fervices, as that they will runne with them into any difloyall accon.

*Eudox.* This grevance, Irenæus, is allfo complayned of in Ingland, but how can yt bee remedied ? fince the fervice muft followe the tenure of the landes, and the landes were geven awaye by the Kinges of England to thofe Lords, when they firft conquered that Realme : and to fay the truth, this allfo woulde be fome prejudice to the Prince in her Wardfhip.

*Iren.* I doe not meane this by the Princes warde,

but by fuche as fall into the handes of the Irifh
Lordes : for I could wifhe and this I woulde enforce,
that all thofe wardfhips were in the Princes dis-
poficon ; for then yt might be hooped, that fhe,
for the univerfall reformacon of that realme, woulde
take better order for the bringinge up of thofe wardfhips in good nourture, and not fuffer them to come
into fo bad handes. And thoughe thefe thinges
bee alreadie paffed awaye by her progenitors former
graunts unto thofe faid Lords, yet I coulde finde a 1230
way to remedie a greate parte thereof, as hereafter,
when fytt tyme ferveth, fhall appeare. And fince
wee are entred into fpeache of fuch grauntes of
former princes to fondrie perfons of that Realme of
Ireland, I will mencon unto you fome other, of like
nature to this, and of like inconvenyence, by which
the Kinges of England paffed unto them a greate
parte of their prerogatyves ; which though then yt
were well intended, and perhappes well deferued of
them which receaved the fame, yet nowe fuch a gapp 1240
of mifcheife lyeth open thereby, that I could wifhe it
weare ftopped. Of this forte are the grauntes of the
Countyes Palletynes in Ireland, which though at
firft were graunted upon good confideracon when
they were firft conquered, for that thofe lands lay
then as a very border to the wylde Irifhe, fubject
to contynewall invafion, foe as yt was needefull to
geve them greate pryviledges to the defence of the
inhabitantes thereof; yet nowe that it is noe more
a border but frontyerd with enemyes, whie fhould 1250
fuch priviledges be any more contynewed ?

1. 1242, '*well ftopped*' : l. 1247, '*is*,' in our MS.

*Eudox.* I would gladlie knowe what you call a county Pallentyne, and whence yt is foe called.

*Iren.* Yt was as I fuppofe firft named Pallatyne of a Pale, as yt were of a pale and defence to their innere landes, foe as now yt is called the Englifh Pale, and thereof allfo is a Palfgrave named, that is an Earle Palentyne. Others thincke of the Latyne, Palare, that is, to foraige or outrune, becaufe that marchers and borderers ufe comonly foe to doe. ₁:
Soe as to have a County Pallentyne is in effecte but to have a priviledge to fpoile the Enemyes borders adjoyninge. And furely foe yt is ufed at this day, as a priviledged place of fpoiles and ftealthes ; for the County of Typperarie, which is nowe the only county Pallentyne in Ireland, is, by abufe of fome bad ones, made a receptacle to rob the reft of the Countryes about yt. By meanes of whofe priviledges none will follow theire ftealthes, foe as yt, beinge fcytuate in the very Topp of all the land, is made ₁ nowe a border, which how inconvenyent yt is, let every man judge. And though that right noble man, that is the lord of that libertye, doe payne himfelfe all that he may to yeilde equall Juftice unto all, yet cann there not but greate abufes lurke in foe inward and abfolute a priviledginge, confideracon whereof is to be refpected carefully, for the next fucceffion. And much like unto this graunte there are alfo other priviledges graunted unto moft of the Corporacons there ; that they fhal not be bounde to ₁ any other goverment then theire owne, that they fhall not be charged with any garrifons, that they

l. 1270, '*lap*' : l. 1273, '*endevour.*'

ſhall not be be travaelled forth of their owne fran-
chiſes, that they may buye and ſell with theves and
Rebelles, that all amercemêts and fynes which ſhalbe
ympoſed upon them ſhall come unto themſelves.
All which, though att the tyme of theire firſt graunte
they were tollerable, and perhapes reaſonable, yet
nowe are moſt unreaſonable and inconvenyent. But
all theſe will eaſilie be cutt of with the ſuperior power 1290
of her Majeſtys prerogatyve, againſt which her owne
grauntes are not to be pleaded nor enforced.

*Endox.* Nowe truelie, Irenius, yee have meſeemes,
very well handled this pointe touchinge incon
venyences in the Com̃on Lawe there, by you
obſerved ; and yt ſeemeth that you have had a
myndefull regard unto the thinges that may concerne
the good of that Realme. And yf you cann aſwell
goe through with the Statute Lawes of that lande,
I will thincke you have not loſt all your tyme there. 1300
Therefore, I praye you, nowe take them to you in
hande and tell us what you thincke to bee amiſſe in
them.

*Iren.* The Statutes of that realme are not manie,
and therefore wee ſhall the ſooner rune through
them. And yet of thoſe fewe there are ſondrie
impertinent and unneceſſarie : the which perhappes
though at the tyme of the makinge of them were
very needeful, yet nowe through chainge of tyme
are cleane antiquated, and altogether idle : As that 1310
which forbiddeth any to weare theire beardes all on
theire upper lip, and none under the chynne, and
that which putteth away ſaffron ſhirts and ſmockes,

l. 1310, '*idle*' not in MS.

and that which reftrayneth the ufinge of guylte
bridles and pettronells, and that which appointed to
the recorders and Clarkes of Dubline and Drodagh
[= Drogheda], to take but ijd. for the Coppie of a
playnte, and that which comaundeth bowes and
arrowes, and that which maketh that all Irifhmene
that fhall converfe amonge the Englifhe fhalbe
taken for fpies, and foe punifhed, and that which
forbiddeth perfons ameanable to lawe to enter and
diftrayne in the lands in the which they have tittle ;
and many other the like which I coulde rehearfe.

*Eudox.* Thefe, trulie, which you have repeated,
feeme very fryvolous and fruitles ; for by the breach
of them little dammage or inconvenience cann come
to the Comon-Wealthe, nether, indeede, yf any trans-
greffe them, fhall he feeme worthie of punifhment,
fcare of blame, favinge be that they abide by the
names of lawes.   But lawes ought to be fuche, as
that the keepinge of them fhould be greatlie for the
behoofe of the Comon-Wealth, and the violatinge of
them fhould be very haynous, and fharply punifhable.
But tell us of fome more weightie diflikes in the
Statutes then thefe, and that may more behouefull
importe the reformacon of them.

*Iren.* There is one or twoe ftatutes which make
the wrongfull deftrayninge of any mans goods againft
the forme of Comon Lawe to be fellony.   The which
ftatutes feeme furelie to have benn at firfte meant
for the greate good of that Realme, and for
reftrayninge of a fowle abufe, which then raigned
comonly amongft that people, and yet is not

1. 1330, '*faving for that they beare the name of lawes*' not in our MS.

altogether layed afide ; that when any one was
indebted to another, he would firft demaunde his
debt, and, yf he were not paied, he would ftreighte
goe and take a diftres of his goods or Cattell, where
he could finde them, to the value : which he would
keepe tyll he were fatisfied, and this the fimple 1350
Churle (as they call him) doth comonly ufe to doe
yet, thorough ignorance of his mifdoing, or evill
ufe that hath longe fettled amongeft them. But
this, though it be fure moft unlawfull, yet furely
me feemes to hard to make it death, fince there is
no purpofe in the partie to fteale the others goods,
or to conceale the diftres, but doth yt openly, for
the moft parte before witneffes. And againe, the
fame ftatutes are foe flackelie pende, befides that
latter of them is fo vnfenfiblye contryved that yt 1360
fcarfe carieth any reafon in yt, that they are often
and very eafily wrefted to the fraude of the fubjecte ;
as yf one goinge to diftrayne upon his land or
Tenemente, where lawfully he may, yet yf in doinge
thereof he tranfgres the leafte point of the Comon
Lawe, he ftreightlie comitteth fellonie. Or if one by
any other occafion take any thing from another, as
boyes ufe fometimes to cap one another, the fame is
ftraight fellony. This is a very harde lawe.

*Eudox.* Neverthelesse the evill ufe of diftrayninge 1370
another mans goods, you will not deny but is to be
abolifhed and taken awaye.

*Iren.* Yt is foe, but not by takinge awaye the
fubjecte withall ; for that is to violent a medycine,

1. 1348, ‘*and chattels*’ : ll. 1366-9, ‘*Or . . . fellony*’ not in our
MS.

fpeciallie this ufe beinge permitted, and made lawfull
to fome, and to other fome, death.  As to moft of
the Corporate Townes there, it is graunted by theire
charter, that they may, every man by himfelfe,
without an officer (for that were more tollerable)
for any debt, to diftrayne the goods of any Irifhe, 1 ?
beinge founde within theire liberty, or but paffinge
through theire Townes.  And the firft permiffyon
of this was for that in thofe tymes when that graunt
was made, the Irifhe were not amefnable to lawe,
foe as yt was not faiftie for the Townefman to goe
to him forth to demaund his debt, nor poffible
drawe him into lawe, foe that he had leve to be
his owne bayliffe, to arreft his faide debtors goods
within his owne franchife.  The which the Irifh
feinge, thought yt as lawfull for them to diftrayne 1 ?
the Townefmans goods in the countrey where they
founde yt.  And foe [by] enfample of that graunt to
Townes-men, they thought yt lawfull, and made yt
an ufe to diftrayne one anothers goods for fmale
debtes.  And to fay truth, me thinkes yt hard for
every tryflyng debt of 2 or 3s. to be dryven to lawe,
which is foe farre from them fometymes to be
fought ; for which me thinkes yt were an heavy
ordinance to geve death, efpecyally to a rude man
that is ignorant of Lawe, and thinketh a common ufe 14
or graunt to other men a lawe for himfelfe.

*Eudox.* Yea, but the Judge, when it commeth
before him to tryall, may eafilie defide this doubte,
and lay open the intent of the lawe by his better
difcrecon.

1. 1398, ' *methinkes it an.*

*Iren.* Yea, but yt is daingerous to leave the fenfe of a lawe unto the reafon or will of Judges, whoe are men and may bee mifcaryed by affeccons, and many other meanes. But the lawes ought to be like to ftony tables, playne, ftedfaft, and ymmoveable. 1410 There is allfo fuche another. ftatute or twoe, which make Coigne or lyverye to bee treafon, no leffe inconvenient then the former, beinge, as yt is penned, howe ever the firft purpofe thereof were expedient ; for thereby nowe noe man cann goe into anothers howfe for Lodginge, nor to his owne Tenants howfe to take vi&tuall by the waye, notwithftandinge that there is no other meanes for him to have lodgings or horfe meate, nor mans meate, there beinge noe Innes, nor none otherwife to bee bought for money, 1420 but that he is indaingered to that Statute of Treafon, whenfoever he fhall happen to falle out with his Tennant, or that his faid hofte lift to complaine of grevance, as oftentymes I have feene them very malifhiouflie doe thorowe the leaft provocation.

*Eudox.* I doe not well knowe, but by geffe, what ye doe meane by thefe termes of Coigne and Lyvery : therefore I praye you explaine them.

*Iren.* I knowe not whether the wordes be Englifhe or Irifhe, but I fuppofe them rather to be auncyent 1430 Englifhe, for the Irifhemen cann make no derivacon or analogie of them. What lyverie is, wee by Comon ufe doe knowe well enough, that it is allowance of horfemeate, as commonly they ufe the word in ftabline, as to keepe horfes at lyverye; the which worde, as I geffe, is deryved of lyveringe or

l. 1407, ' *a judge* ' in our MS. : l. 1421, ' *endammaged.* '

delyveringe forth theire nightlie foode. Soe in greate howfes, the lyvery is faide to be ferved up for all night, that is theire eveninges allowance of drinke. And lyvery is allfo called the proper garment which a ferving man weareth, foe called, as I fuppofe, for that yt was delyvered or taken from him at pleafure : So yt is apparant, that by the worde Lyverie is there meante horfe-meate, like as by the word Coigny is under-ftood mans meate : But whence the worde is deryved is very hard to tell. Some fay of coyne, for that they vfed Comoditye in theire Coignes, not only to take meate, but coyne allfo ; and that that takinge of money was fpecyally meante to be prohibited by that ftatute : But I thinke rather this word Coignye is deryved of the Irifhe. The which is a comon ufe amongeft the cheife landelords, to have a comon fpendinge upon theire Tennants ; for all theire tennants, beinge comonly but tennants att will, they ufe to take of them what victuall they lift, ffor of victualls they were wounte to make fmale reconinge: neither in this was the Tennante wronged, for yt was an ordinarie and knowen cuftome, and his lord comonly ufed foe to covenante with him, which yf at any tyme the tennante difliked, he might freelie departe at his pleafure. But nowe by this ftatute the Irifhe lord is wronged, for that he is cutt of from his cuftomary fervices, of the which this was one, befides many other of the like, as Cuddie, Coffherie, Bonnagh, Shragh, Sorehin, and fuch others ; the which I thinke at firft were cuftomes

l. 1440, '*upper*' : l. 1448, '*commonly*.'

brought in by the Englifhe upon the Irifhe, the
which were never wonte, and yet are loath to
yeilde any certen rent, but onlye fuch fpendinges : 1470
for theire comon fayinge is, Spende me and defende
me.

*Eudox.* Surelie I take yt as you faye, that therein
the Irifhe Lord hath wronge, fince yt was an
auncyent cuftome, and nothinge contrarie to lawe,
for to the willinge there is no wronge done : And
this right well I wott, that, even here in England,
there are in many places as ftrange Cuftomes as that
of Coygnie and lyverye. But I fuppofe by your
fpeache, that yt was the firft meaninge of the State 1480
to forbid the violent takinge of victualls upon other
mens Tenants againft theire willes, which furelie is a
greate outraige, and yet not foe greate me feemes, as
that yt fhoulde be made Treafon : for confideringe
that the nature of Treafon is concerninge the royall
eftate or perfon of the prince, or practizinge wyth his
enimies, to the derogacon and dainger of his crowne
and dignitie, yt is hardlie wrefted to make this
treafon. But as you erft faid, Better a mifcheife
then an inconvenience.                                 1490

*Iren.* Another ftatute I remember, which havinge
been an ancyent Irifhe cuftome is nowe upon
advifement made an Englifhe lawe, and that is
called the Cuftome of Kincougifh, which is, that
every heade of every fept and every cheife of every
kindred or familie, fhould be required anfwerable and

---

l. 1478, '*large*': l. 1485, '*concerning the realme*': ll. 1491-2,
reverfed in Dr. Morris's text '*Englifhe*' and '*Irifh*': ll. 1496,
'*anfwerable*'. . . *crime*' not in MS.

bound to bring foorth every one of that fept and kindred under it at all times to be juftified, when he fhould be required or charged with any treafon, felony, or other haynous crime.

*Eudox.* Whic, furely this feemes a very neceffary lawe. For confidering that many of them bee fuch lofells and fcatterlinges, as that they cannot eafily by any fheriffe, Conftable, Bayliffe, or other ordinary officer be gotten, when they are challenged for any fuch facte; this is a very good meanes to gett them to be brought in by him that is the heade of the fepte or cheife of that howfe : wherfore I wonder what deepe excepcon ye cann make againft the fame.

*Iren.* True, Eudox., in the pretence of the good of this ftatute, yee have nothinge erred, for yt feemeth very expedient and neceffarie : But the hurte which cometh thereby is greater then the good. For, whileft every cheife of a fepte ftandeth foe bounde to the lawe for every man that is of his bloud or fept that is under him inclufive, every one of his fept is put under him and he is made greate by the comaundinge of them all. For yf he may not comaund them, then that lawe doth wronge that bindeth him to bringe them forth to bee juftified : and yf he may comaund them, then he may comaund them afwell to yll as to good. Hereby the lords and captaines of the countries, the principalls and heades of fepts, are made ftronger, whome yt fhoulde be a moft fpecyall care in pollycie to weaken, and to fett up, and ftrengthen divers of his underlines againft

1. 1506, '*meane*' : l. 1509, '*juft.*'

him, which whenfoever he fhall offer to fwarve from dutye, may be able to bearde him ; for it is very daingerous to leave the comaund of foe many as 1530 fome feptes are, beinge v or vi thowfande perfons, to the will of one man, whoe may leade them to what he will, as he himfelfe fhall be inclyned.

*Eudox.* In very deede, Irenius, yt is very daingerous, efpecially feinge the difpoficon of thofe people not allwayes inclynable to the beft. And therefore I holde yt noe wifedome to leave unto them, to much comaund over theire kindred, but rather to withdrawe theire followers from them afmuch as may bee, and to gather them under the commaund of lawe by 1560 fome better meane then this cuftome of Kincougifh. The which word I woulde bee glad to knowe what yt namely fignifieth, for the meaninge thereof I feeme to underftand reafonable well.

*Iren.* It is a worde mingled of Englifhe and Irifh together, fo as I am partlye led to thinke, that the cuftome thereof was firft Englifhe and afterwardes Irifhe ; for fuche an other lawe they had here in Englande, as I remember, made by Kinge Alured, that every gentleman fhould contynually 1570 bringe forth his kindred and followers to the lawe. So Kin is Englifhe and Coughifh fignifieth affinitie in Irifhe.

*Eudox.* Sithe then that wee have thus reafonablie handled the inconveniences in the lawes, lett us nowe paffe unto your fecond parte, which was, as I remember, of the abufes of Cuftomes ; in which, me feemes, yee have a fayre champion laied open unto you, in which yee may at large ftretch out your

difcourfe into many fweete remembrances of Anti- 158
quities, from whence yt feemeth that the cuftomes
of that natyon proceede.

*Iren.* Indeede, Eudox : you fay very true ; for
all the cuftomes of the Irifhe which I have very
often noted and compared with that I have red,
would mynifter occafion of moft ample difcourfe of
the firft originall of them, and the antiquitie of that
people, which in truth I doe thinke to bee more
auncyent then moft that I know in this ende of the
worlde ; fo as yf yt were in the handlinge of fome 159
man of found judgement and plentifull readinge, it
woulde bee moft pleafant and profitable.    But yt
may bee wee may, at fome other time of meetinge,
take occafion to treate thereof more at large.    Here
only yt fhall fuffice to touch fuch Cuftomes of the
Irifh as feeme offenfive and repugnant to the good
government of that Realme.

*Eudox.* Followe then your owne corfe, for I fhall
the better content my felfe to forbeare my defire
nowe, in hope that you will, as you fay, fome other 16c
time more aboundantly fatisfie yt.

*Iren.* Before wee enter into the treatife of theire
Cuftomes, yt is firft needfull to confider from whence
they fproung ; for from the fundrie mannors of the
nations, from whence that people which nowe are
called Irifhe were derived, fome of the cuftomes
which nowe remayne amongeft them have benn
fetcht, and fince they have benn contynwed amongeft
them ; for not of one nacyon was that people as yt
is, but of fondrie people of different condicons and 161

l. 1600, '*fome . . . time*' not in our MS.

manners: But the cheif which have firft poffeffed, and inhabited yt, I fuppofe to be Scythians.

*Eudox.* How commeth it then to paffe, that the Irifh doe derive themfelves from Gathelus the Spaniard?

*Iren.* They doe indeed, but (I conceive) without any good ground. For if there were any fuch notable tranfmiffion of a colony hether out of Spaine, or any fuch famous conqueft of this king-dome by Gathelus, a Spaniard, as they would faine 1520 believe, it is not unlikely, but the very Chronicles of Spaine (had Spaine then beene in fo high regard as they now have it) would not have omitted fo memorable a thing, as the fubduing of fo noble a realme to the Spaniard, no more then they doe now negleɕt to memorize their conqueft of the Indians, efpecially in thofe times, in which the fame was fuppofed, being nearer unto the flourifhing age of learning and writers under the Romanes. But the Irifh doe heerein no otherwife, then our vaine 1630 Englifh-men doe in the Tale of Brutus, whom they devife to have firft conquered and inhabited this land, it being as impoffible to proove, that there was ever any fuch Brutus of Albion or England, as it is, that there was any fuch Gathelus of Spaine. But furely the Scythians (of whom I earft fpoke) which at fuch tyme as the Northerne Nations overflowed

1. 1612, '*Scythians*'—in Collier and Dr. Morris and other texts there follows here the paragraph commencing '*Scythians, which. . . Scotland*'. This in our MS. comes in further on, in next page. On the other hand, the paragraph '*Eudox. How . . . fpoke,*' on same page (ll. 1613-36), is not in Dr. Morris, but in Collier, etc., etc., and accepted by us.

all Chriftendome, came downe to the Sea cofte, where
enquiringe for other countryes abroade, and gettinge
intelligence of this Countrye of Irelande, findinge
fhippinge convenient, paffed over thither, and arived
in the North parte thereof, which is now called Ulfter,
which firft inhabiting, and afterwardes ftretchinge
themfelves forth into the Ilande as theire nombers
encreafed, named yt all of themfelves Scuttenlande,
which more breiflie is called Scutland, of Scotland.

*Eudox.* I wonder, Irenius, whether you runne fo
farre aftraye ; for whilft wee talke of Ireland, me
thinkes you rippe up the originall of Scotland ; but
what is that to this ?

*Iren.* Surelie very much, for Scotland and Ireland
are one and the fame.

*Eudox.* That feemeth more ftrange ; for wee all
knowe right well that they are diftinguifhed, with
a greate fea runninge betweene them ; or elfe there
are twoe Scotlands.

*Iren.* Never the more are there twoe Scotlands,
but twoe kindes of Scotts there were indeede, as you
may gather out of Buchanan, the one Irine or Irifhe
Scotts, the other Albyne Scotts ; for thofe Scotts
or Scythians arrived, as I fuppofed, in the North
parts of the Ifland, where fome of them afterwards
paffed into the next coafte of Albyne, nowe called
Scotland, which, after much trouble, they poffeffed,
and of themfelves named yt Scotland ; but in
procefs of tyme, as is comonly feene, the denomina-
cōn of the part prevailed in the whole, for the Irifhe
Scotts puttinge away the name of Scotts, were called
only Irifhe, and the Albyn Scotts, leavinge the name

of Albyne, were called only Scotts.   Therefore yt 1670
cometh of fome wryters, that Ireland is called Scotia-
major, and that which nowe is named Scotland, is
called Scotia-minor.

*Eudox.* I doe nowe well underftande your diftin-
guifhing of the twoe fortes of Scotts, and twoe
Scottlands, howe that this which is nowe called
Irelande was auncyently called Erine, and afterwardes of fome wrytten Scotland, and that which
is nowe called Scotland was formerlie called Albyn,
before the cominge of the Scutts thither : But what 1680
other Nations inhabited thother partes of Irelande ?

*Iren.* After this people thus planted in the North,
or before, (for the certentie of tymes in thinges foe
farre from all knowledge cannot bee juftlie avowched)
another nation cominge out of Spaine aryved in the
Weft parte of Irelande, and findinge it wafte, or
weakelie inhabited, poffeffed yt : who whether they
were native Spaniards, or Gaules, or Africans, or
Goathes, or fome of thofe Northerne Nations which
did over-fpred all Chriftendome, it is impoffible to 1690
affirme, onlie fome naked conjectures may be
gathered, but that out of Spaine certenlie they
came, that doe all the Irifhe Cronicles agree.

*Eudox.* You doe verie boldlie, Irenius, venture
upon the hiftories of auncyent tymes, and leane too
confidently unto thofe Irifhe Cronicles which are
mofte fabulous and forged, in that out of them you
dare take in hande to laye open the Originall of a
nation foe antique, as that noe monument remaynes
of her begynninge and inhabitinge there ; fpecially 1700

1. 1700, '*and firft inhabiting.*

havinge bene allwayes without letters, but only bare
tradicons of tymes and remembrances of bardes,
which ufe to forge and falefifye every thinge as they
lifte to pleafe or difpleafe any man.

*Iren.* Trulie I muft confeffe I doe foe, but yet not
foe abfolutelie as yee fuppofe. But I doe herein
relye upon thofe bardes or Irifhe Cronicles, though
the Irifhe themfelves, through their ignorance in
matters of learninge and deepe judgement, doe moft
conftantly beleve and avouch them. But unto them
befides I adde my owne readinge ; and out of them
both togeather, with comparifon of tymes, likenes of
manners and cuftomes, affinitie of words and names,
properties of natures and ufes, refemblances of rights
and ceremonies, monuments of Churches and Tombes,
and many other like circumftances, I doe gather a
likelyhood of truth ; not certenly affirminge any
thinge, but by conferringe of tymes, language, monuments, and fuch like, I doe hunte out a probabilitie
of thinges, which I leave unto your judgement to
beleve or refufe. Nevertheles there bee fome very
auncyent authors which make mencyon of thofe
thinges, and fome moderne, which by comparinge
of them with the prefent tymes, experience, and
theire owne reafon, doe open a wyndow of greate
light unto the reft, that is yet unfene ; as namely,
of the oulder, Cefar, Strabo, Tacitus, Ptolomie, Plinie,
Pompeus Mela, and Berofus : of the latter, Vincen-
tius, Æneas Silvius, Ludus, Buckhanan, for that he
himfelfe, beinge an Irifhe Scott or Picte by nacon,
and beinge very excellently learned, and induftrious
to feeke out the truth of thefe thinges concerninge

the originall of his owne people, hath both fett downe the teftimonies of the auncyents truly, and his owne opinion withall very reafonablie, though in fome thinges he doth fomewhat flatter. Befides, the Bardes and Irifhe Croniclers themfelves, though through defier of pleafinge perhappes to much, and ignorance of arte and pure learninge, they have concluded the truth of thofe tymes ; 1740 yet there appeareth amongeft them fome Reliques of the true antiquitie, though difguifed, which a well eyed man may happilie difcover and finde out.

*Eudox.* How cann there bee any truth in them at all, fince the auncyent nations which firft inhabited Ireland were altogether deftitute of letters, much more of learninge, by which they might leave the veritie of thinges wrytten. And thofe bardes cominge alfoe foe many hundred yeres after, could 1750 not knowe what was done in former ages, nor delyver certenty of any thinge, but what they feyned out of theire unlearned heades.

*Iren.* Thofe bardes indeede, Cefar wryteth, delyver noe certen truth of any thinge, nether is there any certen holde to be taken of any antiquitie which is receaved by tradiccon, fince all men bee lyers, and many lye when they will ; but yet for auncyentnes of the wrytten Cronicles of Ireland, geve me leave to faye fomethinge, not to juftifie them, but to fhowe 1760 that fome of them might fay truth. For where yee fay that the Irifh have allwayes benn without letters, yee are therein much deceaved, for yt is

l. 1740, '*clouded*,'

certen, that Ireland hath had the ufe of letters
very auncientlie, and longe before England.

*Eudox.* Is yt poffible? how comes yt then that
they are fo barbarous ftill, and foe unlearned, beinge
foe olde fcollers? For learninge as the Poett faith,
" Emollit mores, nec finit effe feros :" whence then
I pray you coulde they have thofe letters?              17.

*Iren.* It is harde to faye: for whether they at
theire firft cominge into the lande, or afterwardes
by tradinge with other Nations which hade letters,
learned them of them, or devifed them amongeft
themfelves, yt is nothing doubtfull ; for the Saxons
of Englande are faide to have theire letters, and
Learninge, and learned men, from the Irifhe, and
that alfo appeareth by the likenes of the Carracter,
for the Saxons carracter is the fame with the Irifhe.
Nowe the Scythians never, as I cann reade, of oulde 17
had letters amongeft them : therfore yt feemeth that
they had them from the nacyon which came out of
Spaine, for in Spaine there was (as Strabo wryteth)
letters auncyently ufed, whether brought unto them
by the Phenicians, or the Perfians, which (as yt
appeareth by him) had fome footinge there, or from
Marfeles, which is faide to have bene inhabited by
the Greekes, and from them to have had the Greeke
carracter ; of the which Marfilianns yt is faid, that
the Gaules learned them firft, and ufed them only 17
for the furtherance of theire trades and private
bufines : for the Gaules (as is ftronglie to be proved
by many auncyent and athenticall wryters) did firft

1. 1776, ' *but that they had letters aunciently is nothing doubtfull* ' after
, *doubtfull* ' in Dr. Morris, Collier, etc., but not in our MS.

inhabite all the fea cofte of Spaine, even unto Cales
and the mouth of the Streights, and peopled alfo a
greate parte of Italie, which appeareth by fundrie
Citties and havens in Spaine called of them, as
Portingalia, Gallecia, Galdunum ; and alfo by fundrie
nacons therin dwellinge, which yet have refeaved
theire owne names of the Gaules, as the Rhegnie, 1800
Prefamarie, Tamariti, Cineri, and divers others.   All
which Pompeius Mela, beinge himfelfe a Spaniarde,
yet faith to have defcended from the Celtics of
Fraunce, whereby yt is to be gathered, that that
nacon which came out of Spaine into Ireland were
auncyentlie Gaules, and that they brought with them
thofe letters which they had learned in Spaine, firft
into Ireland, the which fome allfo faye doe muche
refemble the olde Phenicon carraƈter, beinge likewife
diftinguifhed with   pricke   and   accent,   as   theires 1810
auncyentlie; but the further enquirie thereof needeth
a place of longer difcourfe then this our fhorte
conference.

   *Eudox.* Surelie you haue fhowed a greate probabilitie of that which I had thought impoffible to
have benn proved ; but that which you nowe faye,
that Ireland fhoulde have benn peopled with the
Gaules, feemeth much more ftrainge, for all theire
Cronicles doe fay, that the weft and fouth was
poffeffed and inhabited of Spaniards : and Cornelius 1820
Tacitus doth allfo ftronglie affirme the fame, all which
you muft either overthrowe and falfefye, or renounce
your opinion.

   *Iren.* Nether fo, nor foe ; for the Irifh Cronicles, as

1. 1801, ' *Nerii*

I faid unto you, beinge made by unlearned men, and wrytinge thinges accordinge to the apparance of the truth which they conceyved, doe erre in the circum-ftances, not in the matter. For all that came out of Spaine (they beinge no dilligent fearchers into the differences of the Nacyons) fuppofed to be Spaniards, and fo called them ; but the groundworke thereof is nevertheles (as I faide) true and certen, however, they through theire ignorance difguife the fame, or through theire owne vanitie whilft they woulde not feeme to bee ignorant, doe thereupon buylde and enlarge many forged hiftories of theire owne antiquitie, which they delyver to fooles, and make them beleve them for true : as for example, that firft of all one Gathelus the fonne of Cecropes or Argos, who havinge married the Kinge of Egyps his daughter, thence fayled with her into Spaine, and there inhabited : Then that of Nemedus and his fower fonnes, whoe cominge out of Scythia peopled Ireland, and inhabited yt with his 2 fonnes twoe hundred and ffyfty yeares, till he was overcome of the Gyants dwellinge then in Irelande, and at the laft quite banifhed and rooted out. After whome twoe hundred yeres, the fonnes of one Dela, beinge Scythians, arryved there againe, and poffeffed the whole lande, of the which the youngeft, called Slaynius, in the ende made himfelfe Monarch. Laftlie, of the iiij fonnes of Milefius Kinge of Spaine, which conquered the lande from the Scythians, and inhabitinge yt with Spaniards, called yt of the youngeft Heberous, Hibernia : all which are in truth mere fables, and very Melefian

l. 1850, '*Slevius*': l. 1854, '*of the name of the.*'

lyes, (as the lattine proverbe is ;) for there was never fuch a Kinge of Spaine called Milefius, nor any fuche colony feated with his fonnes, as they fayne, that cann ever bee proued.    But yet under thefe tales yee may in manner fee the truth lurke. 1860 For Scythians, here inhabitinge, they name and doe fpeake of Spaniards, whereby appeareth that both thofe nations here inhabited : but whether very Spaniards, (as the Irifhe greatlie affecte), ys noe way to be proved.

*Eudox.* Whence cometh yt then that the Irifhe doe foe greatlie covett to fetch themfelves from the Spaniards, fince the olde Gaules are a more auncyent and much more honorable nation ?

*Iren.* Even of a very defier of newfanglenes and 1870 vanitie, for beinge as they are nowe accompted, the moft barbarous Nation in Chriftendome, they to avoide that reproache woulde deryue them felves from the Spaniards, whom they now fee to bee a very honorable people, and next borderinge unto them : But all that is moft vaine ; for from the Spaniard that nowe is, or that people that now inhabite Spaine, they no wayes can prove themfelves to defcend ; neither fhould it be greatly glorious unto them ; for the Spaniard, that now is, is come from 1880 as rude and falvage nations as they, there beinge, as yt may be gathered by corfe of ages and veiwe of theire owne hiftories (though they therein labored much to enoble themfelves) fcarfe any dropp of the oulde Spanifhe bloode left in them ; for all Spaine

ll. 1877 80, '*or that . . . now is*' not in our MS., but in Collier, Morris, etc.

was firft conquered by the Romaynes, and filled
with Colonies from them, which were ftill encreafed,
and the native Spaniarde ftill cutt of. Afterwards
the Carthaginians in all the longe Punicke Warres,
havinge fpoiled all Spaine, and in the ende fubdued yt whollie to themfelves, did, (as yt is likelye)
roote out all that were affected to the Romaynes.
And laftly the Romaines, havinge againe recovered
that countrye and beate out Hanniball, did doubtles
cutt of all that had favored the Carthaginians, foe
that betwixte them both, to and fro, there was fcarfe a
native Spaniard left, but all inhabited of Romaynes.
All which tempefts of troubles being overblowen,
there longe after arofe a newe ftorme, more dreadfull
then all the former, which over-ranne all Spaine,
and made an infinite confufion of all thinges ; that
was, the cominge downe of the Gothes, the Hunnes,
and Vandalles: and laftly all the Nations of Scythia,
which, like a mountaine flud, did overflowe all Spaine,
and quite drowned and wafht away whatever relictes
there were left of the land-bred people, yea and of all
the Romaynes too. The which Northerne Nations
findinge the complexion of that foile, and the
vehement heate there farr different from theire
natures, toke no felicitie in that country, but from
thence paffed over, and did fpread themfelves into
all Countries in Chriftendome, of all which there
is none but hath fome mixture or fprincklinge, yf
not through peoplinge of them. And yet after all
thofe the Mores and Barbarians, breakinge over out
of Africa, did finally poffeffe all Spaine, or the mofte
parte thereof, and treade downe under theire foule

heathenifhe feete what ever little they founde there
yet ftandinge.  The which, though afterwards they
were beaten out by Ferdinando of Arragon and 1920
Ifabell his wife, yet they were not foe clenfed, but
that through the marriages which they had made,
and mixture,of the people of the lande, during their
longe contynuance there, they had left no pure
drop of Spanifh bloode, noe nor of Romayne nor
Scythian.  Soe that of all nacons under heaven, I
fuppofe, the Spaniard is the moft mingled, moft uncerten, and moft baftardlie : wherefore moft foolifhly
doe the Irifh thinke to enoble themfelves by wreftinge
theire aunceftrie from the Spaniard, whoe is unable 1930
to deryve himfelfe from any nacon certen.

*Eudox.* You fpeake very fharplie, Irenius, in
difhonor of the Spaniard, whome fome other boaft
to be the only brave fouldier under the fkye.

*Iren.* Soe furely he is a very brave man ; nether
is that which I fpeake any thinge to his derogacon,
for, in that I faide he is a mingled people, and
compounded with others, it is no difprayfe ; for I
thinke there is no nation now in Chriftendome, nor
much further, but is mingled, and compounded with 1940
others : Yt was a finguler providance of God, and
a moft admirable purpofe of his wifedome, to drawe
thofe Northerne Heathen Nacons downe into thofe
Chriftian partes, where they might receave Chriftianitie, and to mingle nations foe remote foe miraculouflie,
to make, as it were, one kindred and bloode of all
people, and each to have knowledge of him.

l. 1921, miswritten '*Elizabeth*' in our MS.: l. 1934, '*nation*':
l. 1938, '*it . . . difprayfe*' not in MS.: ll. 1938-41, '*for . . . others,*' ibid.

*Eudox.* Nether have you fure any more difhonered
the Irifhe, for you have brought them from very
greate and auncyent nations, as any were in the 195
worlde, howe ever fondly they affecte the Spaniard.
For both the Scythians and the Gaules were twoe
as mightie nations as ever the worlde brought forth.
But is there any token, denominacon or monument
of the Gaules yet remayninge in Ireland, as there is
of Scythians ?

*Iren.* Yea furelie very many : for there is firft in
the Irifh language many words of Gaules remayninge,
and yet daylie ufed in comon fpeach.

*Eudox.* Wher, what was the Gallifh fpeach ? is 196
there any parte of yt ftili ufed amongeft any nacon ?

*Iren.* The Gallifh fpeeche is the very Brytifhe, the
which was generally ufed heere in all Bryttaine
before the cominge of the Saxons : and yet is
retayned of the Welchmen, the Cornithe men, and the
Bryttains of Fraunce, though tyme, woorking alteracon
of all thinges, and the tradinge and enterdeale with
other nacons rounde about, have chaunged and
greatly altered the dialecte thereof : but yet the
originall wordes appeare to be the fame, as who 1971
hath lyfte to reede in Cambden or Buckanan, may
fee at large.   Befides, there be many places, as
havens, hilles, townes, and caftles, which yet beare
names from the Galles ; of the which Buckanan
rehearfeth above 3 hundred in Scottland, and I
can (I thinke) recount neare as many in Ireland :
Moreover there be of the olde Galles certaine nacons
yett remayninge in Ireland which retaine the olde
denominacons of the Galles, as the Manapij, the

Cauci, the Venti, and others; by all which and 1980
many other very reafonable probabilities, which this
fhorte 'courfe, will not fuffer to be laid forth, it
appeareth that the cheef inhabitantes in the Iland
were Galles, cominge thither firft from Spayne, and
afterwards from befides Tannius, where the Gothes,
Hunnes, and the Getes fat downe, they allfo beinge
(as it is faid) of fome ancient Galles; and laftly
paffinge out of Gallia it felf, from all the fea Coafte
of Belgia and Celtica, into all the fotherne coaftes of
Ireland, which they poffeffed and inhabited, where- 1990
upon it is at this daye, amongft all the Irifhe a
common ufe to call any ftrange inhabitante there
amongft them, Gald, that is, defcended of [or] from
the Gaules.

*Eudox.* This is very lykely, for even fo did thies
Gaules aunciently poffeffe and people all the
Sotherne coaftes of our Bryttaine, which yet retayne
their old names, as the Belgiæ in Somerfetfhier,
Wiltfhier, and parte of Hampefhier, Attrebatij in
Barkfhier, Regni in Suffex and Surrey, with many 2000
others. Nowe thus farr I underftand your opinion,
that the Scythians planted in the Northe parte of
Ireland; the Spaniard (for fo we call them) what.euer
they were that came from Spaine, in the Weft; the
Gaules in the Southe: fo that there now remayneth
onely the Eaft partes towardes England, which I
would be glad to underftand from whom you thinke
them to be peopled.

*Iren.* Mary, from the Bryttons themfelves, of

l. 1985, ' *Tanais* ': l. 2008. '*them* . . . *peopled*' not in our MS.:
*ib.*, '*they were*' for ' *them to be.*'

which though their be lyttle footinge nowe remayning, 2010
by reafon that the Saxons afterwardes and laftly the
Englifhe, dryvinge out all the firft inhabitantes
thereof, did poffeffe and people the land themfelves.
Yet amongft the Tooles, the Brines, the Cavenaghes,
and other nacons in Linfter, there is fome memorie
of the Brytons remayninge ; as the Tooles are called
of the old Brytifh woord Tol, that is, an hilly
Country.   The Brins of the Brytifh woord Brin, that
is, Woody.   And the Cavenaghes, of Caune, that
is, ftronge.   So that in thies three people, the very 2020
denominacon of the old Bryttons doth ftill remayne.
Befides, when any flyeth under the fuccor or
protection of any againft an enemy, he cryeth unto
him, Commericke, that is Brytton Helpe, for the
Brytton is called in his owne language, Commerouye.
Furthermore to prove the fame, Ireland is by
Diodorus Siculus, and by Strabo, called Brytannia,
and a parte of Greate Bryttaine.   Finally, it
appeareth by good Record yet extante that King
Arthure, and before him Gurgunt, had all that Iland 2030
in his alleagiaunce and fubjection : hereunto I could
adde many probabilities of the names of places,
perfons, and fpeeches, as I did in the former, but they
fhould be to longe for this place, and I referve them
for another.   And thus you have hard my opinion,
howe all the Realme of Ireland was firft peopled,
and by what nacon.   After all which the Saxons
fucceedinge, did wholley fubdue it unto themfelves.
For firft Egfryde, longe kinge of Northumberland

---

l. 2016, ‘ *are called*’ not in our MS., or rather ‘ *is called*’ is miswritten
after ‘ *word*’ : l. 2024, ‘ *Cummurreeih* ’ : l. 2025, ‘ *Cummeraig.*’

did utterly waſte and ſubdue it, as appeareth out of 2040
Beda's complaint againſt him. And afterwardes
Kinge Edgarr brought it under his obedience, as
appeareth by auncient Record, in which it is founde
wrytten that he ſubdued all the iſlandes of the North,
even unto Norwaye, and their kings did bringe into
his ſubjeƈtion.

*Eudox.* This rippinge up of Aunceſtries, is very
pleaſinge unto me, and indeed favoreth of good
concciptes, and ſome reading withall. I ſee hereby
howe profitable travill and experience of forraine 2050
nacons, is to him that will apply them to good
purpoſe. Neyther indeed would I have thought, that
any ſuch antiquities could have bene avouched for
the Iriſhe, that maketh me the more to longe to
ſee ſome other of your obſervacons, which you have
gathered out of that Country, and have earſt half
promiſed to put forthe : And ſure in this minglinge
of nacons appeareth (as you earſt well noted) a
wonderfull providence and purpoſe of Almightie
God, that ſtirred up the people in the furtheſt partes 2060
of the world to ſeeke out thies regions ſo remote
from them, and by that meanes bothe to reſtore the
decayed habitacons, and to make himſelfe knowen
to the Heathen. But was their, I praye you, a more
generall Impeoplinge of that Iland, then firſt by the
Scythians, which you ſaye were the Scottes, and
afterwardes by the Affricans, beſydes the Gaules,
Bryttons, and Saxons ?

*Iren.* Yes, there was an other, and that the laſt
and the greateſt, which was by the Engliſh, when 2070

l. 2065, '*winning*' : l. 2067, '*Spanyards.*'

the Earle Strangbowe, havinge conquered that Lande, delivered up the fame into the handes of Henry the fecond, then Kinge, who fent over thither great ftore of gentlemen, and other warlyke people, amongft whom he diftributed the Land, and fetled fuch a ftronge Colonie therein, as never fince could, with all the fubtile practices of the Irifhe, be rooted out, but abyde ftill a mightie people, of fo many as remayne Englifhe of them.

*Eudox.* What is that you fay, of fo many as re- 208 mayne Englifh of them ? Why, are not they that were once Englifh, abydinge Englifhe ftill ?

*Iren.* No, for the moft parte of them are degenerated and growen almoft meare Irifhe, yea and more malicous to the Englifhe then the very Irifhe them felves.

*Eudox.* What heare I ? And is it poffyble that an Englifheman, brought up naturally in fuch fweet civilitie as England affordes, could fynd fuch lyking in that barberous rudenes, that he fhould forgett 209 his owne nature, and forgoe his owne nacon ? howe may this be ? or what I pray you may be the caufe thereof ?

*Iren.* Surely, nothinge but that firft evill ordinance and Inftitution of that Comon Wealthe. But thereof nowe is their no fitt place to fpeake, leaft, by the occation thereof offering matter of longe Difcourfe, we might be drawen from this that we have in hand, namely, the handleinge of abufes in the Cuftomes of Ireland.                    210

*Eudox.* In truthe Irenius, you doe well remember the plott of your firft purpofe ; but yet from that

me feemes, ye have much fwarved in all this longe
difcourfe, of the firft inhabiting of Ireland : for what
is that to your purpofe ?

*Iren.* Truely very materiall ; for if you marked
the courfe of all that fpeech well, it was to fhew by
what meanes the Cuftomes, that nowe are in Ireland,
beinge fome of them indeed very ftraunge and almoft heathenifhe, were firft brought in : and that 2110
was, as I faid, by thofe nacons from whome that
contry was firft peopled ; for the difference of
manners and cuftomes doth followe the difference
of nations and people : the which I have declared
unto you to have bene 3 fpeciall, which feated
themfelves theare ; to wyt, firft the Scythian, then
the Gaules, and laftly the Englifhe. Notwyth-
ftanding that I am not ignorant, that there were
fundry other nacons which got footing in that
Lande, of the which their yet remayne dyvers great 2120
families and feiptes, of whom I will alfo in their
proper places make mencon.

*Eudox.* You bringe your felf, Iren., very well into
the waye againe, notwithftanding that it feemeth that
you were never out of the waye. But nowe that
you have paffed through their antiquities, which I
could have wyfhed not fo foone ended, begine when
yee pleafe, to declare what Cuftomes and manners
have bene deryued from thofe nacons to the Irifhe,
and which of them yee fynd faulte withall. 2130

*Iren.* I will then begin to count their cuftomes
in the fame order that I counted their nacons : and
firft with the Scythian or Scottifh manners. Of the
which there is one ufe amongft them, to keepe their

IX. 6

Cattell, and to live them felves the moſt parte of the yeare in Bollies, paſturinge upon the mountaines and waſt wyld placces; and removing ſtill to freſhe land, as they have depaſtured the former dayes. The which appeareth plaine to be the manner of the Scythians, as you may reede in Olaus Magnus, and 2? Jo. Boemus, and yet is uſed amongſt all the Tartarians and the people about the Caſpian Sea, which are naturally Scythians, to live in heardes as they call them, beinge the very fame that the Iriſhe Bollies are, dryving their cattell continually with them, and feeding onely on their whyt meates.

*Eudox.* What fault can you fynd with this cuſtome? for thoughe it be an olde Scythian uſe, yet it is very behooffull in this Country of Irelande, where their are great mountaines, and waſt deſertes 2 full of graſſe, that the fame ſhould be eaten downe, and nouriſhe many thouſandes of cattell for the good of the whole Realme, which cannot mithinke be any other waye, then by keepinge thoſe Bollies as there ye have ſhewed.

*Iren.* But by this cuſtome of Bolling there grewe in the meane tyme many great enormities unto that Comon waylth. For firſt, if their be any outlawes, or looſe people, as they are never without fome, which live upon the ſtelthes and ſpoyles, they are 2' evermore ſuccered and fynd Releef onely in thoſe Bollies, beinge upon the waſt placces, where eles they ſhould be dryven ſhortly to ſterve, or to come downe to the townes to ſeeke releef, where, by one meanes or another, they would foone be caught. Beſydes,

l. 2146, '*milke and.*'

fuch ftelthes of cattell they bringe comonly to thofe
Bollies, wheare they are receaved readily, and the
theif harbored from daunger of Lawe, or fuch officers
as might light upon him. Moreover, the people that
live thus in thies Bollies growe thereby more bar- 2170
borous, and live more licentioufly then they would in
townes, ufing what meanes they lyft, and practyzing
what mifcheefes and villainies they will, eyther
againft the government theire, generally by their
combinacons, or againft pryvate men, whom they
maligne, by ftealinge their goodes, or murtheringe
themfelves. For theare they thinke them felves
half exempted from Lawe and obedience, and
havinge once tafted freedome, doe, lyke a fteare
that hath bene longe out of his yooke, grudge and 2180
repyne ever after to come under rule againe.

*Eudox.* By your fpeech, Irein. I perceive more
evill come by theis bollies, then good by their
grafinge; and therefore it may well be reformed:
but that muft be in his due courfe: doe you proceede to the next.

*Iren.* They have another cuftome from the
Scythians, that is the wearinge of manteles, and
longe glebbes, which is a thicke curled bufhe of
heare, hanginge downe over their eyes, and mon- 2190
ftroufly difguyfinge them, which are both very badd
and hurtfull.

*Eudox.* Doe you thinke that the mantle cometh
from the Scythians? I would furely thinke other-
wyfe, for by that which I have redd, it appeareth

l. 2166, ' *as* ' misinserted before ' *they* ' in our MS., and ' *as they make* '
not in it, as in Collier, etc.—' *as they make they bringe.* '

that moft nacons in the world auntiently ufed the
mantle.    For the Jewes ufed it, as you may reed of
Elias mantle, of [blank space].    The Caldees alfo
ufed it, as you may reed in Diodorus.    The Egyptians lykewyes ufed it, as yee may reed in Herodotus, 2
and may be gathered by the difcription of Berenice,
in the greek Commentaries upon Callimacus.    The
Greekes alfo ufed it aunciently, as appeareth by
Venus mantle lyned with ftarres, though afterwards
they chaunged the forme thereof into their clookes,
called Pallia, as fome of the Irifhe alfo ufe.    And
the auncient Latines and Romains ufed it, as yee
may reede in Virgill, who was a very great Antiquarie,
that Evander, when Æneas came to him at his feaft,
did intertaine and feaft him on the ground, and lying 2
on manteles.    Infomuch as he ufeth the very woord
mantile for a mantle.

———— Mantilia humi fternunt.

So that it feemeth that the mantle was a generall
habite  to  moft  nacons,  and  not  proper  to  the
Scythians onely, as yee fuppofe.

*Iren.* I cannot deny but aunciently it was common
to moft, and yet fithence difufed and laid away.
But in this latter age of the world, fince the decay
of the Romaine empyre, it was renued and brought 2
in againe by thofe Northerne nacons when, breakinge
out of their could caves and frofen habitacons into
the fweet foyle of Europe, they brought with them
their ufuall weedes, fitt to fheild their could, and that

1. 2201, miswritten '*difcipline*' in our MS : l. 2206, '*doe*': l. 2208,
'*auncient.*'

continuall froſt, to which they had bene at home
inured : the which yet they lefte not of, by reaſon
that they were in perpetuall warres with the nacons
where they had invaded.   But ſtill removing from
place to place, carryed always with them that weede,
as their howſe, their Bedd and their garment.   And, 2230
cominge laſtly into Irelande, they found there more
ſpeciall uſe thereof, by reaſon of the rawe could
clymate, from whence it is nowe growen into that
generall uſe in which that people nowe have it.
Afterward the Affricans ſucceedinge, ſyndinge the
lyke neceſſitie of that garment, continued the lyke
uſe thereof.

*Eudox.* Since then the neceſſitie thereof is ſo
comodious, as ye aledge, that it is inſteed of
howſinge, Bedding, and Clothinge, what reaſon have 2240
you then to wiſhe ſo neceſſary a thinge caſt of ?

*Iren.* Becauſe the comoditie dothe not counter-
vayle the diſcomoditie, for the inconveniences that
thereby doe aryſe are much more many ; for it is a
fitt howſe for an outlawe, a meet Bedd for a Rebell,
and apte Cloke for a theef.   Firſt the outlawe beinge
for his many crymes and villainies baniſhed from the
townes and howſes of honeſt men, and wandring in
waſt places, farre from daunger of Lawe, maketh
his mantle his howſe, and under it covereth himſelf 2250
from the wrathe of heaven, from the offence of the
earthe, and from the ſight of men.   When it raynethe
it is his penthowſe ; when it bloweth it is his tente ;
when it freezeth it is his tabernacle.   In Sommer
he can weare it looſe, in winter he can lappe it cloſe ;

l. 2235, '*Gaules*': l. 2238, '*Sith*': l. 2255, '*weare.*'

at all tymes he can ufe it; never heavie, never
comberfome.    Lykewaies for a Rebell it is as ferviceable; for in his warre that he maketh, if at leaft it
deferve the name of warre, when he ftill flyeth from
his foe, and lurketh in the thicke woodes and ftraigt 22
paffages, wayting for advantages, it is his Bedd, yea,
and almoft all his houfhold ftuffe.    For the wood is
his howfe againft all wethers, and his mantle is his
cave to fleepe in.    Therein he wrappeth himfelf
rounde, and efconfeth himfelf ftrongly againft the
gnattes, which in the Country doe more anoy the
naked rebelles, whylft they keepe the woodes,
and doe more fharply wound them, then all their
enemyes fwordes or fpeares, which can feldome
come nighe them : yea, and often tymes their mantle 22
ferveth them, when they are nighe driven, being
wrapped about their lefte arme infteed of a Target,
for it is hard to cut thorough it with a fwoord.
Befydes it is light to beare, light to throw away,
and, being, as they then comonly, naked, it is to
them all in all.    Laftly, for a theef it is fo handfome,
as it may feeme it was firfte invented for him ; for
under yt he can clenly convey any fytt pillage that
cometh handfomely in his way, and when he goeth
abroad in the night in free-bootinge, it is his beft 22
and fureft frend ; for lyinge, as they often doe, two
or three nightes together abroad, to watch for their
booty, with that they can prettyly fhroud them
felves under a bufh or a backe fyde, tyll they may
conveniently doe their errande : and when all is
doone, he can in his mantle paffe through any

l. 2265, ' *enclofeth* ' : l. 2284, ' *bankes.* '

towne or Company, being clofe hooded over his head, as he ufeth, from knowledg of any to whome he is indaungered.   Befydes all this, he, or any man eles that is dyfpofed to any mifcheef or villainie, 2290 may under his mantle goe privyly armed without fufpicon of any, carry his headpeece, his fkene, or piftole if he pleafe, to be alwaies in a readines. Thus neceffarye and fytting is a mantle for a Badd man.   And furely for a badd hufwyfe it is no leffe convenient, for fome of them that be wandring women, called of them Mona fhut, it is half a Ward-robe ; for in Somer ye fhall fynd her arayed comonly but in her fmocke and mantle ; to be more ready for the light fervices : in Wynter, and in her 2300 travill, it is her cloake and fafegard, and alfo a coverlett for her lewde exercyfe.   And when fhe hathe fylled her veffill, under it fhe can hyde bothe her burden, and her blame; yea, and when her baftard is borne it ferves infteed of all her fwadling cloutes.   And as for all other good women which love to doe but lyttle woorke, howe handfome it is to lye in and fleepe, or to loufe themfelves in the funne fhine, they that have bene but a whyle in Ireland, can well wytneffe.   Sure I am that you 2310 will thinke it very unfitt for good hufwyves, to ftirre in, or to bufy her felf about her hufwyfry in fuch forte as they fhould.   Thies be fome of the abufes for which I would thinke it meete to forbidd all mantles.

*Euaox.*  O evill mynded man, that having reckned

1. 2290, '*villanye to any man*': l. 2297, '*Beantoolhe*': l. 2305, '*inftede of a craddle and.*'

up fo many ufes of mantles, will ye yet wifhe it to
be abandoned ?   Sure I thinke Diogenes difhe did
never ferve his mafter more turnes, notwithftanding he
made [it] his difhe, his cupp, his meafure, his water- 23
pott, then a mantle doth an Irifhe man.   But I
fee they be all to bad intentes, and therefore I will
joyne with you in abolifhinge it.   But what blame
lay you to the glybb? take heed, I pray you, that
you be not too bufie therewith for feare of your owne
blame, feeing our Englifhemē take it up in fuch a
generall fafhion to weare their heare fo immefurably
longe, that fome of them exceed the longeft Irifhe
glybbes.

*Iren.* I feare not the blame of any undeferved 23
myflyke ; but for the Irifh glybbes, I fay that befyde
their falftye, bruitifhnes and fylthines which is not
to be named ; they are [as] fitt mafkes as a mantle
is for a theife.   For whenfoever he hath runne
himfelf into that perill of lawe that he will not be
knowen, he eyther cutteth of his glibb quite, by
which he becometh nothing lyke himfelf, or pullethe
it fo lowe downe over his eyes, that it is very hard
to difcerne his thevifh countenaunce.   And therefore
fit to be truffed up with the mantle. 23

*Eudox.* Truly thies three Scythian abufes, I hould
fitt to be taken away with fharpe pennalties ; and
fure I wonder howe they have bene kepte thus
longe, notwithftandinge fo many good provicons and
orders as have bene devyfed for that people.

*Iren.* The caufe thereof fhall   appeare to you

l. 2327, '*unmeafurably*' : l. 2331, '*liflikes*' : l. 2341, '*hold moft*' :
l. 2345, '*for the reformation of.*'

hereafter. But let us nowe goe forward with our
Scythian Cuftomes. Of the next that I have to
treat of, is the manner of rayfinge their Crye in their
conflictes, and at other troblefome tymes of uprore : 2350
the which is very naturall Scythian, as we may reed
in Diodorus Siculus, and Heroditus, difcrybing the
manner of the Scythians and Parthians cominge to
geve the charge at their battelles : at the which it
is faid, they come running with a terrible yell and
hubbubbe as if heaven and yearth would have gone
together, which is the very Image of the Irifh
hubbub, which their kerne ufe at their firft incounter.
Befydes, the fame Herodotus wryteth, that they ufed
in their battelles to call upon the names of their 2360
Captaines or generalls, and fometymes upon their
greateft kinge difceafed, as in that battell of Tomyris
againft Cyrus : which cuftome to this day manifeftly
appeareth emongft the Irifhe. For at their joyning
of battell, they lykewyes call upon their captaines
name, or the name of his aunceftors. As they under
Oneale crye Landergabo, that is, the bloudy hand,
which is Oneales badge : they under Obrien call
[Laun-laider], which is [the ftrong hand]. And to
their enfample, the old Englifhe alfo which there 2370
remayneth, have gotten up their cryes Scythian
like, as Cromabo, and Butlerabo. And herein alfo
lyeth open an other very manifeft proof that the
Irifhe are Scythes or Scottes, for in all their
incounters they ufe one very comon woord, crying

---

1. 2349, ' *cry* ': l. 2353, ' *Perfians* ': l. 2358, ' *hubbabowe* ' : l. 2369,
[blank space here] : l. 2372, ' *as the Geraldins Crown—alowe and the
Butlers Butleaur—aboue.* '

Ferragh, ferrogh, which is a Scottifhe word, to wyt,
the name of one of their firft kinges of Scottland,
called Fergus (or Ferragus), which fought againft
the Pictes, as you may reed in Buckanan *de rebus
Scoticis* ; but as others wryt, it was longe before, 2380
that the name of their cheef Captayn, under whome
they fought againft the Affricans, the which was then
fo fortunate unto them, that ever fithence they have
ufed to call upon his name in their Battelles.

*Eudox.* Beleeve me Irenius, this obfervacon of
yours is very good and delightfull ; farre beyond the
blynd conceipt of fome, whome I remember have
upon the fame woord Ferragh, made a very blunt
conjecture, as namely Mr. Stanihurft, who though he
be the fame country man borne, that fhould fearch 2390
more nearely into the fecreats of thies thinges, yet
hath ftrayed from the truthe all the heavens wyde
(as they faye,) for he therevpon groundethe a very
groffe imaginacon, that the Irifhe fhould difcend
from the Egiptianes which came into that Iland,
firft under the leadinge of Scota the daughter of
Pharao, whereupon they ufe (faith he) in all their
battailes to call upon the name of Pharaoh, crying
Ferragh, Ferragh. Surely he fhott wyde on the
Bowe hand, and very farre from the marke. For 2400
I would firft knowe of him what auncient ground
of Authoritie he hath for fuch a fencelesse fable, and
if he have any of the rude Irifhe bookes, as it may
be he hath, yet me feemes a man of his learning

l. 2376, ' *Farrih* ': l. 2387, ' *blunt* ': l. 2388, ' *gross* ': ll. 2397—
2404, ' *whereupon . . . . feemes* ' not in our MS., but in Collier
and Morris, etc. : l. 2398, ' *Farrih* ' as before.

fhould not fo lightly have bene carryed away with
old wyves tales from approvance of his owne
Reafon ; for whether Scota be lyke an Egiptià
woord or fmacke of any learning or judgment, let the
learned judge. But his Scota rather comes upon
the Greeke *Scoto*, that is, darkenes, which hath not 2410
let him fee the light of the truthe.

*Iren.* You knowe not, Eudoxus, howe well Mr.
Stanihurft could fee in the darke ; perhappes he
hath owles or cattes eyes, but well I woot he fceth
not well the very light in matters of more wayght.
But as for Ferragh I have tould you my conjecture
onely, and yet thus much I have more to prove a
likelyhood, that there be yet at this day in Ireland,
many Irifh men, chiefly in the Northeren partes,
called by the name of Ferragh. But let that nowe 2420
be : this onely for this place fuffyfeth, that it is a
woord comonly ufed in their hubbubbs, the which,
with all the reft, is to be abolifhed, for that it
difcovereth an affection of Irifhe captenry, which in
this platforme I indevour fpecially to beat downe.
There be other foartes of cryes, all fo ufed among
the Irifhe, which favour greatly of the Scythian
barbarifme, as their lamentacons at their burialles,
with difpairefull outcryes, and imoderate waylinges,
the which Mr. Stanihurft might alfo have ufed for 2430
an argument to prove them Egiptians, for fo in
Scripture it is mentioned, that the Egyptians
lamented for the deathe of Jofeph. Others thinke
this Cuftome to come from the Spaniardes, for that

l. 2420, '*Fareehs*': l. 2422, '*Hubbabowes*': ll. 2431-2, '*for
. . . Egyptians*' not in our MS. or in Dr. Morris, but in Collier, etc.

they doe imefurably bewayle lykewife their dead.
But the fame is not propper Spanifhe, but altogether
heathenifhe, brought in firft thither eyther by the
Scythians, or the Moores, which weare Affricans but
longe poffeffed that Country. For it is the manner
of all Paganes and infidelles to be intemperate in 2440
their waylinges of their dead, for that they had no
faythe nor hope of falvacon. And this ill Cuftome
alfo is fpecially noated by Diodorus Siculus, to have
bene in the Scythians, and is yet amongft the
Northeren Scottes at this day, as you may reade
in their chronicles.

*Eudox.* This is an evill Cuftome alfo, but yet doth
not fo much conferne Civill Reformacon, as abufe
in Religion.

*Iren.* I did not rehearfe it as one of the abufes 2450
which I thought moft worthie of Reformation; but
having made mencon of Irifhe cryes I thought this
manner of Cryinge and howlinge not impertinent
to be noted as uncyvill and Scythians lyke : for by
thies old cuftomes, and other lyke conjecturall fircumftances, the defcentes of nacons can onely be
proved, where other monuments of writinge are not
Remayninge.

*Eudox.* Then I pray you whenfoever in your
difcourfe you meet with them by the way, doe not 246c
fhune, but bouldly touch them ; for befydes their
great pleafure and delight for their antiquitie, they
bringe alfo great profitt and helpe unto civilitie.

*Iren.* Then fythenes you will have it foe I will

l. 2435, '*unmeafurably*' : ll. 2445-6. '*as . . . chronicles*' not in our
MS. or Dr. Morris, but in Collier, etc. : l. 2453, '*lewd crying.*'

heare take occation, fince I lately fpake of their
manner of Cryes in joyninge of Battaile, to fpeake
fomewhat alfo of the manner of their Armes, and
Array in battayle, with other Cuftomes perhappes
woorth the notinge. And firft of their Armes and
Weapons, amongft which their broad fwordes are 2470
proper Scythian, for fuch the Scythes ufed comonly, as
you may reed in Olaus Magnus. And the fame alfo
the old Scottes ufed, as yee may reed in Buchanan,
and in [Solinus], where the pictures of them are in
the fame forme expreffed. Alfo theire fhort bowes,
and lytle quivers with fhorte Bearded arrowes, are
very Scythiä, as ye may reede in the fame Olaus.
And the fame foart, bothe of bowes, quivers, and
arrowes, are at this daye to be feene comonly
among the Northern Irifhe, whofe Scottifhe bowes 2480
are not paft 3 quarters of a yard longe, with a
ftringe of wrethed hempe flackly bente, and whofe
arrowes are not above half an elline longe, tipped
with fteele heades, made lyke comon broad arrowes
heades, but many more fharpe and flender, that
they enter into an armed mä or horfe moft
cruelly, notwithftanding that they are fhott forth
weakely. Moreover, their longe broad fheeldes,
made but with wicker roddes, which are comonly
ufed amongft the faid Northeren Irifhe, but fpecially 2490
of the Scottes, and brought from the Scythians, as
ye may reede in Olaus Magnus, Solinus, and others ;
lykewyes their goinge to battaile without armor on
their bodies or heades, but trufting onely to the
thicknes of their glybbes, the which they fay will

l. 2474, [blank space] : l. 2480, ' *Irifhe-Scotts.*'

fometymes beare of a good ftroke, is meare falvage
and Scythian, as ye may fee in the faid Images of
the old Scythes or Scottes, fet forth by Herodianus
and others.   Befydes, their confufed kinde of march
in heapes, without any order or aray, their clafhing 250
of fwordes together, their fierce runninge upon their
enemyes, and their manner of fight, refembleth
altogether that which is redd in all hiftories to have
bene ufed of the Scythians.   By which it may
almoft infallably be gathered, together with other
fircumftances, that the Irifhe are very Scottes or
Scythes oridgionall, though fince intermingled with
many other nacons repairinge and joyninge unto
them.   And to thefe I may alfo add an other very
ftronge conjecture which cometh to my mynde, that 251
I have often obferved there amongft them, that is,
certaine relidgious Ceremonies, which are very fuperftitious, yet ufed amongft them, the which are alfo
wrytten by fundry Authores, to have bene obferved
amongft the Scythians, by which it may very
vehemently be prefumed that the   nations were
aunciently all one.   For Plutarch as I remember, in
his Treatife of Homere, indeavouringe to fearch out
the truth, what countryman Homere was, proveth it
moft ftrongly, as he thinketh, that he was an Italian 252
borne ; for that in diftributing of a facrifice of the
Greekes, he omitted the [blank] called [blank]
[loyne,] the which all the other Grecians, fave the
Italians, doe ufe to burne in their facrifice : alfo for
that he maketh the entralles to be rofted on fyve
fpites, the which was the proper maner of the

l. 2520, ' *Aeolian* ' : l. 2521, ' *deferibing* ' : l. 2524, ' *Aeolians*.'

Ætolians, who only, of all the nations and Cuntryes
of Gretia, ufed to facrifice in that forte, wheras all
the reft of the Greekes ufed to roft them upon three
fpites, by which he inferreth, neceffarily, that Homere 2530
was an Ætolian. And by the fame reafon may I as
reafonably conclude, that the Irifh ar defcended from
the Scythians; for that they ufe even to this day,
fome of the fame Ceremonyes which the Scythians
aunciently ufed. As for example, yee may reade in
[Lucian] in that fweet dialogue which is intituled
Toxaris or of frendfhipp, that the comon oath of the
Scythians, was by the fword, and by the fyer, for that
they accounted thefe two fpecyall devyne powers,
which fhould worke vengance on perjurors. So doe 2540
the Irifh at this day, when they goe to any battayle,
fay certayne prayers or charmes to ther fwordes,
making a croffe therewith upon the earth, and
thrufting the poyntes of ther blades into the
grownd ; thinking therby to have the better fucceffe
in fight. Alfoe they ufe to fwere comonly by their
fwordes. Likewife at the kindling of Candles, they
fay certayne prayers ; and ufe fome other fuper-
ftitius rightes, which fhowe that they honor the
fyer and the light ; for all thofe Northerne nations, 2550
having bene ufed to be anoyed with much could
and darkeneffe, are wont therfore to have the fyer
and the fonne in great veneracon : like as otherwife
the Moores and Egiptians, which are much offended
and greved with much extreame heate of the funne,
doe every morning, when the funne aryfeth, fall to
curfing and banning of him as ther plague and cheife

l. 2536, [blank in our MS.] ; l. 2547, ' *the fire and.*'

fcourge. [Alfo the Scythians ufed when] they would
binde any folemne vowe or combynacon, to drawe a
bowle of blood, together vowing therby to fpend their 256
laft blood in that quarrell, as ye may reade in
Buckhanan ; and fome of the Northerne Irifhe, lykewife : as ye may alfo reade in the fame booke, in
the tale of Arfacomas, that it was the manner of
the Scythians when any on[e] of them was heavily
wronged, and would affemble unto him any forces
of people, to joyne with him in his revenge, to fit
in fome publick place for certayne dayes upon an
oxe hide, to which there would reforte all fuch
perfons as being difpofed to take armes would enter 257
into his armes, would take pay or ioyne with him
in his quarrell. And the fame ye may lykewife
reade to have bene the auncyent manner of the
wilde Scottes, which are indeed the very naturall
Irifh. Moreover, the Scythians ufed to fweare by
ther Kinges hand, as Olaus fheweth. And foe doe
the Irifh ufe to fwere by their Lordes hand, and,
to forfweare it, hould it more cryminall then to
fweare by god. Alfo the Scythians fayd, that they
were once every yere turned into wolves, and foe it 258
is wrighten of the Irifh ; thoughe Mafter Camden in
a better fence doe fuppofe it was a diffeaze, called
Licanthropia, foe named of the wolfe. And yet
fome of the Irifh doe ufe to make the wolf their
goffopp. The Scythians alfo ufed to feeth the
flefhe in the hyde ; and fo doe the North Irifhe yet.
The Scythians likewife ufed to boyle the bloode of

l. 2586, Substantially Dr. Morris's text agrees, but our MS. some-
what differently arranges the sentences in these two pages.

the beaft lyvinge, and to make meate thereof : and foe doe the Irifhe ftill in the North. Manye fuch cuftomes I could recounte unto you, as of 2590 there ould manner of marrying, of burying, of dauncing, of finging, of feaftinge, of curfing, though Chriftians have wyped out the moft parte of them, by refemblance whereof yt might playnely appere to you that the nacons ar the fame, but that by the reckoning of thefe fewe, which I haue tould unto you, I finde my fpeech drawen out to a greater lenth then I fuppofed. Thus much only for his tyme, I hope, fhall fuffice you, to thinke that the Irifhe are auncyently deduced from the 2600 Scythians.

*Eudox.* Surely, Irenius, I have in theefe fewe wordes heard that from you which I would have thought had bene impoffible to have bene fpoken of tymes foe remote, and cuftomes foe auncyent : with delight whereof I was all that while as it were entranced, and carryed farr from my felfe, as that I am now right forrye that yee ended foe foone. But I marvayle much howe it cometh to paffe, that in foe long contynuance of tyme, and many 2610 ages come betwene, yett any jott of thofe ould rightes and fuperftitious cuftomes fhould remayne amongeft them.

*Iren.* It is noe caufe of wounder at all ; for it is the manner of all barbarous nacons to be very fuperftitious, and diligent obfervors of ould cuftomes and antiquities, which they receyve by contynuall tradicon from ther parentes, by recording of ther

l. 2598, *'purpofed.*

bardes and cronicle[s], in their fonges and by dayly
ufe and enfample of ther elders.                          26

*Eudox.* But have you I pray you obferved any
fuch cuftomes amongft them, brought likewife from
the Spanyardes or Gaules, as thofe from the
Scythians? that may fure be very materiall unto
your firft purpofe.

*Iren.* Some perhapps I have; and whoe that will
by this occafion marke and compare ther cuftomes
fhall finde many more.   But ther are fewer I thinke,
remayning of the Gaules or Spanyardes then of the
Scythians, by reafon that the partes, which they 26
then poffeffed lying upon the Coaft of the Wefterne
and Southerne Sea, were fithence contynually
vifited with ftrangers and forreyne people, repayring
thither for trafficke, and for fifhing, which is very
plentifull upon the coaftes: for the trade and
enterdeale of feacofte nacons one with another
worketh more civility and good fafhions, all fea
men being naturally defirous of new fafhions, then
the Inland dwellers which are feldome feene of
forreyners; yet fome of them as I have noted, 26
I will recounte unto you.   And firft I will, for
the better creditt of the reft, fhewe you one out
of ther Statutes, amongft which it is enacted that
noe man fhall weare his beard but only on the
upper lyp, like mufchachios, fhaving all the reft
of his chinne.   And this was the auncient manner

l. 2627, 'occafion more diligently marke': l. 2631, 'then poffeffed'
not in our MS., but in Collier, Morris, etc.; l. 2635, 'thefe': ll. 2637-8,
'all . . . fafhions' not in our MS., but in Collier, Morris, etc.:
l. 2644, 'but,' from Dr. Morris, not in our MS.

of the Spanyardes, as yett it is of all the Mahometans, to cut all ther beardes clofe, fave onely mufchachos, which they weare longe. And the caufe of this ufe was for that they, being 2650 bred in an hot country, found much hayre on ther faces and other partes to be noyous unto them : for which caufe they did cutt yt moft away, like as contraryly all other nacons, brought upp in could countryes doe ufe to nourifh ther hare, to keep them the warmer, which was the caufe that the Scythians and Scottes woare glibbes, as I fhewed you, to keep ther heades warme, and long beardes to defend ther faces from could. From them alfo I thinke came faffron fhirtes and fmockes, which 2660 was devifed by them in thofe hotte countryes, wher faffron is very coṁon and rife, for avoyding that evill which coṁeth of much fwetnes, and longe wearing of lynnen. Alfo the women amongft the ould Spanyardes had the charge of all hufhould affayres, both at home and abroad, as Boemius wrighteth, though now theife Spanyardes ufe it quite otherwife. And foe have the Irifh women the truft and care of all thinges, both at home, and in the feilde. Likewife rownd lether targettes, 2670 as the Spanyarde fafhion, who ufed it, for the moft part, paynted, which in Ireland they ufe alfoe, in many places, colored after ther rude fafhion. Moreover ther manner of ther womens ryding on the wrong fyde of the horfe, I meane with ther faces toward their right fyde, as the Irifh

l. 2649, ' *they* ' from Collier, Morris, etc. : l. 2652, ' *noyfome* ' : l. 2663, ' *fweating.* '

ufe, is, as they fay, ould Spanifh, and as fome fay
Africane, ffor amongft them the women (they fay)
ufe to ride acroffe : Alfo the deep fmock fleve
hanging to the grownd, which the Irifh women 268
ufe, (they fay), was ould Spanifh, and is ufed yet
in Barbary : and yett that fhould feme rather
to be an ould Irifh fafhion ; for in Armory the
fafhion of the Manche, which is geven in armes
by many, being indeed nothing ells but a fleve,
is fafhioned much like to that fleve. And that
Knightes in ould tymes ufed to weare ther miftres
favor or loves fleve, upon ther armes, as appereth
by that is wrighten of Sir Launcelott, that he
wore the fleve of the fayre mayd of Afteroth in 269
a tourney, whereat Quene Guenouer was much
difpleafed.

*Eudox.* Your conceit is very good, well fitting
for things foe farre from certayntye of knowledge
and learning, only upon lykelyhoodes and conjectures. But have you any cuftomes remayning
from the Gaules or Bryttans ?

*Iren.* I have obferved a few of eyther ; and
whoe will better fearch into them may find more.
And firft the profeffion of their Bardes was, as
Cæfar writeth, ufuall amongft the Gaules ; and 270
the fame was alfo comon amongft the Brittans,
and is not yett altogether left of with the Walfhe,
which are ther pofterity. ffor all the fafhions
of the Brittons, as he teftifieth, were much like.
The longe dearts came alfo from the Gaules, as

1. 2683, '*Englifh*': l. 2687, '*auncient*': l. 2690, '*Afteloth*': l. 2694,
'*farre growne*': l. 2705, '*Gaules and.*'

ye may read in the fame Ceafaer, and in John
Boemius.    Likewife the faid Jo. Boemius wrighteth,
that the Gaules ufed fwordes, a hanfull broad, and
foe doe the Irifh nowe.    Alfo that they ufed 2710
long wicker fheilds in battell that fhould cover
their whole bodyes, and foe doe the Northerne
Irifh.    But becaufe I have not feen fuch fafhioned
targettes in the Southerne partes, but only amongft
thofe Northerne people, and Irifh Scottes, I doe
thinke that they were brought in rather by the
Scythians, then by the Gaules.    Alfoe the Gaules
ufed to drincke ther enymyes blood, and to paynte
themfelves therewith : foe alfoe they wright, that
the ould Irifh were wonte, and foe have I fene 2720
fome of the Irifh doe, but not theire enymyes but
frendes bloode.    As namely at the execution of
a notable traytor at Lymbricke, called Murrogh
Obrien, I faw an ould woman, which was his
fofter mother, tooke up his heade, whilft he was
quartered, and fucked up all the blood running
thereout, faying, that the earth was not worthy
to drincke it, and therewith alfo fteeped her face
and breft, and tare her heare, crying and fhriking
out moft terribly.                                     2730

*Eudox.* Yee have very well runne thorough fuch
cuftomes as the Irifh have deryved from the firft
ould nacons which inhabited that land, namely,
the Scythians, the Spanyardes, the Gaules, the
Brittanes.    It nowe remayneth that you now take
in hand the cuftomes of the ould Englifh which

---

1. 2708, ‘ *Likewife* . . . *Boemius*’ not in our MS., but in Collier,
Morris, etc,

are amongſt the Iriſh : of which I doe not thinke
that yee ſhall have much to find fault with any,
conſideringe that by the Engliſhe moſt of the ould
badd Iriſh Cuſtomes were aboliſhed, and more cyvill
faſhions brought in their ſteade.

*Iren.* You thinke otherwiſe, Eudox : then I doe ;
for the cheifeſt abuſes which are nowe in that
realme, are growne from the Engliſh, that are now
much more lawleſſe and lycencious then the very
wild Iriſh : ſo that as much care as was then by
them had to reforme the Iriſh, ſo much and more
muſt nowe be uſed to reforme them ; ſoe much
tyme doth alter the manners of men.

*Eudox.* That ſemeth very ſtrange which you ſay,
that men ſhould ſoe muche degenerate from their
firſt natures as to grow wild.

*Iren.* Soe much can libertye and ill examples
doe.

*Eudox.* What liberty had the Engliſh ther, more
then they had here at home ?   Were not the lawes
planted amonge them at the firſt, and had they not
governors to curbe and keepe them ſtill in awe and
obedience ?

*Iren.* They had, but it was ſuch for the moſt part,
as did more hurt then good ? for they had governors
for the moſt part of them ſelves, and comonly out of
the two familyes of the Geraldines and the Butlers,
both adverſaryes and corivales one againſt the other.
Who though, for the moſt part, they were but
deputyes under ſome of the Kinges of Englands

l. 2741, '*in*' miswritten '*vpp*' in our MS. : l. 2747, '*Iriſh*' miswritten '*Engliſh*' in our MS.

fonns, brethren, or other nere kinfmen, who were
the Kinges leiutenantes, yet they fwayed foe much
as they had all the rule, and the others but the
tytle. Of which Butlers and Geraldines, albeit I 2770
muft confeffe they were very braue worthy men,
as alfo of other the peres of that realme, made
Lorde Deputyes, and lord Juftices and fignories
at fundry times, yet thorough greatnes of their late
conquefts and feignories they grewe infolent, and
evill bente both that regall authority, and alfo ther
private powers, one againft another, to the utter
fubverfion of them felves and ftrenthining of the
Irifh againe. This you may reade playnly difcovered
by a letter written from the Citizens of Corke out of 2780
Ireland, to the earle of Shreffburye then in England,
and remayning yet upon recorde, both in the Tower
of London, and alfoe amongft the Cronicles of Ireland.
Wherein it is by them complained, that the Englifh
Lords and Gentlemen, who then had great poffeffions
in Ireland, began thorough pride and infolencye, to
make private warrs one againft another, and, when
the other parte was weake, they would wage and
drawe in the Irifh to take ther part, by which
meanes they both greatly encoraged and enabled 2790
the Irifh, which till that tyme had bene fhut upp
within the mountaynes of Slewlougher, and weakened
and difabled them felves, in foc much that there
revenews were wonderfully impayred, and fome of
them, which are ther reckoned to have bene able to
have fpent xij or xiij hundred poundes per annum,

ll. 2774-5, ' *at fundry . . . feignories* ' not in our MS., but in Collier,
Morris, etc. : and so ll. 2784-6, ' *Wherein . . . Ireland.* '

of owld rent, that I may fay noe more, befides
ther comodetyes of Creekes and havens, were now
fcarce able to difpend the third part.   From which
diforder, and thorough ther huge calamityes which 280
have come vpon them therby, they are now
almoft growne to be almoft as lewde as the Irifh:
I meane of fuch Englifh as were planted towardes
the Weft; for the Englifh pale hath preferved it
felfe, thorough nearenes of the ftate, in reafonable
civilitye, but the reft which dwell abouc in Connagh
and Munfter, which is the fweeteft foyle of Ireland,
and fome in Leinfter and Ulfter, ar degenerate and
growen to be as very Patchcockes as the wild Irifhe,
yea, fome of them haue quite fhaken of ther Englifh 281
names, and put on Irifhe that they might be altogether Irifhe.

*Eudox.* Is it poffible that any fhould foe farr
growe out of frame that they fhould in foe fhort fpace,
quite forgett ther Country and ther owne names?
that is a moft dangerous LETHARGIE, much worfe
then that of MESSILA CARVINUS, who, being a
moft learned man, thorough ficknes forgot his
owne name.   But can you counte us any of this
kynde?                                              282

*Iren.* I cannot but by the reporte of the Irifhe
themfelves, who report, that the Macmaghons, in the
North, were auncyently Englifh; to witt, defcended
from the Fitz Urfulas, which was a noble family in
England, and that the fame appered by the fignificacon
of their Irifh names.   Lykewife that the Macfwinies,
now in Ulfter, were aunciently of the Veres of England,

---

l. 2803, '*planted above.*'

but that they themfelves, for hatred of the Englifh,
foe difguifed ther names.

*Eudox.* Could they ever conceyve any fuch devilifh 2830
diflike of ther owne naturall Country, as that they
would be afhamed of ther name, and bite of the
dugge from which they fuckcd lyfe?

*Iren.* I wote well ther fhould be none : but prowd
heartes doe oftentymes, like wanton coultes, kicke at
ther mothers, as we reade Alcibiades and Themiftocles
did, who, being banifhed out of Athens, fledd unto
the Kinge of Afia, and ther ftirred him upp to warr
againft ther Country, in which warrs they them
felves wer cheiftaynes. Soe that, they fayd, did theife 2840
Macfwynes and Macmahons, or rather Veres or Fitz
Urfulaies, for private defpite, turne themfelues againft
England. For at fuche tyme as Robert Vere, Earl
of Oxford, was in the Barons warrs againft King
Richard the feconde, thorough the mallice of the
Peeres, banifhed the realme and profcribed, he with
his kynfman Fitz Urfula fledd into Ireland, wher
being profecuted, and afterwardes in England put
to death, his kinfmen there remayning behinde in
Ireland, rebelled, and confpiring with the Irifhe, did 2850
quite caft of ther Englifhe names and alleigaunce ;
fince which tyme they have fo remained, and have
euer fithence bene counted meere Irifh. The verye
like is alfo euer foe reported of Macfwynes, Mackmahons and Mackfhchaies of Mounfter, howe they
lykewife were auncyently Englifh, and ould followers
to the Earle of Defmond, untill the raigne of King
Edward the fourth : at which tyme the Earle of

ll. 2852-4, '*fo . . . alfo,*' from Collier, Morris, etc., but not in our MS,

Defmonde that then was, called Thomas, being
thorough falfe fubbornacon, as they fay, of the 2860
Queene for fome offence, by her againſt him conceyved, brought to his death at Tredagh moſt
unjuſtly, notwithſtanding that he was a very good
and founde fubieᴄte to the kinge.    Therupon all his
kinſemen of the Garaldines, which then was a mighty
family in Mounſter, in reveng of that huge wronge,
roſe into armes againſt the kinge, and utterly
renownced and forfware all obedience to the Crowne
of England ; to whom the fayd Mackſwynes, Mack-
fhchayes, and Mackmahons, ther fervantes and 2870
followers, did the like, and have euer fithence fo
contynued.    And with them, they fay, all the people
of Mounſter went, and many other of them, which
were mere Engliſh, thenceforth ioyned with the
Iriſh againſt the King, and termed themfelves very
Iriſh, taking on them Iriſhe habites and cuſtomes,
which would never fince be cleane wyped awaye, but
the Contagion thereof hath remayned ſtill amongſt
ther poſterityes.    Of which forte, they fay, be moſt
of the furnames which end in an, as Shinian, 2880
Mangan, &c. the which nowe account them felves
naturall Iriſh.    Other great howſes ther bee of the
ould Engliſhe in Ireland, which thorough lycentious
converſinge with the Iriſh, or marrying, or foſtering
with them, or lacke of meete nurture, or other fuch
unhappy occaſions, have degendred from ther auncyent

---

1.  2862,  '*Drogheda*' :  l.  2868,  '*forſooke*' :  l.  2875,  '*meere*' :
ll. 2875-6, '*againſt . . . Iriſh*' not in our MS., but in Collier, Morris,
etc. : l. 2877, '*could*': l. 2880, '*Heenan*' (Collier), '*Hernan*' (Morris),
before '*Shinian*' : l. 2882, '*meere*' : l. 2886, '*degenerated*.'

dignityes, and are nowe growen as Irifh as Ohanlans breach, (as the proverbe ther is,) of which forte ther are two moft pittifull exfamples above the reft: to witt the Lord Breningham, who being the moft 2890 auncyent Barron in England, is nowe waxen the moft falvage Irifh, naming himfelfe Irifh like Noccorifh : and the other the greate Mortimer, who forgetting howe great he was once in England, or Englifh at all, is now become the moft barbarous of them all, and is now called Macnemarra; and [not] much better then he is the ould Lord Courrie, who having lewdly wafted all the land and fignoryes that he had and aliened them unto the Irifhe, is himfelfe alfo now growne quite Irifhe.                                          2900

*Eudox.* In truth this which you tell is a moft fhamfull hearing, and to be reformed with moft fharpe fenfures in foe greate perfonages, to the terrour of the meaner : for wher the lords and chiefe men wax fo barbarous and baftard like, what fhalbe hoped of the pefantes, and bafer people ? And hereby fure you have made a fayre waye unto your felfe to lay open the abufes of ther vile cuftomes, which yee have now next to declare, the which, noe doubte, but are very bad and barbarous, 2910 being borowed from the Irifh, as there apparell, ther language, their riding, and many other the lyke.

*Iren.* Yee cannot but thinke them fure to be very brute and uncyvill ; for were they at the beft that they weare of ould, when they were brought in, they fhould in foe long an alteracon of tyme feeme very ftrang and uncouth.  For it is to be

l. 2890, ' *Bremechame* ' : l. 2897, ' *Courcye* ' : l. 2899, ' *allyed.* '

thought, that the ufe of all Englande, was in the raigne of Henry the feconde, when Ireland was firft planted with Englifhe, very rude and barberous, foe 292c as yf the fame fhould be nowe ufed in England by any, it would feme worthy of fharpe correction, and of newe lawes for reformacon ; but it is but even the other day fince England grewe cyvill : therfore in countyng the evill cuftomes of the Englifhe ther, I will [not] have regard whether the beginninge thereof were Englifhe or Irifh, but will have refpect only to the inconvenyence thereof. And firft I have to find faulte with the abufe of language, that is, for the fpeaking of Irifhe amongft the Englifh, 293c which as it is unnaturall that any people fhould love another language more then ther owne, foe it is very inconvenient, and the caufe of many other evills.

*Eudox.* It femeth ftrang to me that the Englifh fhould take more delight to fpeake that language then ther owne, whereas they fhould (me thinkes) rather take fcorne to acquainte ther tonges therto : for it hath alwayes bene the ufe of the conqueror to difpofe the language of the conquered, and to 294c force him by all meanes to learne his. So did the Romains alwayes ufe, infomuch that ther is almoft not a nacon in the world, but is fprinkled with their language. It were good therfore (me thinkes) to fearch out the originall courfe of this evill ; for, the fame beinge difcovered, a redreffe thereof wilbe the more eafily provided : for I thinke it were ftrange, that the Englifh being foe many, and the Irifh foe

l. 2923, '*for*' : l. 2940, '*difpife*' : l. 2945, '*caufe.*'

fewe, as they then were left, the fewer fhould drawe
the more unto their ufe.                              2950

*Iren.* I fuppofe that the chiefe caufe of bringing
in the Irifh language, amongft them, was fpecially
ther foftering, and marrijng with the Irifh, which
are twoe moft dangerous infections ; for firft the
child that fucketh the milke of the nurfe, muft of
neceffity learne his firft fpeach of her, the which
being the firft that is enured to his tongue, is after
moft plefing unto him, infomuch as though he afterwardes be taught Englifh, yet the fmacke of the
firft will alwayes abide with him ; and not only of 2960
the fpeach, but of the manners and condicons.    For
befydes the yonge children bee like apes, which
affect and Imitate what they have feene done before
them, fpecially by their nourfes whom they love foe
well : moreover they drawe into themfelves, together
with ther fucke, even the nature and difpofition of
ther norfes : for the mind followeth much the tem-
perature of the body ; and alfoe the wordes are the
image of the minde, foe as, the[y] proceeding from
the minde, the mynd muft be needes affected with 2970
the wordes.    Soe that the fpeach being Irifh, the
hart muft needes be Irifhe ; for out of the aboundance of the hart, the tonge fpeaketh.    The next is
the marryinge with the Irifh, which how dangerous
a thinge it is in all comonwelths appeareth to every
fympleft fence ; and thoughe fome greate ones have
ufed fuch matches with ther vaffales, and have of
them neverthcleffe rayfed worthie yffue, as Telamon
did with Tecmiffa, Alexander the greate with Roxane,
and Julius Cefar with Cleopatre, yet the example is 2980

fo perillous, as it is not to be ventured : for in ftead
of thofe fewe good, I could counte unto them infinite
many evell. And indeed how can fuch matching but
bring forth an evill race, feing that comonly the child
taketh moft of his nature of the mother, befydes
fpeach, mannors, and inclynation, which are for the
moft part agreable to the condicons of ther mothers ?
for by them they are firft framed and fafhioned
foe as [if] they receyve any thing from, them they
will hardly ever after forgoe. Therfore are theife
twoe evill cuftomes of foftering and maryinge with
the Irifhe moft carefully to be reftrayned ; for of
them twoe, the third, that is the evill cuftome of
language which I fpake of, cheifly, proceedeth.

*Eudox.* But are ther not lawes alredye appointed,
for avoyding of this evill ?

*Iren.* Yes, I thinke there be ; but as good never
a whit as never the better. For what doe ftatutes
avayle without penaltyes, or lawes without charge of
execution ? for foe ther is another like lawe enackted
againft wearing of Irifh apparell, but never the more
it is obferved by any, or executed by them that
have the charge : for they in ther private difcrefions
thinke it not fitt to be forced upon the pore wretches
of that Countrye, which are not worth the price of
Englifh apparell, nor expediente to be practyfed
againft the better forte, by reafon that the Country
(fay they) doe yeeld noe better : and were ther
better to be had, yet theife were fitter to be ufed, as
namely, the mantle in travelling, becaufe ther be noe
Innes wher meate or beding might be had, foe that

1. 2981, ' adventured' : l. 3007, ' abler' : l. 3011, ' meete bedding.'

his mantle ferves him then for a bed : the lether quilted Jacke in jorninge and in Campinge, for that it is fitteft to be under his fhirte of maile, for any occafion of fuddayne fervice, as ther happen many, and to cover his thine bretch on horfbacke. The great lynnen rowle which the women weare, to keepe ther heades warme after cutting their hayre, which they ufe in any ficknefle. Befydes ther thicke foulded lynnen fhirtes, ther longe fleved 3020 fmocke, ther halfe-fleved coates, ther filken fillottes, and all the reft, they will devife fome coulor for, eyther of neceffity, or of antiquity, or of comlyneffe.

*Eudox.* But what couler foever they alledge, me thinke it is not expedient, that the execution of a lawe once ordayned fhould be left to the difcreffion of the officer, but that, without partialitie or regard, yt fhould be fulfilled afwell on Englifhe as Irifhe.

*Iren.* But they thincke this pricifenes in refor-macon of apparell not to be foe materiall, or greatly 3030 pertinent.

*Eudox.* Yes furely but yt is ; for mens apparell is comonly made accordinge to theire condicons, and theire condicons are oftentymes governed by theire garmentes : for the perfon that is gowned is by his gowne put in mynde of gravitie, and alfo reftrayned from lightnes by the very aptnes of his weede. Therefore yt is wrytten by Ariftotle, then when Cyrus had overcome the Lydeans that were a warlike nacon, [and] devifed to bringe them to a 3040 more peacable life, he chaunged theire apparrell and muficke, and in fteade of theire fhorte warlike coate,

l. 3027, '*judge or officer*' : l. 3037, '*vnaptnefs.*'

clothed them in longe garmentes like wyves, and in
fteade of theire warlike muficke, appointed to them
certen lafcyvious layes, and loos gigges, by which
in fhorte fpace theire mindes were [fo] mollified and
abated, that they forgot theire former feircenes, and
became moft tender and effeminate : whereby it
appeareth, that there is not a little in the garment
to the fafhioninge of the mynde and condicons. But 305(
bee [all] thefe, which you have defcribed, the fafhions
of the Irifhe weedes ?

*Iren.* Noe : all thefe which I have rehearfed to
you, bee not Irifh garmentes, but Englifhe ; for
the quilted leather Jacke is oulde Englifhe ; for
yt was the proper weede of the horfeman, as you
may reade in Chaucer, where he defcribeth Sir
Thopas apparrell and armor, when he went to
fighte againft the gyant, which fhecklaton, is that
kinde of gilden leather with which they ufe to 306
Imbroder theire Irifhe Jackes. And there likewife
by all that difcripcon yee may fee the very fafhion
and manner of the Irifhe horfeman moft lively fett
out, in his longe hofe, his fhoes of coftlie cordwaine,
his hacqueton, and his haberjon, with all the reft
thereunto belonginge.

*Eudox.* I furely thought that that manner had
bene kindly Irifhe, for yt is farre differinge from that
we have nowe ; as alfo all the furniture of his horfe,
his ftronge braffe bytt, his fliding raynes, his fhanke 307
pillyon without ftirruppes, his manner of mountinge,
his fafhion of rydinge, his charginge of fpeare aloft
above hande, [and] the forme of his fpeare.

l. 3073, ' *head.*'

*Iren.* Noe fure ; they bee native Englifhe, and
brought in by the Englifhe men firft into Ireland:
nether is the fame yet accounted an uncomelie
manner of rydinge ; for I have hearde fome greate
warryors fay, that, in all thefe fervices which they·
had feene abroade in forraygne countreyes, they
never fawe a more comelie horfeman then the Irifh 3080
man, nor that cometh on more bravely in the
charge; nether is his manner of mountinge unfemely,
though he lacke ftirrops, but more readie then with
ftyrropes ; for in his gettinge up, his horfe is ftill
goinge, whereby he gayneth way. And therefore
the ftyrrop was called foe in fcorne, as yt were
a ftayre to gett up, beinge derived out of the oulde
Englifhe worde fty, which is, to mounte.

*Eudox.* It feemeth then that you finde no faulte
with this manner of rydinge ; whie then woulde 3090
you have the gilded jacke layed awaye?

*Iren.* I would not have that laied away, but
the abufe thereof to bee put awaye ; for beinge
ufed to the ende that it was framed, that is, to
be worne in warre under a fhirte of male, yt
is allowable, as alfo the fhirte of mayle, and all
his other furniture : but to be worne daylie att
home, as in Townes and civill places, yt is a
rude habitt and moft uncomelie, feeminge like a
players painted coote.                    3100

*Eudox.* But yt is worne, they faye, likewife of
Irifhe footemen ; howe doe you allowe of that ?
for I fhoulde thinke yt were unfeemelye.

---

l. 3083, '*wante*': l. 3088, '*to gett up, or*': l. 3091, '*quilted*' :
l. 3101, '*likewife*' from Collier, Morris, etc.

*Iren.* Noe, not as yt is ufed in warre, for yt is then worne likewife of footmen under their fhirts of mayle, the which footmen they call Galloglaffes; the which name doth difcover him to bee allfo auncyent Englifhe, for *Gallogla* fignifies an. Englifhe fervitor or yeoman. And he being fo armed, in a longe fhirte of mayle downe to the 311c calfe of his legge, with a longe broade axe in his hande, was then *pedes gravis armaturæ*, and was infteade of the armed footeman that nowe weareth a Corfelett, before the corflett were ufed, or allmoft invented.

*Eudox.* Then him belike you allowe in your ftreighte reformacon of oulde cuftomes.

*Iren.* Both him and the kearne allfo (whome only I toke to bee the proper Irifhe fouldyer) cann I allowe, foe that they ufe that habite and cuftome 312c of theires in the warres onely, when they are ledd forth to the fervice of their Prince, and not ufuall[y] at home, and in civill places, and befides doe laye afide the evill wylde ufes which the galloglaffes and kerne doe ufe in theire evill trade of lief.

*Eudox.* What be thofe?

*Iren.* Marry, thefe be the moft loathlie and barbarous condicons of any people, I thincke, under heaven; for, from the tyme that they enter into that coorfe, they doe ufe all the beaftlie behavior that 3130 may bee to oppreffe all men: they fpoile afwell the fubjecte as the enemye; they fteale, they are cruell

---

ll. 3105-6, '*under . . . footmen,*' and ll. 3107-8, '*for . . Englifh,*' not in our MS., but in Collier, Morris, etc.: l. 3117, '*common*': l. 3127, '*lothfome.*'

and bloodye, full of revenge, and delighte in deadlye execucon, licenfious, fwearers, and blafphemers, comon ravifhers of weomen, and murtherers of children.

*Eudox.* Thofe bee moft villanous condicons; I mervayle then that ever they bee ufed or imployed, or allmoft fuffered to lyve: what good cann there bee then in them?    3140

*Iren.* Yet fure they are very valiaunt, and hardye, for the moft parte greate endurors of colde, labor, hunger, and all hardnes, very actyve and ftronge of hande, verye fwyfte of foote, very vigillant and circumfpecte in theire enterprifes, very prefent in perills, very greate fcorners of death.

*Eudox.* Truelie, by this that yee faye, yt feemes the Irifhman is a very brave fouldier.

*Iren.* Yea truelie, eaven in that rude kinde of fervice hee beareth himfelfe very couragiouflie. But 3150 where he cometh to experience of fervice abroade, or is putt to a peece, or a pyke, he maketh as worthie a fouldier as any nacon he meeteth with. But lett us I pray you turne againe to our difcourfe of evill cuftomes amongeft the Irifhe.

*Eudox.* Me feemes, all this which you fpeake of, concerneth the Cuftomes amongeft the Irifhe very materially; for theire ufes in warre are of noe fmale importance to be confidered, afwell to reforme thofe which are evill, as to confirme and contynew thofe 3160 which are good. But followe you your owne coorfe, and fhewe what other theire Cuftomes you have to diflike of.

l. 3143, '*hardinefs*': l. 3149, '*furely*': l. 3156, '*thinkes.*'

*Iren.* There is amongeft the Irifhe, a certen kinde of people called the bardes, which are to them infteade of Poetts, whofe profeffion is to fett forth the prayfes and difprayfes of men in theire Poems or rymes ; the which are had in foe high regarde and eftimacon amongeft them, that none dare difpleafe them for feare to runne into reproach 317 through theire offence, and to be made infamous in the mouthes of all men. For theire verfes are taken up with a generall applaufe, and ufuallye fonnge att all feafte meetings, by certen other perfons whofe proper function that is, which alfo receave for this fame, greate rewardes, and reputacon befides.

*Eudox.* Doe you blame this in them, which I would otherwife have thought to have ben worthie of good accompte, and rather to have ben 318 mayntayned and augmented amongeft them, then to have ben difliked ? for I have reade that in all ages Poetts have bene had in fpecyall reputacon, and that me feemes not without greate caufe; for befides theire fweete invencons, and moft wyttie layes, they are alwayes ufed to fett forth the praifes of the good and vertuous, and to beate downe and difgrace the bad and vicyous. Soe that many brave younge mindes have oftentymes, through the hearinge the prayfes and famous Eulogies of 319 worthie men fonge and reported unto them, benn ftirred up to affecte the like comendacons, and foe to ftryve unto the like defertes. Soe they fay

1. 3168, '*requeft*' : 1. 3186, '*prayfes of the*' in Collier, Morris, etc.

that the Lacedemonians were more enclyned to defire of honor with the excellent verfes of the Poett Tyrteus, then with all the exhortacons of theire Captaines, or authorities of theire rulers and Magiftrates.

*Iren.* It is moft true that fuch Poettes, as in theire wrytinge doe labor to better the Manners 3200 of men, and through the fweete bayte of theire nombers, to fteale into the younge fpirittes a defire of honor and vertue, are worthy to be had in greate refpecte. But thefe Irifh bardes are for the moft parte of another mynde, and foe far from inftructinge younge men in Morrall difcipline, that they themfelves doe more deferve to be fharplie decyplined; for they feldome ufe to chufe unto themfelves the doinges of good men, for the ornamentes of theire poems, but whomefoever they finde to bec moft 3210 lycentious of lief, moft bolde and lawles in his doinges, moft daungerous and defperate in all partes of difobedience and rebellious difpoficon, him they fett up and glorifie in theire rymes, him they prayfe to the people, and to younge men make an example to followe.

*Eudox.* I mervayle what kinde of fpeaches they cann finde, or what face they cann put on, to prayfe fuch lewde perfons as lyve fo lawleflie and licenfiouflie upon ftealthes and fpoiles, as moft of them doe; or 3220 howe can they thincke that any good mynde will applaude the fame?

*Iren.* There is none foe bad, Eudoxus, but that

l. 3201, '*of men*' from Collier, Morris, etc. : l. 3203, '*are worthy*,' ibid. : l. 3222, '*applaude or approve*,' ibid.

fhall finde fome to fauor his doinges ; but fuch
licentious partes as thefe, tendinge for the moft parte
to the hurte of the Englifh, or mayntenance of theire
owne lewd libertye, they themfelves, beinge moft
defirous therto, doe moft allowe.    Befides thefe
evill thinges beinge deckt and fuborned with the
gay attyre of goodlie wordes, may eafilie deceave and 32
carry awaye the affeccon of a younge mynde, that
is not well ftayed, but defirous by fome bolde
adventure to make profe of himfelfe ; for beinge
(as they all bee) brought up idlelie, without awe of
parents, without precepts of mafters, without feare
of offence, not beinge directed, nor imployed in anye
courfe of lief, which may carry them to vertue, will
eafilie be drawen to followe fuch as any fhall fett
before them : for a younge mynde cannot reft ; yf
he bee not ftill bufied in fome goodnes, he will 32
finde himfelfe fuch bufines as fhall foone bufye all
about him.    In which yf he fhall finde any to prayfe
him, and to geve hym encorragement, as thofe
Bardes and rymers doe for little rewarde, or a fhare
of a ftollen cowe, then waxeth he mofte infolent and
halfe mad with the love of himfelfe, and his owne
lewde deedes.    And as for wordes to fett forth
fuch lewdenes, yt is not hard for them to geve a
goodlie glofe and paynted fhowe thereunto, borrowed
even from the prayfes which are proper unto vertue 32
yt felfe.    As of a moft notorius theife and wicked
outlawe, which had lyved all his tyme of fpoiles and
robberies, one of theire Bardes in his praife findes,
That he was none of thofe idle mylkefoppes that

l. 3229, '*attired*' (Collier) : l. 3253, '*will fay.*'

was brought up by the fyer fide, but that moft of
his dayes he fpent in armes and valiant enterprifes;
that he did never eate his meate before he had
wonne yt with his fworde ; that he laye not flugginge
all night in a cabben under his mantle, but ufed
comonly to kepe others wakinge to defend theire 3260
lyves, and did light his Candle at the flame of theire
howfes to leade him in the darknes ; that the day
was his night, and the night his daye ; that he loved
not to lye longe woinge of wenches to yealde to him,
but where he came he toke by force the fpoile of
other mens love, and left but lamentacon to theire
lovers ; that his muficke was not the harpe, nor
layes of love, but the Cryes of people, and clafhinge
of armor ; and that fynally, he died not wayled of
manye, but [made] many wayle when he died, that 3270
dearlye bought his death.   Doe you not thinke,
Eudoxus, that many of thefe prayfes might be
applied to men of beft defert ? yet are they all
yeilded to mofte notable traytors, and amongeft
fome of the Irifh not fmallye accompted of.   For
the fame, when yt was firft made and foung vnto
a perfon of high degree, they were bought as their
manner is, for fortie crownes.

*Eudox.* And well worth fure.   But tell me I pray
you, have they any arte in their compoficons? or 3280
bee they any thinge wyttye or well favored, as poems
fhoulde bee ?

*Iren.* Yea truly ; I haue caufed diuers of them
to be tranflated vnto me that I might underftande
them ; and furelye they favored of fweete witt and
good invencon, but fkilled not of the goodly orna-

mentes of Poetrie : yet were they fprinckled with
fome prettye flowers of theire owne naturall devife,
which gave good grace and comlines unto them, the
which yt is greate pittye to fee foe good an ornament 3290
abufed, to the gracinge of wickednes and vice, which
woulde with good ufage ferve to bewtifie and adorne
vertue.    This evill cuftome therefore needeth reformacon.    And nowe next after the Irifh Kerne, me
feemes the Irifh Horfe boyes woulde come well in
order, the ufe of which though neceffarye (as tymes
nowe bee) doe enforce, yet in the reformacon of that
Realme they fhoulde be cutt of.    For the caufe
whie they muft bee nowe permitted is the wante
of convenient innes for lodginge of travellers on 3300
horfbacke, and of Oftelers to tende theire horfes by
the waye.    But when thinges fhalbe reduced to a
better paffe, this needeth fpecially to be reformed ;
for out of the frye of thefe rakehelly horfeboyes,
growinge up in knavery and villany, are theire
kerne contynewally fupplied and mayntayned.    For
hauinge benn once brought up an idle horfeboye, he
will never after falle to labor, but is only made fitt
for the halter.    And thefe allfo (the which is one
fowle over-fight) are for the moft parte bred up 3310
amongeft Englifhmen, and Souldyers, of whome
learninge to fhoote a peece, and beinge made acquainted with all the trades of the Englifhe, they
are afterwardes, when they become kerne, made
more fytt to cutt theire throates.    Next to this
there is another much like, but much more lewde
and difhoneft ; and that is, of theire Carrowes, which

l. 3295, ' *boyes or Cuilles* ': l. 3297, ' *the thorough* ': l. 3317, '*Kearroghs.*'

is a kinde of people that wander up and downe
gentlemens howfes, lyvinge only upon Cardes and
dyce, the which, though they have little or nothinge 3320
of theire owne, yet will they playe for much moneye,
which if they wynne, they wafte moft lightlie, and
yf they loofe, they paye as flenderlye, but make
recompence with one ftealth or another, whofe only
hurte is not, that they themfelves are Idle Loffelles,
but that through gayminge they drawe others to like
lewdnes and idlenes. And to thefe maye bee added
another forte of like loofe fellowes, which doe paffe
up and downe amongeft gentlemen by the name
of Jefters, but are in deede notable Roges, and 3330
partakers not only of many ftealthes by fettinge
forth other mens goodes to bee ftollen, but allfo
pryvie to many trayterous practizes, and common
Carryers of newes, with defier whereof you woulde
wonder howe muche the Irifhe are fedd : for they
ufe comonly to fende up and downe to knowe
newes, and yf any meete another, his fecond worde
is, What newes? In foe much that hereof is toulde
a pretty jeft of a Frenchman, whoe havinge bene
fometyme in Ireland, where he marked theire greate 3340
enquirye for newes, and meetinge afterwardes in
Fraunce an Irifhman whome he knewe in Ireland,
firft faluted him, and afterwardes thus merelye : Sir,
I praye you (quoth he) tell me of curtefie, have
you hearde yet any thinge of the newes that ye fo
much enquired for in your Countrye ?

*Eudox.* This argueth fure in them a greate defier
of innovacon, and therefore thefe occafions which
norifhe the fame are to be taken awaye, as namelie,

thefe Jeftcrs, Carrowes, Mora-fhite, and all fuch 3350
ftraglers, for whom me feemes the fhorte riddance
of a Marfhall were meeter then any ordinance or
prohibicon to reftraync them.   Therefore, I praye you,
leave all this brablement of fuch loofe Runnagates,
and paffe to fome other Cuftomes.

*Iren.*  There is a greate ufe amonge the Irifhe, to
make greate affemblies togeather upon a Rath or
hill, there to parlie (as they faye) about matters and
wronges betwene Townefhip and Townefhip, or one
private perfon and another.   But well I wott, that 336
knowe, yt hath bene oftentymes approved, that in
thefe meetinges many mifcheifes have benn both
practized and wrought : for to them doe comonly
reforte all the fcumme of loofe people, where they
may freelie meete and conferre of what they lift,
which ells theye could not doe without fufpicon or
knowledge of others.  ·  Befides, at thefe parlies I have
divers tymes knowen that many Englifhmen, and
other good Irifhe fubjectes, have benn villanouflie
murdered, by movinge one quarrell or another 337
amongeft them.   For the Irifhe never come to
thofe Rathes but armed, whether on horfebacke or
on foote, which the Englifh nothinge fufpectinge, are
then comonly taken at advantagge like fheepe in the
pynfolde.

*Eudox.*  It may bee Iren : that abufe maye bee in
thefe meetings.   But thefe rounde hilles and fquare
bawnes, which you fee foe ftronglie trenched and
throwen up, were (they faye) at firft ordayned for

l. 3350, '*Beantvoilles*'; Todd and Collier have '*Mona-fhules.*' See
Glossary, *s.v.* : l. 3364, '*bafe.*'

the fame purpofe, that people mighte affemble them- 3380
felves thereon ; and therefore auncientlyc they were
called Folkmotes, that is, a place for people to
meete or talke of any thinge that concerned any
difference betwene parties and Townefhipes, which
feemeth yet to me very requifite.

*Iren.* You fay very true, Eudox: the firft makinge
of thefe high hilles was at firft indeede to very good
purpofe for people to meete ; but though the tymes
when they were firft made, might well ferve to good
occafions, as perhappes they did then in England, 3390
yet thinges being fince altred, and nowe Ireland
much differing from that ftate of England, the goode
ufe that then was of them is nowe turned to abufe ;
for thofe hills wherof you fpeake, were (as ye may
gather by reading) appointed for two fpecial ufes, and
built by two feverall nations. The one are thofe which
you call Folke-motes, the which were builte by the
Saxons, as the woorde bewraieth ; for it fignifieth in
Saxone a meeting of folke or people, and thofe are
for the moft parte in forme fower fquare, well trenched 3400
for the meetinge of that [blank]. The others that
are rounde, were caft up by the Danes, as the name
of them doth betoken ; for they are called Daneraths,
that is, hilles of the Danes, the which were by them
devifed, not for parlies and Treaties, but appointed as
fortes for them to gather unto in troblefome tyme,
when any tumult aroie ; for the Danes, beinge but
a fewe in comparifon of the Saxons, ufed this for

---

ll. 3391-2, '*yet . . . England*,' and ll. 3394-9, '*hilles . . . and
thofe*,' not in MS., but in Collier, Morris, etc. : l. 3407, '*trouble*' :
l. 3408, ' *Saxons in England.*'

theire fafetie.　They made thefe fmale rounde hilles, foe ftronglye fenced, in every quarter of the hundred, 341c to the ende that yf in the night, or at any other tyme, any crye or uprore fhoulde happen, they might repayre with all fpeede unto theire owne forte, which was appointed for theire quarter, and there remayne fayfe, tyll they coulde affemble themfelfes in greate ftrengthe : for they were made fo ftronge, with one fmale entrance, that whofoever came thither firft, were he one or twoe, or like fewe, he or they might reft faife, and defend themfelves againft manie, tyll more fuccor came unto them ; and when they were 342c gathered to a fufficient nomber they marched to the next fort, and foe forward tyll they mett with the perill, or knewe the occafion thereof.　But befides thefe twoe fortes of hilles, there were auncientlie divers others ; for fome were rayfed, where there had bene a greate battayle, as a memorye or trophes thereof ; others, as monuments of buryalls of the carcaffes of all thofe that were flaine in any fyghte, upon whome they did throwe up fuch rounde mounts, as memorialls for them, and fometimes did caft up 343c great heapes of ftones, as you may read the like in many places of the Scripture, and other whiles they did throw up many round heapes of earth in a circle, like a garland, or pitch many long ftones on ende in compaffe, every of which they fay, betokened fome worthie perfon of note there flayne and buried ; for this was theire auncyent cuftome, before Chriftianitie came in amongeft them that church-yardes were inclofed.

l. 3412, ' *any troublous crye* ' : ll. 3431·4, ' *as . . . long* ' from Collier, Morris, etc.

*Eudox.* Yee have very well declared the originall of thefe mountes and greate ftones encompaffed, 3440 which fome vaynely terme the olde Gyants Tryvetts, and thincke that thefe huge ftones woulde not ells bee brought into order or reared up without the ftrengthe of gyants. And others as vaynelie thincke that they were never placed there by mans hand or arte, but only remayned there fince the beginninge, and were afterwards difcovered by the deluge, and layed open by the wafhinge of the waters, or other like cafuallytie. But lett them dreame their owne 3450 imaginacons to pleafe themfelves ; but yee have fatisfied me much better, both by that I fee fome confirmacon thereof in the Holy Wrytt, and allfo remember that I have red in many hiftoryes and Cronicles the like mounts and ftones oftentimes menconed.

*Iren.* There bee many greate authorities, I affure you, to prove the fame ; but as for thefe meetinges on hilles, whereof wee were fpeakinge, yt is verye inconvenient that any fuch fhoulde be permitted, fpecially in a people foe evill mynded as they nowe 3460 bee and diverflie fhowe themfelves.

*Eudox.* But yt is very needefull me feemes for many other purpofes, as for the countrye to gather togeather when there is any impoficon to be laied upon them, to the which they then all agree att fuch meetings to cutt and devide upon themfelves, accordinge to theire holdinges and abilities. Soe as yf att thefe affemblies there bee any officers, as Conftables, Bayliffes, or fuch like amongeft them, there cann be noe perill or doubte of fuch bad practifes.

1. 3449-50, '*lett them with their dreames and vayne imaginations pleafe.*'

*Iren.* Nevertheles, daungerous are fuch affemblies, 3470
whether for ceffe or ought ells, the Conftables and
Officers beinge allfo of the Irifhe ; and yf there
happen there to bee of the Englifh, even to them
they may proue perillous.    Therefore for avoydinge
of all fuch evill occafions, they were beft to be
abolifhed.

*Eudox.* But what is that which you call ceffe ? yt
is a word fure unufed amongeft us here ; therefore I
pray you expounde the fame.

*Iren.* Ceffe is none other but that your felfe called 3480
impoficon, but yt is in a kinde unacquainted perhappes unto you.    For there are ceffes of fondry
fortes ; one the ceffinge of fouldiors upon the
country ; for Ireland beinge a country of warr as
yt is handled, and all wayes full of fouldyors, they
which have the goverment, whether they finde yt
the moft eafe to the Queenes purfe, or moft ready
meanes at hande for the victualinge of fouldiors, or
that neceffitie enforceth them thereunto, doe fcatter
the army abrode the country, and place them in 3490
townes to take theire victualls of them, att fuch
vacant tymes as they lye not in campe, nor are
otherwife imployed in fervice.    Another kinde of
Ceffe, is the impofinge of provifion for the Governors
houfe keepinge, which though yt be moft neceffary,
and be allfo, for avoyding of all the evilles formerly
therein ufed, lately brought to a compoficon, yet yt
is not without greate inconveniences, no leffe then
here in England, or rather much more.    The like
Ceffe is allfo charged upon the country fometymes 3500

l. 3491, ' *villages* ' (Collier).

for victuallinge of the fouldyors, when they lie in
garrifon, at fuch tymes as when there is none remayninge in the Queenes ftore, or that the fame
cannot convenientlie bee conveyed to theire place
of garrifon.   But thefe twoe are not eafie to be
redreffed when neceffity thereto compelleth ; but as
the former, as yt is not neceffary, foe yt [is] moft
hurtfull and offenfyve to the poore Country, and
nothinge convenient to the fouldyor himfelfe, whoe
during his lyinge at Ceffe, ufeth all kinde of out- 3510
ragious diforder and villanie, both towards the poore
men that victell and lodge them, and allfo to all
the reft of the Country round about them, whome
they abufe, fpoile, and afflicte by all the meanes
[they] cann invent : for they will not only not content themfelves with fuch victualls as theire hoftes
doe provide them, nor yet as the place will afford, but
they will have theire meate provided for them, and
*aqua vitæ* fent for ; yea and money befides layed at
his trencher, which yf he wante, then about the 3520
howfe he walketh with the wretched poore man
and the fillye poore wief, whoe are glade to purchafe
theire peace with any thinge.   By which vyle manner of abufe, the country people, yea and the very
Englifh which dwell abrode and fee, and fometimes
feele thefe outrages, growe into greate deteftacon of
the fouldyor, and thereby into hatred of the very
goverment, which draweth upon them fuch evilles :
And therefore this yee may alfo joyne with the
former evill cuftomes which yee haue to reprove in 3530
Ireland.

l. 3514, '*abufe, oppreffe and.*'

*Eudox.* Trulie this is one not the leaſt, and
though the perſons, of whom yt is uſed be of better
note then the former rogiſh ſorte which yee reckoned,
yet the faulte [is] no leſſe worthye of a Marſhall.

*Iren.* That were a hard corſe, Eudoxus, to redres
every abuſe by a Marſhall : yt would ſeeme to you
evill ſurgery to cutt of every unſounde ſicke parte
of the body, which, beinge by other due meanes
recovered, might afterwards doe very good ſervice to 3540
the body againe, and haply helpe to ſave the whole :
Therefore I thincke better that ſome good ſalve for
redres of this evill be ſought forth, then the leaſt
parte ſuffred to periſhe.  But hereof wee have to
ſpeake in another place.   Nowe we will proceede to
the other like defeſtes, amonge which there is one
generall inconvenience which rayneth allmoſt throughout all Ireland : and that of the Lords of land, and
fre-holders, whoe doe not there uſe to ſett out theire
lands to farme, or for terme of yeres, to their teñants, 3550
but only from yere to yere, and ſome during pleaſure;
nether indeede will the Iriſhe teñant or huſband
otherwiſe take his lande then ſo longe as he liſt
himſelfe.  The reaſon hereof in the teñant is, for
that the landlords there uſe moſt ſhamefully to racke
theire tenants, layinge upon him coygnie and livery
at pleaſure, and exaſtinge of him beſides his covenante, what he pleaſe.  So that the poore huſband-
man either dare not binde himſelfe to him for longer
tyme, or that he thincketh by his contynuall libertie 3560
of chainge to keepe his landlorde the rather in awe
from wronginge of him.  And the reaſon whie the

ll. 3540-1, '*afterwards . . . haply*' from Collier, Morris, etc.

landlord will not longer covenante with him is, for that he daylie looketh for chainge and alteracon, and hovereth in expeƈtacon of newe worldes.

*Eudox.* But what evill cometh hereby to the comonwealth ? or what reafon is yt that any landlord fhould not fett, nor any teñante take his land as himfelfe lift ?

*Iren.* Marry, the evilles that cometh hereby are 3570 greate, for by this meanes both the landlord thinketh that he hath his teñante more at commaund, to followe him into what accon foever he will enter, and allfo the teñant, beinge left at his liberty, is fitt for every variable occafion of chainge that fhalbe offered by tyme : and fo much allfo the more willinge and ready is hee to runne into the fame, for that he hath no fuch eftate in any his holdinge, no fuche buyldinge upon any farme, no fuch cofts ymployed in fencing and hufbandinge the fame, as might with- 3580 holde him from any fuch willfull corfe, as his lords caufe, and his owne lewde difpoficon may carry him unto. All which he hath forborne, and fpared foe much expence, for that he had no former eftate in his tenement, but was only a teñante at will or little more, and foe at will may leave yt. And this inconvenience maye be reafon enough to ground any ordinance for the good of a Comon-wealth, againft the private behoofe or will of any landlord that fhall refufe to graunte any fuch terme or eftate unto 3590 his teñante as may tend to the good of the whole Realme.

l. 3570, '*thereby*' : l. 3571, '*meane*': l. 3573, '*fhall*' : l. 3582, '*or*': l. 3584, '*firme.*'

*Eudox.* Indeede me feemes yt is a greate will-
fullnes in any fuch landlord to refufe to make any
longer farmes to theire tenants, as may, befides the
generall good of the Realme, be alfo greatly for
theire owne profit and avayle : For what reafonable
man will not thinke that the tenement fhalbe made
much the better for the lords behoofe, yf the tenante
may by fuch meanes be drawen to buylde himfelfe 360
fome handfome habitacon thereof, to dytch and en-
clofe his grounde, to manure and hufband yt as good
farmers ufe ? For when his tenants terme fhalbe
expired, yt will yeilde him, in the renewinge his
leafe, both a good fyne, and allfo a better rente.
And alfo it wil be for the good of the tenent likewife, whoe by fuch buyldinges and inclofures fhall
receave many benefitts : firft, by the handfomenes
of his howfe, he fhall take greate comforte of his
lief, more faife dwellinge, and a delight to keepe his 361
faide howfe neate and cleanely, which nowe beinge,
as they comonly are, rather fwyne-fteades then
howfes, is the chiefeft caufe of his foe beaftlie
manner of life, and faluaige condicon, lyinge and
lyvinge together with his beafte in one howfe, in
one rowme, and in one bed, that is the cleane ftrawe,
or rather the fowle dounghill. And to all thefe
other comodities he fhall in fhorte tyme finde a
greater added, that is his owne wealth and riches
encreafed, and wonderfully enlarged, by keepinge 362
his cattle in enclofures, where they fhall allwayes
have frefh pafture, that nowe is all trampled and

---

1. 3600, '*fuch good*': l. 3606, '*And . . . be*' from Collier, Morris,
etc. : l. 3608, '*his*' in our MS., miswritten.

over runne ; warme cover, that nowe lyeth open to
all weather ; faife beinge, that nowe are contynually
filched and ftollen.

*Iren.* Yee have well, Eudoxus, accompted the
comoditics of this one good ordinance, amongeft
which this that yee have named laft is not the
leafte : for all thother beinge moft beneficiall
both to the Landlord and the tenantes, this chiefly 3630
redoundeth to the good of the comonwealth, to have
the lande thus inclofed, and well fenced.   For yt is
both a principall barre and impeachment unto theves
from ftealinge of cattle in the night, and allfo a
gaule againft all rebelles and outlawes, that fhall
rife up in any nombers againft government ; for the
theefe thereby fhall have much adooe, firft to bringe
forth, and afterwards to dryve [away] his ftollen
pray but through the comon high wayes, where he
fhall foone bee defcryed and mett wythall : And the 3640
rebell or open enemye, yf any fuche fhall happen,
either at home, or from abroade, fhall eafilie be
founde when he cometh forth, and be well encoun-
tered withall by a fewe in foe ftraight paffages and
ftronge enclofures.   This, therefore, when we come
to the reforminge of all thefe evill cuftomes before
menconed, is needefull to be remembred.   But nowe
by this tyme me feemes that I have well runne
through the evill ufes which I have obferved in
Ireland.   Neverthelcs I will note that many more 3650
there bee, and infinitely many more in the private

l. 3626, ' *counted*': l. 3650 sq., ' *And howbeit there oe many more abufes
woorthie the reformation both in publicke and in private amongeft them,
yet thefe, for that they are the more generall,*' etc.   Morris).

abuſes of men.  But thoſe that are moſt generall, and tendinge to the hurte of the comon wealth, as they have come to my remembrance, I have as breifly as I could rehearſed unto you.  And therefore I thincke beſt that wee paſſe to our thirde parte, in which wee noted inconvenience that is in religion.

*Eudox.* Surelie you have very well handled theſe twoe former, and yf you ſhall as well goe thorough the thirde likewiſe, yee ſhall meritt a very good meede. 366c

*Iren.* Little have I to ſaye of religion, both becauſe the partes thereof bee not many, yt ſelfe beinge but one, and my ſelfe have not been much converſant in that callinge, but as lightlye paſſinge bye I have ſeene or hearde : Therefore the faulte which I finde in religion is but one, but the ſame univerſall thoroughout all that countrye ; that is, that they are all Papiſts by theire profeſſion, but in the ſame foe blindlie 3670 and brutiſhlie informed, for the moſt parte, as that you would rather thincke them Atheiſts or Infidelles, for not one amongeſt an hundred knoweth any ground of religion, and any Article of his faythe, but canne perhappes ſay his pater noſter, or his Ave Maria, without any knowledge or underſtandinge what one worde thereof meaneth.

*Eudox.* This is truly a moſte pyttifull hearinge that ſo many ſowles ſhulde falle into the Devilles handes at once and lacke the bleſſed comfort of 3680 the ſweete goſpell and Chriſts deare paſſyon.

l. 3657, '*inconveniences . . . are*': l. 3673, '*for*' is miswritten '*but*' in our MS.

Aye me, how cometh yt to paffe, that beinge a people, as they are, tradinge with foe many nacons and frequented of foe many, yet they have not tafted any parte of thofe happie Joyes, nor once bene lightned with the morning ftarre of truth, but lye mellinge in fuch fperituall darknes hard by hell mouthe, ever ready to fall in, yf God happilie helpe not?

*Iren.* The generall faulte cometh not of any 3690 late abufe either in the people or their priefts, whoe can teach [noe] better then [they] knowe, nor fhowe noe more light than they have feene, but in the firft inftruccon, and planting religion in all that Realme, which was I reade in the tyme of Pope Caleftine, whoe, as yt is wrytten, did firft fende ouer thether Pallidaius, whoe thence decreafinge, he afterwards fent over St. Patricke, beinge by nacon a Brytton, whoe converted the people, beinge then infidelles, from paganifme, and 3700 Chriftened them: in which Popes tyme and longe before, yt is certen that religion was generally corrupted with theire popifh trumpery. Therfore what other could they learne, then fuche trafhe as was taught them and drincke of that Cuppe of fornicacon [with] which the purple harlott had then made all nacons drounken?

*Eudox.* What, doe you then blame and finde faulte with foe good an acte in that good Pope, as the reducinge of fuch a greate people to 3710 Chriftendome, bringing foe many fowles to Chrifte? yf that were ill, what is good?

l. 3687, '*weltring*': l. 3694, '*inftitution*.'

*Iren.* I doe not blame the Chriftendome of them :
for to bee fealed with the marke of the Lambe,
by what hand foe ever yt bee done rightlie, I
hould yt a good and gracious marke, for the
generall profeffion which [they] then take upon them
at the Croffe and fayth in Chrifte.    I nothinge
doubte but through the powerfull grace of that
mighty Savior [it] will worke falvacon in many 3720
of them.    But nevertheless fince they drouncke
not of the pure fpringe of life, but only tafted
of fuch troubled waters as were brought unto
them, the dragges thereof have brought a greate
Contagion in theire fowles, the which daylie en-
creafinge and beinge ftill more augmented with
theire owne lewde lyves and filthie converfacon,
hath nowe breed in them this generall difeafe that
cannot but only with very ftronge purgacons, bee
clenfed and carried awaye.                              3730

*Eudox.* Then for this defecte you finde no
faulte with the people themfelves, nor with the
preifts which take the charge of fowles, but with
the firft ordinance and inftitucon thereof.

*Iren.* Not fo, Eudox : for the finne or ignorance
of the preifte fhall not excufe the people, nor
the authoritie of theire greate paftor, Peters fucceffor,
fhall not excufe the preifte, but they all fhall dye
in theire finnes : for they have all erred and gone
out of the waye together.                               3740

*Eudox.* But yf this ignorance of the people
bee fuch a burthen unto the Pope, is yt not a
like blott to them that nowe holde that place, in

l. 3713, '*chriftening*' : l. 3724, '*bredd.*'

that they which nowe are in the light themfelves
fuffer a people under theire charge to wallowe in
fuch deadly darkenes? for I doe not fee that the
fault is changed but the faultynes.

*Iren.* That which you blame, Eudoxus, is not
I fuppofe any fault of will in thefe godly fathers
which have charge thereof, nor any defecte of 3750
zeale for reformacon, but the inconvenience of the
tyme and troublous occafions, wherewith that
wretched Realme hath bene contynually turmoyled;
for inftruccon in religion needeth quiett tymes,
and ere wee feeke to fettle a founde difcypline
in the cleargie, wee muft purchafe [peace] unto the
layetie, for yt is yll tyme to preach amongeft
fwords, and moft hard, or rather ympoffible, yt
is to fettle a good opinion in the myndes of
men for matters of religion dowbtfull, which have 3760
dowbtles evill opinion of ourfelves; for ere a newe
be brought in, the oulde muft be removed.

*Eudox.* Then belike yt is meete that fome fitter
tyme bee attended, that God fende peace and
quietnes there in Civill matters before yt be
attempted in ecclefiafticall. I would rather have
thought that as yt is faid, correccon fhoulde
begynne at the howfe of God, and that the care
of the foule fhould have benn preferred before the
care of the bodye.                                          3770

*Iren.* Moft true, Eudoxus, the care of the fowle
and fowle matters are to be preferred before the
care of the body, in confideracon of the worthines
thereof, but not in the tyme of reformacon; for

l. 3747, '*fault-matter.*'

yf you ſhoulde knowe a wicked perſon dangerouſlie
ſicke, havinge nowe both ſowle and body greatly
diſeaſed, yet both recoverable, would you not
thincke yt ill advertiſement to bringe the preacher
before the phiſicon ? for yf his body were neglected,
yt is like that his languiſhinge ſowle being 378c
diſquieted by his diſeaſefull body, would utterly
refuſe and loath all ſpirituall comfort. But yf
his body were firſt recured, and brought to good
frame, ſhould there not then bee founde beſt tyme
to recure his ſowle alſo ? Soe yt is in the ſtate
of a Realme : Therefore as I ſaide yt is expedient,
firſt to ſettle ſuch a coorſe of governent there,
as thereby both Civill diſorders and eccleſiaſticall
abuſes may be reformed and amended, whereto
needeth not any ſuch greate diſtance of tymes, 379c
as yee ſuppoſe I requier, but one joynte reſolucon
for both, that each might ſecond and confirme the
other.

*Eudox.* That wee ſhall ſee when wee come
thereto : in the meane tyme I conſider thus much,
as you have delyvered, touchinge the generall faulte
which yee ſuppoſe in religion, to weete, that it is
popiſhe ; but doe you finde no particular abuſes
therein, in the miniſters thereof ?

*Iren.* Yes verilie ; for 'what ever diſorders yee 3800
ſee in the Church of England yee may finde
there, and many more : namelie, groſſe ſymonie,
greedy covetouſnes, fleſhlic incontinence, careles
ſlougth, and generally all diſordered lief in the
comon clergiemen. And beſides all theſe, they
have theire owne particular enormities ; for all

the Irifhe preifts, which now enjoye the church
lyvings there, arc in a manner mcere laymen, foe
like Laymen [that they] lyve like laymen, followe all
kindes of hufbandrye and other worldly affaires, as 3810
the other Irifhe laymen doe. They nether reade
fcriptures, nor preach to the people, nor mynifter
the Sacrament of Comunion ; but the Baptifme they·
doe, for they chriften yet after the popifh faffhion,
and with the popifh lattine myniftracon, only
they take the tythes and offeringes, and gather
what fruits ells they may of theire lyvinge ; the
which they convert as badly. And fome of them
they faye pay as due tributts and fhares of theire
lyving to their Bifhoppes, (I fpeake of thofe which 3820
are Irifh) as they receave them dulye.

*Eudox.* But is that fuffered amongeft them ?
It is wonder but that the governors redres fuch
fhamefull abufes.

*Iren.* Howe can they, fince they knowe them
not ? for the Irifhe Bifhops have theire cleargie
in fuch awe and fubjeccon under them, that
they dare not complaine of them, foe as they
may doe to them what they pleafe, for they
knowinge theire owne unworthynes and incapacitie, 3830
and that they are therefore removable att theire
bifhops will, yeilde what pleafeth him, and he
taketh what he lifteth : yea, and fome of them
whofe dyocefes are in remote partes, fomewhat
out of the worldes eye, doe not att all beftowe
the benefices, which are in theire owne devocon,

1. 3808, ' *laymen, faving that they have taken holy orders, but otherwife,*'
etc. (Collier) : l. 3836, ' *donation.*'

upon any, but keepe them in theire owne hands, and fett theire owne fervants and horfeboyes to take up the Tythes and frauﬆs of them, with the which fome of them purchafe greate lands, and 384⟨ buylde fayre caﬆells upon the fame. Of which abufe yf any queﬆion bee moved, they have a very feemelic coulor of excufe, that they have no worthie myniﬆers to beﬆowe them upon, but keepe them foe unbeﬆowed for any fuch fufficient perfon as any ſhall bringe unto them.

*Eudox.* But is there no lawe or ordinance to meete with this mifcheife? nor hath yt never before benne looked into?

*Iren.* Yes, it feemes yt hath; for there is a 385⟨ ﬆatute there enaﬆed in Ireland, which feemes to have benn grounded upon a good meaninge—That whatfoever Engliſheman beinge of good converſacon and fufficiency, ſhalbee brought unto any of thofe Byſhops, and nominated unto any lyvinge within theire dyoces that is prefently voide, that he ſhall without contradiccon bee admytted thereunto before any Iriſhe.

*Eudox.* This is furelie a very good lawe, and well provided for this evill, whereof yee fpeake . 386⟨ and whie is not the fame obferved?

*Iren.* I thincke yt is well obferved, and that none of the biſhops tranfgres the fame, but yet yt worketh no reformacon hereof for many refpeﬆs. Firﬆ there are no fuch fufficient Engliſhe myniﬆers fent over as might bee prefented to any byſhop for any lyvinge, but the moﬆe parte of fuch Engliſhe as come over thither of them felves are

either unlearned, or men of fome bad note, for
which they have forfaken England. So as the 3870
Biffhop, to whome they fhalbe prefented, may juftly
rejecte them as incapable and infufficient. Secondly,
the Biffhop himfelfe is perhappes an Irifhe man,
whoe beinge made judge by that lawe of the
fufficiency of the mynifter, may at his owne will,
diflike of the Englifheman, as unworthye in his
opinion, and admytt of any other Irifhe whome
he fhall thincke more fitt for his turne. And yf
he fhall at the inftance of any Englifhman of
counteñance there, whome he will not difpleafe, 3880
accept of any fuch Englifhe minifter as fhalbe
tendred unto him, yet he will under hand carry
fuch a hard hande over him, or by his officers
wring him fo fore, that he will foone make him
weary of his poore lyvinge. Laftlye, the benefices
themfelves are fo meane, and of foe fmale proffitt
in thofe Irifhe countryes, through the ill hufbandry
of the Irifhe people which inhabite them, that
they will not yeilde any competent maynetenance
for any honeft mynifter to lyve upon, fcarflie to 3890
buy him a gowne. And were all this redreffed,
as happely yt might bee, yet what good fhould
any Englifhe mynifter doe amongft them, by
preachinge or teachinge which either cannot
underftande him, or will not heare him? Or what
comfort of lief fhall he have, where his parifhioners
are foe infacyable, foe intractable, foe ill-affected
to him, as they ufually bee to all the Englifh?

l. 3878, '*meete*': ll. 3883-4, '*or . . . wring him*' not in our MS.,
but in Collier, Morris, etc. : l. 3897, '*unfociable.*'

or fynally, how dare allmoft any honefte mynifters, that are peacefull civill men, comit his faifetie to the handes of fuche neighbors, as the boldeft captaines dare fcarfelye dwell by? 390

*Eudox.* Little good then I fee is by that ftatute wrought, howe ever well intended; but the reformacon thereof muft growe higher, and be brought from a ftronger ordinance then the comaundement or penaltye of a lawe, which none dare enforme or complaine of when yt is broken : but have you any more of thefe abufes in the cleargie?

*Iren.* I coulde perhappes reckon more, but I perceave mye fpeach to growe to longe, and thefe may fuffice to judge of the generall diforders which raigne amongft them ; as for the particulers, they are too manie to bee reckoned. For the cleargie there, except fome fewe grave fathers which are in high place about the ftate, and fome others which are lately planted in theire new colledge, are generally bad, lycentious, and moft difordered. 391

*Eudox.* Yee have then, as I fuppofe, gone through thefe three firft partes which ye purpofed unto your felfe, to wyte, the inconveniences which ye obferved in the lawes, in the cuftomes, and in the religion of that Land. The which me feemes, you have foe thoroughlie touched, as that nothinge more remayneth nowe to be fpoken thereof. 392

*Iren.* Not fo thoroughlie as ye fuppofe, that nothinge more can remayne, but foe generally as I purpoft; that is, to lay open the generall evilles of that realme, which doe hinder the good reformacon thereof; for to accounte the particuler faultes of 393

private men, fhould be a worke infinite ; yet fome
there bee of that nature, that though they bee in
pryvate men, yet theire evill reacheth to a generall
hurte, as the extorcon of fheriffes, fubfheriffes, and
theire bayliffes, the corrupcon of victuallers, ceffors,
and purveyors, the diforders of fhenefcalles, captaines,
and theire fouldyers, and many fuch like : All which
I wil only name here, that theire reformacon may bee
mynded in place where yt mofte concerneth.   But
there is one very foule abufe which, by the waye, 3940
I may not omitt, and that is in captaines, whoe
notwithftandinge that they are fpecyallic imployed
to make peace thorough ftronge execucon of warre,
yet they doe foe dandle theire doinges, and dally in
theire fervice to them coïnytted, as yf they would not
have the enemye fubdued, or utterly beaten downe, for
feare leafte afterwardes they fhould neede imployment,
and foe be difcharged of paye: for which caufe fome
of them that are layed in Garrifon doe fo handle
the matter, that they will doe noe greate hurte to 3950
the enemyes, yet for colour fake fome men they will
kill, even halfe with the confent of the enemy, being
perfons either of bafe regard, or enemies to the enemy,
whofe heades eftfones they fende in to the Governor
for a commendacon of theire greate endevors, telling
howe waightie a fervice they have performed by
cuttinge of fuch and fuch daingerous Rebelles.

*Eudox.* Trulye this is a pretty mockerye, and not
to be permitted by the Governors.

*Iren.* Yes, but how cann the Governors knowe 3960

l. 3931, '*worke too*' : ll. 3951-3, '*yet . . . enemy*' from Collier,
Morris, etc.

readily what perfons thofe weare, and what the
purpofe of theire killinge was ? yea, and what will
yee faye, if the captaines doe juftifye this theire
courfe by enfample of fome of theire Governors,
whoe, under Benedicite, I doe tell yt to you, doe
practife the like fleights in theire goverments ?

*Eudox.* Is yt poffible ? Take heed what you faye,
Irenius.

*Iren.* To you, you only, Eudoxus, I doe tell yt, 397
and that even with greate heartes greife, and inward
trouble of mynde, to fee her Majeftie foe much
abufed by fome whome they put in fpecyall truft
of theire affayres : of which fome, beinge marfhall
men, will not doe allwayes what they may for
quietinge of things, but will rather wincke at fome
faultes, and fuffer them unpunifhed, leafte they
havinge put all thinges in that affurance of peace
that they might, they fhoulde feeme afterwards not
to be needed, nor contynued in theire goverments
with foe greate a charge to her Majeftie. And 398
therefore they doe cuñingly carry theire coorfe of
goverment, and from one hande to another doe
bandy the fervice like a Tennys-balle, which they will
never ftrike quite awaye, for feare leafte afterwards
they fhould want fportes.

*Eudox.* Doe you fpeake of under magiftrates,
Irenius, or of principall governors ?

*Iren.* I doe fpeake of noe particulars, but the
truth may be founde out by tryall and reafonable
infighte into fome of theire doinges. And yf I 399
fhoulde faye there is fome blame thereof in fome of

l. 3966, miswritten '*light*' in our MS.: l. 3972, '*fhe.*'

the principall Governors, I thincke I might allfo
fhewe fome reafonable proffe of my fpeach. For by
that which I and many have obferved, the like might
be gathered. As for enfample, fome of them feinge
the ende of theire goverment to drawe nighe, and
fome mifcheefe or troublous practife growinge up,
which afterwards may worke trouble to the next
fucceding governor, will not attempt the redres or
cuttinge of thereof, either for feare they fhoulde leave 4000
the Realme unquiet att the ende of their goverment,
or that the next that cometh fhoulde receave the fame
to quiett, and foe happely wynne more prayfe thereof
then they before. And therefore they will not as I
fay, feeke at all to redres that evill, but will eyther
by graunting proteccon for a tyme, or houldinge
fome enparlance with the rebell, or by treaty of
comiffioners, or other like devifes, onely fmother and
keepe downe the flame of the mifcheife, foe as yt
may not breake out in theire tyme of goverment : what 4010
comes afterwards they care not, or rather wifhe the
worft. This coorfe hath bene noted in fome governors.

*Eudox.* Surelie Irenius this, yf yt were true, fhould
bee worthye of an heauy judgment : but yt ys
hardlye to be thought, that any governor fhould foe
much either envye the good of that realme which is
putt into his hande, or defraude her Majeftie, whoe
trufteth him foe much, or maligne his fucceffor
which fhall poffeffe his place, as to fuffer an evill to
growe up, which he might tymelye have kept under, 4020
or perhaps to nourifhe yt with colloured countenance,
or fuche fynifter meanes.

l. 4015, '*would.*'

*Iren.* I doe not certenly avouch, Eudoxus : but
the fequell of thinges doth in a manner prove, and
playnely fpeake foe much, that the governors ufually
are envyous one of anothers greater glorie, which
yf they woulde feeke to excell by better governinge,
it fhoulde be a moft laudable emulacon. But they
doe quite otherwife : for this (as yee maye marke,)
is the comon order of them, that whoe cometh next 403
in place will not followe that coorfe of government,
how ever good, which his predeceffor helde, or for
defdaine of himfelfe, or dowbte to have his doinges
drowned in another mans prayfe, but will ftraighte
take a way quite contrarye to the former : as yf the
former thought by keepinge under the Irifhe, to
reforme them, the next, by difcontynencinge the
Englifhe will curry favor with the Irifhe and foe
make his government feeme plaufable in veiwe, as
havinge all the Irifhe at his comaund : but he that 404
comes next after will perhappes follow neither thone
nor thother, but will dandle thone and thother in
fuche forte, as he will fucke fweete out of them
both, and leave bitternes to the poore lande, which
yf he that comes after fhall feeke to redres, he
fhall perhappes finde fuch croffes as he fhalbe
hardly able to beare, or doe any good that might
worke difgrace of his predeceffors. Enfamples hereof
yee maye fee in the governors of late tymes
fufficientlye, and in others of former tymes more 405
manifeftlie, when the government of that Realme
was comytted fometymes to the Geraldynes, as

---

l. 4023, '*foe much*' not in our MS., but in Collier, Morris, etc., and
is not needed.

when the Howfe of Yorke helde the Crowne of England ; fometymes to the Butlers, as when the Howfe of Lancafter gott the fame. And other whiles, when an Englifhe governor was appointed, he perhappes founde enemies of both. And this is the wretchédnes of that fatall kingdome which, I thincke, therefore in old tyme was not called amiffe *Ranna* or *Sacra* Infula, takinge *Sacra* for accurfed. 4060

*Eudox.* I am forrie to heare foe much as yee reporte; and nowe I begynne to conceave fomewhat more of the caufe of her contynuall wretchednes then heretofore I founde, and I wifhe that this in-convenyence were looked into : for fure me feemes yt is more waightie then all the former, and more hardly to be redreffed in the governor then in the governed ; as a maladie in a vitall parte is more incurable then in an externall.

*Iren.* You faye very true ; but nowe that wee 4070 have thus ended all the abufes and inconveniences of that goverment, which was our firft parte, it followes next to fpeake of the feconde part, which was of the meanes to cure and redres the fame, which wee muft labor to reduce to the firft begynninge thereof.

*Eudox.* Right foe Irenius : for by that which I have noted in all this your difcourfe, yee fuppofe that the whole ordinance and inftitucon of that realmes goverment was, both att firft when yt was placed, evill plotted, and allfo fince, through other over- 4080 fighte, rune more out of fquare, [to] that diforder which yt is nowe come unto ; like as twoe indirect

l. 4073, '*that . . . part*' not in our MS., but in Collier, Morris, etc.

IX. 10

lynes, the further they are drawn out, the further
they goe afunder.

*Iren.* I doe fee, Eudoxus, and as yee faye, foe
thincke, that the longer that goverment thus con-
tynueth, in the worfe cafe will that Realme bee;
for yt is all in vayne that they nowe ftryve and
endeavor by fayre meanes and peaceable plotts to
redres the fame without firft removinge all thofe 409
inconveniences, and newe framinge, as yt were in the
forge, all that is worne out of fafhion : for all other
meanes wilbe but loft labor, by patchinge up one hole
to make many ; for the Irifh doe ftrongly hate and
abhor all reformacon and fubjeccon to the Englifhe,
by reafon that, havinge bene once fubdued by them,
they were thruft out of all theire poffeffions. Soe as
nowe they feare, that yf they were againe brought
under, they fhoulde likewife be expelled out of all,
which is the caufe that they hate Englifhe goverment, 410
accordinge to the fayinge, Quem metuunt oderunt :
therefore the reformacon muft nowe be with the
ftrength of a greater power.

*Eudox.* But, me thinckes, that might bee by
makinge of good lawes, and eftablifhinge of newe
ftatuts, with fharpe penalties and punifhments for
amendinge of all that is prefently amiffe, and not as
ye fuppofe, to begynne all as yt were anewe, and
to alter the whole forme of the goverment ; which
how daingerous a thinge it is to attempte, you 411
your felfe muft needs confeffe, and they which have
the managinge of the Realmes whole pollycie,

---

l. 4087, ' *courfe* ' : ll. 4102-3, ' *the ftrength of* ' not in our MS., but
in Collier, Morris, etc.

cannot, without greate caufe, feare and refrayne :
for all innovacon is perillous, in foe much as though
yt be meante for the better, yet foe many accidents
and fearefull events maye come betweene, as that
it may hazard the loffe of the whole.

*Iren.* Very true, Eudoxus ; all chainge is to be
fhunde, where the affayres ftand in fuch ftate as that
they may contynue in quietnes, or bee affured at all 4120
to abide as they are.  But that in the Realme of
Ireland wee fee muche otherwife, for every day wee
perceave the troubles growinge more upon us, and
one evill growinge upon another, in foe much as
there is noe parte founde nor affertayned, but all have
theire eares upright, wayting when the watchworde
fhall come that they fhoulde all rife generally into
rebellyon, and caft awaye the Englifhe fubjeccon.
To which there nowe little wanteth ; for I thincke
the worde be alreadye geven, and there wanteth 4130
nothinge but oportunitie, which trulye is the death
of one noble perfon, whoe, beinge himfelfe moft
ftedfaft to his noble Queene and his Countrye,
coaftinge upon the Southe Sea, ftoppeth the ingate
of all that evill which is looked for, and holdeth
in all thofe which are at his backe, with the terror
of his greatnes, and thaffurance of his moft
immoveable loyalltye : And therefore where you
thincke, that good and founde lawes might amend
and reforme thinges amiffe there, you thincke furely 4140
amiffe.  For yt is vayne to prefcribe lawes, where
no man careth for keepinge of them, nor feareth the

---

l.  4138, '*honourable*' : ll.  4142-3, '*nor . . . them*' from Collier,
Morris, etc.

daunger for breaking of them. But all the realme is firſt to be reformed, and lawes afterwards to be made for keepinge and contynuinge yt in that reformed eſtate.

*Eudox.* Howe then doe you thincke is the reformacon thereof to begynne, yf not by lawes and ordinances?

*Iren.* Even by the ſworde ; for all thoſe evilles 41 muſt firſt be cutt awaye with a ſtronge hande, before any good cann bee planted ; like as the corrupt branches and unwholſome lawes are firſt to bee pruned, and the fowle moſſe clenſed or ſcraped awaye, before the tree cann bringe forth any good fruicte.

*Eudox.* Doe you blame me, even nowe, for wyſhinge Kerne, Horſe-boyes, and Carrowes to be cleane cutt of, as too violent a meanes, and doe your ſelfe nowe preſcribe the ſame medicyne ? Is not the ſworde the moſt violent redres that may 41 bee uſed for any evill?

*Iren.* It is ſoe ; but yet where no other remedye maye be found, nor no hope of recovery had, there muſt needes this violent meanes bee uſed. As for the looſe kinde of people which you woulde have cutt of, I blamed yt, for that they might otherwiſe perhappes bee brought to good, as namely by this way which I ſett before you.

*Eudox.* Is not your waye all one with the former, in effecte, which you founde falte with, ſave onely 41 this ods, that I ſaye by the halter, and you ſaye by the ſworde ? what difference is there ?

l. 4153. '*boughes*': l. 4157, '*Kearooghs*': l. 4159, after '*ſame*' '*too violent a*' miswritten again from previous line in our MS.

*Iren.* There is furely greate, when you fhall underftand yt; for by the fworde, which I named, I doe not meane the cuttinge of of all that nacon with the fworde, which farr bee yt from me, that ever I fhould thincke foe defperatelie, or wifhe foe uncharitablie, but by the fworde I meane the Royall power of the Prince, which ought to ftretch yt felfe forth in ther cheife ftrengthe to the redreffinge and 4180 cutting of of thofe evilles, which I before blamed, and not of the people which are evill. For evill people by good ordynance and goverment may be made good; but the evill that is of yt felfe evill, will never become good.

*Eudox.* I praye you then declare your minde at large, howe you woulde wifhe that fworde, which you meane, to bee ufed to the reformacon of all thofe evilles.

*Iren.* The firft thinge muft bee to fende over into 4190 that realme fuch a ftronge power of men, as that fhall perforce bringe in all that rebellyous rout of loofe people, which either doe nowe ftande out in open armes, or in wanderinge companies doe keepe the woodes, fpoilinge and infeftinge the good fub-jecte.

*Eudox.* You fpeake nowe, Iren., of an infynite charge to her Majeftie, to fende over fuch an armye as fhoulde treade downe all that ftandeth before them on foote, and laye on the grounde all the 4200 ftiffe-necked people of that lande; for there is nowe but one Outlawe of any greate reckoninge, to wytt, the Earle of Tyrone, abroade in armes, againft whome you fee what huge charges fhee hath bene att this laſt yere, in ſendinge of men, providinge of viƈtualls, and makinge heade againſt him : yet there is little or nothinge at all done, but the Queenes treaſure ſpente, her people waſted, the poore countrye troubled, and the enemye nevertheles brought into no more ſubjeccon then he was, or lift [421] outwardlye to ſhowe, which in effeƈte is none, but rather a ſcorne of her power, and emboldeninge of a proude Rebell, and an encouragement unto all like lewdelie diſpoſed traytors that ſhall dare to lifte up theire heele againſt theire Soveraigne Lady. Therefore yt were harde counſell to drawe ſuch an exceedinge charge upon her, whoſe event ſhould be ſoe uncerten.

*Iren.* True indeede, yf the event ſhoulde bee uncerten ; but the certentie of theſſeƈte hereof ſhalbe [422] ſoe infallable as that noe reaſon cann gayne ſay yt, nether ſhall the charge of all this armie, which I demaund, bee much greater then ſoe much as in this laſt twoe yeres warres hath vainlye benn expended. For I dare undertake that it hath coſt the Queene above 200000 poundes allready, and for the preſent charge, that ſhee is nowe att there, amounteth to very nere 2000 poundes a monthe, whereof caſt yee the couⁿte ; yet nothinge is done. The which ſome, had yt benn imployed as yt ſhoulde bee, woulde have [423] effeƈted al this that I now goe aboute.

*Eudox.* Howe meane you to have yt imployed, but to be ſpent in the paye of ſouldyors, and proviſion of viƈtuall ?

*Iren.* Right ſoe, but yt is nowe not diſburſed at

4217. '*exceedinge great*' Collier, Morris, etc. : l. 4228, ' 12000.'

once, as yt might bee, but drawen out into a longe
length, by fendinge over nowe 20000 poundes, and
next halfe yere 10000 pounds ; foe as the fouldyer
in the meane tyme, is for wante of due provifion of
victuall, and goode payement of his due, fterved 4240
and confumed ; that of a 1000, which came over
luftie able men, in halfe a yere there are not lefte
500.   And yet is the Queenes charge never the les,
but what is not paied in prefent mony is accompted
in debte, which will not be longe unpaied ; for the
Captaine, halfe of whofe fouldyors are deade, and
thother quarter never muftered, nor feene, comes
fhortlye to demand payement here of his whole
accoumpte, where, by good meanes of fome greate
ones, and privie fharinge with the officers and 4250
fervants of other fome, he receiveth his debte, much
leffe perhapps then was due, yett much more indeede
then he juftlye deferved.

*Eudox.* I take this, fure, to be no good hufbandrye ;
for what muft needes be fpent, as good fpent at once,
where is inough, as to have it drawne out into longe
delaies, feinge that thereby both the fervice is much
hindered, and yett nothinge faved : but yt may be
the Queenes treafure in foe greate occafions of huge
difburfements as yt is well knowne fhee hath beene 4260
at lately, is not alwaies foe readye, nor foe plentifull,
as yt cann fpare foe greate a fome together, but
beinge paide as yt is, now fome and then fome, yt is
noe great burden unto her, nor any great ympoverifh-
ment to her coffers, feinge by fuch delaye of time that
it daylie cometh in foe faft as fhee poureth it out.

l. 4243, '*a whit the*' Collier, Morris, etc. : l. 4256, '*parteth.*'

*Iren.* Yt may be as you faide, but for the goeinge
through of foe honorable a courfe, I doubt not
but yf the Queenes coffers be not foe well ftored,
which wee are not to looke into, but that the whole 4276
realme which now, as thinges are ufed, doe feele a
continuall burthen of that wretched realme hange-
inge upon theire backes, would, for a finall ryddance
of that trouble, be once troubled for all ; and pute
to all theire fhouldiers, and helpinge hands, and
hartes alfoe, to the defrayinge of that charge, moft
gladfullie and willinglye ; and furely the charge, in
effeȼt, is nothinge to the infinite greate good which
fhold come thereby, both to the Queene, and all
this realme generallye, as when tyme ferveth fhalbe 4286
fhewed.

*Eudox.* How manye men then would you require
to the finnifhing of this which yce take in hand ?
and how longe fpace would you have them inter-
tained ?

*Iren.* Verely, not above ten thoufand footemen,
and a 1000 horfe, and all thofe not above the
fpace of one year and a halfe ; for I would ftill,
as the heate of the fervice abateth, abate the
nomber in paye, and make other provifion for them, 4296
as I will fhow.

*Eudox.* Surely, yt femeth not much that you
require, nor noe longe time : but how would you
haue them ufed ? would you leade forth your armye
againft the enymie, and feeke him where he is to
fight ?

*Iren.* No, Eudox., it would not be, for it is well

l. 4297, ' *it* . . . *be* ' from Collier, Morris, etc.

knowne that he is a flying enimye, hidynge himfelf
in woodes and bogges, from whence he will not
draw forth, but into fome ftraight paffage or peril- 4300
lous forde where he knowes the armye moft needes
paffe ; there will he lye in wait, and, if hee finde
advantage fitt, will dangerouflye hazard the troubled
fouldier.    Therefore to feeke him owte that ftill
flyeth, and follow him that cann hardlye be found,
were vaine and bootleffe ; but I would devide my
men in garrifon upõ his countrye, in fuch places
as I would thincke might moft annoy him.

*Eudox.* But how can that bee, Iren., with foe few
men ? for thenemy, as ye now fee, is not all in 4310
one countrye, but fome in Ulfter, fome in Connaug,
and others in Leinfter.    So as to plainte ftronge
garrifons in all thefe places fhould neede many
moe men then you fpeake of, or to plainte all in
one, and to leave the reft naked, fhould be but to
leave them to the fpoyle.

*Iren.* I would wifh the chiefe power of the armye
to bee garrifoned in one countrye that is ftrongeft,
and the other upon the reft that are weakeft : As
for example, the Earle of Terrone is now counted 4320
the ftrongeft ; upon him would I laye 8000 men
in garrifon, 1000 upon Pheagh Mac-Hugh and the
Cavanaghes, and 1000 upon fome partes of Con-
naghe to be at the direction of the Governor.

*Eudox.* I fee now all your men beftowed, but in
what places would you fett theire garrifon that they
might rife out moft convenientlye to fervice ? and
though perhaps I am ignorant of the places, yet

l. 4322, ' *Feughe* ' : l. 4323, ' *Kevanaghs.* '

I will take the mapp of Ireland before me, and
make my eyes in the mean while my fchole-maifters, 4330
to guid my underftandinge to judge of your plott.

*Iren.* Thefe 8000 in Ulfter I would devide likewife into foure parts, fo as theire fhould be 2000
footmen in everye garrifon ; the which I would
thus place. Upon the Blackwater, in fome convenient place, as high upon the ryver as might bee,
I would laye one garrifon. Another would I put at
Caftleliffer, or Caftlefine thereaboutes, foe as they
fhould have all the paffages upon the river to Loghfoyle. The third I would place aboute Fermaugh or 4340
Bondroife, foe as they might lye betweene Connaugh
and Ulfter, to ferve upon both fides, as occafion
fhalbe offered ; and this therefore would I have
ftronger then any of the reft, becaufe yt fhould
be moft enforced, and moft ymployed, and that
they might put wardes at Ballafhanon, Belike, and
all thofe paffages. The reft would I fett aboute
Monnaghan or Belterbert, foe as yt fhould fronte
both upon thenymie that waye, and alfoe keepe
the countye of Cavan and Meath in awe from 4350
paffinge of ftraglers, and out gaders from thofe
partes, whence they ufe to come forthe, and oftentymes worke much mifchiefe. And to everye of
theife garifons of 2000. footemen, I would have
200. horfemen added, for thone without thother
can do but litle fervice. The foure garrifons, thus
beinge placed, I would have to bee victualled
aforehand for half a yeare, which you will faie to

1. 4337, ' *I would lay,*' from Collier, Morris, etc. : l. 4340, ' *Fearne-
munnaghe* ' : l. 4348, ' *Moneham.*'

be harde, confideringe the corruption and ufuall waft of victualls. But why fhould they not be afwell 4360 victualed for foe longe tyme, as the fhipes are ufuallye for a yeare, and fometymes twoe, feinge it is eafier to keepe them on land then on water? There breade would I have in flower, fo as it might be baked ftill to ferve there want. There drinke alfoe there brewed within thē, from tyme to tyme, and theire beef befor hande barrelled, the which maye be ufed as it is needed ; for I make noe doubt but of frefhe victuall they will fometimes purvay themfelves amongft theire enymies Creete. 4370 Here unto would I alfoe have them have a ftore of hofe and fhooes, with fuch other neceffaries as maye be needfull for fouldiers, foe as they fhall have no occafion to looke for reliefe from abroade, or occafion fuch trouble, for their contynuall fupplye, as I fee and have often proved in Ireland to be more coumberous to the Deputy, and more daungerous to them that releif them, then half the leadinge of an Armye ; for the enemy, knowinge the ordinarye wayes by which theire relief moft be brought them, 4380 ufeth comōnlye to drawe himfelfe into the ftraught paffages thitherwarde, and oftentymes doth daunger-oufly diftres them : befides, the pay of fuch force as fhould be fent for theire convoye, the charge of the carryages, the exactions of the countrye fhalbe fpared. But onely every halfe yeare the fupplye brought by the Deputye himfelf, and his power, whoe fhall then vifite and overlooke all thofe garrifons, to fee what is needed, to change what is expedient,

l. 4377, ' *comberfome* ' : l. 4378, ' *retayne.* '

and to directe what he fhall beft advife.    And thefe 4390
fowre garrifons yffuinge forth, at fuch convenient
tymes as they fhall have intelligence or efpeiall upon
the enemie, will foe drive him from one fteade to
another, and tennis him amongft them, that he
fhall finde noe where faif to keepe his creet, nor
hide himfelf, but flyinge from the fyer fhall fall
into the water, and out of one daunger into āother,
that in fhorte tyme his Creet, which is his moft
fufteniance, fhalbe waifted with prayeinge, or killed
with drivinges, or ftarved for want of pafture in 4400
the woodes, and he himfelfe brought fo low, that
he fhall have no harte nor abbilitye to endure
his wretchedneffe, the which will furely come to
paffe in verie fhort fpace ; for one winters well
followinge of him will foe plucke him on his knees,
that he will never be able to ftand up againe.

*Eudox.* Doe you then thinke the winter tyme
fitteft for the fervices of Ireland ? how falls it then
that our moft imployment be in fomer, and the
armyes then ledd comonlye foorth ?                    4410

*Iren.* It is furely mifconceyved ; for yt is not
with Ireland as with other countryes, where the
wars flame moft in fommer, and the helmets glyfter
brighteft in the faire fonnefhine : But in Ireland
the winter yeildeth beft fervices, for then the trees
are bare and naked, which ufe both to cloath and
howfe the kerne ; the ground is could and wett,
which ufeth to be his beddinge ; the ayre is fharpe
and bitter, which ufeth to blow through his naked
fides and legges ; the kyen are barren and without 4420

l. 4393, '*fide*' : l. 4398, '*fpace*' : l. 4414, '*funnefhine.*'

milke, which uſeth to be his onelye foode, neyther yſ
he kill them then will they yeild hime fleſh, nor yſ
hee keepe them will they give him foode ; beſides
then being all in calf for the moſt parte, they will,
through much chaſing and driuinge, caſt all theire
calues, and looſe all their milke, which ſhould releif
him the next ſommer after.

*Eudox.* I doe well underſtand your reaſon ; but
by your leave, I have hard yt other wiſe ſaide,
of ſome that weare outlawes, that in ſommer they 4430
kept themſelfes quiet, but in winter they would
plaie theyre partes, and when the nights weare
longeſt, then burne and ſpoyle moſt, foc that they
might faſlye returne before daye.

*Iren.* I have likewiſe harde and likewiſe ſene
proofe thereof trewe : but that was of ſuch outlawes
as war eyther abiddinge in well inhabited countrye,
as in Mounſter, all a-bordringe to the Engliſh
pale, as Pheah Mā Hugh, the Cavanaghes, the
Mores, the Dempſes, the Ketinges, the Kellies, 4440
or ſuch like : For for them indeed the night
is the fitteſt tyme for ſpoyleing and robbinge,
becauſe the nightes are then, as ye ſaid, longeſt
and darkeſt, and alſo the countryes all aboute
are then fulle of corne, and good proviſion to
be everye where gotten by them ; but it is far
otherwiſe with a ſtronge peopled enymye, that
poſſeſſe a whole countrye, for thother beinge but
a fewe, are indeede privillye lodged, and kept
in out villages and corners nigh the woodes and 4450
mountaynes, by ſome of theire privie freinds, to

l. 4426, ‘*retayne*’ : l. 4441, ‘*winter.*’

whom they bringe theire fpoyles and ftealthes,
and of whom they continuallye receive fecreete
releif; but the open enymye haveinge all his
countrye wafted, what by him, and what by the
foldiers, finddeth them fuccor in noe places. Townes
there are none of which he may gett fpoile,
they are all burt; Countrye houfes. and farmers
there are none, they be all fleed; breade he hath
none, he plowed not in fommer; flefh he hath, 4460
but if he kill yt in winter, he fhall want milke in
fomer, and fhortly want life. Therefore yf they
bee well followed but one winter, yee fhall have
litle worke to doe with them the next fommer.

*Eudox.* I doe now well perceave the dyfference,
and doe verelye thinke that the winter tyme is
there fytteft for fervice: withall I perceave the
manner of youre handlinge the fervices, by drawe-
inge fudden draughtes upon the enimye, when he
looketh nott for you, and to watch advantage upon 4470
him, as he doth uppon you. By which ftraight
keepinge of them in, and not fufferinge them longe
at anye tyme to reft, I muft needes thinke that
they moft fone be brought low, and dryven to
greate extremyties. All which when you have
perfourmed, and brought them to the verye laft
caft, fuppofe that eyther they will offer to come
in unto you and fubmitt themfelves, or that fome
of them will feeke to withdraw themfelves, what is
youre advife to doe? will you have them receaved? 4480

*Iren.* Noe; but at the beginynge of thefe warrs,
and when the garrifons are well planted and

1. 4462, '*and . . . life*' from Collier, Morris, etc.

fortyfied, I would wifh a proclamacon wear made
generally to come to there knowledge, that
what perfons foever would within twentye dayes
abfolutelye fubmite themfelves, exceptinge onely
the verye principall and ringeleaders, fhould finde
grace : I doubt not, but upon the fetlinge of
thefe garrifons, fuch a terror and nere confideracon
of there perilous eftate will be ftricken into moft 4490
that they will covett to draw awaye from theire
leaders.  And againe I well knowe that the rebells
themfelves (as I faw by proof in the Defmonds
warrs) will turne awaye all theire rafcall people,
whom they thinke unfervifeable, as ould men,
woemen, children, and hyndes, which they call
churles, which would onelye waft theire victualls,
and yeild them no ayde ; but theire cattell they
will furely keepe awaye : Thefe therefore though
pollicye would turne them backe againe, that 4500
they might the reyther confume and afflict the
other rebells, yett in a pittifull comifferation, I
would wifhe them to be received ; the reyther for
that this bafe forte of people doth not for the
moft parte rebell of himfelfe, have no harte
thereunto, but is of force drawne by the grand
rebels into theire action, and caryed awaye with
the violence of the ftreame, ells he fhould bee
fure to loofe all that he hath, and perhappes his
life alfoe ; the which now he caryeth with them, in 4510
hope to enjoy them theire, but he is there by
the ftronge rebells themfelves turned out of all,
foe that the conftraint hereof maye jn him deferve
pardon.  Likewife yf anye of there able men or

gentlemen fhall then offer to come awaie, and
to bringe there creete with them, as fome no doubt
may fteale them away prevelye, I wifhe them alfoe
to be receaved, for the difablinge of thenymye,
but withall, that good affurance maye be taken
of theire true behayvor and abfolute fubmiffion, 4520
and that they then be not fuffered to remaine anye
longer in thofe parts, no nor about the garifon,
but fent awaye into the inner parts of the realme,
and difperfed in fuch forte as they fhall not come
togeather, nor eafelye retorne yf they would : For
if they might be fuffered to remaine about the
garrifon, and there inhabite, as fhall offer to
till the ground, and yeild a greate parte of the
profitt thereof, and of theire cattell, to the coronell,
wherewith they have heretofore tempted manie, 4530
they would (as I have by experience knowen) bee
ever after fuch a gall and inconvenyence to them,
as that theire profitt fhould not recompence theire
hurte ; for they will privilie releive theire freindes
that are forth ; they will fend the enymye fecrett
advertifement of all there purpofes and jorneyes
which they meane to make upon them ; they will
alfo not ftick to drawe the enimye upon them,
yea and to betraye the forte it felf, by difcoverye
of all the defects and difadvantages yf anye bee, 4540
to the cuttinge of all theire throts.  For avoydinge
whereof and manye other inconveniences, I wifh
that they fhould be carried farr from thence into
fome other parts, foe as I faide, they come and
fubmitt themfelves, upon the firft fommons : but
afterwards I would have none received, but lefte

to their fortonne and miferable end : my reafon is,
for that thofe which afterwards remaine without,
are ftoute and obftinate rebells, fuch as will never
bee made dutyfull and obedient, nor brought to 4550
labor or civill converfation, havinge once tafted
the licenfius life, and beinge acquainted with fpoyle
and outrages, will ever after be readye for the
like occafions, foe as there is no hope of theire
amendement or recoverye, and therefore nedefull
to be cutt of.

*Eudox.* Surelye of fuch defperat perfons, as will
follow the courfe of theire owne follye, there is
noe compafion to bee hadd, and for the others
yee have purpofed a mercifull meanes, much more 4560
then they have deferved : but what fhall bee the
conclufion of this warr ? for you have prefixed
a fhorte tyme of theire contenewance.

*Iren.* The end I affure mee will be verie fhorte,
and much foner then cann bee, in foe great trouble
(as yt femeth) hoped for, although there fhould
none of them fall by the fword, nor be flaine by
the foldier, yett thus beinge keepte from manurance,
and theire cattle from runinge abroade, by this
hard reftrainte, they would quicklye confume 4570
themfelves, and devoure one an other. The proof
whereof I faw fufficientlye enfampled in thofe
late warrs in Mounfter ; for notwithftandinge that
the fame was a moft ritch and plentyfull countrye,
full of corne and cattell, that you would have
thought they would have beene hable to ftand
longe, yett care one yeare and a half they weare
brought to fuch wretchednes, as that anye ftonye

IX.                                    11

herte would have rewed the fame. Out of everye
corner of the woode and glenns they came  4580
creepeinge forth upon theire handes, for theire
legges could not beare them ; they looked
Anatomies [of] death, they fpake like ghoftes,
crying out of theire graves ; they did eate of
the carrions, happye wheare they could find them,
yea, and one another foone after, in foe much
as the verye carcaffes they fpared not to fcrape
out of theire graves ; and if they found a plott
of water-creffes or fhamrockes, theyr they flocked
as to a feaft for the time, yett not able long  459
to contynewe therewithall ; that in fhorte fpace
there were none almoft left, and a moft populous
and plentyfull countrye fuddenly lefte voyde of
man or beaft : yett fure in all that warr, there
perifhed not manye by the fworde, but all by
the extreamytie of famyne which they themfelves
hadd wrought.

*Eudox.* It is a wonder that you tell, and more
to bee wondred how yt fhould foe fhortly come to
paffe.  460

*Iren.* It is moft true, and the reafon alfoe very
readye ; for ye muft conceive that the ftrength
of all that nation is the Kearne, Gallowglaffe,
Stocagh, Horfman, and Horfeboy, the which haveing
ben never ufed to have any thinge of theire owne,
and now livinge of others, make no fparre of anye
thinge but havocke and confufion of all they meete
with, whether yt bee theire frindes goods, or there
foes. And if they happen to gett never foe greate

1. 4599, '*foe fhortly*' from Collier, Morris, etc.

ſpoyles at anye tyme, the ſame they ſpoyle and waſte 4610
at a tryce, as naturallye delightinge in ſpoyle, though
it doe themſelves noe good. On thother ſide, whatſoever they leave unſpent, the ſoldier, when hee cometh
there, he havocketh and ſpoyleth likewiſe, ſoe that
betweene them both nothinge is verye ſhortlye lefte.
And yett this is verye neceſſarye to be donne, for the
ſonne finyſhinge of the warr ; and nott onely this in
this wiſe, but alſo all thoſe ſubjects which border
upon thoſe parts, are eyther to bee removed and
drawne awaye, or likewiſe to bee ſpoyled, that the 4620
enymie may finde no ſuccor therebye : for what the
ſoldyer ſpares the rebell will ſurelye ſpoyle.

*Eudox.* I doe now well underſtand you. But now
when all thinges are brought to this paſſe, and all
filled with theſe ruefull ſpectackles of ſoe manye
wretched carcaſes ſtarvinge, goodly countryes waſted,
ſoe huge a deſolation and confuſion, as even I that
doe but heare yt from you, and doe picture it in my
mynd, doe greatlye pittye and commiſerate it, yſ it
ſhall happen, that the ſtate of this miſerie and 4630
lamentable image of thinges ſhall bee toulde, and
felingelye preſented to her ſaccred majeſtye, beinge
by nature full of mercie and clemencye, who is
moſt inclynable to ſuch pittyfull complants, and
will not indure to here ſuch tragidyes made of her
people and poore ſubjects as ſome about her maie
inſinuate ; then ſhee perhapps, for verye compaſſion
of ſuch calamityes, will not onely ſtopp the ſtreame of
ſuch violence, and returne to her wonted myldnes, but
alſoe cone them litle thankes which have beene the 4640
aucthors and counſellers of ſuch blodye plattformes.

Soe I remember that in the late goverment of that
good lord Graye, where after longe travell and
many perillous affaies, he hadd brought thinges
almoft to this paffe that ye fpeake of, that yt was
even made readye for reformation, and might have
ben brought to what her majeftye would, like
complainte was made againft him, that he was a
bloodye man, and regarded not the life of her
fubjectes noe more then dogges, but hadd wafted 4650
and confumed all, foe as now fhee had nothinge
left; but to reigne in theire afhes: her Majefties
eare was fonne lent thereunto, all fuddenlye turned
topyfe turvie; the noble Lord eftfoones was blamed;
the wretched people pittied; and newe counfells
plotted, in which it was concluded that a generall
pardon fhould be fent over to all that would accepte
of yt: upon which all former purpofes were blancked,
the Governor at a baye, and not onely all that greate
and longe charge which fhee hadd before beene at, 4660
quite loft and cancelled, but alfoe all that hope of
good which was even at the doore putt backe, and
cleane fruftrate. All which whether yt be trew, or
noe, your felfe cann well tell.

*Iren.* Too trewe, Eudox., the more the pittye,
for I may not forgett foe memorable a thinge:
neyther cann I be ignorante of that perillous devife,
and of the whole meanes by which it was compaffed,
and verye cunninglye contrived, by foweinge firft
dyffenfion betweene him and an other noble per- 4670
fonage, wherein they both at length found how
notablie they had beene abufed, and how therebye,

l. 4652, ' *her Majeftes.*'

under hand, this univerfal alteracon of thinges
was brought aboute, but then to late to ftaie
the fame; for in the meane tyme all that was
formerly done with longe labour and great toyle,
was (as you faye) in a moment undone, and that
good Lord blotted with the name of a bloody man,
whom, who that well knewe, knewe to be moft
gentle, affable, lovinge and temperate; but that the 4680
neceffitye of that prefent ftate of thinges enforced
him to that violence, and almoft changed his verrye
naturall difpofition. But otherwife he was fo farre
from delighting in blood, that oftentymes he fuffred
not juft vengeance to fall where it was deferved :
and even fome of thofe which were afterwardes his
accufers, had tafted to much of his mercye, and
were from the gallowes brought to be his accufers.
But his courfe indeede was this, that he fpared
not the heades and principalls of any mifchevous 4690
practize or rebellion, but fhewed fharpe judgement
on them, cheifly for an example fake, that all the
meaner fort, which alfo were then generally infected
with that evill, might by terror thereof be reclaymed,
and faved, yf it were [poffible]. For in the laft
confpiracye of fome of the Englifh Pale, thinke you
not that there were many more guyltie then [they]
that felt the ponifhement? or was there any almoft
clere from the fame? yet he towched onely a fewe
of fpeciall note; and in the triall of them alfo 4700
even to prevent the blame of crueltie and parciall
proceadinge as feekinge their blood, which he, in his

---

ll. 4687-8, ' *had* . . . *accufers*' from Collier, Morris, etc. : ll. 4695-7,
*For . . . were,' ibid,* : l. 4702, '*dealing.*'

great wifedome (as it feemeth) did fore-fee would
be objected againft him ; he, for avoydinge thereof,
did ufe a fingular difcretion and regarde. For the
Jury that went upon their triall, he made to be
chofen out of their neereft kinnefmen, and their
Judges he made of fome their owne fathers, of others
their uncles and deareft freindes, who when they
coulde not . but juftly condemne them, yet uttered 4710
their judgment in aboundance of teares, and yett
even herein he was accompted bloody and cruell.

*Eudox.* Indeede fo have I heard it often fo fpoken,
but I perceyve (as I alwaies verely thought) that it
was moft unjuftly ; for hee was alwaies knowne to
be a moft juft, fincere, godly, and right noble man,
far from fuche ftearneneffe, far from fuche unrighteous-
nes. But in that fharpe execucon of the Spaniards
at the forte of Seuawick, I heard it fpecially noted,
and, if it were trewe as fome reported, furely it was 4720
a great towche to him in honor, for fome fay that he
promifed them life ; others that at the leaft he did
put them in hope thereof.

*Iren.* Both the one and the other is moft untrue ;
for this I can affure you, my felf beinge as neare
them as any, that hee was fo farre from promifinge
or putting [them] in hope, that when firft their
Secretary, called, as I remember Segnor Jeffrey, an
Italian [being] fent to treate with the Lord Deputie
for grace, was flatly refufed ; and afterwardes their 4730
Coronell, named Don Sebaftian, came forth to intreate

---

1. 4713, '*it heere*' = in England ; but our text, '*it often*,' is surely
preferable to Dr. Morris's reading? l. 4719, '*Smerwicke*' : l. 4728,
'*Geffray*' : l. 4730, '*denyed.*'

that they might part with their armes like fouldiers,
at leaft with their lyves, accordinge to the cuftome
of warre and lawe of Nations, it was ftrongely denyed
him, and tolde him by the Lord Deputie him felfe,
that they coulde not iuftly pleade either cuftome of
warr, or lawe of Nations, for that they were not
any lawfull enemyes ; and if they were, willed them
to fhewe by what comiffion they came thither into
another Princes domynio..s to warre, whether from 4740
the Pope or the Kinge of Spayne, or any other.
Then when they faide they had not, but were onely
adventurers that came to feeke fortune abroade, and
ferve in warrs amongeft the Irifhe, who defired to
entertayne them, it was then tolde them, that the
Irifhe them felves, as the Earle and John of Des-
monde with the reft, were no lawfull enemyes, but
Rebells and traytors ; and therefore they that came
to fuccor them no better then rogues and runnagates,
fpecially cominge with no licence, nor commiffion 4750
from their owne Kinge : fo as it fhoulde be dis-
honorable for him in the name of his Queene to
condicon or make any tearmes with fuche rafcalls,
but left them to their choyce, to yielde and fubmytt
them felves, or no. Wherupon the faid Coronell did
abfolutely yeild him felfe and the fort, with all therein, and craved onely mercy, which it being thought
good not to fhew them, both for daiunger of themfelves yf, being faved, they fhould afterwardes joyne
with the Irifhe, and alfo for terror of the Irifh, who 4760
were muche imboldned by thofe forreyne fuccours,
and alfo put in hope of more ere longe ; there was
no other way but to make that fhort ende of them

which was made.　Therefore moſt untruly and maliciouſly doe theis evill tongues backbite and ſclaunder the ſacred aſhes of that moſt juſt and honorable perſonage, whoſe leaſte vertue, of many moſt excellent which abounded in his heroicke ſpirit, they were never able to aſpire unto.*

*Eudox.* Truly, Iren : I am right glad to be thus 4770 ſatisfied by you in that I have often heard queſtioned, and yet was never hable, to choke the mouthe of ſuche detractors with the certayne knowledge of their ſclaunderous untruthes : neither is the knowledge thereof impertinent to that which we formerly had in hand, I meane to the through proſecutinge of that ſharpe courſe which yee have ſett downe for the bringing under of thoſe rebells of Ulſter and Connaght, and preparinge a waye for their perpetuall reformacon, leaſt happely, by any ſuche ſyniſter 4780 ſugeſtions of creweltie and to muche bloodſhed, all the plott might be overthrowne, and all the coſt and labour therein imployed be utterly loſt and caſt away.

*Iren.* Yee ſay moſt true ; for after that lordes callinge away from thence, the two lorde Juſtices contynued but a while : of which the one was of mynde, as it ſeemed, to have contynued in the footinge of his predeceſſor, but that he was curbed and reſtrayned.　But the other was more myldely 4790

---

* In our own day Sir John Pope Hennessy has revived these old mendacities.　See our new Life of Spenser in Vol. I. for a critical handling of his ‘ Sir Walter Raleigh in Ireland,’ 1883 (Kegan Paul, Trench, & Co.), than which a more audaciously one-sided or malignant book has never been written.　Sir John does presume on the ignorance of his readers.—G.

difpofed, as was meete for his profeffion, and willinge
to have all the woundes of that comonwealth healed
and recured, but not with the heed as they fhoulde
bee.　After, when [he] was gone Sir John Parrott,
fucceedinge, as it were, into another mans harveft,
founde an open way to what courfe he lift, the
which he bent not to that poynt which the former
governors intended, but rather quite contrary, as it
were in fcorne of the former, and in a vayne vaunt
of his owne councells, with that which he was to 4800
willfully carried ; for he did treade downe and dis-
grace all the Englifhe, and fett up and countenance
the Irifhe all that he coulde, whether thinkinge
thereby to make them more tractable and buxome
to the goverment, wherein he thought muche amyffe,
or prively plotting fome other purpofes of his owne,
as it partly afterwardes appeared.　But furely his
manner of goverement coulde not be founde nor
holfome for that Realme, beinge fo contrary to the
former.　Forit was even as two phefitions fhoulde 4810
take one fick bodie in hande at two fundry tymes ;
of which the former woulde minifter all thinges
meete to purge and keepe under the bodie, the
other to pamper and ftrengthen it fodaynely agayne,
whereof what is to be looked for but a moft
daungerous relapfe?　That which we now fee through
his Rule, and the next after him, happened thereunto, beinge now more daungeroufly fick then ever
before.　Therefore by all meanes it muft be fore-
feene and affured, that after once entring into this 4820
courfe of reformacon, there bee afterwardes no remorfe

l. 4792, '*pityfull woundes,*'

or drawinge back for the fight of any fuche ˉuefull
obiect as muft therupon followe, nor for compaffion
of their calamitics, feeinge that by no other meanes
it is poffible to recure them, and that theis are not
of will, but of veric urgent neceffitie.

*Eudox.* Thus farre then you have now procceded
to plant your garrifons, and to direct their fervices ;
of the which nevertheles I muft needes conceive
that there cannott be any certayne direction fett 4830
downe, fo that they muft followe the occafions which
fhalbe [daylic] offred, and diligently awayted.   But,
by your leave Iren., notwithftandinge all this your
carefull fore-fight and provifion, me thinkes I fee
an evill lurk unfpied, that may chaunce to hazard
all the hope of this great fervice, if it be not veric
well looked unto ;  and that is, the corruption of
their captaynes : for though they be placed never
fo carefully, and their companyes filled never fo
fufficiently, yet may they (if they lift) difcarde when 4840
they pleafe, and fende away fuche as will willingly
be ridd of that daungerous and harde fervice ;  the
which well I wott, is their comon cuftome to doe,
when they are laide in garrifon, for then they may
better hide their defaultes, then when they are in
campe, where they are contynually eyed and noted
of all men.   Befides, when their pay cometh, they will
(as they ufe) detayne the greateft porcons thereof
at their pleafurc, by an hundred fhiftes that neede
not here be named, thorough which they oftentymes 4850
deceyve the fouldior, abufe the Queene, and greatly
hinder the fervice.   So that lett the Queene pay

l. 4848, '*fay*.'

never fo fully, the mufter-mafter view them never fo
diligently, lett the deputie or generall looke never
fo exactly, yet they can cozen them all. Therefore
mefeemes it were good, yf at leaft it be poffible, to
make fome provifion for this inconvenience.

*Iren.* It will furely be very harde ; but the cheifeft
helpe for prevencon hereof muft be the care of the
coronell that hath the goverment of all his garifon, 4860
to have an eye to their alteracon, to knowe the
nomber and names of the fick fouldiors, and the
flayne, to marke and obferve their rankes in their
dayly rifinge forthe to fervice, by which he cannot
eafely bee abufed, fo that he him felf be a man of
fpeciall affuraunce and integritie. And therefore
good regarde is to be had in the chofinge and
appoynting of them. Befides, I would not by any
meanes that the captaynes fhould have the payeinge
of their fouldiors, but that there fhoulde a pay- 4870
mafter be appoynted, of fpeciall truft, which fhould
pay every man accordinge to his captaynes tickett,
and the accompt of the clarke of his bande : for by
this meanes the captayne will never feeke to falfify
his alteracons, nor to dyminifhe his companyes, nor
to deceyve his fouldiors, when nothinge thereof
fhalbe for his gayne. This is the manner of the
Spanyardes captaynes, who never hath to meddle
with his fouldiors pay, and indeede fcorneth the
name as bafe, to be counted his fouldiors pugadore ; 4880
whereas the contrary amongeft us hath brought
thinges to fo bad a paffe, that there is no captayne,
but thinkes his band very fufficient, yf he can mufter

l. 4867, ' *greate.*'

iii<sup>xx.</sup> [ = three score], and ſticks not to ſay openly,
that he is unworthie to have a captayneſhip, that
cannot make it ccccc<sup>li.</sup> by the yere, the which they
right well verifie by the proofe.

*Eudox.* Truly I thinke this is a verie good
meane to avoide that inconvenience of captaynes
abuſions. But what ſay you of the coronell ? what 4890
authoritie thinke you meete to be gyven him ?
whether will you allowe him to protcĉt, to ſauſe
conduĉt, [and] to have marſhall lawe as they are
accuſtomed ?

*Iren.* Yea verely, but all theis to be lymited with
verie ſtraight inſtruĉtions. As thus for protcĉtions,
that hee ſhall have authority after the firſt proclamation, for the ſpace of twentie dayes, to protcĉt all
that ſhall come unto them, and then to ſende us to
the Lord Deputie, with their ſauf conduĉt or paſſe, 4900
to be at his diſpoſicon ; but ſo as none of them
turne back agayne, beinge once comen, but be
preſently ſent away out of the countrie, unto the
next ſhereff, and ſo conveyed in ſauftie. And likewiſe for marſhall lawes, that to the ſouldior it be
not extended, but by triall formerly made of his
cryme, by a Jury of his fellowe ſouldiors as it ought
to be, and not raſhly, at the will or diſpleaſure of the
coronell, as I have ſometyme ſeene to lightly. And
as for other of the rebells that ſhall light into their 4910
handes, that they be well aware of what condicon
they be, and what holding they have. For, in the
laſt generall warres there, I knewe many good free-
holders executed by marſhall lawe, whoſe land was

ll. 4897-8, ' *that . . . to* ' from Collier, Morris, etc.

thereby faved to their heires, which fhoulde otherwife have efcheated to her Majeftie. In all which, the greate difcrefion and uprightnes of the coronell him felf is to be the chiefeft ftay bothe of all theis doubtes, and for many other difficulties that may in the fervice happen.                                                        4920

*Eudox.* Your caufion is verie good ; but now towchinge the arche-Rebell him felf, I meane the Earle of Tyrone, if he, in all the tyme of theis warrs, fhould offer to come in and fubmytt him felf to her Majeftie, woulde you not have him receyved, gyvinge good hoftages, and fufficient affurance of him felf ?

*Iren.* No, marry ; for there is no doubt, but he will offer to come in, as he hath done dyvers tymes alreadie, but it is without any intent of true fub- 4930 miffion, as the effect hath well fhowed ; neither indeede can he now, if he woulde, come in at all, nor gyve that affurance of him felf that fhould be meete, for being, as he is, very fubtill headed, feinge him felf now fo farr engaged in this bad action, can you thinke that by his fubmiffion he can purchafe to him felf any fauftie, but that hereafter, when thinges fhalbe quieted, theis his villanyes wilbe ever remem- bered ? and whenfoever he fhall treade awry (as needes the moft righteous muft fome tymes) ad- 4940 vantage wilbe taken thereof, as a breache of his pardon, and he brought to a reconinge for all former matters : befides, how harde it is for him now to frame him felfe to fubjection, that havinge once fett before his eyes the hope of a kingdome, hath ther- unto founde not onely encoragement from the greateft

Kinge of Chriftendome, but alfo founde great fayntnes in her Majefties withftandinge [him], whereby he is animated to thinke that his power is to defende him, and offende further then he had done, when fo 494 ever he pleafe, lett every reafonable man judge. But yf he him felf fhould come in, and leave all other his accomplices without, as Adonel, Macmahon, Mackuyre, and the reft, he muft needes thinke that then, even they will eare longe cut his throate. which having drawen them all into this occafion, now in the mydeft of their trouble gyveth them the flipp ; wherby he muft needes perceyve how impoffible it is for him to fubmytt himfelfe. But yet if he woulde fo doe, can he gyve any affurance of 49! his good obedience ? For how weake holde there is by hoftages, hath to often been proved, and that which is fpoken of takinge Shan Oneales fonnes from him, and fetting them up againft him, is a very perilous councell, and not by any meanes to be put in proofe ; for were they lett forth and coulde overthrowe him, who fhoulde afterwardes overthrowe them, or what affurance can be had of them ? It wilbe like the tale in Æfope of the wilde horfe, who, havinge enmytie againft the Stagg, came to a man 49( to defire his aide againft his enemye, who yeilding therunto mounted upon his back, and fo following the Stagg ere longe flew him, but then when the horfe woulde have him alight, he refufed, but kept him ever after in his fervice and fubjection. Suche, I doubt woulde be the profe of Shane Oneales fonnes. Therefore it is moft daungerous to attempt any fuche

l. 4944, '*Maguecirhe.*'

plott, for even that very manner of plott, was the meanes by which this traytorous Earle is now made great : for when as the laft Oneale, called Turlagh 4970 Lenagh, began to ftand upon fome ticle termes, this fellow, then called Baron of Dungañon, was fett up (as it were)· to beard him, and countenaunced and ftrengthened by the Queene fo farr, as that he is now hable to kepe her felf play : muche like unto a gamefter which havinge loft all, borroweth of his next fellowe gamefter that is the moft wynner, fomewhat to maynetaync play, which he, fetting unto him agayne, fhortly therby wynneth all from the wynner.

*Eudox.* Was this rebell then fett up at firft by 4980 the Quene (as you faie), and now become fo unduetifull ?

*Iren.* He was I affure you the [moft] outcaft of all the Oneales then, and lifted up by her Majeftie out of the duft, to that he hath now wrought him felfe unto ; and now he playeth like the frozen fnake, who beinge for compaffion relieved by the hufbandman, foone after he was warme began to hiffe, and threaten danger even to him and his.

*Eudox.* He furely then deferveth the ponifhment 4990 of the fnake, and fhoulde worthely be hewed to peeces. But yf you like not the fetting Shane Oneales fonnes againft him, what fay you then to that advife which I hearde was gyven by fome, to drawe in the Scotts, to ferve againft him ? how like you that advife ?

*Iren.* Much worfe then the former ; for who that

l. 4970, ' *Tyrrelaghe O'Neale* ' : l. 4980, ' *Eudox. Was . . . undutifull*' from Collier, Morris, etc. : l. 4992, ' *rayfing up of.*'

is experienced in thofe partes and knoweth not that
the Oneales are neerely alied unto the Mac Oneales
of Scotland, and to the Earle of Argill, from whom 5000
they ufe to have all ther fuccors of thofe Scottes and
Redfhanks ? Befides, all thefe Scottes are, through
long continuance, intermingled and alied to all the
inhabitants of the North ; fo as ther is no hope they
will ever be wrought to ferve faithfully againft ther
ould frends and kinfmen ; And if they would, how
when the warrs are finifhed and they have over
throwen him, fhall they themfelves be put out ?
Do not all know, that the Scotts were the firft
inhabitants of all the North, and that thofe which 5010
are now called North Irifh were indede very Scotts,
which challing the ancient inheritance and dominion
of that country to be their owne anciently. This
were then but to leape out of the pan into the
fier ; for the chiefeft caveat and provifon in the
reformacon of the North muft be to keepe out the
Scotts.

    *Eudox.* Indede, I remember that in your difcours
of the firft peopling of Ireland, you fhewed that the
Scithian or Scotts were the firft that fat downe in 5020
the North, wherby it femes they may challeng fome
right therin. How comes it then that Oneale claimes
the dominion therof, and this Earle of Tirone faith
the right is in him ? I pray you refolve me herin ;
for it is very needefull to be knowne, and maketh
moft unto the right of the war againft him, whos
fucceffe ufeth commonly to be according to the
juftnes of the caus, for which it is made : for if
Tiron have any right in that Seigniory me feemes

it fhould be wrong to thruft him out : or if (as I 5030 remember you fayd in the beginning) that Oneale, when he acknowleged the King of England for his liege Lord and Soveraigne, did, as he allegeth, referve in the fame commiffion all his feigniories and rights unto him felf, it fhould be accoumpted unjuft to thruft him out of the fame ?

*Iren.* For the right of Onele in the Seigniory of the North, it is furely none at all : for befides that the Kings of England conquered all the realme, and therby invefted all the right of that land to 5040 themfelves and ther heires and fucceffours for ever, fo as nothing was left in Onele but what he received back from them, Onele himfelf never had any auncient Seigniory in that country, but what by ufurpation and incrochment, after the death of the Duke of Clarence, he got upon the Englifh, whos lands and poffeffions being formerly wafted by the Scotts, under the leading of Edward le Bruce, as I formerly declared unto you, he eftefones entred into, and fithence hath wrongfully detayned, through the 5050 others occupations and greate affaires which the Kings of England fone after fell into here at home, fo as they could not intend to the recovery of that country of the North, nor reftrayning the infolency of Oneale ; who, finding none now to withftand him in that defolation, made himfelf Lord of thos few poeple that remained there, upon whom ever fithence he hath contenewed the firft ufurped power, and nowe exacteth and extorteth upon all men

1. 5030, miswritten '*wrought*' in our MS. : l. 5040, '*therby affumed and.*'

what he lift : foe that nowe to fubdue or expell an 506c
ufurper, fhould be no unjuft enterprize nor wrongfull
war, but a reftitution of an auncient right unto the
croune of England, from whence they were moft
unjuftly expelled and long kept out.

*Eudox.* I am very glad herein to be thus fatisfyed
by you, that I may the better fatisfy them whom
I have often heard to obiect thefe doubts, and
flaunderoufly to barck at the courfes that are held
againft that traiterous Earle and his adherence.
But now that you [have] thus fettled your fervice 507(
for Ulfter and Connaght, I would be glad to
heare your opinion for the profecuting of Feagh
McHugh, who being but a bafe villaine, and of
himfelf of no power, yet fo continually troubleth
that ftate, notwithftanding that he lyeth under
ther nofe, that I difdaine his bould arrogancy,
and thinck it to be the greateft indignity to the
Quene that may be, to fuffer fuch a caytiffe
play fuch reakes, and by his enfample not onely
to give hart and incoragement to all fuch bold 508(
rebells, but alfo to yeild them fuccor and refuge
againft her Majeftie, whenfoever they fly into his
Comerick : wherfore I would firft wifh, befoore
you enter into your plot of fervice againft him,
that you fhould lay open by what means he, being
fo bafe, firft lifted him felf up to this dangerous
greatneffe and how he maynteyneth his part againft
the Quene and her power, notwithftanding all that
hath bin don and attempted ageinft him. And
whether alfo hee have any pretence of right in the 509(

l. 5079, ' *Rex*,' Collier and Morris : l. 5083, ' *Cummerreighe.*'

lands he houldeth, or in the warrs that he maketh for the fame?

*Iren.* I will fo, at your pleafure, and fince you defire to know his beginning, I will not only difcover the beginning of his private houfe, but alfo the originall of all his Sept of the Birnes and Tooles, fo far as I have learned the fame from fome of them felves, and gathered the reft by reading: This poeple of the Birnes and Tooles (as before I fhewed you my conjecture) difcended from the 5100 auncient Britons, which firft inhabited all thofe eaftern parts of Ireland, as ther names do betoken; for Brin in the Britons language fignifieth wooddy, and Toll hilly, which names, it femeth, they tooke of the country which they inhabited, which is all very mountaine and wooddy.    In the which it femeth that ever fithence the comming in of the Englifh with Dermonigile, they have continewed: Whether that ther country being fo rude and mountaynous was of them defpifed, and thought 5110 [un]woorthy the inhabiting, or that they were receaved to grace by them, and fuffred to injoy ther lands as unfit for any other, yet it femeth that in fome places of the fame, they did put foote, and fortifyed with fundry caftles, of which the ruins there do only now remayne, fince which time they are growne to that ftrength, that they are able to lift up hand againft all the eftate; and now lately, through the boldneffe and late good fucceffe of this Feagh McHugh, they are fo far 5120

1. 5103, '*hillye*': l. 5104, '*hole, valley, or darke*': l. 5108, '*Deurmind-ne-Galh.*'

imboldned, that they threaten perill even to Dublin,
over whos neck they continewally hang.    But touching your demand of thefe Feaghs right unto that
countrey, or the feignory which he claimes therin,
it is moft vaine and arrogant.    For this you cannot
be ignorant of, that it was part of that which was
given in inheritance by Dermot McMurrogh, Kinge
of Leinfter, to Strangbow with his daughter, and
which Strangbow gave over to the King and his
heires, fo as the right is abfolutely now in her 5130
Majeftie ; and if it were not, yet could it not be in
this Feagh, but in Obrin, which is the ancient Lord
of all that countrey ; for he and his aunceftours were
but followers unto O Brin, and his grandfather, Shane
Mac Turlogh, was a man of meaneft regard among
them, neither having wealth nor power.    But his
fonn Hugh Mac Shane, the father of this Feagh,
firft began to lift up his head, and through the
ftrength and great fatneffe of Glan-Malor, which
adioyneth unto his houfe of Ballenecan, drew unto 5140
him many theeves and outlawes, which fled unto the
fuccor of the glenn, as to a Sanctuary, and brought
unto him part of the fpoyle of all the country,
through which he grew ftrong, and in fhort fpace
getting to him felf a great name therby amongeft
the Irifh, in whos footing this his fonn continewing
hath, through many unhappy occafions, increafed his
name, and the opinion of his greatneffe, fo that now
he is become a dangerous enemy to deale withall.

l. 5127, ' *Deurmind* ' : ll. 5132-4, ' *which* . . . *O'Brin* ' from Collier,
Morris, etc. : l. 5135, ' *Tirrelaghe* ' : l. 5139, ' *Maleeirh* ' : l. 5140,
' *Ballinecorrih.* '

*Eudox.* Sure, I commend him, that being of him 5150
felf of fo bace a condicon, hath through his owne
hardeneffe lifted himfelf to the height that he now
dare front princes, and make tearmes with great
potentates ; the which as it is honorable to him,
fo it is to them moft difgracefull, to be bearded of
fuch a bafe varlet, that being of late growne out
of the dunghill beginneth now to overcrow fo high
mountaines, and make him felf great proteĉtor of
all outlawes and rebells that will repayre unto him.
But do you thincke that he is now fo dangerous an 5160
enemy as he is counted, or that it is fo hard to take
him doune as fome fuppofe ?

*Iren.* No verelye, there is no great reckoninge to
bee made of him ; for hadd he ever beene taken in
hand, when the reft of the Realme, or at leaft the
parts adjoyninge, hadd beene quiet, as the honorable
gentleman that nowe governeth there, I meane Sir
Willyam Ruffell, gave a notable attempte thereunto,
and hadd worthylie performed yt, yf his courfe hadd
not bene croffed unhappelye, he could not have 5170
ftood thre moneths, nor ever have looked up againft
a very meane power : but now all the parts about
him being up in a madding moode, as the Mores in
Leafe, the Cavanaghes in the county of Wexford,
and fome of the Butlers in the county of Killkenny,
they all flock unto him, and draw unto his country,
as to a ftrong hould where they thinck to be fafe
from all that profecute them : And from thence they
do at ther pleafures breake out into all the borders
adjoyning, which are well poepled countries, as the 5180

l. 5155, miswritten *'grateful'* in our MS,

countys of Dublin, of Kildare, of Carlough, of
Kilkenny, of Wexford, with the fpoyles whereof
they victell and ftrengthen them felves, which fhould
in fhort time be ftarved, and fore pined ; fo that
what he is of him felf you may hereby perceive.

*Eudox.* Then, by fo much as I gather out of your
fpeach, the next way to end the warrs with him, and
to roote him quite out, fhould be to keepe him from
invading of thos countries adjoyning, which as I
fuppofe, is to be donn, by drawing all the inhabitants 519
of thos next borders away, and leaving them utterly
waft, or by planting garifons upon all thos frontieres
about him, that, when he fhall breake forth, may fet
upon him and fhorten his retourn.

*Iren.* You conceive very rightly, Eudox., but for
the difpoepling and driving away all the inhabitants
from the countries about him, which ye fpeake of,
fhould be great confufion and trouble, afwell for the
unwillingneffe of them to leave ther poffeffions, as
alfo for placing and providing for them in other 520
countries, me feemes, the better courfe fhould be by
planting of garrifons about him, the which, when
foever he fhall looke forth, or be drawne out with
defire of the fpoyle of thos borders, or for neceffity
of victuall, fhall be alwayes ready to intercept his
going or coming.

*Eudox.* Where then do you wifh thes garrifons to
be planted, that they may ferve beft againft him ;
and how many in every garifon ?

*Iren.* I my felf, by reafon that, as I told you, I 521

am no marſiall man, I will not take upon me to direct
ſo dangerous affaires, but only as I underſtand by
the purpoſes and plotts, which the Lord Grey who
was well experienced in that ſervice, againſt him
did lay doune : to the performance whereof he only
required a 1000. men to be layd in 4. garriſons : that
is, at Ballincore, 200 footemen and 50. hors, which
ſhould ſhut him out of his great glenn, whereto he
ſo much truſteth ; at Knocklough 200. footemen
and 50. hors, to anſwer the county of Carlo ; at 5220
Arclo or Wicklo 200 footemen and 50 horſemen,
to defend all that ſide towards the ſea ; in Shelelagh
100 footemen which ſhould cut him from the
Cavernaghes, and the county of Wexford ; and
about the 3 caſtles 50. horſmen, which ſhould defend
all the county of Dublin ; and 100 footemen at
Talbotts toune, which ſhould keepe him from breaking
into the county of Kildare, and be alwayes on his
neck on that ſide : the which garriſons, ſo lade, will
ſo buſy him, that he ſhall never reſt at home, nor 5230
ſtirr forth abrode but he ſhall be had ; as ·for his
Creete they can not be above ground, but they muſt
nedes fall into ther hands or ſterve, for he hath no
faſtneſſe nor refuge for them, or his partakers of the
Mores, Butlers, and Cavanaghes.  They will ſone
leave him, when they ſee his faſtneſſe and ſtrong
places thus taken from him.

*Eudox.* Surely this ſemeth a plot of great reaſon,
and ſmall difficulty, which promiſeth hope of a
ſhort end.  But what ſpeciall directions will you 5240

l. 5217, '*Ballinecorrih*' : l. 5220, '*Caterlaghe*' : l. 5221, '*and . . .*
*horſemen,*' Collier, Morris, etc.

fet doune for the ferviccs and rifings out of thes garrifons?

*Iren.* None other then the prefent occafions fhall minifter unto them, and as by good fpialls, whereof ther they cannot want ftore, they fhall be drawne continually upon him, fo as one of them fhall be ftil upon him, and fometimes all at one inftant bayte him. And this I affure my felf, will demand no long time, but will be all finifhed in the fpace of one yere; which how fmall a thing it is, unto the 5250 eternall quietneffe which fhal therby be purchafed to the realme, and the great good which fhould grow to her Majeftic, fhould me thinck readily draw on her Highneffe to the undertaking of the enterprife.

*Eudox.* You have very well me femes, Irenius, plotted a courfe for the atchieving of thes warrs now in Ireland, which feme to afk no long time, nor great charg, fo as th'effecting thereof be committed to men of fome truft, and fome ex- 5260 perience, afwell in the fayd country as in the manner of thos ferviccs; for if it be left in the hands of fuch raw captaines as are ufually fent out of England, being thereto preferred only by frendfhip, and not chofen by fufficienfy, it will fone fall to the ground.

*Iren.* Therfore it were meete me thincks that fuch captaines onely were hereto imployed, as have formerly ferved in that country, and bin at leaft lieftenants unto other captaines there. For other- 5270 wife, being brought and transferred from other ferviccs abroade, as in France, in Spaine, and in

the Low-countries, though they be of good experience
in thofe, and have never fo well deferved, yet in
thefe they will be new to feeke, and, before they
have gathered experience, they fhall buy it with
great loffe to her Majeftie, either by hazarding of
ther companies, through ignorance of the places, and
manner of the Irifh fervices, or by lofing a great
part of the time which is required hereunto, being 5280
but fhort, in which it might be finifhed, before they
have almoft taken out a new leffon, or can tell what
is to be donn.

*Eudox.* You are no good frend to new captaines
it femes, Irenius, that you bar them from the credit
of this fervice : but to fay truth, me thincks it were
mete, that any one, before he come to be a captaine,
fhould have bin a foldier ; for, *Parere qui nefcit,
nefcit imperare.* And befides, ther is great wrong
done to the ould fouldier, who from all means 5290
of advancement (which is due unto him) is cut of,
by fhuffling in thes new cutting captaines into ther
places, for which he hath long ferved, and perhaps
better deferved. But now thos that have thus
as I fuppofe finifhed all the war, and brought all
things to that low eb which you fpeake [of], what
courfe will you take for the bringing in of that reformation which you intend, and recovering all thinges
from this diffolute eftate, in which mee thincks I
behould them now left, unto that perfect eftablifhment 5300
and new comonwealth which you have conceived, of
which fo great good may redounc to her Majeftic,

ll. 5274-6, '*in* . . . *experience*' from Collier. Morris, etc. : l. 5299,
'*defolate.*'

and an affured peace be confirmed ? for that is that
wherunto we are now to looke, and do greatly long
for, being long fince made weary with the huge
charg which you have lade upon us, and with the
ftrong indurance of fo many complaints, fo many
delayes, fo many doubts and dangers, as will hereof
I know well, arife : unto the which before you come,
it were mete me thincks that you fhould take fome 5310
order for the fouldier, which is now firft to be dis-
charged and difpofed of, fome way ; the which if
you do not well fore-fee, may grow to a great inconvenience, as all this that we fuppofe you have quit
us from, by the loofe leaving of fo many thoufand
fouldiers, which from hence forth will be unfit for
any labor or other trade, but muft either feke fervice
and imployment abroade, which may be dangerous,
or ells will perhaps imploy them felves here at home,
as may bee difcomodious. 5320

*Iren.* You fay very true ; and it is a thing much
mifliked in this our comon-wealth that no better
cours is taken for fuch as have bin imployed once in
fervice, but that retourning, whether maymed, and fo
unable to labor, or otherwife, though hole and found,
yet afterward unwilling to worke, or rather willing
to make worke for the hang-man. But that nedeth
an other confideration ; but to this that we have now
in hand, it is far from my meaning to leave the
fouldier fo at randome, or to leave that·waft realme 5330
fo weake and deftitute of ftrength, which may both
defend it againft others that might feke to fet upon

l. 5327, '*fett the hangman a woorke*' : l. 5330, '*fo . . . randome*'
from Collier, Morris, etc.

it, and alfo kepe it from that relaps which I before
did forecaft. For it is one fpeciall good of this plot
which I would devife, that fix thoufand fouldiers of
thofe whom I have now imployed in that fervice,
and made throughly acquainted both with the ftate
of the country, and manners of the people, fhould
henceforth be ftill continewed, and for ever mayntayned of the country, without any charg to her 5340
Majeftie; and the reft that either are ould, and
unable to ferve longer, or willing to fall to thrifte,
(as I have fene many fouldiers after ther fervice to
prove very good hufbands,) fhould bee placed in parts
of the lands by them woonn, at fuch rate, or rather
better then others, to whom the fame fhall be let.

*Eudox.* Is it poffible, Irenius? can ther be any
fuch means devifed that fo many men fhould be
kept ftill for her Majefties fervice without any charg
to her Majeftie at all? Surely this were an exceed- 5350
ing great good, both to her Heighneffe to have fo
many ould fouldiers alwayes ready at call, to what
purpofe foever fhe lift to imploy them, and alfo to
have that land therby fo ftrengthned, that it fhall
neither feare any forreigne invafion, nor practife,
which the Irifh fhall ever attempt, but fhall kepe
them under in continewall awe and firme obedience.

*Iren.* It is fo indede. And yet this truly I do
not take to be any matter of great difficulty, as I
thinck it will alfo fone appere unto you. And firft 5360
we will fpeake of the North part, for that the fame
is of moft weight and importance. So fone as it
fhall appere that the enemy is brought doune, and

l. 5346, '*fett.*'

the ftoute rebell either cut of, or driven to that
wretchedneffe that he is no longer able to hould up
hand, but will come into any condicions, which I
affure my felf will be before the end of the fecond
Winter, I wifh that there be a generall proclamation
made, that whatfoever outlawes will frely come in,
and fubmit themfelves to her Majefties mercy, fhall 5370
have liberty fo to do, where they fhall either find
that grace they defier, or retourn againe in fafety:
upon which it is likely that fo many as furvive,
will come in to fue for grace, of which who fo are
thought mete for fubjection, and fit to be brought
to good, may be receaved, or ells all of them, for
I thinck that all will be but a very few; upon
condicon and affurance that they will fubmit themfelves abfolutely to her Majefties ordinance for them,
by which they fhall be affured of life and liberty, 5380
and be onely tied to fuch condicons as fhall bee
thought by her mete for contayning them ever after
in due obedience.   To the which condicons I nothing
doubt but that they will all moft readily, and upon
ther knees fubmit them felves, by the proofe of that
which I faw in Mounfter.   For upon the like proclamation ther, they all came in tagge and ragge,
and when as afterwards many of them were denyed
to be receaved, they bad them doe with them what
wolde, for they would not by noe meanes retorne, 5390
nor goe forth.   For in that cafe who will not accept
almoft of any conditions, rather then dye of hunger
and miferye?

l.  5366,  '*his head*':  l.  5390,  '*for . . . not*' from Collier, Morris,
etc.

*Eudox.* It is very lykely fo. But what then is the ordinance, and what be the condicions which you will purpofe unto them, that fhall referve unto them an affurance of lyfe and libertye?

*Iren.* Soe foone as they have given the beft affurance of them felves which may be required, which muft bee I fuppofe fome of their principall men to 5400 remaine in hoftage one of another, and fome other for the reft, for other furetye I reckon of none that may bynde them, neyther of wyfe, neyther of children, fynce then perhappes thay wold gladly be rydd of both from the famine; I would have them firft unarmed utterly, and ftript quite of all there warlike weapons, and then, thefe conditions fett downe and made knowne unto them; that thay fhalbe brought and removed with fuch creete as they have, into Lympfter, wher thay fhalbe placed, and have 5410 land given them to occupy and to lyve uppon, in fuch forte as fhalbecome good fubjectes, to labour thenceforth for there lyvinge, and to apply them felves unto honeft trades of Civility as thay fhall everye one be founde meete and able for.

*Eudox.* Where then, a Gods name, will you place them in Lynfter? or will you finde out any new land ther for them that is yet unknowen?

*Iren.* Noe, I will place them in all the countrye of the Birnes and Tooles, which Feagh McHugh hath, 5420 and in all the landes of the Cavanghes, which are now in rebellion, and all the landes which will fall to hir Majeftie there-aboute, which I knowe to be very fpacious and large yeanough to

l. 5396, '*propofe*': l. 5410, = *Leinfter*.

contayne them, being very nere twenty or thirty
myles wide.

*Eudox.* But what then will ye doe with all the
Birnes, the Tooles, and the Cavanaghes, and all thofe
that now are joined with them ?

*Iren.* At the fame very tyme, and in the fame 5430
manner that I make that proclamation to them of
Ulfter, will I alfoe have yt made to thefe; and uppon
ther fubmiffion therunto, I will take lyke affurance
of them as of thother.   After which I will tranflate
all that remaine of them unto the places of the other
in Ulfter, with there Creete, and what els they have
left them, the which I will caufe to be devided
amongeft them in fome meete forte, as each may
therby have fomewhat to fuftayne him felfe a while
withall, untill, by his further travell and labor of 5440
the yearth, he fhalbe able to provide himfelfe
better.

*Eudox.* But will you then give the lande frely unto
them, and make them heires of the former Rebells ?
foe may you perhapps make them heires alfo of
their former villanies and diforders; or how els will
you dyfpofe of them ?

*Iren.* Not fo; but all the landes I will give unto
Englifhmene whom I will have drawne thither, whoe
fhall have the fame with fuch eftates as fhalbe thought 5450
meete, and for fuch rente as fhal eft-fones bee
rated : under every of thofe Englifh men will I place
fome of thofe Irifh to be the tenanntes for a certayne
rent, accordinge to the quantyty of fuch lande as
every man fhall have allotted unto him, and fhalbe

---

1. 5434-5, '*After . . . others*' from Collier, Morris, etc.

founde able to meete, wherin this fpecial regard
fhalbe hadd, that in noe place under any lande lorde
there fhall remaine of them planted together, but
dyfperfed wide frome there acquintances, and fcat-
tered far abroad thorough all the country : for that 5460
is the evill which I nowe fynde in all Ireland, that
the Irifh dwell altogether by there feptes, and feverall
nacions, fo as they may practife or confpire what
they will ; wheras if there were Englifh fhedd
amongeft them and placed over them, thay fhould
not bee able once to ftyrr or murmur, but that yt
fhould be knowne, and thay fhortned accordynge to
there demerite.

*Eudox.* Ye have good reafon ; but what rating of
rentes meane you ? to what end doe you purpofe the 5470
fame ?

*Iren.* My purpofe is to rate the rente of all thofe
landes of her Majeftie in fuch forte, unto thofe
Englifh men as fhall take them, as thay may be
well able to lyve thereuppon, yeilding hir Majeftie
a reafonable cheiferie, and alfo give a competent
maintenance unto the garrifons, which fhall ther be
left amongeft them ; for thefe foldiors (as I told you)
remayning of the former garrifons, I caft to mantaine
uppon the rent of thofe landes which fhalbe efcheated, 5480
and to have them devided through all Ireland in fuch
places as fhalbe thought moft convenient, and occafion
may require. And this was the courfe of the
Romaines obferved in the conqueft of England, for
thay planted of ther legions in all places convenient,
the which thay caufed the country to mantayne,

l. 5456, ‘ *weelde* ’: l. 5484, ‘ *ufed.* ’

cuttinge uppon every porcion of land a reafonable
rente, which thay called Romeftot, the which might
nott furcharge the tennante or freholder, and defray
the pay of the garrifon : and this hath beene alwais 5490
obferved in all princes in all countries to them newly
fubdued, to fett garrifons amongeft them to contayne
them in dutye whofe burden they made them to
beare ; and the want of this ordinaunce in the firft
conqueft of Ireland by Henry the Second, was the
caufe of foe fhorte decay of that goverment, and the
quicke recovery againe of the Irifh.    Therfore by all
meanes it is to be provided for.    And this is it that
I would blame, if it fhould not mifbecom me, in
the late plantying of Munfter, that noe care was had 5500
of this ordinaunce, nor any ftrenth of a garrifon
provided for, by a certayn alowance out of all the
fayd landes, but only the prefent profit loked unto,
and   the   faf   continewance   therof   ever   herafter
neglected.

    *Eudox*. But ther is a band of foldioures layed in
Mounfter, to the mayntenance of which, what odds
is there whethere the Quene, receiving the rent of
the countrye, doe give pay at hir pleafure, or that
ther be a fettled allowance appoynted unto them out 5510
of ther landes there ?

    *Iren*. There is great oddes, for nowe that fayd rent
of the country is not ufually applied to the pay of
the foldyars, but it is, (every other occafion comming
betwene,) converted to other ufes, and the foldier
in times of peace difcharged and neglected as un-
neceffary; wheras if the fayd rent were appoynted
and ordayned by an eftablifhment to this end only,

it fhould not bee turned to any other ; nor in troublous times, upon every occafion, her Majeftie be fo 5520
trobled with fendinge over newe foldiers as fhe now
is, nor the country ever fhould dare to mutine, having
ftill the foldiar in ther necke, nor any forraine enymy
dare to invade, knowinge ther fo ftronge a garrifon
allwais to receave him.

*Eudox.* Sith then you thinkee this Romefcott of
the pay of the foldier uppon the lande to be both
the redyeft way to the foldier, and leffe troblefome to hir Majeftie, tell us, I pray you, how
ye wold have the fayd landes rated, that both a 5530
rente may rife therout unto the Queene, and alfo
the fouldiours receive pay, which (me feemes) wilbe
harde ?

*Iren.* Firft we are to confider how much lande
there is in all Ulfter, that according to the quantitye
thereof we may ceffe the fayd rente and alowance
yffuing thereout. Ulfter, as the auncient recordes of
that realme doe teftyfie, doeth contayne Nine Thoufand
plough landes, every of which plowe landes contayneth fix fcore acres, after the rate of xxi. foot to 5540
every pearch of the fayd acre, which amounteth in
the whole unto 124000 acres, every of which plowe
landes I will rate at xlvjs. 8d. by the yeare ; which
is not much more then 1d. for an acre, the which
yerly rent amounteth in the whole to xviij[000]l,
befides 6s. 8d. chiefrie out of every plow-land. But
becaufe the county of Louth, being a parte of Ulfter,
and contayning in yt vij. h. and xij. plow-landes, is not

---

l. 5544, ' 1½d.': l. 5546, '*befides . . . plow-land*' from Collier,
Morris, etc.

wholy to efcheat unto her Majeftie as the reft, thay
having in all thefe warrs continewed for the moft parte 5551
ductyfull, though otherwife a great parte therof is now
under the rebels, ther is an abatement to be made
out of iiij h. or v h. plowe landes, as I eftimat the
fame, the which are not to pay the whole yearly
rente of xl [vis. 8d.] out of every plow land, like as
the efcheated landes doe, but yet fhall pay for ther
compofition of ceffe towardes the maintenance of the
foldier xxs. out of every plow lande: foe as ther is to
be deducted out of the former fome iij h. yearly, the
which may neverthelesse be fupplied by the rent of 5561
the fyfhings, which are exceding great in Ulfter, and
alfoe by an increafe of rente in the beft landes, and
thofe that lye in the beft places nere the fea-coft.
The which xviii [thoufand] pounds will defray the
entertaynment of xv. hundred foldyers, with fome
overplus toward the pay of the victualls which are
to be imployed in victualing of thefe garrifons.

*Eudox.* So then, belike, ye meane to leave
xvc. = 1500) foldyers in garrifon for Ulfter, to
be payed principally out of the rent of thofe 5571
landes which fhall there efcheat unto her Majeftie.
The which, wher I pray you, will you have them
garrifoned ?

*Iren.* I will have them devided into 3 parts ; that
is, vc. (= 500) in every garrifon, the which I will
have to remayne in thre of the fayd places where
they were before appoynted ; to weete, vc. (= 500)
at Straban and about Loghfoyle, and foe as thay
may hold all the paffages of that parte of the country,

1. 5559; '200 *or* 300*l.* ': l. 5576, '*fame.*'

and fome of them be put in wardes, uppon all the 5580
ftraights thereabouts, which I know to be fuch, as
may ftope all paffages into the country one that
fide ; and fome of them alfoe upon the Bann, up
towardes Logh Sidney, as I formerly directed.   Alfo
other v.c. at the fort uppon Logh-earne, and wardes
taken out of them which fhalbe layde at Farman-
nagh, at Belicke, at Ballifhannon, and on all the
ftraightes towardes Connagh, the which I knowe doe
fo ftrongly commaunde all the paffages that way,
as that none cann paffe from Ulfter into Connaght, 5590
without ther leave.   The laft v.c. fhall alfo remaine
in their forte in Monoghan, and fome of them be
drawen into wardes, to kepe the keyes of all that
country, both downwardes, and alfo towardes Orlyes
countrie, and the pale ; as fome at Enifkilline, fome
at Belterbert, fome at the Blacke forte, and fo alonge
that river, as I formerly fhowed in the firft plantyng
of them.   And moreover at every of thefe fortes, I
wold have the feate of a towne layed forth and
incompaffed, in which I wold wifh that there fhould 5600
inhabitants of all fortes, as merchantes, artificeres,
and hufbanmen, to be placed, to whome ther fhold
be charters and franchifes graunted to incorporat
them.   The which, as it wilbe no matter of difficulty
toe draw out of England perfones which wold very
gladly be fo placed, fo would it in fhort fpace turne
thofe partes to great commodity, and bring ere longe
to her Majeftie much profit ; for thofe places are
fite for trade and traffique, having moft convenient

l. 5586, '*out* . . . *which*' from Collier, Morris, etc. : l. 5599, '*ftate*,'
and fo in MS., but '*feate*' from Collier, etc., accepted.

outgates by [rivers] to the fea, and ingates to the 5610
richeſt partes of the lande, that thay wold fone bee
enriched, and mightily enlarged, for the very feating
of the garrifons by them, befides, the fafty and
affurance which they ſhall worke unto them, will alfoe
draw thither ſtore of people and trades as I have
fene enfampled at Mariburgh and Phillipſtowne in
Leinſtor, wher by reafon of thofe two fortes, though
ther were but fmale wardes left in them, there are
two good townes now growen, which are the greateſt
ſtay of both thofe two countries.                      5620

*Eudox.* Indeed me femes 3 fuch townes, as ye
fay, would doe very well in thofe places with the
garrifons, and in ſhorte fpace wold be fo augmented,
as thay wold be able with little [helpe] to inwall
them felves ſtrongley : but, for the plantyng of all
the reſt of the country, what order will yee take ?

*Iren.* What other then as I fayd to bringe people
out of England, which ſhould inhabit the fame ;
whereunto though, I doubt not, but great troupes
would be ready to runn, yet for that in fuch cafes, 5630
the worſt and moſt decayed men are moſt ready to
remove, I would wiſhe them rather to be chofen out
of all partes of this realme, either by difcrefion of
wife men therunto appointed, or by lott, or by the
drumme, as was the ould ufe in fending forth of
Collinies, or fuch other good meanes as ſhall in ther
wifedome be thought meteſt. Amongſt the cheife
of which I wold have the lande fet into fegniores, in
fuch fort as yt is now in Mounſter, and devided into
hundredes and pariſhes, or wardes, as it is in England, 5640

1. 5610, ' *rivers* ' from Morris, for ' *divers.* ',

and layed out into fheires as yt was aunciently ; *vizt.* the countie of Downe, the countye of Antrim, the countie of Lowth, the countye of Armagh, the countie of Cavan, the countye of Colrane, the countie of Monaghon, the countye of Tiron, the countie of Fermannagh, the countie of Donegall, being in all 10. Over all which I wifh a Lord Prefident and a Counfell to bee placed, which may keepe them afterwardes in awe and obedience, and minifter unto them juftic and equity. 5650

*Eudox.* Thus I fee the whole purpofe of your plott for Ulfter, and now I defire to heare your like opinion for Cannagh.

*Iren.* By that which I have already fayd of Ulfter, yee may gather my opinion for Cannagh, beinge very anfwereable unto the former. But for that the landes, which fhall efcheat unto hir Majeftie, are not fo intyrelie togeather as that thay cann be accounted unto one fome, it nedeth that thay be confidered feverally. The province of Cannagh contayneth in 5660 the whole, as appeareth by recorde at Dubline, vii thoufand and twoe hundred plowe landes of the former meafure, and is of late devided into fix fheires or countyes : the countie of Clare, the countye of Letrim, the county of Rofcaman, the county of Galway, the county of Maio, the county of Sligoh. Of the which, all the county of Slygoh, all the county of Maio, the moft parte of the county of Rofcomon, the moft parte of the countie of Lictrim, a great parte of the county of Galway, and fome of 5670 the county of Clare, is lyke to efcheate unto hir

l. 5665, ' *Leutrum* ' : l. 5666, ' *Gallowaye* ' : *ib.*, ' *Sleugho.* '

Majeſtie for the rebellion of there preſent poſſeſſors. The which two counties of Sligoh and Maio are ſuppoſed to contayne almoſt iij [thouſand] plowe landes, the rate wherof, ratablie to the former, I valewe almoſt at vj [thouſand] li. p. ann. The countie of Roſcomon, ſavinge what pertayneth to the howſe of Roſcomon and ſome fewe other Engliſh there lately ſeted, is all out, and therfore it is wholy lykwiſe to eſcheat to her Majeſtie, ſavinge thoſe 5680 porcons of the Engliſh inhabitantes ; and even thoſe Engliſh doe, as I underſtand by them, pay as much rente to hir Majeſtie as is ſet uppon thoſe in Ulſter, countyng ther compoſition money therwithall, ſo as it may runn all into one reconinge with the former two countyes : So that this countye of Roſcomon, contayning xij.c. plowe landes, as yt is accounted, amounteth to ij [thouſand] iiijc. poundes by the yeare, which with the former twoe countyes rent maketh about viij [thouſand] li. for the former wanted 569c ſomwhat. But what the eſcheated landes of the countyes of Galway and Lietrim will riſe unto is yet uncertayne to define, till ſurvay thereof be made, for that thoſe landes are intermingled with the Earle Clanricard, and others [lands] ; but it is thought that thay be thone halfe of both thoſe countyes, ſoe as thay may bee counted to the valewe of one whole countye, which contayneth above one thouſande plow-landes (for ſo many the leaſt county of them comprehendeth,) which maketh 570( two thouſand poundes more, that is, in all, x or xi thowſand poundes. Thother two counties muſt

l. 5679, '*one*': l. 5690, '8300*li.*' : l. 5701, '2000 *li.*'

remaine till ther efcheates appeare, the which lettyng
paffe as yet unknowne, yet thus much is knowne to
be accounted for certayne, that the compofition of
thefe twoe counties, beinge rated at xxs. everye
plowe lande, will amounte to above xiij [thoufand]
li. more: all which being layd togeather to the
former, may be reafonably eftimated to rife unto
xiij [thoufand] poundes, the which fome, togeather 5710
with the rēt of the efcheated landes in the twoe laft
countyes, which cannot yet be valued (beinge, as
I doubt not, leffe than a thowfand poundes more)
will yeild largely unto a thowfand men and ther
victuallers, and a thowfand pounds over towards the
Governor.

*Eudox.* Ye have me thinckes, made but an eftimate
of thofe lands of Cannaght even at a very venter, fo as
it fhould be harde to build any certaintye of charge
to be raifed uppon the fame.                    5720

*Iren.* Not altogeather yet uppon uncertantyes ;
for thus much may eafily appeare unto you for
certayne, as the compofition money of every plowelande amounteth unto ; for this I would have you
principally underftande, that my purpofe is to rate
all the landes in Irelande at xxs. every plowelande,
for there compofition towardes the garrifon. The
which I knowe, in regard of being freed from all
other charges whatfoever, wilbe redyly and moft
gladly yeilded unto. Soe that there beinge in all 5730
Ireland (as appeareth by there old rentes) 43920
plowelandes, the fame fhall amounte to the fomme

---

likewife of 43920 poundes, and the reft to be reared
of thefcheated landes which fall to hir Majefty in
the faid provinces of Ulfter, Connoght, and that
parte of Leinfter under the rebels; for Mounfter wee
deale not withall.

*Eudox.* But tell me this, by the way, doe you then
lay compofition uppon thefcheated landes as you doe
uppon the reft? for foe me thinckes, you recken all 5740
togeather.   And that fure were to much to pay
vij nobles out of every plowe lande, and compofition
money befides, that is xxs. out of every plowelande.

*Iren.* Noe, you miftake me ; I put onely vij
nobles rent and compofition both uppon every
plowe lande efcheated, that is xls. for compoficon,
and vjs. viijd. for cheifery to hir Majeftie.

*Eudox.* I doe now conceiue you ; procede then
I pray you, to the appointing of your garrifons in
Cannaght, and fhew us both howe many and where 5750
you would have them placed.

*Iren.* I wold have one thoufand laide in Cannaght
in two garrifons; namely, v.c. in the county of Maio,
about Clan McCoftulaghes, which fhall kepe Mayo
and the Burckes of McWilliam Enter : thother v.c.
in the county of Clanricarde, about Garrandough,
that thay may contayne the [Conhors] and the [blank]
Burkes ther, the Kellies and Macknyars with all
them about ; for that garrifon which I formerly
placed at Lougharne will ferve for all occafions in 5760
the county of Sligah, being nere adjoyning therunto,
fo as in one nighets march they may be allmoft

----

l. 5754, ' *Coftalors* ': l. 5754, ' *the Moores* ': l. 5757, [blank] : l. 5758,
illegible in our MS.

in any place thereof when need fhall requier them.
And like as in the former places of garrifon in
Ulfter, I wifhed iij corporat townes to be planted,
which under the fafegarde of the ftrenth fhall dwell
and trade fafely with all the country about them,
foe would I alfoe wifh to be in this of Connaght ;
and that befides, there were another eftablifhed at
Athlone, with a convenient warde in the caftle there 5770
for ther defence.

*Eudox.* What fhould that need, feing that the
Governor of Cannagh ufeth to ly there alwaies,
whofe prefence wilbe a defence to all that townefhip.

*Iren.* I know he doth foe, but that is much to be
dyfliked that the Governor fhould lye fo farre of, in
the remoteft place of all the province, wheras it
were meter that he fhould be continually abidinge
in the middeft of his charge, that he might both 5780
looke out alike into all places of his goverment, and
alfo be foone at hande in any place, where occafion
fhall demaunde him ; for the prefence of the Governor
is (as you fayd) a great ftay and brydle vnto them
that are ill difpofed : like as I fee it is well obferved
in Mounfter, wher the dayly good thereof is continually apparant ; and, for this caufe alfoe doe I
greatly miflike the lorde Deputies feating at Dubline,
being the outeft corner in the realme, and left neding
the awe of his prefence ; wheras, me feemes it were 5790
fitter, fince his proper care is of Leinfter, though he
hath care of all befides generally, that he fhould feat
himfelfe about Athie, or therabouts, uppon the fkirt

l. 5788, ' *diflike.*'

of that unquiet contry, fo as that he might fit, as it were, at the very mayne maft of the fhipp, whenc he might eafly overlooke and fome tymes overreach the Mores, the Butlers, the Dempfes, the Ketines, the Conners, Ocarrell, Omoloy, and all that heape of Irifh nations which ther ly hudled togeather without any to over-rule them, or contayne them in 5800 dutye. For the Irifh man, I affure you, feares the goverment noe longer then he is within fight or reach.

*Eudox.* Surely me thinckes herin you obferve a matter of much importance, more then I have heard ever noted ; but fure that femes fo expedient, as that I wonder it hath beene hertofore over omitted ; but I fuppofe the inftance of the cittizens of Dublin is the greateft let there.

*Iren.* Truly, then it ought not fo to bee ; for noe cau[f]e have they to feare that it wilbe any hinder- 5810 ance for them; for Dubline wilbe ftill, as it is, the key of all paffages and tranfportacons out of England thither, to noe leffe profit of thofe citizens then it now is, and befides other places will herby receave fome benefytt. But let us now, I pray you, come to Lynfter, in the which I wold wifh the fame courfe to be obferved as in Ulfter.

*Eudox.* You meane for the leavinge of the garrifons in there fortes, and for planting of Englifh in all thofe countryes betwene the county of Dubline and 5820 the county of Wexforde ; but thofe waft wild places, I thinke, when thay are woone unto her Majeftie, that ther is none that wilbe hafty to feek to in-habite.

ll. 5794-5, ' *as it were*,' Collier, Morris, etc. : l. 5806, ' *ever*.'

*Iren.* Yes ynough, I warrante, for though the whole tracte of the countrie bee mountaine and wodie, yet there are manie goodlie vallies amongft them, fytt for fayre habytation, to which thofe mountaines adjoyned wilbe a greate increafe of pafturage ; for that countrie is a verie great foyle 5830 of cattell, and verie fitt for breed : as for corne it is nothing naturall, fave onelie for barlie and oates, and fome places for rye, and therfore the larger peniworth may be allowed vnto them, though other wyfe the wyldnes of the mountaine pafturage doe recompence the badnes of the foile, foe as I doubt not but it will finde inhabitants and undertakers enough.

*Eudox.* How much then doe you thinke that all thofe landes which Pheagh McHugh holdeth under 5840 him may amount unto, and what rent may be reared therout to the mayntenance of the garrifons that fhalbe layd there?

*Iren.* Truly, it is ympoffible by aime to tell yt, and as for experience and knowledge, I doe not thinke that there was ever any of the particulars thereof, but yet I will, if it pleafe you, geffe therat, uppon grounde only of there judgment which have formerly devided all that countrye into twoe fhcires or coun- tyes, namely the county of Wickloe, and the county 5850 of Fernes : the which twoe I fee noe caufe but thay fhould holy efcheat to her Majefty, all but the barrony of Arclo which is the Earle of Ormwoodes auncient inheritance, and hath ever bene in his poffeffion ; for all the whole lande is the Quenes,

l. 5829, ' *adjoyning* ': l. 5853, ' *Ormond-is.*'

unleffe there be fome graunt of any parte therof
to be fhowed from hir Majeftie : as I thinke there
is only of New Caftle to Sir Henry Harrington,
and of the caftle of Fernes to Sir Thomas Mafterfon,
the reft, being almoft thirty miles over, I doe fuppofe 5860
canne contayne noe leffe then two thoufande plowelandes, which I will eftimat at iiij [thoufand] li.
rent, by the yeare.   The reft of Leinfter, being vij
countyes, to weete, the countye of Dubline, Killdare,
Catherlogh, Wexford, Kilkenye, the Kinges and the
Queenes countye, doe containe in them 7400. plowelandes, which amounteth to fo many poundes for
compofition to the garrifon, that makes in the
whole xi [thoufand] iiijc. l., the which fome will
yeild pay unto a thowfand fouldiars, little wantynge, 5870
which may be fupplied out of other landes of the
Cavenaghes, which are to be efcheated to her Majeftie
for rebellione of ther poffeffions, though otherwife ·
indeed they be of hir owne auncient demaine.

*Eudox.*   It is a great reafon.   But tell us now
where you wold wifh thofe garrifons to be laied,
whether alltogeather, or to be dyfperfed in fundry
places of the country ?

*Iren.* Mary, in fundry places, to weete, in this
forte, or much the like as may be better advifed, 5880
for cc. in a place I doe thinke to be enough for
the fafegarde of the countrie, and kepinge under
all fudden upftartes, that fhall feeke to trouble the
peace thereof : therfore I wifhe [200.] to be layede
at Ballinocros for the kepinge of all bade perfons

---

l. 5865, ' *Katarlaghe* ': l. 5873, ' *poffeffours* ' Collier, Morris, etc. :
. 5885, ' *Ballinecorrih.* '

from Glammalour, and all the faftenes thereaboutes,
and alfo to conteynne all that fhalbe planted in
thofe lands thenceforthe. Another 200. at Knock-
loughe in there former place of garrifon, to kepe
the Brifkagh and all thofe mountaines of the Cava- 5890
naghes ; 200. more to lye at Fearnes, and upwardes,
inwardes upon the Slane ; 200. to be placed at the
forte of Leix, to reftraine the Mores, Offorie, and
Ocarroll ; other 200. at the forte of Ofaley, to
carbe the Oconnors, Omoloys in [Mac] Coghlane
Maccughejan, and all thofe Irifh nations borderinge
thereaboute.

*Eudox.* Thus I fee all your thoufande men beftowed
in Leinfter : what faye you then of Meath, which is
the firfte parte ?                                         5900

*Iren.* Meath, which conteyneth bothe Eftmeath
and Weftmeath, and of laite the Analy, nowe called
the countye of Langforde, is accoumpted therunto :
But Meath it felfe (accordinge to the ould recordes)
4320. plowelandes, and the countye of Langford
947., which in the whole make 5267 plowlandes,
of which the compofitiõ monye will amounte like-
'wife to 5267 li. to the maintenance of the garrifone.
But becaufe all Meath, lyinge in the bofome of that
kingdome, is alwayes quiet ynough, yt is needeleffe 5910
to put anye garrifon there, foe as all that charge
may be fpared. But in the countye of Longforde
I wifhe 200. footemen and 50. horfemen to be
placed in fome cõvenient feate betwene the Annalie
and the Breine, as aboute Lough Silone or fome

---

1. 5890, '*Brifkelagh* ': l. 5896, '*Maccagvhan* ' : l. 5915, '*Brenie*
. . . *Sillon.*'

like place of that ryver, foe as they myght keepe
both the Oneales, and alfoe the Ofarralles, and all
that outfkirte of Meathe in awe; the which ufe
upone everye lighte occafion to be ftirringe, and
having contynuall enmitye amongefte themfelves, 592c
doe therby oftentymes troble all thofe partes, the
charge wherof beinge 4400 and odde poundes is to
be cut oute of that compofitione money for Meath
and Longforde, the overplus, beinge almoft 2000 li.
by the yeare, will come in clearly to her Majeftie.

*Eudox.* It is worth the harkening unto. But
nowe that you have done with Meath, proceed I
praye you to Mounfter, that wee may fee howe it
will rife ther for the manteynance of the garrifone.

*Iren.* Monfter conteyneth by recorde at Dublyne 593c
16000 plowlandes, the compofitione whereof, as the
refte, will make 16000 li. by the yeare, out of the
which I would have 1000. foldyers to be mainteyned
for the defence of that province, the charge, which
with the victualers wages, will amount to 12000 li.
by the yeare; thother 4000 li. will defray the charges
of the Precydence and the Confell of that province.

*Eudox.* The reckininge is eafye; but in this accompt, by your leave, me thinkes you are deceaved,
for in this fome of the compofitione money you 594c
accompt the landes of the undertakers of that province, whoe are, by ther graunte frome the Queene
to be free frome all fuch impofitions whatfoever,
exceptinge there only rente, which is furely ynoughe.

l. 5917, ' *O Relyes* ': l. 5922, ' 3400 ': ll. 5930-1, These two lines,
' *Monfter* . . . 16000 ' are written before ' *Eudoxus* ' and again here,
in our MS.

*Iren.* Yee faye true, I did foe; but the fame 20 s.
for everye plolande I ment to have deducted out
of the rente due upone them to her Majeftie, which
is noe hindrance, nor charge at all more to her
Majeftie then it nowe is, for all that rente which
fhe receves of them, fhe putteth forth againe to the 5950
mayntenaunce of the Prefidencie there, the charge
whereof yt doth fcarfelye defraye ; whereas in this
accompte bothe that charge of the Prefidencye, and
alfoe of 1000 foldyors more, fhalbe maynteyned.

*Eudox.* It fhould be well, if it coulde be brought
to that. Nowe wher will you [have] your 1000 men
garryfoned ?

*Iren.* I would have 100 of them placed at the
Bantrie where is a mofte fytt place, not onlye to
defende all that fide of the countrye weft parte frome 5960
forraine invafion, but alfoe to anfwere all occafions
of trobles, to which that countrye, being foe remote,
is verye fubiecte. And furelye here alfoe would be
placed a good towne, havinge both verye good haven
and plentifull fifhinge, and the land beinge already
efcheated to her Majeftie, but beinge forcaible kepte
from her by a rough tayle kerne that proclaimes
hime felfe the baftarde fonne of the Erle of Clancar,
beinge called Donell Mac Chartie, whom it is meet
to forfee to cut of ; for [as] whenfoever the Erle 5970
fhall dye, all thofe landes, after hime, are to come to
her Majefty, he is like to make a foule ftire there,
though of hime felfe of noe power, yet through
-fupportance of fome others whoe lye in the winde,
and looke after the fall of that inheritance. Another

l. 5959, '*Baintrie*' : l. 5967, '*rag tayle.*'

100 woulde I have placed at Caftlemaine, which
fhould kepe all Defmonde and Kerrye, for it an-
fwereth them both moft convenyentlye : Alfoe
aboute Kylmore in the countye of Corke would I
have 200 placed, which fhoulde breake that nefte 5980
of theves there, and anfwere equallye both the
countye of Lymbricke, and alfoe the countye of
Corke : Another 100 whold I have lye at Corke,
afwell to comand the towne, as alfoe to be readye
for anye forreine occafione : likewife at Waterforde,
would I place 200, for the fame reafones, and alfoe
for other privic caufes, that are noe leffe importante.
Moreover on the fide of Arlo, nere to Mafkrye
Werke, which is the county of the Bourkes, aboute
[Kill-patricke,] would I have 200 to be garrifoned, 5990
which fhoulde fkowre both the White Knightes
countrye and Arlo, and Mufkrye Wherkes, by which
places all the paffages of theeves doth lye, which
convaie there ftealthe from Mounfter downwardes
towards Tipperarie, and that Englifhe Payle, and
from the Englifh Pale alfoe uppe unto Mounfter,
whereof they ufe to make a comon trade. Befides
that, ere longe I doubte the countye of Tipperarie
yt felfe will neade fuch a ftrength in yt, which were
good to be there readye before the evill fall, that 6000
is daylye of fome expected : and thus you fee all
your garrifones placed.

*Eudox.* I fee it right well, but lett me I praye
you, by the waye afke the reafone whic in thofe
cytics of Mounfter, namely Waterforde and Corke,
you rather placed garryfons then in all the others in

1. 5988-9, ‘ *Mofcria Whirke*’ : l. 5990, [blank].

Irelande ?   For they maye thinke them felves to have great wrounge to be fo charged above all the refte.

*Iren.* I will tell you : thofe two cytties, above all the refte, doe offer an ingate to the Spanyarde mofte 6010 fytlie ; and alfoe inhabytants of them are mofte ill affected to the Englifhe government, and mofte frendes to the Spanyardes ; but ʻyet, becaufe they fhall not take exceptione to this, that they are charged above all the refte, I will alfoe laye a charge upon the others likewife ; for in deede it is no reafon that the corporate Townes, enjoyinge great franchifes and priviledges from her Majeftie, and livinge therby not only fafe, but drawinge to them the wealth of all the lande, fhould live fo free as not to be partakers of the 6020 burthen of this garryfone for there owne fafetye, fpecially in this time of trouble, and feinge all the refte burdened ; and therfore, I will thus charge them all ratably, accordinge to there abilities, towardes there mayntenance, the which her Majeftie may yf fhe pleafe, fpare oute of the charge of the refte, and referve towards her owne coftes, or adde to the charge of the Prefydence in the Northe.

| Waterford | 100. | Clonmell | 10. | Dundal[k]e | 10. |
| Corke | 100. | Cafhell | 10 | Mollinger | 10. 6030 |
| Lymricke | 50. | Fedred | 10. | Newry | 10. |
| Galwaye | 50. | Kilkiny | 25. | Trime | 10. |
| Kinfaile | 10. | Wexford | 25. | Ardrye | 10. |
| Dinglecufhe | 10. | Treddagh | 25. | Kells | 10. |
| Youchall | 10. | Roffe | 25. | Dubline | 100. |
| Kilmallocke | 10. | | | | |

Suma 490.   [Wrong=630].

l. 6028, '*other*' : l. 6030, ' *Corke* 50 ': l. 6031, ' *Fetherte* ' : l. 6034, ' *Dingellechooifhe* ' : ib., '*Drogheda* ' : l. 6037, Morris, ' 580.'

*Eudox.* It is eafie, Iren : to laye a charge upone any towne, but to forfee howe the fame maye be anfwered and defrayed is the chefe parte of good 604 advifemente.

*Iren.* Surely this charge which I put upon them I knowe to be foe refonable, as that it will not much [be] felte ; for the porte townes which have benefitte of fhippinge maye cutte it eafelye of there tradinge, and in inlande townes of their corne and cattall : nether doe I fee, but fince to them the benefitte of peace doth redownde, that they fpecially fhould beare the burden of ther fafegardes and defence, as wee fee all the townes of the lowe 605 countries doe cut upone them felves an excife of all thinges towardes the maintenance of the warre that is made in ther behalfe, to which thoughe the[y] feare not to be compared in riches, yett are to be charged accordinge to their poverty.

*Eudox.* But now that yowe have fett upone thefe forces of foldyers, and provided well as you fuppofe, for ther paye, yett there remaineth to forcafte howe they may be vitualed, and where purvayance therof may be made ; for in Irelande yt felfe I cannot 606 fee howe anye thinge almofte is to be had for them, beinge airedye foe pittifullye wafted as it is with this fhorte tyme of warre.

*Iren.* For the firfte two yeares indeed it is needefull that they be vitualled out of Englande throughlye, from halfe yeare to halfe yeare, afor-hande. Which time the Englifhe Paile fhall not be burdened at all, but fhall have tyme to recover

ll. 6053-4, '*they are not,*' Morris ; '*thefe are not,*' Collier.

them felves ; and Mounfter alfoe, beinge reafonablie
well ftored, will by that tyme, if God fend fefonable 6070
wether, be throughly well furnifhed to fupplye a
greate parte of that charge, for I knowe there is a
great plentye of corne fent over fea from thence,
the which if they myght have fayle for at home,
they would be glad to have money fo neare hande,
fpeciallye yf they were ftraightlye reftrayned from
tranfportinge of it.   Thereunto alfoe there wilbe a
great healpe and furtherance gyven to the puttinge
forwarde of hufbandrye in all meate places, as hereafter fhall in due place appeare.   But hereafter, 6080
when thinges fhall growe to a better ftrengthe, and
the country be replenifhed with corne, as in fhorte
fpace yt will if it be well folowed, for the country
people themfelves are greate plowers, and fmale
fpenders of corne, then woulde I wifhe there fhould
be good ftore houfes and magafines erected in all
thofe great places of garrifons, and in all greate
townes, afwell for the victuallinge of foldyers and
fhipps, as for all occafions of fudden fervices,
as alfoe for preventinge of all tymes of dearth and 6090
fcarfitye : and this want is much to be complayned
of in Englande above all other countryes, whoe,
truftinge to much to the ufuall bleffinge of the
earth, doe never forcafte anye fuch hard fefaons,
nor any fuch fudden occafions as thefe troblefome
tymes maye everye daye bringe forthe, when it
wilbe too late to gather provifione from abroad,
and to bringe perhapes from farre for the furnifhinge
of fhipes or foldyers, which peradventure maye need

---

l. 6070, miswritten '*wilbe*' in our MS.

to be prefently imployed, and whofe wante maye 610
(which God forbid) happ to hazarde a kingdome.

*Eudox.* In deed the wante of thofe magafynes of
victualls, I have harde oftentymes complayned of in
England, and wondred at in other countreyes, but
that is nothinge nowe to oure purpofe ; but as for
thefe garrifons which yee have nowe fo ftronglye
planted throughout all Irland, and everye place
fwarminge with foldyers, fhall there be noe end of
them ? For nowe thus beinge me femeth, I doe fee
rather a countrye of warre then of peace and quiet, 611
which ye erfte pretended to worke in Irelande ; for
if you bringe all thinges to the quietnes which yee
faid, what nead then to maintaine foe great forces as
ye have charged upon it ?

*Iren.* I will unto you, Eudox. in privitye difcover
the drifte of my purpofe : I mean (as I toulde you)
and doe well hoppe therby bothe to fettle an eternall
peace in that country, and alfoe to make yt very
profitable to her Majeftie, the which I fee mufte be
broughte in by a ftronge hande, and foe contenued 612
untill it growe into a ftedfaft courfe of governmente,
the which in this forte will nether be defyculte nor
dangerous ; for the foldyers beinge once broughte
in for the fervice into Ulfter, and havinge fubdued
it and Connaught, I will not have hyme to laye
downe his armes anye more, tyll he have effected
that which I purpofe : that is, firfte to have this a
generall compofitione for the mayntenance of thefe
througheout all the realme, in regarde of the trobles

l. 6101, '*happlye*' : l. 6121, '*runne*': l. 6122, '*difficile*' : l. 6129,
'*troublous.*'

tymes, and daylye danger which is threatned to this 6130
realme by the Kinge of Spaine : and thereupone to
beftowe all my foldyers in [fuch] fort as I have
donne, that noe parte of all Irlande fhalbe able to
dare foe much as quinch. Then will I bring eftfones
in my reformacon, and thereupon eftablifhe fuch an
order of governmente as I may thinke metefte for the
good of that realme, which beinge once eftablifhed,
and all thinges put into a righte ·way, I dowbt not
but they will rune one farely. And though they
would ever feeke to fwarve afyde, yet fhall they not 6140
be able without forraine violence once to remoove,
as you your felfe fhall fone, I hope, in your owne
reafone readelye conceve ; which if it fhall ever
appere, thene maye her Majeftie at pleafure withdrawe fome of the garrifone, and torne ther paye
into her purfe, or if fhe will never pleafe foe to
doe (which I would rather wifh), then fhall fhe
have a nomber of brave oulde foldyers alwayes
readye for anye occafion that fhe will ymploe
vnto, fuppliinge there garrifones with frefh ones 6150
in there fteed ; the maintenance of whome fhalbe
noe more charge to her Majeftie then nowe the
realme is ; for all the revinue thereof, and muche
more, fhe fpendeth, even in the mofte peaceable
tymes that are there, (as things nowe ftande). And
in tyme of warre, which is fure nowe everye
vij yeare, fhe fpendeth infynite treafure befides to
fmale porpofe.

*Eudox.* I perceve your porpofe ; but nowe if you
have thus ftrongly made waye vnto your reformacon, 6160
as that I fee the people foe humbled and prepared

that they will and mufte yeald to any ordynance that fhalbe geuen them, I doe much defire to under-ftand the fame; for in the begiñinge you promifed to fhewe a mean howe to redreffe all thofe incon-veniences and abufes, which you fhewed to be in that ftate of governmente, which nowe ftandeth ther, as in the lawes, coftomes, and religione : wherin I woulde gladlye knowe firfte, whether, in fteed of thofe lawes, you would have newe lawes made ? 617 for nowe, for oughte that I fee, you maye doe what you pleafe.

*Iren.* I fee, Eudox. that yowe well remember our firfte porpofe, and doe rightlye contynue the courfe thereof. Firfte therfore to fpeake of lawes, fince we firfte begane with them, I doe not thinke yt convenient, though nowe it be in the power of the Prince to change all the lawes and make newe ; for that fhould bread great troble and confufione, afwell in the Englifhe now dwellinge and to be 618 planted, as alfoe in the Irifhe. For the Englifhe, havinge bene trained upp alwayes in the Englifhe governement, will hardely be enduced unto any other, and the Irifhe wilbe better drawne to the Englifhe, then the Englifhe to the Irifhe governmente. Ther-fore fince wee cannot nowe applic lawes fitte to the people, as in the firfte inftitutione of comone-welthes it ought to be, wee will applye the people, and fitt them to the lawes, as it mofte conveniently maye be. The lawes therfore we refolve fhall abyde in 619 the fam forte that they doe, bothe Commone Lawes and Statutes, onlye fuche defectes in the Comone

1. 6183, '*enured.*'

Lawe, and inconveniens in the Statutes, as in the
begininge wee noted, and as men of deep infighte
fhall advife, may be changed by fome other newe
actes and ordynances to be [by] a Parlyamente
there confirmed : as thofe of tryalls of Ples of the
Crowne, and private righte betwene parties, colorable
convaiances, [and] acceffaries.

*Eudox.* But howe will thofe be redreffed by Parli- 6200
mente, when as the Irifhe, which fwaye mofte in
Parlamente, as you faid, fhall oppofe them felves
againfte them?

*Iren.* That maybe well avoyded : for nowe that
foe manye free-holders of Englifhe fhalbe eftablifhed,
they togeather with Burgeffes of townes, and fuch
other loyall Irifhe men as may be preferred to be
Knightes of the fhire, and fuch like, wilbe able to
beard and counterpofe the refte ; whoe alfoe, beinge
nowe broughte more in awe, will the more eafelye 6210
fubmite to anye fuch ordynances as fhalbe for the
good of them felves, and that realme generallye.

*Eudox.* You fay well, for the increffe of the
Freeholders, for ther nombers will hereby be greatlye
augmented ; but howe fhall it paffe throughe the
higher houfe, [which] will ftyll confifte all of
Irifhe?

*Iren.* Marie, that alfoe maye be redreffed by
example of that which I hard was donne in the
like cafe, by Kinge Edwarde the Theerd, as I 6220
remember, whoe, beinge greatly barred and croffed
by the billes of the Clargie, they beinge then by
reafone of the Lord Abbote and others, too many

---

l. 6197, ' *tromles* ' (*sic*) in our MS. : l. 6220, ' *bearded* ' : l. 6221, ' *Lordes*.

and ſtronge for them, ſoe he could not for there
forwardnes, order and reforme thinges as he deſiered,
was adviſed to dyrecte forth his writtes to certaine
Gentlemen, and of the beſte abilitye and truſte,
intitlinge them therin Barrons, to ſerve and ſytt as
Barrons in the next Parlyment. By which meanes
he had ſoe manye Barons in his Parlamente, as 6230
were able to weighte downe the Clarge and there
frendes : the which Barons they ſaye, were not afterwardes lordes, but onelye Barronits, as ſundrye of
them doe yett retayne the name. And by the like
deviſe her Majeſtie maye nowe likewiſe curbe and
cut ſhorte thoſe Iriſhe unrulye lordes that hinder
all good procedinges.

*Eudox.* It ſemeth noe leſſe then for reforminge
of all thoſe inconveniente ſtatutes which yee noted
in the beginninge, and redreſſinge of all thoſe evell 6240
coſtomes, and laſtelye, for ſettinge ſounde religione
amongeſt them : mee thinkes yee ſhould not neade
anye more to over-goe thoſe particulers againe,
which you menconed, nor anye other which might
beſides be remembred, but to leave to the reformacon
of ſuch a Parlamente, in which, by the good care
of the Lorde Deputye and Conſell, they maye all
amende. Therfore nowe that you maye come to
that genarall reformacon which you ſpake of, and
bringinge in of all that eſtabliſhement, by which 6250
you ſaid all men ſhould be conteyned in duetie ever
after, without the terror of warlike forces, or violēt
wreſtinge of thinges by ſharpe punyſhmente.

1. 6226, '*of the*,' Collier, Morris, etc. : l. 6231, '*were*' miswritten
'*was*' in our MS. : l. 6232, '*remaine*,' Collier, Morris, etc.

*Iren.* I will foe at your pleafure, the which me
femes by noe meanes can be better plotted, then
by example of fuche other Realmes as have ben
annoyed with the like evelles, Ireland nowe is, and
ufeth ftyll to be. And firfte in this Realme of
England, yt is manifefte, by the reporte of the
Cronycles and other aunciente writers, that it was 6260
greatly infeƈted with robbers and outclawes, which
lurked in woodes and fafte places, whence they vfed
often tymes to breake forth into the highe wayes,
and fometymes into fmale villages to robbe and
fpoyle. For redreffe wherof it is written that Kinge
Allured, or Alfride, whoe then raigned, did devide
the relme into fhires, and the fhires into hundredes,
[and the hundredes] into rapes, Rapentackes, and
wapentackes into tythinges : So that tenn tythinges
made an hundred, and five made a laythe or wea-
pentacke, of which tenn, eache one was bounde for 6270
another, and the eldeft or beft of theme, whom they
called the Tythingman or Bouroughfolder, that is,
the eldeft plege, became furetye for all the refte.
Soe that if anye one of theme did ftarte into anye
undutiful aƈtione, the Burroughfolder was bounde
to bringe hyme forth, whoe joyninge eftefones with
all his tythinge, would folowe the loofe perfone
through all places, till they brought hyme in. And
if all the tythinge fayled, then all the lathe was
charged for the tythinge, and if that lathe fayled, then 6280
all the hundreth was demanded for theme ; and if
the hundreth, then the fhire, whoe joyninge eftfones

l. 6272, ‘*Burfe-holder*’: l. 6280, miswritten ‘*tythe*’ in our MS., and
so onward.

altogether, would not reft tyll they had founde oute
and delyvered in, that unlawfull felowe which was
not ameanable to lawe.    And herin yt femed, that
that good Saxon Kinge folowed the Confell of
Jethro to Moyfes, who advifed hyme to devide the
people into hundreds, and to fette Captaines and
wife men of truft over them, which fhoulde take
the charge of them, and eafe hyme of that burden. 6290
And foe did Romulus, as you may reade, devyde
the Romaines into trybbes, and the tribbes into
centuryons or hundreds.    By this ordynaunce this
Kinge brought this realme of Englande, which
before was moft trooblefome, unto that quiet ftate,
that noe one badd perfon could ftirre that he was
[not] ftreighte taken hould of by thofe his tythinge,
and ther Burrowfolder, whoe beinge his neighboure
or next kindfeman was pryvie to all his wayes, and
loked narrowly to his life.    The which inftitutione 6300
yf it were obferved in Irland, would worke that
effecte which it did then in Englande, and kepe all
men within the Compaffe of duetie and obedyence.

*Eudox.* This is contrary to that you faid before ;
for, as I remember, you faid that ther was a greate
difproportione betwene Englande and Irlande, foe
as the lawes which were fittinge of the one would
not fitt the other.    Howe comes it then nowe,
that ye would transferre a principall inftitutione from
England to Irland ?    6310

*Iren.* This lawe was not made by a Norman

---

1. 6284, '*undutifull*': ll. 6295-6, '*unto . . . ftirre*' from Collier,
Morris, etc.: l. 6296, '*ftarte*': l. 6297, '*of his owne*': l. 6305, '*you
. . . that*' from Collier, Morris, etc.

conqueror, but by a Saxon Kinge, being at what tyme England was verye like to Irland, as nowe it ftandes : for it was, I tould you, annoyed greatly with robbers and outlawes, which trobled the whole realme, everye corner havinge in it a Robyn Hoode, that kept all woodes, and fpoiled all paffingers and inhabitants, as Irland nowe haith ; foe as, me femeth, this ordynance would fitt verye well, and bring them all into one.                                  6320

*Eudox.* Then, when you have thus tithed the comanaltye, as you fay, and fet Burrowfolders over them all, what would you doe when yee came to the gentlemẽ ? would you hold the fame corfe ?

*Iren.* Yee, marye, moft fpecially ; for this you mufte knowe, that all the Irifhe almofte bofte them felves to be gentlemẽ, noe leffe then the Welchmen ; for if he cane deryve hymfelfe from the heade of a fept, as moft of them can, they are [so] experte by there Bardes, then foe holdeth hyme felfe 6330 a gentlemã, and thereupon fcorneth eftfones to worke, or vfe anye harde laboure, which he faith is the liefe of a peffant or churle ; but thenceforth either becometh a horfeboye, 'or a ftocage to fome kerne, inuring hyme felfe to his weapone, and to the generall traide of ftealinge, (as they count it). Soe that if a gentleman, or anye worthye yoman of them, have anye childrene, the eldefte of them perhappes fhalbe kepte in fome order, but all the refte fhall fhifte for them felves, and fall to this 6340

l. 6320, ' *awe* ': l. 6330, ' *then* ' miswritten ' *&* ': l. 6332, ' *handye* ': l. 6335, miswritten ' *endevoringe* ': l. 6336, ' *gentell*,' Morris ; ' *gentlemanly*,' Collier : ib., ' *as . . . it* ' from Collier, Morris, etc.

occupacon.   And it is a commen ufe amongeſt ſome
of there beſte gent [lemen] tenantes ſonnes, that ſoe
ſoone as they are able to uſe there weapons, they
ſtreight gether to themſelves three or foure ſtrauglers,
or kernes, with whome wanderinge a while idellye vpe
and downe the countrye, takinge onlye meate, he
at laſte falleth unto ſome badde occaſione that he
ſhalbe offrede, which beinge once made knowen,
he is thenceforthe counted a mane of worth, in whom
there is corrage ; whereupon there drawe to hime 6350
manye other like looſe younge men, which, ſtirringe
hime up, with encouragement, provoke hyme ſhortlye
to flatte rebellion ; and this happens not onlye
in the ſonnes of gentle[men], but oftentymes by
there noblemen, ſpecially there baſe borne ſonnes,
as there are ſewe without ſome of them.   For they
are not onlye not aſhamed to acknowledge them,
but alſoe to boſte of them, and uſe them in ſuch
ſecrett ſervices as they themſelves will   not   be
ſeen in, as to plauge there enemyes, ſpoyle there 6360
neighbores, to opreſſe and cruſh ſome of [their]
owne to ſtubborne freholders, which are not tractable to theire badde willes.   Two ſuch baſtardes of
the Lord Roches there are nowe out in Mounſter,
whom he doth not only countenance but alſoe
pryvilye mainteyne and relyve mightely amongeſt
his tenantes.   Such other is therof the Erle of
Clancarte in Deſmond, and manye otheres in many
other places.

   *Eudox.* Then   it   ſemeth   that   this   ordynance of 6370

1.  6344, '*three or foure*' from Collier, Morris, etc. : l. 6361. '*and
cruſh.*' *ibid.* : l. 6366, '*againſt.*'

tythinge them by the pole is not only fitt for the
gentlemen, but alfoe for the noblemen, whom I
would [have] thought to have bene foe honourable
mynded, as that they fhould not need fuche a bafe
kinde of lyvinge, beinge bounde to there allegance,
[who] fhould rather have held in and ftayed all
others from undutifulnes, then need to be forced
thereunto them felves.

*Iren.* Yet foe it is,. Eudox : but yet becaufe that
noblemẽ cannot be tythed, there beinge not manye 6380
tythinges of them, and becaufe a Barrowe holder
over them fhould not only be a great indignitye,
but alfoe a danger to adde more power to them
then they have, or to make one the comander
of tenne, I holde it meet that there were onclye
fewerties taken of them, and one bounde for another,
wherbye, if anye fhall fwarve, his fewerties fhall for
fafegarde of ther bandes bringe hyme in, or feeke
to ferve upon him : and befydes, I would wifh them
all to be fworne to her Majeftic, which they never 6390
yet were, but at the firft creatyon ; and that oath
would fure contayne them greatly, or the breach
of yt bringe them to fhorter vengence, for God
ufeth to punifhe perjurye fharply. So I read, in
the raigne of Edward the 2, and alfo of Henry
the 7, when the tymes were very broken, that
there was a corporate oath taken, of all the lordes
and beft gentlemen of fealty to the Kinge, which
nowe is noe lefle nedfull, becaufe many of them
are fufpeected to have taken an other oath privylye 6400
to fome badd purpofe, and therupon they have
receaved the Sacramentc, and ben fworne to a

preift, which they thinke bindeth them more then theire alleagance to their Prince, or love of their countrye.

*Eudox.* This tythinge of the comon-people, and takinge furetyes of lordes and gentlemen, I like very well, but that yt wilbe very troblefome : fhould yt not be as well to have them all booked, and the lordes and gentlemen to take all meaner forte upon 6410 themfelves ? for they are beft able to bringe them in, whenfoever any of them ftarted out.

*Iren.* This inded Eudoxus hath bene hitherto, and yet is a comon order amongft them, to have all the people booked by the lords and gentlemen, but yt is the worft order that ever was devifed ; for by this bokinge of men, all the inferyour fort are brought under the commaundes of theire lords, and forced to followe them into any actyon whatfoever. Now this ye are to underftand, that all the rebellyons 6420 which ye fee from tyme to tyme hapen in Ireland, are not begune by the comon people, but by the lords and captaines of countryes, upon pride or wilfull obftinacye againft the government, which whenfoever they will enter into, they drawe with them all their people and fuch followers, as thinke themfelves bound to goe with them, becaufe they have boked them and undertaken for them. And this is the reafone that you have fewe fuch badd occafyons here in England by reafon that the noble 6430 men howeever they fhould hapen to be evill difpofed, have no comande at all over the comynalty, though dwellinge under them, becaufe every man ftandeth

1. **6424,** '*againft the government*,' Collier, Morris, etc.

upon himfelfe, and buildeth his fortunes upon his owne fayth and firme affurance : the which this manner of tythinge the powles will worke alfo in Ireland. For by this the people are broken into many fmall parts, like lytle ftreames, that they canot eafely come together into one heade, which is the princypall regard that is to be had in Ireland to 6440 kepe them from growinge into fuch a head, and adheringe unto greate men.

*Eudox.* But yet I canot well fee how this can be brought about, without doinge greate wronge unto the noble men there ; for at the conqueft of the realme, thofe greate fignoryes and lordfhips were given them by the King, that they fhould bee the ftronger againfte the Irifh, by the multitude of followers and tennauntes under them : all which hould their tenementes of them by fealtye, and fuch 6450 fervices, wherby they are by the firft graunte of the King, made bound unto them, and tyed to rife out with them upon all occafyons of fervice. And this I have often heard, that when the Lord Deputies have rayfed any generall oftinges, the noble men have claymed the leadinge of them, by graunt from the Kings of England under the Greate Seale exhibyted ; fo as the Deputye[s] would not refufe them to have the leadinge of them, or yf they did, they would fo worke, as none of they[r] followers 6460 fhould rife forth to the oftinge.

*Iren.* Yee fay very true ; but will ye fee fruite of thofe grauntes? I have knowne when thofe lords have had the leadinge of theire owne followers under them to the generall oftinges, that they have for the fame cut upon every plowland within their country forty fhillinges or more, wherby fome of them have gathered above vij. or viij. c. li., and others much more into there purfe, in lieue wherof they have gathered unto themfelves a nomber of lofe kernes out of all 647c parts, which they have caryed forth with them, to whome they never gave penny of entertaynment, allowed by the contry or forced by them, but let them feed upon the contryes, [and] extorte upon all men where they cam ; for that people will never afke better entertaynment then to have a coullour of fervice or imployment geven them, by which they will powle and fpoile fo outragioufly, that the very enemy cannot doe much worfe : and befides turne them to the enemy. 648c

*Eudox.* It femes the firft intents of thefe grauntes was againft the Irifhe, which nowe fome of them ufe againft the Queene her felfe : But now what remedye is there for this ? or how can thefe grauntes of the Kings be avoyded, without wronge of thofe lords which had thofe landes and lordfhips geven them ?

*Iren.* Surely they may be well enough ; for moft of thofe lords, fince the firft grantes from the Kings by whome thefe landes were geven them, have fence beftowed the moft parte of them amongft theire kins- 6490 folke, as everye lord perhaps in his tyme hath geven one or another of his principall caftells to his yonger fonnes and other to others, as largly and as amply as they were given to him ; and others they have fold, and others bought, which were not in theire

1. 6466, '*within . . . country*' from Collier, Morris, etc. : l. 6479, '*and they alfo fometimes,*' *ibid.*

firſt grauntes, which nowe nevertheleſſe they bringe
within the compas therof, and take and exacte upon
them, as theire firſt demeanes of all thoſe kindes of
ſervices, yea and the very wilde Iriſhe exactyons as
Coynie and Lyverye for him, and ſuch like, by which 6500
they pole and utterly undoe the pore teñantes and
frehoulders under them, which ether through ignorãce
knew not theire tennors, or through greatnes of
theire newe lords dare not chalenge them ; yea, and
ſome lords of countryes alſo, as greate ones as
themſelves, are nowe by ſtronge hand brought under
them, and made theire vaſſalls.    As for example
Arundell of the Strande in the County of Corke,
who was auncyently a greate lord, and able to ſpend
3500 li. by the yeare, as apeareth by good recordes, 6510
is nowe become the Lord Barryes man, and doth
to him all thoſe ſervices, which are due unto her
Majeſtic.    For reformacon of which, I wiſh that theire
were a commiſſyon graunted forth under the Great
Seale, as I have ſeene one recorded in the ould
councell Boke in Mounſter : that was ſent forth in
the tyme of Sir William Drurye unto perſons of
ſpecyall truſt and judgment to enquire thoroughout
all Ireland, beginninge in one countye firſt and ſo
reſtinge a while untill the ſame were ſetled, by the 6520
verdicte of a ſounde and ſubſtantyall jurye, howe
every man houldeth his landes, of whome and by
what tennor, ſo that everye one ſhould be admitted
to ſhewe and exhibite what right he hath, and by
what ſervices he houldeth his lande, whether in
cheife or in ſoccage, or in knight ſervice, or els

l. 6502, '*unto*': l. 6513, '*I wiſh,*' Collier.

foever. Therupon would apeare, firft howe all thofe greate Englifh lords do claime thofe greate fervices, what fignoryes they ufurpe, what wardfhips they take from the Queene, what landes of hers they 6530 conccalde : and then, howe thofe Irifh captaines have encroched upon the Queenes frehoulders and tennantes, how they have tranflated the teñors of them from Englifh houldinge into Irifhe Taniftre, and defeated her Majeftie of all her right and duetyes which are to acrew to her therabout, as wardfhipps, liveryes, marriages and fines of allye-nacons, with many other comodyties ; which nowe are kepte and conceald from her Majefty to the vallowe of 60000 li. yearely, I dare undertake, in 6540 all Ireland, by that which I knowe in one countye.

*Eudox.* This, Iren. would feme a dangerous commiffion, and redy to ftirre uppe all the Irifh in rebellion, who knowinge that they have nothinge to fhewe for all thofe lands which they hould, but theire fwordes, would rather drawe them then fuffer theire landes to be thus drawne away from them.

*Iren.* Neyther fhould theire landes be taken away from them, nor the uttermoft advantages enforced againft them : But this by deferetyon of the com- 6550 miffioners fhould be made knowne unto them, that it is not her Majefties meaninge to ufe any fuch extremetye, but onely to reduce thinges into order of Englifh lawe and make them hould theire landes of her Majeftye and to reftore to her her due ferviees, which they detayne out of thofe landes

l. 6528, '*greate*' (1st) from Collier, Morris, etc. : l. 6532, '*of countryes*,' *ibid.* : ll. 6543-4, '*in rebellion*,' *ibid.* : l. 6547, '*drawne*,' *ibid.*

which were auncyently helde by her Majeftye. And
that they fhould not onely [not] be thruft out, but
alfo have eftates and grauntes of theire landes newe
made to them frō her Majeftye, fo as they fhould 6560
thenceforth hould them rightfullye, which they nowe
ufurpe moft wrongfully ; and yet withall I would wifh
that in all thofe Irifh countryes there were fome
land referved to her Majeftyes free difpofytyon for
the better contayninge of the reft, and enterminglinge
them with Englifh inhabytantes and cuftomes, that
knowledg might ftyll be had by them of all theire
doinges, fo as no manner of practife or confpiracye
fhould be in hand amongft them, but notice fhould
be given therof by one meanes or another, and theire 6570
practifes prevented.

*Eudox.* Truly neither can the Irifh, nor Englifh
lords, thinke themfelves wronged, or hardly delt
withall herin, to have that indeed which is none of
their owne at all, but her Majeftyes abfolutely, geven
unto them with fuch equall condicons, as that both
they may be affured therof, better then they are, and
alfo her Majeftye not defrauded of her right utterly ;
for yt is a greate grace with a prince, [to] take that
with condicons which is abfolutely her owne. Thus 6580
fhall the Irifh be well fatisfied, and as for the greate
men which had fuch grauntes made them at firft by
the Kings of England, [it] was in regard they fhould
kepe out the Irifh, and defend the Kings right, and
his fubjectes : but now fcinge that, in fted of de-
fendinge them, they robb and fpoyle them, and, in
ftead of kepinge out the Irifh, they doe not onely

l. 6559, '*nowe*' : l. 6565, '*entermeddling.*'

make the Irifh theire teñantes in thofe lands, and
thruft out the Englifh, but alfo they themfelves
become mere Irifh, with marrying with them, 6590
fofteringe with them, and combinynge with them
againft the Queene ; what reafon is there but thofe
grauntes and prefedentes fhould be eyther revoked,
or at leaft reduced to theire firft intencon for which
they were graunted ? for furely in my opinyon they
were more fharpely to be chaftifed and reformed
then the wilde Irifh, which, beinge very rude at the
firft, are nowe become fomwhat more civill, when
as Englifh, from Englyfhe are growene to be wilde
and mere Irifhe.                                        6600

*Iren.* Indede as you faye, Eudox : thefe do need
a fharper reformacon than the very Irifh, for they are
much more ftuborne, and difobediente to lawe and
governement, than the Irifh be; and more mallytious
than the Englifh that are dayle fent over.

*Eudox.* Is that poffible ? I pray you, howe comes
yt to paffe ? what might be the reafon herof ?

*Iren.* Mary, they faye that the land is theires,
onely by right, beinge firft conquered by theire
aunceftors, and that they are wronged by the newe 6610
Englifhe men's entringe theire unto, whom they
call *la fa Bona,* that is in Englifh with a greate
reproch as they would rate a dogge.    [And for]
that fome of youre aunceftors were in tymes paft
(when they were Civill and uncorrupted) deputyes

l. 6592, '*is there,*' Collier, Morris, etc. : l. 6593, '*priviledges,*' *ibid.*:
l. 6597, '*rude,*' *ibid.* : ib., '*wilde*' : ll. 6597-8, '*at . . . firft,*' *ibid.*:
l. 6599, '*civilitye,*' *ibid.* : l. 6609, '*right*'—miswritten '*Englifh*' in
our MS. : l. 6611, '*intruding*' : l. 6612, '*Alloonagh.*'

and Juſtices of the land, they thinke that the like
authoritye ſhould be comytted unto you and the
charge of the Realme lefte in theire hands ; which,
for that they ſe now otherwiſe diſpoſed and that
truſt not given them (which theire aunceſtors had) 6620
they thinke them ſelves greately indignyfyed and
diſgraced therby, and ſo growe both diſcontented
and undutyfull.

*Eudox.* In truth, Irenyus, this is more than ever
I hard, that the Engliſh-Iriſh there ſhould bee
worſe then the wild Iriſhe : O Lord, howe quickly
doth that country alter mens natures ! It is not
for nothinge I perceave that I have heard, that the
Councell of England thinke yt not good polycye
to have that realme reformed, or planted with 6630
Engliſh, left they ſhould growe ſo undutyfull as
the Iriſh, and become much more dangerous : as
apeareth by the example of the Lacyes in the tyme
of Edward the Second, which you ſpake of, that
ſhoke of theire religion to theire naturall Prince,
and turned to Edward le Bruce, deviſinge to make
him Kinge of Ireland.

*Iren.* No tymes have bene without bad men :
But as for that purpoſe of the Councell of England,
which ye ſpeake [of,] that they ſhould kepe that 6640
Realme from reformacon, I thinke, they are moſt
lewdlye abuſed, for theire greate carfulnes and
earneſt endeavors do witneſſe the contrarye. Neyther
is yt [the] nature of the countrye to alter a mans
manners, but the badd mindes of them, whom

l. 6635, '*allegiannce,*' Collier, Morris, etc.; l. 6636, '*and . . . Bruce,*'
*ibid.*

havinge bene brought uppe at home under a ftraight
rule of dutye and obedyence, beinge alwayes
reftrayned by fharpe penaltyes from lewde behavior,
fo foone as they come thither, where they fee lawes
fo flackely tended, and the hard [reftraint] which 6650
they were ufed unto nowe flacked, they growe more
lofe and careleffe of theire dutye.     As yt is the
nature of all men to love libertye, fo they become
flatt libertynes, and fall to flatt licentyoufnes, more
bouldly daringe to difobay the lawe, through pre-
fumptyon of favor, and freindfhippe, then any Irifh
dare.

*Eudox.* Then yf it be fo, me thinkes your late
advifement was very evell, whereby you wifhed the
Irifh to be fowed and fprinckled with the Englifh, 6660
[and] in all the Irifhe countryes to have Englifh
planted amongft them, for to bringe them to Eng[lifh]
fafhons, fince the Englifh be foner drawne to the
Irifhe, then the Irifh to the Englifh : for as I
faid before, [if] they much rune with the ftreame,
the greater number will carry awaye the leffe :
Therefore me femes by this reafon yt fhould be
better to parte the Irifhe and Englifh, then to mingle
them together.

*Iren.* Not fo, Eudox : but where there is no 6670
good ftaye of government, and ftronge ordinances
to hold them, there inded the fewer will followe
the more, but where there is due order of difcipline
and good rule, there the better fhall goe foremoft,
and the worft fhall followe.     And therfore fince
Ireland is full of her owne nacon, that may not

1. 6654, 'all,' Collier, Morris, etc.: l. 6664, 'you,' *ibid.*

be rooted [out], and fomewhat ftored with Englifh alredy, and more to be, I thinke yt beft by an unyon of maners, and conformytye of mindes, to bringe them to be one people, and to put awaye 6680 the diflikefull conceipt both of the one, and of thother, which wilbe by no meanes better then by this interminglinge of them : that neyther all the Irifh may dwell together, nor all the Englifh, but by tranflatynge of them and fcatteringe them in fmall numbers amongft the Englifh, not onely to bringe them by dayly converfatyon unto better likinge of each other, but alfo to make both of them leffe able to hurte. And therfore when I come to the tythes, I will tythe them one with 6690 another, and for the moft parte will make the Irifh man the tything-man, wherby he fhall take the leffe exceptyon to partiallitye and yet be the more tyed therby. But when I come to the Head Borough, which is the head of the lath, him will I make an Englifhman, or Irifh man of no fmall affurance : as alfo when I come to apointe the Elderman, that is the head of the hundreth, him will I furely chufe [to be] an Englifh man of fpecyall regarde, that may be a ftay and piller of 6700 all the Boroughs under him.

*Eudox.* What do you meane by your hundred ? and what by your Borough ? By that, which I have red in auncyent recordes of England, one hundred did contayne a hundred villages, or as fome faye a c. plowlandes, beinge the fame which the Saxons called Cantred ; the which cantred, as I finde it recorded

l. 6683, '*by this*,' Collier, Morris, etc.

in the blacke boke of Irelande, did contayne 30,
Villattas terræ, which fome call, quarters of land,
and every Villatta can maintayne 400 cowes in 6710
pafture, and the 400. cowes to be devided in 4
heardes, fo as none of them fhall come nere another:
every Villata contayneth 17 plowlandes, as is there
fet downe. And by that which I have red of a
Borough, it fignyfieth a free towne, which had a
principall officer, called a head borough, to become
ruler, and undertake for all the dwellers under him,
havinge for the fame franchifes and priviledges
graunted them by the King, wherof yt was called a
free boroughe, [and] of the lawyer *Franciplegiũ*.         6720

*Iren.* Both that which ye fayde, Eudox: is true,
and yet that which I fayd not untrue; for that
which ye fpeake of devidinge the contrey into
hundreds, was a devife of the lands of the Realme,
but this which I tell, was of the people, who were
thus devided by the poll: fo that an c. in this fence
fignyfyeth a c. pledges, which were under the
comand and afurance of theire alderman, the which,
as I fuppofe, was alfo called a waapentacke, fo
named of touchinge the weapon or fparke of theire 6730
alderman, and fwearinge to folowe him faythfully,
and ferve theire Prince trulye. But others thinke that
a weapontacke was ten hundreds or Boroughs: likewife a boroughe, as I here ufe yt, and as the ould
lawes ftill ufe yt, is not a borough towne, as they
nowe call yt, that is a franchift towne, but a mayne
pledge of c. free perfons, therfore called a fre
borough or as ye fay *Franciplegiũ*: For Borh in
ould Saxon fay fignyfieth pledges or furetyes, and

yet yt is fo ufed in fome fpeches, as Chaucer 6740 fayth St. John to *barrowe*, that is for affurance and warrantye.

*Eudox.* I conceave the difference. But now that ye have thus devided the people into thefe tythinges, and hundreds, howe will you have them fo preferved and continued? for people do often chaunge theyr dwellinges, and fome muft dye, whilft otherfome doe growe up into ftrength of yeares, and become men.

*Iren.* Thefe hundreds I would [wifh] to affemble themfelves once every yeare with theire pledges, and 6750 to prefent themfelves before the juftices of peace, which fhalbe thereunto apointed, to be furvayed and nombred, to fe what change hath happened fince the yeare before; and, the defectes to fuply of thofe yonge plantes late growne uppe, which are diligently to be overloked and vewed of what con-dicon and demeanor they be, fo as pledges may be taken for them, and they put into order of fome tythinge: of all which alteracons note is to be taken, and bookes made thereof accordingly. 6760

*Eudox.* Now mee thinkes Irenius, ye are to be warned to take good hede, leafte unawares ye fall into the inconveniencyes which you formerly founde faulte with in others; namely, that by this bokinge of them, you do not gather them into another head, and havinge broken theire former ftrength, do not againe unite them more ftronglye: for every Alder-man, havinge all his fre pledges of his hundred under his comand, may me thinkes, yf he be yll difpofed, drawe all his companye into any evill 6770

ll. 6746-7, '*often . . . doe,*' Collier, Morris, etc. : l. 6765, '*a new,*' *ibid.*

actyon.   And likewife, by this affemblinge of them
once a yeare unto theire Alderman by theire weapon-
tackes, take heede leaft ye alfo give them occafyon
and meanes to practife any harme in any confpiracye.

*Iren.* Neyther of both is to be doubted ; for the
aldermen and headborrowes will not be fuch men
of power and countenance of themfelves, beinge to
be chofen thereunto, as neede to be feared : Neither,
yf he were, is his hundred at his comaund further
then his Princes fervice ; and alfo every tything man 678c
may controll him in fuch a cafe.   And as for the
affemblinge of the hundred, much leffe is any danger
therof to be doubted, feinge yt is before a juftice
of peace, or fome high conftable to be therunto
apointed : fo as of thefe tythinges there can no
peryll enfue, but a certayne affurance of peace and
greate good ; for they are thereby withdrawne from
theire lords, and fubjected to theire Prince.   Moreover for the [better] breakinge of thefe heades and
fectes, which I tould you was one of the greateft 679c
ftrengthes of the Irifhe, me thinkes, yt fhould do
very well to renewe that ould ftatute that was made
in the reigne of Edward the Fourth in England,
by which yt was comaunded, that wheras all men
that ufed to be called by the name of theire fectes,
accordinge to theire feverall nacons, and had no
furnames at all, that from thenceforth each one
fhould take unto himfelfe a feverall furname, eyther
of his trade or facultye, or of fome quallety of his
bodye or mynde, or of the place where he dwelte, fo 6800
as everye one fhould be diftinguifhed from other,

l. 6793, blank.

or from the moft parte, wherby they fhall not onely not depend upon the head of their fecte, as nowe they doe, but alfo fhall in fhorte tyme learne quyte to forgett this Irifh natyon. And herewithall would I alfo wifh all the Oes and the Mackes which the head of the fectes have taken to theire names, to be utterly forbiden and extinguyfhed ; for that the fame beinge an ould manner (as fome fayth) firft made by O Brin, for the ftrengthninge of the Irifh, 6810 the abrogatinge therof will afmuch infable them.

*Eudox.* I like this ordinaunce very well ; but now that you have thus devided and diftinguifhed them, what other order will you take for theire maner of lyfe ? for all that, thoughe perhaps yt may kepe them from difobedyence and difloyaltye, yet will yt not bringe them from theire barbarifme and favadge lyfe.

*Iren.* The next [thing] that I will doe fhalbe to apointe to every one, that is not able to live of his 6820 frehoulde, a certayne trade of lyfe, to which he fhall find himfelfe fittefte, and fhalbe thought ableft, the which trade he fhalbe bounde to followe, and live onely therupon. All trades therfore [it] is to be underftode [are to be] of iij kindes, manuell, intellectuall, and mixed, th'one containinge all fuch as nede the exercyfe of bodely labor to the performance of theire profeffyon ; th'other confiftinge onely of the exercyfe of the witte and reafon ; the third parte of bodely labor, and parte of the witte, but dependinge 6830 [moft] of induftrye and carefulnes. Of the firft forte

---

1. 6806, ' *Oes* '--miswritten ' *Oathes* ' in our MS. : l. 6829, '*fort*,' Collier, Morris, etc.

be all handycrafts and hufbandryc labor.  Of the feconde be all fcyences, and thofe which are called the liberall Arts.  Of the thirde is marchandize and chafferye, that is, buyinge and fellinge ; and without all thefe iij there is no comonwealth can almoſt confyſt, or at the leaſte be perfecte.  But the wretched realme of Ireland wanteth the moſt princypall of them, that is, the intellectuall ; therfore in fekinge to reſtore her ſtate yt is fpecyall to be loked unto.  But becaufe of hufbandrye, which fupplyeth unto us all thinges neceffarye for foode, whereby we cheifly live, therfore yt is firſt to be provided for.  The firſt thinge then that we are to drawe thefe newe tythed men unto, ought to be hufbandrye.  Firſt, becaufe yt is the moſt eafye to be learned, nedinge onely the labor of the bodye.  Next, becaufe yt is moſt naturall and moſt needefull ; then, becaufe it is moſt naturall ; and laſtly, becaufe yt is moſt enemy to warre, and moſt hateth unquietneſſe, as the Poet fayth,

—— " bella execrata collonis : "

But hufbandrye beinge the nurfe of thrifte, and the daughter of induſtrye and labor, deteſteth all that may worke her fcathe, and deſtroy the travell of her hands, whofe hope is all her lives comforte unto the plough : therfore are all thofe Kearne, Stochaus, and Horſboyes, to bee drawen and mad to imploye that ableneſſe of bodye, which they [were] wonte to ufe to thefte and villainye, hencforth to labor and

---

1. 6839, ‘*reforme*,’ Collier, Morris, etc.: 1. 6847, ‘*generall*,’ *ibid.* : 1. 6847, ‘*moſt . . . and*,’ *ibid.*: 1. 6854, ‘*hinderaunce*’: 1. 6856, ‘*Stokaghs*’: 1. 6857, ‘*driven*,’ Collier, Morris, etc.

huſbandryc.  In the which, by that tyme they have 6860
ſpentc but a lytlc payne, they will find ſuch ſwetenes
and happy contentment, that they will hardly afterwardes bc hayled away from yt, or drawne to their
wonted leude lyfe in theivcry and rogerye.  And
bcinge thus once entered thcrunto, they arc not
oncly to be countenanced and encoradged by all
good meancs, but alſo provided that theire children
after them may be brought up in the ſame, and
ſuccecd in the rome of theire fathers.  To which end
there is a Statute in Ircland alrcdy well provided, 6870
which comaundcth that all the ſonncs of huſbandmē
ſhalbe trayned uppe in theire fathers trade, but yt is,
God wot, very ſlenderly lokcd unto.

*Eudox.* But do you not counte, in this trade of
huſbandrye, paſturinge of cattell, and kepinge of
theire cowes? for that is reckoncd as parte of hus-
bandrye.

*Iren.* I knowe yt is, and nedfull to be uſed, but I
doe not meanc to allowe any of thcſe able bodyes,
which arc able to uſe bodely labor, to followe a fewe 6880
cowes graſinge, but ſuch impotente perſons, as beinge
unable for ſtronge travell, arc yet able to drive cattell
to and froe the paſture ; for this kepingc of cowes
is of yt ſelf a very idle lyfe, and a fit nurſery for
a theiſe.  For which cauſe, ye remember, I diſlyked
the Iriſhman for kepinge of Bollyes in Som͂er upon
the mountayne, and lyvinge after that ſavadg forte.
But yf they will alwayes fede any cattle, or kepe
them on the mountaynes, let them make ſome

---

l. 6860, '*induſtry*' : l. 6863, '*to*' miswritten '*from*' in our MS. :
l. 6873, '*executed*,' Collier, Morris, etc.: l. 6888, '*algates*,' *ibid*.

townes nere to the mountaynes fyde, where they may 689
dwell together with neighbors, and be converfante in
the vewe of the world.    And, to fay truth, though
Ireland be by nature counted a greate foyle of
pafture, yet had I rather have fewer cowes kept,
and men better mannred, then to have fuch huge
increafe of cattell, and no increafe of condicons.    I
would therfore wifh that there were fome ordinaunce
made amongft them, that whatfoever kepeth twentye
kine fhold kepe a plough goinge, for otherwife all
men would fall to pafturinge, and none to hufbandrye, 690(
which is a greate caufe of this dearth nowe in
England, and a caufe of the ufuall ftealthes nowe
in Ireland : For loke in all countreyes that live in
fuch forte by kepinge of cattell, and you fhall find
that they are both very barbarous and uncivill, and
greatly given to warre.    The Tartaryans, the Mufco-
vites, the Norwayes, the Gothes, the Armenyans, and
many other do witnes the fame.    And therfore fince
nowe we purpofe to drawe the Irifh from defire
of warre and tumults, to the love of peace and 691(
civylitye, yt is expediente to abridge theire cuftome
of heardinge, and augment their trade more of
tyllinge and hufbandrye.    As for other occupacons
and trades, they ned not to be enforced to, but
every man bound onely to followe that he thinks
himfelfe apteft for.    For other trades of artificers
wilbe occupied for very neceffityes, and conftrayned
ufe of them ; and fo likewife will marchandize for
the gaine therof ; but learninge and bringing up in
liberall fcyences, will not come of yt felfe, but muft 6920

---

l. 6896, ' *of good*,' Collier, Morris, etc.

be drawne on with ſtraight lawes and ordinaunces : And therfore yt were mete that ſuch an acte were ordayned, that all the ſonnes of lords and gentlemen, and ſuch others as are able to bringe them up in learninge, ſhould be trayned uppe herin from theire childhodes. And for that end everye pariſh ſhalbe forced to kepe one pettye ſcholemaſter, adjoininge unto the pariſh charge, to be the more in veiwe, which ſhould bringe up theire children in the firſt rudiments of letteres : and that, in every country or 6930 baroncy, they ſhould kepe another able ſcholemaiſter, which ſhould inſtructe them in gramer, and in the princyples of ſcyences, to whom they ſhold be compelled to ſend theire youth to be diſcyplyned, wherby they will in ſhorte tyme growe uppe to that civyll converſaſyon, that both the children will loath the former rudnes in which they were bred, and alſo theire parentes will, even by the enſample of theire yonge children, perceave the foulnes of theire owne brutiſhe behavior compared to theires : for learninge 6940 hath that wonderfull power of yt ſelfe, that yt can ſoften and temper the moſt ſterne and ſavadge nature.

*Eudox.* Surely I am of your minde, that nothing will bringe them from theire uncivill life ſoner then learninge and diſcypline, next after the knowledge and feare of God. And therfore I doe ſtill expecte, that ye ſhould come thereunto, and ſet ſome order for reformacon of religion, which is firſt to be reſpected ; accordinge to the ſayinge of CHRIST, " Firſt ſeke the kingdome of heaven, and the righteoufnes 6950 therof."

*Iren.* I have in mynde ſo to doe ; but let me,

I pray you, firſt finiſh that which I had in hand, wherby all the ordinances which ſhall after be ſet downe for religion may abid the more firmely, and be obſerved more diligently. Now that this people is thus tythed and ordred, and every one bound to ſome trade of lyfe, which ſhalbe particulerly entred and ſet downe in tythinge bookes, yet perhaps there wilbe ſome ſtraglers and runagates which will not of 696c themſelves come and yeld themſelves to this order, and yet after the well finiſhinge of the preſent warre, and eſtabliſhinge of the gariſons in every ſtronge place of the countrye, where theire wonted refuge was moſt, I ſuppoſe there will fewe ſtand out, or yf they doe, they will ſone be brought in by the eares : But yet afterwardes, leaſt any one of theſe ſhould ſwarve, or any that is tyed to a trade ſhould after- wardes not followe the ſame, according to this inſtitutyon, but ſhould ſtraggle upp and downe the 697c countrye, or mich in corners amongſt theire freinds idllye, as Carrowe, Bardes, Jeſters, and ſuch like, I would wiſh that there were a Provoſt Marſhall apointed in everye ſheire, which ſhould continually walke thorough the countrey, with half a dozen, or halfe a ſcore horſemen, to take up ſuch loſe perſons as they ſhould finde thus wandringe, whom he ſhould puniſh by his owne authoretye, with ſuch paynes as the perſons ſhould ſeeme to deſerve : for yf he be but once ſo taken idelye roginge, he 698o may puniſhe him more lightlye, as with ſtockes, or ſuch like : but yf he be found agayne ſo loytringe, he may ſcorge him with whips, or roddes, after which

1. 695S, ' *ſome honeſt*,' Collier, Morris, etc.: 1. 6966, ' *ſhortly.*'

yſ he be taken agayne, let him have the bitternes
of the Marſhall lawe. Likewiſe yſ any relickes of
the rebellion be found by him, that eyther have
not come in and ſubmitted him ſelfe to the law,
or that havinge once come in, breake forth againe,
and walke diſorderlye, let them taſt of the ſame
cuppe in Gods name ; for yt was due to them 6990
for theire firſt guilte, and nowe beinge revived by
theire later loſenes, let them have theire firſt deſerte,
as nowe beinge found unfitt to live in a comon-
wealthe.

*Eudox.* This were a good maner ; but me thinkes
yt is an unneceſſarye charge, and alſo unfitte to
continue the name or forme of any marſhall lawe,
when as there is a proper oficer apointed alredy
for theſe turnes, to witt the ſherife of the ſheire,
whoſe particuler ofice yt is to walke contynually 7000
up and downe his Bayliwicke, as ye would have a
marſhall, to ſnatch up all thoſe runagates and un-
profitable members, and to bringe them to his gaole
to be punyſhed for the ſame. Therfore this may
well be ſpared.

*Iren.* Not ſo, me ſemes ; for though the ſherife
have this authorytye upon himſelfe to take upe all
ſuch traytors, and impriſon them, yet ſhall he not
doe ſo much good, nor worke that terror in the
hartes of them, that a marſhall will, whom they 7010
ſhall knowe to have power of life and death in ſuch
caſes, and ſpecially to be apointed for them : Neyther
doth yt hinder but that though yt perteyne to the

---

l. 6987, '*themſelves*,' Collier, Morris, etc.: l. 7000, '*peculiar*': l. 7008,
'*ſtragglers*,' Collier, Morris, etc.

fherife, the fheriffe may do therin what he can, and
yet the marfhall may walke his courfe befydes;
for both of them may doe the more good, and may
terrifye the idle rogue, knowinge that though he
have a watche upon thone, yet he may light upon
th'other.    But this provifo is nedfull to be had in this
cafe, that the fherif may not have the like power 7020
of life as the marfhall hath, and as heretofore they
have bene accuftomed ; for yt is dangerous to give
power of lyfe into the hands of him which may have
benefyte by the partyes death, as, yf the fayd lofe
liver have any goodes of his owne, the Sherife is
to feize therupon, wherby yt hath comen often to
paffe, that fome who have not perhaps deferved
judgemente of death, though otherwife perhaps
offendinge, have bene for theire goods fake caught
up, and caryed ftraight to the boughe ; a thinge inded 7030
pittyfull and very horryble.    Therfore by no meanes
would I wifhe the Sherife to have fuch authoretye,
nor yet to imprifon that loofell tyll the Seffions,
for foe all gaoles might fone be filled, but [to]
fend him to the Marfhall, who, eftfones findinge
him faultye, fhall give him mete correctyon, and
rid him away forthwith.

    *Eudox.* I do nowe perceave your reafon well.
But come we nowe to that wherofe we earft fpake,
I meane, to religion and religious men ; what order 7040
will you fett amongft them ?

    *Iren.* For religion lytle have I to fay, my felf
beinge as I fayde, not profeffed therin, and yt felfe
beinge but one, fo as there is but one waye therin ;

---

l. 7014, '*the fherriffe*,' Collier, Morris, etc.

for that which is true onely is, and the reft are
not at all, yet in plantinge of religion this much
is nedfull to be obferved, that being not fought
forceablie to be impreffed into them with terror
and fharpe penaltyes, as nowe is the manner, but
rather delivered and intymated with myldnes and 7050
gentlenes, fo as yt may not be hated before yt be
underftod, and theire Profeffors difpifed and rejected.
For this I knowe that moft of the Irifh are fo
farre from underftandinge the popifh religion as
they are of the proteftantes profeffyon ; and yet do
they hate that though unknowne, even for the
very hatred which they have of the Eng[lifh], and
of theire government.    Therefore yt is expedient
that fome difcreete minifters of theire owne contrymen be firft fent amongft them, which by theire 7060
mild perfwafyons and inftructyons, as alfo by theire
fober lyfe and converfacon, may drawe them firft
to underftand, and afterwardes to imbrace, the
doctrine of theire falvacon ; for yf that the auncyent
godly fathers, which firft converted them, beinge
infidells, to the faith, were able to drawe them
from infidelyte and paganfye to the true beliefe
in CHRIST, as S. Pattricke, and S. Columb, how
much more the godly teachers bringe them to the
true underftandinge of that which they alredy 7070
profeffe? wherin yt is greate wonder to fee the
odds which is betweene the zeale of Popifh Preifts,
and minifters of ye Gofpell ; for they fpare not

l. 7046, 'thus,' Collier, Morris, etc.: l. 7051, 'afore': ll. 7065-6,
'which . . . faith,' Collier, Morris. etc.: ll. 7067-8, 'to . . . Columb,'
ibid. : l. 7069, 'more cafelie fhall,' ibid.

to come out of Spaine, from Rome, from Rhemes,
by longe toyle and dangerous travell hither,
where they knowe perill of death awayteth them,
and no rewarde nor ritches is to be found, onely
to drawe the people to the Church of Rome ;
whereas fome of our idle minifters, having a way
for credit and eftymacon therby opned unto them, 7080
and having the livinges of the country offred them,
without paines, without perill, will neither for the
fame, nor for any love of God, nor zeale of religion,
nor for all the good which they might doe by
winninge of fo many foules to God, be drawne
forth from theire warme neaftes and theire fwete
loves fydes to loke out into Gods harveft, which
is even redy for the fickle, and all the feildes
yellowe longe agoe : doubtleffe thefe good ould
fathers will, I feare me, rife uppe in the day of 7090
judgment to condemne them.

*Eudox.* Surely, yt is greate pittye, Irin[i]us, that
there are none chofen out of the mynifters of
Eng[land], good fober, and difcreete men, which
might be fent over thither to teach and inftructe
them, and that there ys not afmuch care had of
theire foules as of theire bodyes ; for the care of
both lyeth upon the Prince.

*Iren.* Were there never fo many fent over thither
they fhould do fmall good tyll one enormity be 7100
taken from them, that is, that both they be reftrayned from fendinge theire yonge men abroade to
other Univerfytyes beyond feas, as Rhemes, Doway,
Lovaine, and the like, and that others from abroade

---

l. 7079, '*fome of*,' Collier, Morris, etc.

be reſtrayned for cominge to them ; for their lurk-
inge ſecretly in theire houſes and in corners of the
countrye do more hurte and hindrance to religion
with theire private perſwaſyons, then all the others
can doe with theire publicke inſtructyons ; and
though for theſe latter there be a good ſtatute theire 7110
ordeyned, yet the ſame is not executed, and as for
the former theire is noe lawe nor order for theire
reſtrainte at all.

*Eudox.* I mervell that yt is no better loked unto
and not onely this, but alſo that which, I remember,
you mencyoned in your abuſes concerninge the
profittes and revenues of the lands of fugitives
in Ireland, which by pretence of certaine collorable
conveyances are ſent continuallye over unto them,
to the comfortinge of them and others againſt her 7120
Majeſtye, for which here in Eng[land] there is good
order taken : and why not then aſwell in Ireland ?
For though there be no ſtatute there yet enacted
therefore, yet might her Majeſtye, by her onely
prorgative, ſeize the fruictes and profites of thoſe
fugitives lands into her handes, tyll they came over
to teſtefye theire true allegeance.

*Iren.* Indeed ſhe might ſo doe ; but the combrous
tymes do perhaps hinder the regarde therof, and of
many other good intencons.                                    7130

*Eudox.* But why then did they not minde yt in
peaceable tymes ?

*Iren.* Leave we that to theire grave conſideracons,
but procede we forwarde. Next care in religion is
to builde up and repaire all the ruine[d] churches :

l. 7131, '*why then*' from Collier, Morris, etc.

ther, the moſt parte ly even with the grounde, and
ſome [that] have bene lately repayred and thatched
are ſo unhandſomely patched, and thatched, that
men doe even ſhun the places for the uncomlynes
thereof : therfore I would wiſh that there were order 7140
taken to have them builte in ſome better forme,
according to the churches of England ; for the out-
ward ſhewe, aſſure your ſelfe, doth greatly drawe the
rude people to the reverencinge and frequye[n]tinge
therof, what ever ſome of our to nice foles ſaye, there
is nothinge in the ſemely forme and comly order of
the church.     And, for ſo kepinge and continuynge
them, there ſhould likewiſe Church-wardens of the
graveſt men in the pariſhe be apointed, as there be
here in England, which ſhould take the yearely 7150
charge both hereof, and alſo of the ſchole-houſes,
which I wiſhed to be builded nere to the ſayd
churches ; for maintenance of both which, yt were
mete that ſom ſeverall porcon of land were allotted,
ſeinge no more mortmaines are to be loked for.

*Eudox.* Inded me ſemes it would be ſo convenyente ; but when all is done, how will you have
this churche ſerved, or your myniſters mayntayned ?
ſince the livinges (as you ſayd) are not ſufficient
ſcarce to make them a newe gowne, much leſs to 7160
yeelde meete maintenaunce accordinge to the
dignitye of theire degree.

*Iren.* There is noe waye to helpe that, but to
laye two or three of them together, untill ſuch

l. 7138, ' *are . . . thatched* ' from Collier, Morris, etc. : l. 7143,
' *aſſure your ſelfe,*' *ibid.*: l. 7148, ' *Church-wardens,*' *ibid.*: ll. 7159-61,
' *ſince . . . maintenance,*' *ibid.*

tyme as the contreye growe more ritche and better inhabited, at which times the tythes and other obvencons will alfo be more agmented and better vallued : But now that we have thus gone through all theire forts of trades, and fet a courfe for theire good eftablifhment, let us yf you pleafe, goe next 7170 to fome other nedfull pointes of other publicke matters, no leffe concerninge the good of the comon-wealth, though but accydently dependinge on the former.   And firft I wifh that order were taken for the cuttynge downe and openinge of all paces thorough woodes, fo that a wide waye of the fpace of c. yardes might be layde open in every of them for the fafety of travellers, which ufe often in fuch perillous places to be robbed, and fometymes murthered.   Next, that bridges were builte upon all 7180 rivers, and all the fordes marred and fpilte, fo as none might paffe anye other waye, but by thofe bridges, and every bridge to have a gate and a fmall gatehoufe fett theron ;  wherof this good will come that no night ftealthes, which are comonly driven in bywayes and by blinde fordes unufed of any but fuch like, muft be conveyed out of one contrye into another, as they ufe, but that they muft paffe by thofe bridges, where they may be hapely encountred, or eafely tracked, or not fuffred to paffe at all, by 7190 meanes of thofe gatehoufes therin : Alfo that in all ftreights and narrowe paffages, as betwene twoe bogges, or through any deepe forde or under any mountayne fyde, there fhould be fome litle fortillage, or wodden caftell fett, which fhould kepe and comand

l. 7167, ‘*oblations*’ : l. 7187, ‘*fhall*,’ Collier, Morris, etc.

that ftreight, wherby any rebells that fhould com in
the contrye might be ftopped the way, or paffe
with greate perill. Moreover, that all high wayes
fhould be fenced on both fydes, leavinge onely fortye
foote bredthe for paffage, fo as none fhould be able 7200
to paffe but thorough the high waye, wherby theeves
and night robbers might be the more eafely purfued
and encountred, when there fhalbe no other waye
to drive theire ftollen cattell but therin [as] I
formerly declared. Further, that there fhould in
fondrye convenyent places, by the highe waye [be]
townes apointed to be builte, the which fhould be
fre borrowes, and incorporate under Baylifes, to be
by theire inhabitants well and ftronglie trenched, or
otherwife fenced with gates at eache fyde therof, to 7210
be fhutte nightlye, like as there is [in] many places
in the Englifh Pale, and all the wayes about yt to
be ftrongly fhut uppe, fo that none fhould paffe but
thorough thofe townes : To fome of which yt were
good that the priviledge of a markett were given,
the rather to ftrengthen and enable them to theire
defence, for nothinge doth fooner caufe civillitye in
any countrye then many market townes, by reafon
that the people repayringe often thither for theire
neds, will daylye fe and learne civyll manners of the 7220
better forte. Befydes, there is nothinge doth more
ftaye and ftrengthen the contrye then fuch corporate
townes, as by profe in many rebellyons have bene
proved, in all which when the countryes have
fwarved, the townes have ftood ftil and fafte, and
yelded good releife to the fouldiors in all occafyons

l. 7199, '*fenced and fhut up*,' Collier, Morris, etc.: l. 7224, '*feene.*'

of fervice. And laftly there doth nothinge more
enrich any contry or realme then many townes ; for
to them will people drawe and bringe the fruiéte of
theire trades, afwell to make money of them, as to 7230
fuply theire nedfull ufes ; and the contrymen will
alfo be the more induftrious in tyllage, and rearinge
all hufbandrye comodityes, knowing they fhall have
redy fale for them at thofe townes : and in all thofe
townes fhould there convenyent inns be erééted for
the lodginge and harboringe of all travellers, whoe
are nowe oftentimes fpoyled by lodginge abroade in
weake thatch houfes, for wante of fuch fafe places to
fhrowde themfelves in.

*Eudox.* But what profitt fhall your markett townes 7240
reape of their markett, wheras each one may fell
theire corne and cattell abroade in the countrye,
and make theire fecrett bargaynes amongft themfelves, as nowe I underftand they ufe ?

*Iren.* Inded, Eudox : they doe fo, and thereby
no fmall inconvenyence doth rife to the comon-
wealth ; for nowe when any one hath ftolne a cowe
or a garon, he may fecrettly fell yt in the countrye
without privytie of any, wheras yf he brought yt
into a market towne yt would perhaps be knowne, 7250
and the theife difcovered. Therfore yt were good
that a ftraight ordinance were made, that none
fhould buy or fell any cattell but in fome open
markett (there beinge nowe markett townes everye
where at hand) upon a greate penaltye neyther
fhould they likewife by any corne to fell the

1. 7229, '*will all the,*' Collier, Morris, etc. : l. 7233, '*fhall have,*'
*ibid.* : l. 7240, ' *townes,*' *ibid.*

fame againe, unleffe yt were to make malte therof ;
for by fuch engroffinge and regratinge we fee the
dearth that nowe comonly raigneth here in England
to have bene caufed.    Hereunto alfo is to be added 726
that good ordinance, which I remember was once
proclaymed throughout all Ireland.    That all men
fhould marke theire cattell with an open feverall
marke upon theire flanckes or buttocks, fo as yf
they hapned to be ftollen, they might apeare
whofe they were, and they which fhould buy them
might therby fufpecte the owner, and be warned to
abftayne from byinge of them of a fufpected perfon
with fuch an unknowne marke.

    *Eudox.* Surely thefe ordinances feme very ex- 727
pedient, but fpecyally that of fre townes, of which
I wonder that there is fuch fmall ftore in Ireland,
and that in the firft peoplinge and plantinge therof
they were neglected and omytted.

    *Iren.* They were not omitted ; for there were,
thoroughe all places of the country convenyente,
many good townes feated, which thorough that
inundacon of the Irifh, which I firft tould of, were
utterly wafted and defaced, of which the ruines are
yet in many places to be fene, and of fome no figne 728
at all remayninge, fave onely theire bare names, but
theire feates are not to be founde.

    *Eudox.* But how then cometh yt to paffe, that
they have never fince recovered, nor theire habitacon
bene reedified, as of the reft which have bene noe
leffe fpoyled and wafted ?

    *Iren.* The caufe therof was for that, after theire

l. 7270, ' *ordinances* ' miswritten ' *evidences* ' in our MS.

dcfolacon, they were begged by gentlemen of the
Kings under collours to repaire them and gather
the poore relickes of the people againe together, 7290
of whome havinge obtayned them, they were fo
farre from reedyfying of them, as that by all
meanes they have endeavored to kepe them wafte,
leaft that, beinge repayred, theire charters may be
renewed, and the burgeffes reftored to theire landes,
which they had nowe in theire poffeffyon ; much
like as in thofe oulde monuments of abbyes, and
religious houfes, we fee them likewife ufe to doe :
for which caufe yt is judged that King Henry the
Eighth beftowed them upon them, knowinge that 7300
thereby they fhould never be able to rife againe.
And even fo do thofe Lords, in thefe ould pore
corporate townes, of which I could name diverfe
but for kindling of difpleafure. Therefore as I
wifhed many corporate townes to be erected, fo
would I againe wifh them to be free, not dependinge upon the fervice, nor under the comandment
of any but the Governor. And beinge fo, they
will bothe ftrengthen all the countrye round about
them, which by theire meanes wilbe the better 7310
replenifhed and enriched, and alfo be as contynuall
houldes for her Majefty, yf the people fhould revolt
and breake out againe ; for without fuch yt is eafye
to forrey and over-ronne the whole lande. Let be,
for example, all thofe freboroughes in the Lowe-
countryes, which are nowe all the ftrength therof.
Thefe and other like ordinances might be delivered

l. 7294, '*might*,' Collier, Morris, etc. : l. 7303-5, '*of* . . . *townes*,'
*ibid.*

for the good eſtabliſhment of this realme, after yt
is once ſubdued and reformed, in which yt might
afterwardes [be] very eaſely kepte and maintayned 7320
with ſmall care of the Governor and Councell there
apointed, ſo as that yt ſhould in ſhort ſpace yeld
a plentyfull revenewe to the crowne of England;
which now doth but ſucke and conſume the
treaſurye therof, through thoſe unſound plattes
and changfull orders which are daylye deviſed
for her good, yet never effectually proſecuted or
performed.

*Eudox.* But in all this your diſcorſe I have not
marked any thinge by you ſpoken touchinge the 7330
appointment of the principall officer, to whome
you wiſh the charge and performance of all this
to be comitted : onely I obſerved ſome foule abuſes
by you noted in ſome of the late Governors, the
reformacon wherof you lefte for this preſente
tyme.

*Iren.* I delight not to lay open the blames of
greate magiſtrates to the rebuke of the worlde, and
therefore theire reformacon I will not medle with,
but leave unto the wiſdome of greater heades to be 7340
conſidered ; onely this much I will ſpeake generally
herof, to ſatisfye your deſyre, that the Government
and cheife majeſtracye I wiſh to continue as yt
doth, to weete, that yt be ruled by a Lord Deputye
or Juſtices, for that it is a very ſafe kinde of rule :
But therewithall I wiſh that over him there were
placed a Lord Leiftenante, of ſome of the greateſt
perſonages in England (ſuch an one I could name)
upon whom the eye of all England is fixed, (and our

laft hopes nowe reft) who beinge intituled with that 7350
dignitye, and beinge alwayes here refidente, may
backe and defend the good caufe of the government
againft all malignors, which ells will, through theire
cuñing workinge under hand, deprave and pull backe
whatfoever things fhalbe well beguñe or intended
there, as we comonly fee by experyence at this daye, to
the utter ruyne and defolacon of the pore Realme, and
this Leiftenancye fhould be no difcountenauncing of
the Lord Deputye, but rather a ftrengthninge and
maintayninge of all his doinges ; for now the cheife 7360
evill in that government is, that no Governor is
fuffred to goe one with any one courfe, but upon
the leaft informacon here of this or that, he is
eyther ftoped or croffed, and other courfes apointed
him from hence which he fhall runne, which how
[in]convenient yt is, is at this hower to well felte.
And therfore this fhould be one principle in the
apointment of the Lord Deputies authoritye, that yt
fhould be more ample and abfolute then yt is, and
that he fhould have an uncontrouled power to doe 7370
any thinge that he, with the advifement of the
Councell, fhall thinke mete to be don : for yt is not
poffible for the Councell here, to directe a Governor
there, who fhalbe forced oftentymes to followe the
neceffitye of prefent occayfons, and to take the
foddayne advantage of tyme, which beinge once
lofte will not bee recovereu ; whilft, thorough expect-
inge directyon from hence, the delayes wherof are
oftentymes through greater affaires moft irkfome, the
oportunytyes there in the meane tyme paffe awaye, 7380

1. 7372, '*fhould*,' Collier, Morris, etc.

and greate danger often groweth, which by fuch timely prevencon might eafely be ftopped. And this I remember is worthely obferved by Matchavell in his difcorfes upon Lyvye, where he comendeth the manner of the Romans government, in giving abfolute power to all theire Confules and Governors, which yf they abufed, they fhould afterwards derly anfwere : And the contrary therof he reprehendeth [in] the State of Venice, of Florence, and many other principalytyes of Ittalye, who ufe to lymytt theire 7390 cheife officers fo ftraightlye, as that therby they have oftentymes loft fuch happy occafyons as they could never come unto againe. The like wherof, who fo hath bene converfante in that government of Ireland, hath to often fene theire great hinderance and hurt. Therfore this could I wifh to be redreffed, and yet not fo, but that in particuler thinges he fhould be reftrayned, though not in generall government ; as namely in this, that no ofices fhould be fould by the Lord Deputy for money, nor no pardons, 7400 nor no protectyons bought for rewarde, nor noe beves taken [for] captencyes of contryes, nor no fhares of bifhopricks for nominatinge theire bifhops, nor no forfaytures, nor difpenfacons with penall ftatuts geven to theire fervants or freindes, nor no fellyng of lycences for exportacon of prohibited warres, and fpecyally of corne and flefhe, with many the like ; which nede fome manner of reftrainte, or els very greate truft in the honorable difpofytyon of the Lord Deputye.

l. 7391. '*they have,*' Collier. Morris, etc.: l. 7392, '*loft fuch happy,*' *ibid.* : ll. 7395-6, '*hindraunce and,*' *ibid.* : l. 7400, '*for money,*' *ibid.*

Thus I have, Eudox : as breifly as I could, and as 7410
my remembrance would ferve, rund through the ftate
of that whole contrye, both to let you fee what it
nowe is, and alfo, what yt may be by good care
and amendment : not that I take upon me to change
the pollicye of fo greate a kingdome, or prefcribe
rules to fuch wife men as have the handlinge therof,
but onely to fhewe you the evills, which in my fmall
experience I have obferved to be the cheife hindrance
of the reformacon therof; and by the way of conference to declare my fimple opinyon for redreffe 7420
therof, and eftablifhinge a good courfe for that
government ; which I do not deliver for a perfecte
plotte of myne owne invenfyon to be onely followed,
but as I have learned and underftood the fame by
the confultacons and actyons of very wife Governors
and Counfellors whome I have fometymes heard
treate therof.   So have I thought good to fett downe
a remembraunce of them for myne owne good, and
your fatisfactyon, that who lift to overloke them,
although perhaps much wifer then they which have 7430
thus advifed of that ftate, yet at leafte, by comparifon
hereof, may perhaps better his owne judgment,
and by the light of others foregoinge, he may
followe after with more eafe, and hapely finde a
fayrer waye thereunto then they which have gone
before.

*Eudox.* I thanke you, Irenyus, for thys your gentle
paynes ; withall not forgettynge nowe in the fhuttyng
uppe to put you in mynd of that which you have

---

l. 7414, '*upon me*,' Collier, Morris, etc. : l. 7426, '*heard*,'
*ibid.*

formerly halfe promyfed—herafter when we fhall 744c
meete agayne upon the like good occafyon, ye will
declare unto us thofe your obfervacons which ye have
gathered of the Authoretyes of Ireland.

finys 1596 : E. S.

l. 7443. '*Antiquities,*' Collier, Morris, etc., but plainly '*Authoretyes*'
=on the national history—in our MS.

## II.

# LETTERS

FROM

## *Spenſer*

('*IMMERITO*')

TO

## *Gabriel Harvey*

1579-1580.

# NOTE.

The first of these Letters is drawn from the original book, whose title-page is given opposite.

The second, with added quotation from Harvey's answer, is taken from the book whose title-page is similarly given on *verso* of the other.

A return to the originals corrects a number of little misprints and mis-spellings or modernizings in prior reprints, even in Dr. Morris's ('Globe'). It is to be noted that in the first Letter the date is '5 of October,' which may be queried '16th,' (p. 264, l. 91,) and by error 2579 for 1579. See the Life in Vol. I. on these Letters and related matters.

A. B. G.

# ¶ TVVO OTHER

very commendable Let-
ters, of the fame mens vvri-
ting, both touching the forefaid
Artificiall Verfifying, and certain other particulars;

*More lately delivered vnto the*
*Printer.*

CHARITAS.

# IMPRINTED AT LON-

don, by H. Bynneman, dvvelling
in Thames Streate, neere vnto
Baynardes Caftell.

*Anno Domini* 1580.

*Cum gratia & priuilegio Regiæ Maieftatis.*

# ¶ THREE PROPER

and wittie, familiar Letters:
lately paſſed betvveene tvvo V-
niuerſitie men : touching the Earthquake in Aprill laſt, and our Engliſh
reſourmed Verſifying

*With the Preface of a well-willer to
them both.*

CHARITAS.

# IMPRINTED AT LON-

don, by H. Bynneman, dvvelling
in Thames Streate, neere vnto
Baynardes Caſtell.

*Anno Domini.* 1580.

*Cum gratia & priuilegio Regiæ Maieſtatis.*

# LETTERS

FROM

## SPENSER (IMMERITO) TO
## GABRIEL HARVEY.

### TO THE WORSHIPFULL HIS VERY SINGU-
### LAR GOOD FRIEND, MAISTER G. H.

#### FELLOW OF TRINITIE HALL IN CAMBRIDGE.

OOD Master G. I perceive by your
moſt curteous and friendly Letters
your good will to be no leſſe in 10
deed, than I alwayes eſteemed. In
recompence wherof, think I beſeech
you, that I wil ſpare neither ſpeech,
nor wryting, nor aught elſe, when-
ſoever, and whereſoever occaſion
ſhal be offred me : yea, I will not ſtay, till it be
offred, but will ſeeke it, in al that poſſibly I may.
And that you may perceive how much your Counſel
in al things prevaileth with me, and how altogither
I am ruled and over-ruled thereby : I am now 20

determined to alter mine owne former purpofe, and
to fubfcribe to your advizement : being notwithftanding refolved ftil, to abide your farther refolution.
My principal doubts are thefe.   Firft, I was minded
for a while to have intermitted the uttering of my
writings : leafte by over-much cloying their noble
cares, I fhould gather a contempt of myfelf, or elfe
feeme rather for gaine and commoditie to doe it, for
fome fwcetneffe that I have already tafted.   Then
alfo, mefeemeth, the work too bafe for his excellent 30
Lordfhip, being made in Honour of a private Perfonage unknowne, which of fome yl-willers might be
upbraided, not to be fo worthie, as you knowe fhe is :
or the matter not fo weightie, that it fhould be offred
to fo weightie a Perfonage : or the like.   The felfe
former Title ftil liketh me well ynough, and your
fine Addition no leffe.   If thefe, and the like doubtes,
maye be of importaunce in your feeming, to fruftrate
any parte of your advice, I befeeche you without the
leaft felfe love of your own purpofe, councell me 40
for the befte : and the rather doe it faithfullye, and
carefully, for that, in all things I attribute fo muche
to your judgement, that I am evermore content to
annihilate mine owne determinations, in refpecte
thereof.   And indeede for your felfe to, it fitteth
with you now, to call your wits and fenfes togither,
(which are alwaies at call) when occafion is fo fairely
offered of Eftimation and Preferment.   For, whiles
the yron is hote, it is good ftriking, and minds of
Nobles varie, as their Eftates.   *Verùm ne quid durius.* 50
    I pray you bethinke you well hereof, good
Maifter G. and forthwith write me thofe two or three

fpecial points and caveats for the nonce, *De quibus in fuperioribus illis mellitiffimis longiffimifque Litteris tuis.* Your defire to heare of my late beeing with hir Majeftie, mufte dye in it felfe. As for the twoo worthy Gentlemen, Mafter *Sidney* and Mafter *Dyer*, they have me, I thanke them, in fome ufe of familiarity : of whom, and to whome, what fpeache paffeth for youre credite and eftimation, I leave your 60 felfe to conceive, having alwayes fo well conceived of my unfained affeftion and zeale towardes you. And nowe they have proclaimed in their ἀρειωπάγῳ a generall furceafing and filence of balde Rymers, and alfo of the veric befte to : in fteade whereof, they have, by authoritie of their whole Senate, prefcribed certaine Lawes and rules of Quantities of Englifh fillables for Englifh Verfe : having had thereof already great practife, and drawen mee to their faftion. Newe Bookes I heare of none, but only 70 of one, that writing a certaine Booke, called *The Schoole of Abufe*, and dedicating it to Maifter *Sidney*, was for hys labor fcorned : if at leafte it be in the goodneffe of that nature to fcorne. Suche follie is it, not to regarde aforehande the inclination and qualitie of him to whome wee dedicate oure Bookes. Suche mighte I happily incurre entituling *My Slomber* and the other Pamphlets unto his honor. I meant them rather to Maifter *Dyer*. But I am, of late, more in love wyth my Englifhe Verifying than with 80 Ryming : whyche I fhould haue done long fince, if I would then haue followed your councell. *Sed te folum jam tum fufpicabar cum Afchamo fapere : nunc Aulam video egregios alere Poëtas Anglicos.*

Maifter E. K. hartily defireth to be commended unto your Worfhippe : of whome what accompte he maketh, your felfe fhall hereafter perceive, by hys paynefull and dutifull Verfes of your felfe.

Thus much·was written at Weftminfter yefter-night : but comming this morning, beeyng the 90 fixteenth of October, to Myftreffe *Kerkes*, to have it delivered to the Carrier, I receyved youre letter, fente me the lafte weeke : whereby I perceive you otherwhiles continue your old exercife of Verfifying in Englifhe : whych glorie I had now thought fhoulde have bene onely ours heere at London and the Court.

Trufte me, your Verfes I like paffingly well, and envye your hidden paines in this kinde, or rather maligne, and grudge at your felfe, that woulde not 100 once imparte fo muche to me. But once, or twice you make a breache in Maifter *Drants* Rules : *quod tamen condonabimus tanto Poëtæ, tuæque ipfius maximæ in his rebus autoritati.* You fhall fee when we meete in London (whiche, when it fhall be, certifye us) howe faft I have followed after you in that Courfe : beware, leafte in time I overtake you. *Veruntamen te folum fequar, (ut fæpenumero, fum profeffus,) nunquam fanè affequar dum vivam.*

And nowe requite I you with the like, not with 110 the verye beft, but with the verye fhorteft, namely, with a few Iambickes : I dare warrant they be pre-cifely perfect for the feete (as you can eafily judge), and varie not one inch from the Rule. I will imparte yours to Maifter *Sidney* and Maifter *Dyer* at my nexte going to the Courte. I praye you, keepe

mine clofe to yourfelfe, or your veric entire friendes,
Maifter *Prefton*, Maifter *Still*, and the refte.

## Iambicum Trimetrum.

Unhappie Verfe, the witneffe of my unhappie ftate, 120
 Make thy felfe fluttring wings of thy faft flying
 Thought, and fly forth unto my Love wherfoever
  fhe be :

Whether lying reaftleffe in heavy bedde, or elfe
 Sitting so cheereleffe at the cheerfull boorde, or elfe
 Playing alone careleffe on hir heavenlie Virginals.

If in Bed, tell hir, that my eyes can take no refte :
 If at Boorde, tell hir, that my mouth can eate no
  meate :
 If at hir Virginals, tell hir, I can heare no mirth.

Afked why? say: Waking Love fuffereth no fleepe :
 Say, that raging Love dothe appall the weake 130
  ftomacke :
 Say, that lamenting Love marreth the Muficall.

Tell hir, that hir pleafures were wonte to lull me
  afleepe :
 Tell hir, that hir beautie was wonte to feede
  mine eyes :
 Tell hir, that hir fweete Tongue was wonte to
  make me mirth.

Nowe doe I nightly wafte, wanting my kindely refte :
 Nowe doe I dayly ftarve, wanting my lively foode :
 Nowe doe I alwayes dye, wanting thy timely
  mirth.

And if I wafte, who will bewaile my heavy chaunce?
And if I ftarve, who will record my curfed end?
And if I dye, who will faye : *this was Immerito ?* 140

I thought once agayne here to have made an
ende, with a heartie *Vale* of the beft fafhion : but
loe, an ylfavoured myfchance.    My laft farewell,
whereof I made great accompt, and muche marvelled
you fhoulde make no mention thereof, I am nowe
tolde (in the Divels name) was thorough one mans
negligence quite forgotten, but fhoulde nowe un-
doubtedly have beene fent, whether I hadde come,
or no.    Seeing it can now be no otherwife, I
pray you take all togither, wyth all their faultes : 150
and nowe I hope, you will vouchfafe mee an
anfweare of the largeft fize, or elfe I tell you true,
you fhall bee verye deepe in my debte : notwyth-
ftandying, thys other fweete, but fhorte letter, and
fine, but fewe Verfes.    But I woulde rather I might
yet fee youre owne good felfe, and receive a
Reciprocall farewell from your owne fweete mouth.

*Ad ornatiffimum virum, multis jam diu*
NOMINIBUS CLARISSIMUM G. H. IMMERITO
*fui, mox in Gallias navigaturi,* εὐτυχεῖν.            160

Sic malus egregium, fic non inimicus Amicum :
Sicque novus veterem jubet ipfe Poëta Poëtam,
Salvere, ac cœlo, poft fecula multa fecundo
Jam reducem, cœlo mage, quàm nunc ipfe, fecundo
Utier.    Ecce Deus, (modò fit Deus ille, renixum
Qui vocet in fcelus, et juratos perdat amores)

Ecce Deus mihi clara dedit modò figna Marinus,
Et fua veligero lenis parat Æquora Ligno,
Mox fulcanda, fuas etiam pater Æolus Iras
Ponit, et ingentes animos Aquilonis——            170
Cunƈta viis fic apta meis : ego folus ineptus.
Nam mihi nefcio quo mens saucia vulnere, dudum
Fluƈtuat ancipiti Pelago, dum Navita proram
Invalidam validus rapit huc Amor, et rapit illuc.
Confiliis Ratio melioribus ufa, decufque
Immortale levi diffeffa Cupidinis Arcu.
Angimur hoc dubio, et portu vexamur in ipfo.
Magne pharetrati nunc tu contemptor Amoris,
(Id tibi Dii nomen precor haud impune remittant)
Hos nodos exfolve, et eris mihi magnus Apollo.    180
Spiritus ad fummos, fcio, te generofus Honores
Exftimulat, majusque docet fpirare Poëtam,
Quàm levis eft Amor, et tamen haud levis eft Amor
    omnis.
Ergo nihil laudi reputas æquale perenni,
Præque facrofanƈta fplendoris imagine tanti,
Cætera, quæ vecors, uti Numina, vulgus adorat,
Prædia, Amicitias, urbana peculia, Nummos,
Quæque placent oculis, formas, fpeƈtacula, Amores,
Conculcare foles, ut humum, et ludibria fenfus.
Digna meo certè Harveio fententia, digna         190
Oratore amplo, et generofo peƈtore, quam non
Stoica formidet veterum Sapientia vinclis
Sancire æternis : sapor haud tamen omnibus idem
Dicitur effæti proles facunda Laërtæ,
Quamlibet ignoti jaƈtata per æquora Cœli
Inque procellofo longùm exful gurgite ponto,
Præ tamen amplexu lachrymofæ Conjugis, Ortus

Cœleſtes Divûmque thoros ſpreviſſe beatos.
Tantùm Amor, et Mulier, vel Amore potentior. Illum
Tu tamen illudis : tua Magnificentia tanta eſt :     200
Præque ſubumbrata Splendoris Imagine tanti,
Præque illo Meritis famoſis nomine parto
Cætera, quæ Vecors, uti Numina, vulgus adorat,
Prædia, Amicitias, armenta, peculia, nummos.
Quæque placent oculis, formas, ſpeſtacula, Amores,
Quæque placent ori, quæque auribus, omnia temnis.
Næ tu grande ſapis, Sapor at ſapientia non eſt :
Omnis et in parvis benè qui ſcit deſipuiſſe,
Sæpe ſuperciliis palmam ſapientibus aufert.
Ludit Ariſtippum modò tetrica Turba Sophorum,     210
Mitia purpureo moderantem verba Tyranno
Ludit Ariſtippus diſtamina vana Sophorum,
Quod levis emenſi male torquet Culicis umbra :
Et quiſquis placuiſſe Studet Heroibus altis,
Deſipuiſſe ſtudet ſic gratia creſcit ineptis.
Denique laurigeris quiſquis ſua tempora vittis,
Inſignire volet, Populoque placere faventi,
Deſipere inſanus diſcit, turpemque pudendæ
Stultitiæ laudem quærit. Pater Ennius unus
Diſtus in innumeris ſapiens : laudatur at ipſa     220
Carmina veſano ſudiſſe liquentia vino.
Nec tu pace tua, noſtri Cato Maxime sæcli,
Nomen honorati ſacrum mereare Poëtæ,
Quantamvis illuſtre canas, et nobile Carmen,
Ni ſtultire velis, ſic S[t]ultorum omnia plena,
Tuta ſed in medio ſupereſt via gurgite, nam Qui
Nec reliquis nimium vult deſipuiſſe videri,
Nec ſapuiſſe nimis, Sapientem dixeris unum.
Hinc te merſerit unda, illinc combuſſerit Ignis.

Nec tu delicias nimis afpernare fluentes,　　　　　230
Nec ferò Dominam, venientem in vota, nec Aurum.
Si fapis, ablatum, (Curiis ea, Fabriciisque
Linque viris miferis miferanda Sophifmata : quondam
Grande fui decus ii, noftri sed dedecus ævi :)
Nec fectare nimis.　Res utraque crimine plena.
Hoc bene qui callet, (fi quis tamen hoc bene callet)
Scribe, vel invito fapientem hunc Socrate folum.
Vis facit una pios : Juftos facit altera : et altra
Egregiè cordata, ac fortia pectora : verùm
Omne tulit punctum, *qui mifcuit utile dulci.*　　240
Dii mihi, dulce diu dederant : verum utile nunquam :
Utile nunc etiam, ô utinam quoque dulce dediffent.
Dii mihi (quippe Diis æquivalia maxima parvis)
Ni nimis invideant mortalibus effe beatis,
Dulce fimul tribuiffe queant, fimul utile : tanta
Sed Fortuna tua eft : pariter quæque utile, quæque
Dulce dat ad placitum : fævo nos fydere nati
Quæfitum imus eam per inhofpita Caucafa longè,
Perque Pyrenæos montes, Babilonaque turpem,
Quòd fi quæfitum nec ibi invenerimus, ingens　　250
Æquor inexhauftis permenfi erroribus, ultrâ
Fluctibus in mediis focii quæremus Ulyffis.
Paffibus inde Deam feffis comitabimur ægram,
Nobile qui furtum quærenti defuit orbis.
Namque finu pudet in patrio, tenebrisque pudendis
Non nimis ingenio Juvenem infœlice virentes,
Officiis fruftra deperdere vilibus Annos,
Frugibus et vacuas fperatis cernere fpicas.
Ibimus ergo ftatim : (quis eunti faufta precetur ?)
Et pede Clibofas feffo calcabimus Alpes.　　　　260
Quis dabit interea conditas rore Britanno,

Quis tibi Litterulas ? quis carmen amore petulcum ?
Mufa sub Oebalii defueta cacumine montis,
Flebit inexhaufto tam longa filentia planctu,
Lugebitque facrum lacrymis Helicona tacentem.
Harveiusque bonus, (charus licet omnibus idem,
Idque fuo merito, prope fuavior omnibus unus,)
Angelus et Gabriel, (quamvis comitatus amicis
Innumeris, geniûmque choro ftipatus amæno)
*Immerito* tamen unum abfentem fæpe requiret,          270
Optabitque, Utinam meus hic *Edmundus* adeffet,
Qui nova fcripfiffet, nec Amores conticuiffet
Ipfe fuos, et fæpe animo verbisque benignis
Faufta precaretur, Deus illum aliquando reducat, &c.

> *Plura vellem per Charites fed non licet per Mufas.*
> *Vale, Vale plurimùm, Mi amabiliffime Harveie, meo*
> *cordi, meorum omnium longè chariffime.*

I was minded alfo to have fent you fome Englifh
verfes : or Rymes, for a farewell : but by my Troth,
I have no fpare time in the world, to thinke on 280
fuch Toyes, that you know will demaund a freer
head, than mine is prefently. I befeeche you by
all your Curtefies and Graces let me be anfwered
ere I goe : which will be, (I hope, I feare, I thinke)
the next weeke, if I can be difpatched of my Lorde.
I goe thither, as fent by him, and maintained moft
what of him : and there am to employ my time,
my body, my minde, to his Honours fervice. Thus
with many fuperhartie Commendations and Re-
commendations to your felfe, and all my friendes 290
with you, I ende, my laft Farewell, not thinking

any more to write unto you, before I goe : and
withall committing to your faithfull Credence the
eternal Memorie of our everlafting friendfhip, the
inviolable Memorie of our unfpotted friendfhippe,
the facred Memorie of our vowed friendfhip : which
I befeech you Continue with ufuall writings, as you
may, and of all things let me heare some Newes
from you.  As gentle M. *Sidney*, I thanke his good
Worfhip, hath required of me, and fo promifed to 300
doe againe.  *Qui monet, ut facias, quod jam facis ;*
you knowe the reft.  You may alwayes fend them
moft fafely to me by *Miftreffe Kerke*, and by none
other.  So once againe, and yet once more, Farewell moft hartily, mine owne good *Mafter H.* and
love me, as I love you, and thinke upon poore *Immerito*, as he thinketh uppon you.

Leycefter House, this 5 of October, 1579.
*Per mare, per terras,*
*Vivus, mortuufque*                                    310
*Tuus Immerito.*

## TO MY LONG APPROOVED AND SINGULAR GOOD FRENDE, MASTER G. H.

GOOD Mafter H. I doubte not but you have fome
great important matter in hande, which al this
while reftraineth your Penne, and wonted readineffe
in provoking me unto that, wherein your felfe nowe
faulte.    If there bee any fuch thing in hatching,
I pray you hartily, lette us knowe, before al the
worlde fee it.    But if happly you dwell altogither 320

in *Juſtinians* Courte, and give your ſelfe to be de-
voured of ſecreate Studies, as of all likelyhood you
doe : yet at leaſt imparte ſome your olde, or newe
Latine, or Engliſhe, Eloquent and Gallant Poeſies
to us, from whoſe eyes, you ſaye, you keepe in a
manner nothing hidden.   Little newes is here
ſtirred : but that olde greate matter ſtill depending.
His Honoure never better.   I thinke the *Earthquake*
was also there wyth you (which I would gladly
learne) as it was here with us : overthrowing divers 330
old buildings and peeces of Churches.   Sure verye
ſtraunge to be hearde of in theſe Countries, and
yet I heare ſome ſaye (I knowe not howe truely)
that they have knowne the like before in their
dayes.   *Sed quid vobis videtur magnis Philoſophis ?*
I like your late Engliſhe Hexameters ſo exceedingly
well, that I alſo enure my Penne ſometime in that
kinde : whyche I fynd indeede, as I have heard you
often defende in worde, neither ſo harde, nor ſo
harſhe, that it will eaſily and fairely yeelde it ſelfe 340
to our Moother tongue.   For the onely, or chiefeſt
hardneſſe, whych ſeemeth, is in the Accente :
whyche ſometime gapeth, and as it were yawneth
ilfavouredly, comming ſhorte of that it ſhould, and
ſometime exceeding the meaſure of the Number, as
in *Carpenter*, the middle ſillable being uſed ſhorte
in ſpeache, when it ſhall be read long in Verſe,
ſeemeth like *a lame Goſling that draweth one legge
after hir* : and *Heaven* being uſed ſhorte as one
ſillable, when it is in verſe ſtretched out with a 350
*Diaſtole*, is like *a lame Dogge that holdes up one
legge*.   But it is to be wonne with Cuſtome, and

rough words muſt be ſubdued with Uſe. For, why a Gods name may not we, as elſe the Greekes, have the kingdome of oure owne Language, and meaſure our Accentes by the ſounde, reſerving that Quantitie to the Verſe? Loe, here I let you ſee my olde uſe of toying in Rymes, turned into your artificial ſtraightneſſe of Verſe, by this *Tetraſticon.* I 360 beſeech you tell me your fanſie without parcialitie.

See yee the blindſoulded pretie God, that feathered
    Archer,
Of Lovers Miſeries which maketh his bloodie game?
Wote ye why, his Moother with a Veale hath
    coovered his Face?
Truſt me, leaſt he my Loove happely chaunce to
    beholde.

    Seeme they comparable to thoſe two, which I tranſlated you *ex tempore* in bed, the laſt time we lay togither in Weſtminſter?

That which I eate did I joy, and that which I
    greedily gorged,
As for thoſe many goodly matters leaſt I for others. 370

    I would hartily wiſh, you would either ſend me the Rules and Precepts of Arte, which you obſerve in Quantities, or elſe followe mine, that M. Philip Sidney gave me, being the very ſame which M. Drant deviſed, but enlarged with M. Sidneys own judgement, and augmented with my Obſervations, that we might both accorde and agree in one : leaſte we overthrowe one an other, and be overthrown of the reſt. Truſte

IX.

me, you will hardly beleeve what greate good liking
and eftimation Maifter *Dyer* had of your *Satyricall* 380
*Verfes*, and I, fince the viewe thereof, having before
of my felfe had fpeciall liking of *Englifhe Verfifying*,
am even nowe aboute to give you fome token, what,
and howe well therein I am able to doe : for, to tell
you trueth, I minde fhortely at convenient leyfure, to
fette forth a Booke in this kinde, whiche I entitle
*Epithalamion Thamefis*, whyche Booke, I dare undertake wil be very profitable for the knowledge, and
rare for the Invention and manner of handling.  For
in fetting forth the marriage of the Thames : I 390
fhewe his firft beginning, and off fpring, and all the
Countrey, that he paffeth thorough, and alfo defcribe
all the Rivers throughout Englande, whyche came
to this Wedding, and their righte names, and right
paffage, &c.  A worke, beleeve me, of much labour,
wherein notwithftanding Mafter *Holinfhed* hath
muche furthered and advantaged me, who therein
hath beftowed fingular paines, in fearching oute
their firfte heades and fourfes : and alfo in tracing
and dogging oute all their Courfe, til they fall into 400
the Sea.  O Tite, fiquid, ego,
              Ecquid erit pretij?

But of that more hereafter.  Nowe, my *Dreames* and
*Dying Pellicane*, being fully finifhed (as I partelye
fignified in my lafte Letters) and prefentlye to bee
imprinted, I wil in hande forthwith with my *Faery
Queene*, whyche I praye you hartily fend me with al
expedition : and your frendly Letters, and long expected Judgement wythal, whyche let not be fhorte, 410

but in all pointes fuche, as you ordinarilye ufe, and I extraordinarily defire. *Multum vale. Weftminfter. Quarto Nonas Aprilis* 1580. *Sed, amabo te, meum Corculum tibi fe ex animo commendat plurimùm : jamdiu mirata, te nihil ad literas fuas refponfi dediffe. Vide quæfo, ne id tibi Capitale fit : Mihi certè quidemerit, neque tibi hercle impunè, ut opinor, Iterum vale, & quam voles fæpè.*

Yours alwayes to commaunde,

IMMERITO. 420

*Poftfcripte.*

I take beft my *Dreames* fhoulde come forth alone, being growen by meanes of the Gloffe (running continually in maner of a Paraphrafe) full as great as my *Calendar.* Therin be fome things excellently, and many things wittily difcourfed of E. K. and the pictures fo fingularly fet forth, and purtrayed, as if *Michael Angelo* were there, he could (I think) nor amende the befte, nor reprehende the worft. I know you woulde lyke them paffing wel. Of my 430 *Stemmata Dudleiana,* and efpecially of the fundry Apoftrophes therein, addreffed you knowe to whome, muft more advifement be had, than fo lightly to fende them abroade : howbeit, truft me (though I doe never very well) yet in my owne fancie, I never dyd better. *Veruntamen te fequor folum : nunquam verò affequar.*

## QUOTATION FROM HARVEY'S REPLY.

But Mafter *Collin Cloute* is not every body, and albeit his olde Companions, *Mafter Cuddy* and *Mafter* 440 *Hobbinoll* be as little beholding to their *Miftreffe Poetrie*, as ever you wift : yet he peradventure by the meanes of hir fpecial favour, and fome perfonall priviledge, may happely live by *Dying Pellicanes*, and purchafe great landes, and Lordfhippes, with the money, which his *Calendar* and *Dreames* have and will affourde him. *Extra jocum*, I like your *Dreames* paffingly well : and the rather, bicaufe they favour of that fingular extraordinarie veine and invention, which I ever fancied mofte, and in a 450 maner admired onelye in *Lucian, Petrarche, Aretine, Pafquill*, and all the moft delicate and fine conceited Grecians and Italians : (for the Romanes to fpeake of, are but verye Ciphars in this kinde :) whofe chiefeft endevour, and drifte was, to have nothing vulgare, but in fome refpecte or other, and efpecially in *lively Hyperbolicall Amplifications*, rare, queint, and odde in every pointe, and as a man would faye, a degree or two at the leafte, above the reache, and compaffe of a common Schollers capacitie. In whiche 460 refpecte notwithftanding, as well for the fingularitie of the manner, as the Divinitie of the matter, I hearde once a Divine, preferre *Saint Johns Revelation* before al the verieft *Metaphyficall Vifions*, and jollyeft conceited *Dreames* or *Extafies*, that ever were devifed by one or other, howe admirable, or fuper excellent foever they feemed otherwife to the worlde. And truely I am fo confirmed in this opinion, that when I bethinke me of the veric notableft, and mofte wonderful Propheticall, or Poeti- 470 call Vifion, that ever I read, or hearde, me feemeth the proportion is fo unequall, that there hardly appeareth anye femblaunce of Comparifon: no more in a manner (efpecially for Poets) than doth betweene the incomprehenfible Wifdome of God, and the fenfible Wit of man.

But what needeth this digreffion between you and me? I dare faye you wyll holde yourfelfe reafonably wel fatisfied, if youre *Dreames* be but as well efteemed of in Englande, as *Petrarches* 480 *Vifions* be in Italy: which I affure you, is the very worft I wifh you. But, fee, how I have the Arte *Memorative* at commaundement. In good faith I had once againe nigh forgotten your *Faerie Queene*: howbeit by good chaunce, I have nowe fent hir home at the lafte, neither in better nor worfe cafe, than I founde hir. And muft you of neceffitie have my judgement of hir indeede? To be plaine, I am voyde of al judgement, if your *Nine Comœdies*, whereunto in imitation of *Herodotus*, you 490 give the names of the *Nine Mufes* (and in one mans fanfie not unworthily) come not neerer *Arioftoes Comœdies*, eyther for the fineneffe of plaufible Elocution, or the rareneffe of Poetical Invention, then that *Elvifh Queene* doth to his *Orlando Furiofo*, which notwithftanding, you wil needes feeme to emulate, and hope to overgo, as you flatly profeffed yourfelf in one of your laft Letters.

Befides that you know, it hath bene the ufual

practife of the moft exquifite and odde wittes in all 500
nations, and fpecially in *Italie*, rather to fhewe, and
advaunce themfelves that way, than any other : as
namely, thofe three notorious dyfcourfing heads,
*Bibiena*, *Machiavel*, and *Aretine* did, (to let *Bembo*
and *Ariofto* paffe) with the great admiration, and
wonderment of the whole country : being in deede
reputed matchable in all points, both for conceyt of
Witte and eloquent decyphering of matters, either
with *Ariftophanes* and *Menander* in Greek, or with
*Plautus* and *Terence* in Latin, or with any other, in 510
any other tong.   But I wil not ftand greatly with
you in your owne matters.   If fo be the *Faerye
Queene* be fairer in your eie than the *Nine Mufes*,
and *Hobgoblin* runne away with the Garland from
*Apollo* : Marke what I faye, and yet I will not fay
that I thought, but there an End for this once, and
fare you well, till God or fome good Aungell putte
you in a better minde.

END OF VOL. IX.

*Hazell, Watson, and Viney, Printers, London and Aylesbury.*

www.ingramcontent.com/pod-product-compliance
Lightning Source LLC
Chambersburg PA
CBHW060611030726
47498CB00005B/1635